1917 Eagles

Book 4 in the British Ace Series

By

Griff Hosker

1917 Eagles Fall

Published by Sword Books Ltd 2014
Copyright ©Griff Hosker Second Edition

The author has asserted their moral right under the Copyright, Designs and Patents Act, 1988, to be identified as the author of this work.

All Rights reserved. No part of this publication may be reproduced, copied, stored in a retrieval system, or transmitted, in any form or by any means, without the prior written consent of the copyright holder, nor be otherwise circulated in any form of binding or cover other than that in which it is published and without a similar condition being imposed on the subsequent purchaser.
A CIP catalogue record for this title is available from the British Library.
Cover by Design for Writers

London Borough of Enfield	
91200000814855	
Askews & Holts	14-Jun-2024
AF HIS	
ENWINC	

Dedication

To the thousands who went over the top at Arras in 1917
The General

"Good morning, good morning," the general said,
When we met him last week on our way to the line.
Now the soldiers he smiled at are most of 'em dead,
And we're cursing his staff for incompetent swine.
"He's a cheery old card," muttered Harry to Jack
As they slogged up to Arras with rifle and pack.

But he did for them both by his plan of attack.

Siegfried Sassoon

Contents

1917 Eagles Fall i
Dedication iii
Chapter 1 2
Chapter 2 10
Chapter 3 16
Chapter 4 23
Chapter 5 29
Chapter 6 36
Chapter 7 43
Chapter 8 49
Chapter 9 56
Chapter 10 62
Chapter 11 70
Chapter 12 75
Chapter 13 84
Chapter 14 91
Chapter 15 96
Chapter 16 102
Chapter 17 109
Chapter 18 116
Chapter 19 122
Chapter 20 129
Chapter 21 135
Chapter 22 141
Chapter 23 147
Chapter 23 154
Chapter 24 160
Chapter 25 168
Chapter 26 174
Chapter 27 182
Chapter 28 189
Chapter 29 199
Chapter 30 205
Chapter 31 213
Chapter 32 221
Epilogue 230
Glossary 231
Historical note 233
Other books by Griff Hosker 237

Chapter 1

Lumpy and I were sat in the waiting room outside General Henderson's office. We had been summoned from the hospital and brought to London by a military escort from the hospital in Essex where we had been recovering from injuries suffered during our flight from France. Flight Sergeant Hutton was convinced that I was going to be given a medal of some description. I was not so certain. I was just grateful that Nurse Beatrice Porter, the woman I knew that I would marry, had been allowed to accompany me; ostensibly it was to look after my broken arm.

I had been annoyed at the summons for I had hoped for some time with Beatrice in the military hospital. It seemed it was not to be. Our goodbye had been perfunctory. Whitehall is not the most romantic place to say goodbye to a loved one and the steely stares of the guards meant a chaste kiss and a quick goodbye. As she hurried through the London streets to the hospital in Hyde Park I cursed General Henderson for his orders.

I cursed him more as we watched the clock in the hall tick slowly around while we cooled our heels, seemingly ignored. I knew that Lumpy was wrong when Captain Ebbs and Lieutenant White arrived. Captain Ebbs kept his head down and avoided looking in my direction while the Lieutenant gave me a wan smile and an apologetic shrug. I knew then that I was in trouble. When we had been rescued from the sea by the Navy we had been harshly interrogated by Captain Ebbs as German spies. I had had to use force with his sergeant to avoid being shot out of hand. Had it not been for Lieutenant White's intervention then things might have gone ill. Luckily the young lieutenant was able to prove that we were not spies and that our injuries had been attended to in the hospital. I had wondered if my actions might come back to haunt me.

"What do you think he wants, sir?"

"Probably our heads as a pair of trophies to hang upon his wall."

"You can't be serious sir! You mean you aren't going to get a medal?"

I laughed, "I will be lucky to keep these pips and avoid gaol!"

The middle-aged captain was only inside for a short time. He came out a little red-faced and bothered. He flashed a look of irritation at me. He was beneath contempt. I can think of many young pilots who could have been in my position. They might not have emerged as undamaged as I was.

The Lieutenant was in a little longer and when he came out he saluted. "Good to see you and the sergeant are up and about."

"And you too, Lieutenant White. Did you put in for that transfer?"

He grinned, "Yes sir! I hope to hear something in the next fortnight."

Just then a sergeant came out into the corridor, "Flight Sergeant Hutton."

The Lieutenant said, "I had better go, sir." He saluted and said, "Good luck, sir."

And then I was alone. I thought back to the moment when I had struck the sergeant and broken the Captain's swagger stick. I could not think how I could have avoided doing anything else. It was bizarre; we had escaped through enemy territory, and crossed the English Channel and yet we had nearly died when we landed in England.

Lumpy was in what seemed like an age and he came out red-faced too. I wondered what was happening in the office. The sergeant said, "Captain Harsker, if you would like to follow me, sir"

When I entered I recognised General Henderson. There was a lieutenant next to him. The sergeant sat down and took up his pen. He would be keeping a record of the meeting. I saluted.

General Henderson returned it and asked, "How is the arm?"

"Itchy."

He laughed, "Good, then it is healing. Sit down." He held his hand out for the notes the sergeant had been making. He scanned them and handed them back. He leaned back and began to fill his pipe. When it was drawing to his satisfaction he pointed at me. "You are a damned fool! For what you and the Flight Sergeant did you should been awarded the V.C." He shook his head, "As it is..." I felt like a real fool at that moment. If I said anything then it would either come out as whining or apologetic. I had done what I had to and I was ready for my punishment. Perhaps I would end up a sergeant again. I could live with that.

"Nothing to say for yourself, eh?"

I shrugged, "It is hard to know what to say, sir. If you want me to apologise then I am afraid I won't. I would do it again! In fact, the only thing I regret is not smacking that arrogant captain as well."

I saw the sergeant hide a smile while the lieutenant looked shocked. Surprisingly enough the General did not react as I would have expected, "Yes, well I can understand that, but better he is in Blighty than in the trenches eh? So what do we do with you?" He shook his head. "You can't stay in England despite the fact that you need sick leave. I need you away for at least a month so that the hubbub can die down. Captain Ebbs was desperate to bring charges but thanks to Lieutenant White's testimony and your sergeant's I think that I can send a report to the captain's C.O. and he will be reprimanded."

He must have seen the relief on my face. I did not want another court-martial. "Quite, Captain Harsker. You made quite an impression on the young lieutenant. He has asked for a transfer to the RFC. Well, you and the Flight Sergeant can travel back to France by train. There was a new bus for you but the broken arm means you can't fly. We'll have a ferry pilot take it over at the end of the week. I'll have my driver take you to Victoria." He leaned over his desk, "Try to avoid upsetting senior officers eh, Captain? Stay in the air. You are in your natural element there."

I stood and saluted, "Sir."

"Oh, and your Flight Sergeant has been put in for the new Military Medal." He grinned, "He didn't hit anyone."

Once outside, Lumpy stood, "Well, sir?"

"We are being sent back to France."

"But your arm, sir. It isn't healed."

"They want us out of the way. We have a travel warrant for the train."

He shook his head, "It's not fair, sir."

"I know but someone once said there is nothing fair in love and war."

When we reached the street the driver had placed our kit bags in the boot of the General's car. I leaned in to the corporal driver. I noticed that it was a woman. I smiled, "Corporal I have to make a detour on the way to the station. I need to call at the hospital which is close to Hyde Park." She frowned. "It is on the way and I promise I shan't be long."

She gave me a searching look. "Is this RFC business?"

I decided that honesty might work. I gave her my most charming smile, "It is heart business. I need to tell my fiancée that I am returning to the front and we won't have any time together now."

I thought for one moment that she would refuse but then she gave me a beaming smile. "You should have said so in the first place."

It was, indeed, a rapid journey. "Entertain the corporal will you sergeant?"

"Yes, sir."

They knew me at the hospital and the porter rang up to the ward for Beatrice. She looked surprised to see me but the look on my face must have given her a premonition. "You are going back to France and the war aren't you?"

I nodded, "The general wants me out of the way until the furore has died down." I didn't care what people thought. I threw my good arm around her and kissed her. "I will be back for Gordy's wedding. We will have a week's leave then."

As she pulled away I saw that, although she was smiling, tears were coursing down her cheeks. "I know but take care, will you? You have nearly died twice and I couldn't bear it if I lost you forever."

"Don't worry, I will return. The flying will soon be limited because of the weather. Besides, with this arm, I will be grounded for a while anyway."

I heard the porter hiss, "Watch out sir, matron!"

I released Beatrice, "I will write!"

She fled inside before Matron could see us. What we had just done was definitely against the Matron's regulations. I slumped into the back seat. The corporal said, as we drove off, "She seems like a nice girl."

As I stared at the wet London streets all I could say was, "She is."

We were dropped at Victoria Station and handed our travel warrants. They allowed us Second Class travel on any train. There was a military pass for each of us. It would not do to be stopped by military police. Lumpy looked up at the departures board. "There's a train in an hour, sir. We have just got time for a cup of tea."

I looked at the board. I did not want to take the train and the boat. If I had to return then I wanted it to be quickly. "We'll get the one to Greenwich instead. It goes in fifteen minutes. You will have to wait for your cup of tea."

He could not believe his ears. "Why Greenwich, sir? We'll be in trouble."

"Come on and I'll explain. I don't want to miss that train." We hurried to the platform. "We will fly the new Gunbus back ourselves. We will get there quicker. I don't know about you but I don't fancy sleeping on a train."

He considered that and nodded, "But you have a broken arm! You can't fly."

"When I fire the Lewis I only fly with one arm. Where is the difference? Come on, Sergeant, pretend we are escaping across France again!"

He suddenly grinned, "You normally make the right decisions sir. Righto, in for a penny, in for a pound."

We made the train with time to spare. It was relatively empty as it was noon and most people were at work. We had the whole compartment to ourselves. Once on the train, I took off my sling and had Lumpy feed my plaster cast arm through the sleeve of my greatcoat. "We'll just tell the flight officer that the General wanted the Gunbus over there sooner rather than later."

"It might not be ready to fly sir."

"All it needs is fuel and we can do that, can't we?"

I was largely convincing myself as well as Lumpy but it sounded a reasonable plan. I had one twinge of pain getting into my coat but it was nothing really. We left the train and Lumpy carried both of our kitbags. I used the station master's telephone to ring the airfield for a vehicle and a lorry arrived an hour later.

When we walked into the squadron office I was delighted to see that I knew the officer from our previous flights and I outranked him! Earlier in the war, I would never have dreamed of using rank but the war had changed me.

"Good to see you again. We are here to take the new FE. 2 over to Number 41 Squadron."

He looked surprised, "We thought we had to wait for a ferry pilot."

I leaned in, tapped the side of my nose and said, "Something big brewing, we were pulled back from leave especially."

He brightened somewhat. Young officers in Blighty lived vicariously through the exploits of those of us in France. He would dine out in this story and it would grow in the telling. "You will be doing us a favour. The Zeppelin raids mean it is asking to be blown up there on the field. I'll just get it fuelled for you. Flight Sarn't, get the new Gunbus fuelled up for Captain Harsker would you?"

"Sir."

"Anything else I can do for you?"

"A couple of flying helmets, goggles and gloves would not go amiss and if you could manage a brew of tea we would be eternally grateful."

Half an hour later we were aboard the familiar Gunbus. We had had tea and we were kitted out well. We had even been given a couple of scarves. The downside was that we were unarmed and we had no way of communicating with each other, save by shouting. But we would be going home. Without the sling, my broken arm ached as I taxied to the end of the airfield. The sling had taken much of the pressure off it. Once we took off I would have to rest it on the side of the cockpit. It was a luxury for Lumpy not to have to spin the propeller and hurl himself on board; the mechanics at the field did it for us. In fact, he would have an easy journey east to France.

I had lied a little to my Flight Sergeant. It was not as easy to fly one-handed as I had made out and I needed to use my broken arm to help us into the air. Again, I felt a twinge or two but once we were airborne I used my one good hand to lift us slowly to our cruising altitude.

Everything had taken slightly longer than I would have expected and I was not certain that we could make the field before dark. One advantage we had was that we knew the route well. The wind was from the west and that enabled us to make the field before the sun set. As we turned to land into the wind I counted the aeroplanes on the field. They were all there. The only one missing was the one which we had burned in the woods near to Ypres.

Our arrival sparked nerves and interest. The sound of an aeroplane flying from the east meant that the gun crews around the field aimed their weapons at the skies. As the rest of the squadron was down it meant that the pilots and gunners were curious about this new and late arrival. The huge Gunbus looks nothing like any German aeroplane and we were recognised for what we were.

When the engine stopped the mechanics raced over to secure the aeroplane. I had taxied as close to the aeroplane park as I could manage. As soon as Lumpy descended he was recognised and the other gunners swarmed over this popular character.

My arm was now aching quite severely and I struggled to climb down from the cockpit. Gordy and Ted greeted me, "We thought you would be on sick leave! We heard you had been wounded."

I held up my left arm, "Just a damaged wing. Nothing to worry about."

We headed for the office, where I saw Archie and Randolph waiting for us. Ted shook his head. "Then why are you back? Operations are winding down at the moment and we will be going back for Gordy's wedding in four weeks. You should have stayed in Blighty."

Gordy looked at me and laughed, "This isn't as simple as it sounds. I am looking forward to hearing this."

Major Archie Leach held out his hand, "Glad you made it Bill! You are the good luck charm of this squadron. Come in and we'll have a wee nip of something just to keep out the cold."

The wee nip turned into two bottles as I went through the whole story of the crash and the escape across the sea. I finished with General Henderson's words. Archie shook his head as he put the last, half-empty bottle away. "Well, you'll no be flying until Doc Brennan gives you the all-clear. You are daft, man. You should have travelled back on the train."

I smiled, I was slightly drunk, "And miss all your smiling faces? I didn't fancy the train and the ferry. Anyway, what have I been missing?"

"Not a great deal. The weather has been awful and we have not managed too many operations but some of the other squadrons have taken a real hammering from the new Fokkers and the Albatros the Boche has recently introduced. I am afraid the Gunbus just can't handle them."

"The Major is right Bill, Ted and I are just glad to get down in one piece after a patrol these days." Just then we heard the gong for dinner. "Anyway, your young lads and Bates will be desperately glad to see you. Poor Bates thought you had gone west and he just moped around. The lads in your flight felt guilty that you had sacrificed yourself for them."

"I had better get changed for dinner then."

I left the office and headed for my quarters. Airman Bates was waiting for me with his normal disapproving look. "I am pleased to see you back, Captain Harsker, but your sergeant has told me of your wound. Get your sling on now." He flourished the sling like a magician.

"I think we can wait until I have dressed for dinner eh?"

"Yes sir but, really, you must look after yourself!"

I was washed and dressed by Bates who took more care of me than a mother would. He was not satisfied until the sling was in place and he had adjusted it for maximum comfort. "There." He brushed some fluff from my tunic. He nodded towards the other officers' quarters. "They all missed you, Captain Harsker. It was like a funeral parlour here until we received the message that you had reached England. We all thought you were dead." He shook his head, "I couldn't go through that again, sir."

Poor Bates had had a breakdown when his last officer had died going over the top. He had transferred to the RFC because he thought it was safer. He was learning that life was equally precarious in the air. "I have learned my lesson, Airman Bates, and I will be careful. I intend to marry Miss Porter."

That brought the smile back to his face. "Well, jolly good sir! That makes up for many things. Now off you go or there will be no dinner left."

Chapter 2

To my embarrassment, I was cheered by the whole mess when I entered. Johnny and Freddie had saved a place between them for me. I could see that Ted and Gordy were put out. I smiled and sat between my two wingmen. Charlie Sharp gave me the thumbs up. His face showed his delight at my return. After we had said Grace I was bombarded with questions from my two young pilots about my escape, my crash and my flight across northern France and Belgium. I noticed that all the other younger officers were listening keenly.

I was glad when we had the toast and were able to retire to the comfortable seats. This time I managed to get my own chair and Gordy and Ted sat close by while Charlie sat on the arm of the settee.

"The Luger came in handy then, sir." Charlie had been my sergeant and could not get into the habit of calling me, while in the mess, Bill.

"It did but, ironically, it almost got me shot when we landed in England."

"That Ebbs sounds like an idiot. He must be one of those armchair generals we hear so much about." Gordy had never been keen on officers when he was a sergeant and now that he was one himself it was only those in our squadron whom he rated.

"Looking at the way the war on the ground is going there must be some of those armchair generals making the decisions right now. We made great advances on the ground in the first days of the Somme offensive and then they made a mess of it."

I remembered Albert. "Some of those who live here seem to have suffered greater losses than we have. We can't change our generals. We just have to do the best that we can. There was an old man called Albert who gave his life so that Lumpy and I could escape. I owe it to him to keep on."

Charlie said quietly, "I don't think any of us thought about giving up but when you fly over the front and see the wasted deaths, it makes you wonder. The fighting has eased off lately and that gives you more time to look when you fly over the front. It scares me."

Gordy waved the mess orderly over. "Enough depressing talk. Did you see Mary when you were in London?" The orderly came. "Same again, Jackson, on my bill."

"Yes, sir."

I shook my head. "I was only there for a couple of hours. Just enough time to get a dressing down from the general. Beatrice said she had caught up with her a couple of weeks ago. They had lunch with my sister, Alice. Beatrice said she was really excited about the wedding." I smiled at the relief on Gordy's face. "Don't worry; it is the women organising the wedding, not us. It will all go swimmingly!"

The sombre mood was lightened by the talk of the wedding for that meant leave. The Major had said that the flight commanders could all have leave in late November, or early December and he, Captain Marshall and the younger pilots would all have the end of December. It was not altruistic; most of the young pilots did not have wives and children. New Year was a better celebration for the single young men. None of the wedding guests would be home for Christmas but I would be able to travel and see my family before I had to return to the front. If Beatrice could manage leave too then I would be able to have my family meet her.

It felt strange, the next morning, not to be flying. It was just Ted and Gordy's flights that were on patrol. As I had been told already the front was quiet. The Somme offensive had ground to a muddy, bloody halt. The patrols were over the front to discourage the Germans from reclaiming any of the precious land our lads had gained.

Lumpy and the armourer, Flight Sergeant Richardson, were busy fitting the Lewis guns to the new bus and I was like a spare part. I walked with Charlie who was also having a rest day. We wandered down the airfield. Charlie had seen a few apples which had not fallen and he wanted to gather them. I was not much use with one working arm. However, I had learned how to fill and light my pipe with one hand. I did so while he collected the latest windfall apples and reached up for the ones still on the tree.

I leaned on the fence as Charlie began to open up. "I have never really thanked you, sir, for giving me my chance to be a pilot and an officer."

"There is nothing to thank me for. I was glad to do it. You deserve it."

"My mum and dad were so proud when I was made an officer. The other lads in the street are all privates or corporals. You know how it is."

I nodded. I did know. His people were like mine, working-class and always keen to brag about their children who had bettered themselves. Charlie was still the same bright lad I had known as a young gunner but he had taken his chance.

"What will you do after the war then, Charlie?"

He put down the bucket which was now full and lit a cigarette. "I haven't given it much thought. This war seems never-ending."

"But it will end. What then?" I knew that Charlie had worked in a factory before the war; most of his uncles and cousins also worked in the grim northern factories.

"I don't think I could go back to the factory. I know cotton is supposed to be in my blood but I have been in the fresh air for the last two years and I like it." He picked up an apple. "I would never have been able to do this if I had worked in a factory, would I? I'd like to fly. Perhaps I will stay on. I like the Royal Flying Corps and I like the blokes I serve with."

"What about a wife? A family?"

"We don't get much chance for that here do we sir? Besides, any woman who wants to marry me would have to let me fly."

He flicked his cigarette stub away and picked up his bucket. We began to walk back. I was thinking about my future. What would I do? I didn't want to stay in the Corps. I wanted a home for me and Beatrice and not a barracks. I heard the drone of engines behind us. The flight was back early. Something was not right. Suddenly Charlie shouted, "Sir, they aren't our lads. It is the Boche!"

He dropped his bucket and began to run. I turned and saw a line of five aeroplanes. They were coming in either to strafe or to bomb us. I heard the bell being rung and the gun crews ran to the guns and their sandbags.

I heard the unmistakable chatter of a machine gun and saw an airman pitched in the air by the nine-millimetre steel-jacketed bullets. The gunner just made the sandbags.

"In there Charlie, you can feed the machine gun!"

We just made it behind the wall of sandbags before the first bullets thudded into them. I ducked down. I was annoyed that I could do nothing. I did not even have my service revolver. The five aeroplanes, which I did not recognise, machine-gunned the gun pits and then climbed. The gunner had managed to cock his Vickers. "Is that it sir? Will they be off?"

As they had flown over I had seen that they were a two-seater and they had bomb racks fitted next to the cockpit. "No, airman, they'll be back. Let's see if you and Lieutenant Sharp can bag one." I watched as they looped to return. Their first run had been to silence the guns. This time they would go for the six parked aeroplanes. I looked around for a weapon. The only one I saw was the Very pistol. I picked it up. It was loaded.

They came in again. This time they flew a little higher and down the centre of the airfield. The heavy Vickers began to pump out bullets. There were tracer rounds which enabled the gunner to be more accurate but the Vickers was a heavier weapon than the Lewis and the gunner and Charlie had to tap the barrel around to follow the flight of the fast-moving Germans. I had a sudden idea. I stepped out and aimed the pistol. Instead of firing it high, I fired at a low trajectory. I had one chance in a thousand of hitting an aeroplane but that was not my main intention.

The gunner was also the bomb aimer and no bullets came in my direction. I fired the pistol and then ducked behind the sandbags. I saw the flare arc over the first two aeroplanes and then, as it dipped just in front of the third aeroplane it exploded. The flash must have terrified and disorientated the pilot who suddenly jerked his bus up into the air. The fourth German kept on coming and when the third aeroplane overcorrected his wingtip caught the fourth German's tail. The crippled German plunged vertically and exploded in a fireball just a hundred yards from us. The explosion and the Vickers hit the other aeroplane which also crashed and exploded on the runway.

I heard the bombs from the first two aeroplanes as they hit our airfield but the fifth, having seen his fellow fliers crash and burn, banked and headed east. Archie came down the airfield. He was shaking his head when he met me. "And don't think for one minute you can claim that one laddie!" The medical team were examining the dead airman. "We were lucky then. Very lucky. They didn't hit any of the buses."

Charlie pointed to the dead and wounded airmen who were being attended to. "They weren't lucky though, were they sir?"

An hour later we heard the familiar drone of Rolls Royce engines. However, I could detect that not all of the engines were running smoothly. I saw the six aeroplanes in the distance. That was a relief; they had all made it but I saw smoke drifting from the engines of two of them. When Ted fired his Very pistol we knew that they had wounded men in the buses. I watched as Senior Flight Sergeant Lowery and every man not attending to the wounded tried to put out the fires on the two German aeroplanes and clear the airfield. There was just enough room for a Gunbus to land but if they were damaged then it could be tricky.

It was with some relief that we saw all six landed safely. We ran over to the most damaged of them. Doc Brennan was still busy with the wounded from the raid.

Ted jumped down. "That was a nightmare. Some of the new Albatros D.III jumped us. They are so fast and manoeuvrable that we didn't have time to make a circle. And they have two machine guns! I have no idea how Paddy McCormack managed to land his."

We went to Paddy's aeroplane. The medical orderly climbed into the cockpit only to return five minutes later shaking his head. Paddy's gunner lay on the ground being attended to. "He must have landed it while in his last dying moment, sir. He's gone." The gunner lay on the ground being attended to, Paddy had given him a chance.

Another young pilot had gone west. The new German aeroplanes were gaining the upper hand and that was no mistake. We lost three gunners and four of the aeroplanes were too badly damaged to fly. The next day it was down to Charlie and the major to take up just five aeroplanes. They stayed well inside our lines. Their intention was to stop the Germans from bombing our field. We were no longer on the offensive but were just hanging on for dear life.

Randolph discovered, after the remains of the two aeroplanes were examined, that they were a type called Albatross CIII. Obviously, the single-seaters we had encountered were a newer version. We buried the four dead Germans but their belongings were collected and dropped, at dusk, two days later over the closest German airfield. The Germans had begun the tradition. This was one of the few opportunities we had had to reciprocate.

And that was the way the Somme Offensive ended. It just petered out. Both sides were like punch-drunk boxers. Neither wanted to quit but they had no strength to carry on. Nature and the French winter determined that there would be little flying until the Spring.

The wedding party, as we were termed, left France on the 25th of November. We would all have to return to the airfield by the 8th of December. It was not long but it would have to be enough. Johnny and Freddie also took leave at that time but they did not come to the wedding.

The day before we were due to leave Airmen Bates came in with that look of his which I now knew meant there was something he was unhappy about. "Come, on then Bates, spit it out!"

He wrinkled his nose at my choice of words, "Well sir, I am pleased that you are going on leave; heaven knows you deserve it, but you need someone to look after you."

I smiled, "Don't worry, John, I have Nurse Porter. She can see to me."

"Sir!" He was shocked, "You cannot have the young lady helping you to dress that would not be acceptable. She is not your nurse now, she is your young lady!"

I shrugged, "Well you are going home on leave so I will just have to manage."

"No sir, I could look after you."

"You mean you would spend the leave looking after me rather than having time with your family?"

He looked at me sadly, "I have no family sir. If I went home… well sir, this is as near to a home as I have." He turned to leave, "Of course, if you don't need me, sir."

"Of course I need you, but I didn't want to take advantage of you."

He looked puzzled, "How sir? I am a gentleman's gentleman; it is what I do."

"Very well then although I am not certain about the available accommodation at the hotel."

He beamed, he was happy now. "Leave that to me, sir. I have dealt with hotel staff before. I shall go and pack our things." He went off to his little room whistling. He was a strange little man but I began to wonder how I had managed before he had been posted to us. He seemed to work in a different way to the rest of us. I wondered what he would do when the war was over. The world would be a different one then. Too many fine young men had gone west for it to be anything else.

Chapter 3

The journey back to England was far jollier than I had expected. Bates looked after us like a faithful sheepdog. The two young pilots were happy to be part of the group and Gordy was as excited as a puppy with two tails. Even Charlie seemed more relaxed and managed to call me Bill!

We had a compartment to ourselves. Bates rarely sat down for he was usually fetching or carrying for one of us. Gordy took out the letter from Mary when we pulled out of the station at Amiens. "Now, it would be inappropriate for us to stay at Mary's and so she has booked four rooms for us at the Lanchester Hotel. It isn't far from the church. Of course, after the wedding, there will be a spare room."

Johnny asked, "Why is that, sir?"

Freddie laughed and nudged him in the ribs. He whispered in his ear and the young lieutenant blushed.

"I will need to get a room for Bates here when we arrive."

Charlie smiled, "He can bunk in with me if you like, Bill."

Bates was outraged, "A very kind offer, sir but I could not take a gentleman's room. Do not worry, Lieutenant Sharp, I know the Lanchester. They have rooms for servants and I am sure I can arrange something. I shall find the conductor and see what time we reach the ship. There is no buffet car aboard this train! The French!"

Charlie laughed after he had left. "A gentleman! We live in a little two up two down house!"

Freddie asked, "Really? Where do the servants live?"

It was Johnny's turn to clip his friend around the ears.

I laughed, "The point Lieutenant Sharp was making was that four of us here were not born gentlemen. We are gentlemen because of our rank. My family are servants. My sister is a housekeeper and my brother-in-law is a butler. If the war hadn't come along then I would have followed in their footsteps. I would be a servant rather than having someone like Bates to take care of me. It takes some getting used to."

"But you are all gentlemen. Some of those who visited our family might have dressed well and spoken well but they were no gentlemen. I think, sir, that being a gentleman is something you are born with and, if you don't mind me saying so, all four of you are gentlemen."

"Thank you, Freddie."

Charlie was probably as excited as the young pilots but for different reasons. He had been lonely as a gunner being a very shy young man but now he was part of a team and he had real friends. For him, the Royal Flying Corps had opened doors, not closed them. In addition, this would be the first wedding he had attended. That was also a cause for excitement, especially as it would be in London, a city that Charlie had never visited before.

Poor Johnny and Freddie looked disappointed when they left us at Victoria. We had really had a good time on the boat and the trains and we had laughed a ridiculous amount at jokes and stories which did not warrant such laughter. That was war.

When we arrived at the Lanchester it was the inestimable Bates who, confidently, took charge. He decided that the rooms we had been allocated were not good enough for someone who had won the Military Cross. He had a word with the manager. We found ourselves in the best four rooms in the hotel while Bates was more than happy with his accommodation. He had a servant's room on the top floor. He even gave us the address of a good restaurant nearby. It was too late to meet with Mary, Beatrice and Alice anyway and the five of us had a boys' night out in London. Bates ensured that we all behaved but he had to help me put a very drunken Lieutenant Sharp to bed. He was simply too big for me to handle on my own.

As he took me back to my room to lay out my clothes for the following day I asked, "What did you get up to Bates?"

"Oh, I just wandered the streets of London. It is such a lively place. You seem to have had a pleasant night."

"Well, Mr Sharp certainly did."

"He is a nice chap, that Lieutenant Sharp. The men in his flight think the world of him. I dare say one night where he is the worse for drink is no bad thing; just so long as he doesn't make it a habit!" I think Bates would have made an excellent teacher!

I forced Bates to take the next day off and enjoy the sights of London while we went to meet Mary and Alice. Trafalgar Square was the place we had chosen as the rendezvous. The four of us were there early admiring the magnificent lions and the monument to a great hero. My dad had never been in the navy but he admired Nelson. I think one of my ancestors must have been a Jack in the Navy.

We felt as though the cares of the world had been lifted from our shoulders but that contrasted with the faces that we saw on the streets.

There were many women dressed in black; the deaths at the front had impacted greatly. We had been at war for just over two years now and almost every home had been touched. We saw few men and the ones we did see were, like us in uniform. We also saw a huge number of staff officers in smart red uniforms with the red band around the caps. We saluted them all but the senior ones, and there were many of them, who seemed not even to notice us. The junior ones seemed almost embarrassed when they saw us, especially when they saw the M.C. on my chest.

The two ladies arrived together. Mary looked the same but Alice was not the little sister I had last seen when she had visited me in the hospital in the summer. She had not only blossomed she had changed. It was as though she had become a butterfly. She was stunning. I knew it was not just me looking at her with proud brother's eyes; I saw officers turning to look as she rushed up to me. She dressed flamboyantly with a hat at a racy angle. I was not sure that mother would have approved of her make-up.

She flung her arms around me and planted a bright red kiss on my cheek. She suddenly seemed to notice my broken arm and she stepped back. "Oh Bill, wounded again! You must take care of yourself!"

I was aware that Mary and Gordy were locked in each other's arms. "Alice, this is Ted and Charlie, they are pilots in my squadron. Ted, Charlie, this is my little sister, Alice."

She squealed with delight, "How delicious! I had worried that when Beatrice came I should be the lemon but here I am with two handsome officers to escort me." She linked Ted and Charlie. "Come on Mary, we have so much to do this morning!"

My sister had become a force of nature and both Ted and Charlie were not only taken aback they were under her spell from the moment she spoke and linked them. She led them off towards Piccadilly. I waited until Mary and Gordy had had some private time and then Mary linked Gordy and me and we followed them.

Mary leaned in and spoke confidentially to me. "Your little sister is a pip, Bill. She has designed and made my wedding dress and dresses for her and Beattie. I don't know what I would have done without her."

"Is she managing down here then?"

"She is already a huge success. Lady Burscough's friend is more than pleased with her. She has had a pay rise already." She paused to kiss me on the other cheek. "There you have two red marks now!" She laughed. I looked over and saw how happy Gordy was. It helped me to make my mind up, finally. I would speak with Beattie before the leave was over. I had delayed long enough. "Beattie's shift finishes at seven so we are meeting her at the Ritz."

"The Ritz? That sounds expensive." Gordy looked worried.

"It is! But we are not having a honeymoon so this will have to do and the wedding breakfast is at my house so we have saved money on that." She became serious. "Oh don't spoil it. It is Alice and Beattie's idea. They wanted to make it a special night. And we couldn't have done it without Bill here."

"Me?"

"Yes, when we tried to book it we were told they were full until Beattie said that you would be one of the guests. She even had the photograph of the King giving you your medal and so they said they could accommodate us and would be proud to do so for a British Ace."

I shook my head. I was just a pilot who had been luckier than most. "I don't like all this fuss."

Gordy laughed, "If it gets us treated like royalty then I am happy enough!"

We had a wonderful day and managed to see just about everything from the Houses of Parliament to Buckingham Palace. Alice insisted on taking us along the expensive shops in Bond Street and Burlington Arcade and then took us to a very fashionable dress shop where she showed us two of her dress designs in the window.

"Of course, until the war is over then we have to think about cost and be less ambitious but when the war is over… just watch me, big brother."

Both Ted and Charlie hung on her every word but it was Charlie who was definitely smitten. I hoped that Alice would not hurt him. I would have to have a word with her later on. I felt responsible for Charlie; he was vulnerable.

Late in the afternoon, we parted. "Should we dress in civilian clothes or evening dress tonight?"

"Don't you dare, our Bill! Wear your uniform and try to wear your hat at a jaunty angle. You are a hero! Look the part!"

Alice kissed us all goodbye as she hurried off to her lodgings. Mary laughed as she kissed Gordy. "She is a peach, Bill!"

Charlie seemed in a dream world as we walked back to the hotel. Ted chuckled. "Your Mary is right, Gordy. She's like a breath of fresh air. I'd forgotten what it was like to laugh."

They went ahead while I lit my pipe. Charlie asked, "Do you know if your sister has a young man, Bill?"

I stopped, "I don't think so why?"

"She's lovely."

"You have only just met her."

He replied, earnestly, "Oh I know. I am just saying she ought to have a young man. Any boy would be honoured to walk out with her. I know I felt ten feet tall when she linked me."

I didn't know what to say. Our Alice just liked fun. Perhaps she had only been pleasant with my two friends because they were my friends. I know Ted hadn't taken any of it seriously but then he was much older than Charlie. I could not do much about it. I would seek the advice of Beatrice; she would know what to say. As we entered the hotel I wondered about Mary's use of '*Beattie*'. Did she want me to call her by a shortened form of her name? I had only ever used Beatrice and she had never corrected me. I tapped my pipe out in an ashtray. I was just like Charlie- I was out of my depth.

Bates was sitting in the lounge drinking a cup of tea and reading a paper when I returned. He folded his paper and stood. "A good day, sir?"

"Excellent and tonight we dine at the Ritz."

He nodded as we went up the stairs to our room. "And they will want you in your uniform I daresay."

"How did you know that?"

He smiled, "Ladies like to be on the arm of a smart and handsome officer. That is you, sir. I will clean your uniform. You really need a decent spare sir."

"I'll go tomorrow and order one then."

"That's the ticket!" We entered my room. "Now I shall draw you a bath and I will have the worst of the marks removed by the time you are finished."

I didn't know how I had managed before Bates. He shaved you so closely, that your face felt like a lady's hand. He had also persuaded me, some time ago, to grow a moustache. He had trimmed it when I returned to the squadron and he did so again.

He stood back to admire me like a painting he had just finished. "There you are, sir. I hope your young lady approves."

"You can ask her yourself at the wedding."

He seemed shocked, "I am invited?"

"Of course, you are a member of the squadron are you not?"

He seemed genuinely touched, "Thank you, sir. I am honoured."

We reached the Ritz before the ladies and stood outside smoking and admiring all the well-dressed bright people who went in. We noticed that, while the women were all young, many of the men were almost old men.

Ted said, "Well I am an ugly old bugger but some of these chaps look positively ancient."

Gordy laughed at him, "You are too stuck in your ways and you are a miserable old man. You'll end your days as a bachelor."

He brightened, "Then I will keep most of my money then?"

When the three ladies arrived, they came by car. Beatrice and Mary got out first and Alice leaned back in to kiss the driver on the cheek. I saw Charlie and his face fell. I think his heart broke in that instant. And then I forgot about Charlie completely for Beatrice was in my arms. "Oh, you look so handsome!" She kissed me full on the lips. She reached up and whispered in my ear. "I have a week's leave starting tomorrow afternoon."

"That is wonderful news." We walked through the entrance past the liveried doorman. Alice had linked Ted and Charlie again. "What about going up to Lancashire for a visit to see my home?"

She gave me a mischievous look. "Why, what is up there that I might want to see?"

I was crestfallen, "Well my family live there and I thought…"

"You thought what?"

"Well you and I, you know, we have been walking out and …"

I knew that I was being teased but I just didn't know how to handle it. "And what? What are your intentions Captain Harsker?"

I was suddenly aware that we were in the sumptuous lobby of the Ritz, all chandeliers and bright lights and the others had stopped to remove their coats. They were all looking intently at me. "Well… er, well I want to marry you."

Alice burst out laughing and came to kiss me on the cheek. "Our Bill, that is the worst proposal I have ever heard. If Beattie accepts it then you are the luckiest man in the world!"

When I looked at Beatrice, I saw that there was a look of joy on her face. She said huskily, "Of course I will and I think it was a lovely proposal. It was just like you." I used my good arm to help her take her coat off and handed it to the attendant. "And now let us go and have some fun!"

It was the most spectacular place I had ever seen. When the manager heard that we were celebrating a proposal of marriage and a wedding he insisted on providing us with Champagne. It delighted Alice. The evening started off really well. Then I noticed that Charlie was looking down in the mouth. I waited until Beatrice and Alice had gone to the cloakroom and I asked, "What's up Charlie?"

"It's your sister. She obviously has a chap. She came in his car!"

Mary had overheard for she was sitting on the other inside of me. She leaned over and touched Charlie's hand. "That chap is the husband of the woman who Alice works with. He is old enough to be her father." She smiled, "And Alice likes you."

The change was remarkable. The grin never left his face all night. We were all a little drunk by the time the evening ended. I would not see Beattie again until the day of the wedding and I hugged her and kissed her as though I would never see her again. We had money for a taxi for the ladies as some rich gentleman had recognised both my medal and my name and insisted on paying the bill at the Ritz. The Head Waiter told us that the old man's only son had died at Ypres. Everywhere we went were reminders of the war and its effects. The war was striking everyone. We had even heard of bombing raids over London! This was a new kind of war. The Germans seemed to be inventing many new ways of killing and it was indiscriminate.

We strolled unsteadily back to our hotel. It was a chilly night but we didn't care. Charlie walked with me. He talked incessantly of the evening and the fun but mainly he spoke of Alice. He was drunk on Alice rather than the Champagne we had consumed and he bombarded me with questions about her. He had fallen for her. This was not a Gunbus this was an infatuation with my little sister who was as unpredictable as the weather. I just hoped that he knew how to land! Otherwise, he could crash and burn.

Chapter 4

There were just the three of us in our carriage as the train chugged north. Charlie had decided to stay on in London for the rest of his leave. It seemed my sister had become more important than his family. Alice seemed quite happy to show Charlie around when she had time from work. Ted went home and we left the love birds in Mary's lovely little house where, I dare say, they would make up for the months apart.

The wedding had been charming. The handful of guests did not detract from the joy on Mary and Gordy's faces. Bates had fussed around them like a mother hen after the ceremony. We had all returned to Mary's to celebrate. She and Beatrice had made huge amounts of food and Bates saw to our every need.

He was still looking after us now as we made our way north. We would only have six days there for the train took a day to reach Burscough and we had to allow two to three days to get back to the airfield and France. A delay would mean that our comrades would not get a full leave.

Beatrice leaned over, "Do you think your mother will like me?"

"She will love you. Why do you ask?"

"Mothers have a tendency to view any woman as a threat."

"Don't be daft. Mum isn't like that. Besides I am sure our Alice has already told her about you."

She seemed mollified by that and we watched the rain-shrouded land as we sped through the factories of the Midlands. I knew that all of them would be churning out material for the war. What would they make once the war was over? It was a sobering thought that this war was costing a fortune. The Gunbus could not be cheap to build and the squadron had got through almost twenty of them with losses and damage.

"Penny for them."

"Oh sorry, I was just thinking about the waste of money that this war is."

"I think it is a greater tragedy that we have damaged and lost so many fine young men. Think of all the futures there will never be. They lie in the mud of Flanders and France."

We both looked up at Bates. He was a thoughtful soul. He listened well and when he spoke his words were worth hearing. "Quite right, Bates, the money is nothing."

He stood. "Now you two talk about something more cheerful. There is a buffet car on this train. I shall go and get us a cup of tea eh?"

Once again we had managed to get a compartment to ourselves. After he had gone we risked talking of a future after the war. Gordy and Mary had made that leap. It was a risk for one never knew where one would fall. But we planned anyway.

After changing trains at Liverpool we managed to get the tea-time train to Burscough. We arrived after dark and, as we pulled into the dimly lit station, I wondered how we would get to the cottage. Bates and I could walk but I couldn't ask Beatrice to do so.

I helped her from the carriage while Bates brought the bags. I saw that there were boxes being unloaded from the guard's van and I recognised old Harry from the hall. "Wait here would you?"

I ran down the platform. "Harry!"

He grinned when he recognised me, "Little Billy Harsker! And aren't you looking smart? Home on leave are you? Your mam and dad aren't expecting you."

I suddenly felt guilty but if I had sent a telegram it might have upset them. "Yes, this is a surprise. Listen, there are three of us. Any chance of a lift?"

He nodded, "Aye if you don't mind sitting in the wagon."

"Anything is better than Shanks' pony."

"Get your stuff on board. It'll be nice to chat to you. We don't have many young lads around here anymore."

Bates had to sit in the back with the boxes but he didn't seem to mind. "Your mam and dad will be glad to see you. When your mam got that telegram we all thought that you were dead."

I had forgotten that when I went missing there would have been a telegram. I felt even guiltier now. I had been so caught up in the wedding and Beatrice that I had forgotten my family at home. "But they know I am alive now don't they?"

"Oh aye, Lord Burscough rang home and her ladyship went to see your mam. But they were all upset for a couple of days. Everybody was. You are quite famous; picture in the paper, met the king." Once again I had a fame I had not sought.

We pulled up outside the cottage which seemed so tiny now. When we had been growing up we thought that having three bedrooms was a luxury. I wondered what Bates and Beatrice would make of it.

As we pulled up my dad came out with a lantern. I saw him shield his eyes as he tried to see who it was. "Is that you Harry? Is there a problem with Jess?" That was typical of my father. He worried about his horses even though he was semi-retired. Jess was one of his favourites.

"No Jack, I picked up your Bill from the station."

I jumped down into the light and shook dad's hand. "Mother, it's our Bill. He's here in the flesh."

I helped Beatrice down. "And this is Beatrice Porter, Dad."

My dad was not often stuck for words but he was then. Beatrice gave him a smile and shook his hand. "I am very pleased to meet you."

Bates appeared and stood quietly behind us. "This is Airman Bates from my squadron."

Harry had placed the bag at the door. "I'll tell your Kath and his lordship that you are back."

"His lordship is home?"

"Aye." He nodded at my arm. "He's picked up a wound too."

He clambered up and clicked his tongue. Jess took the wagon along the track to the main house. The door opened and bathed us in light. My mother stood there looking older and frailer than I remembered. She began to cry as she threw her arms around me and sobbed into my chest. "Our Bill! We thought you were dead! I am glad you are safe."

"I'm too stubborn to die, our mum." She stepped back to look at me. "Could we put up my young lady and my friend? I am sorry I couldn't let you know but…"

My mother's good manners took over, "Of course, come on in. Father, go and put a kettle on for the hot water bottles."

Beatrice was ushered in and Bates, said, "Let me help you with that Mr Harsker" and he and dad disappeared to fill the kettle.

Mum was just taking Beatrice's coat when my words registered with her. "Young lady?"

I took Beatrice's coat from mum and put it on the hook behind the door. I went up to them both and put my arms around them. "Yes, mum, my young lady. We are going to get married."

I glanced at Beatrice and saw the look of apprehension flicker in her eyes. There was a moment of awkward silence and them mum grabbed me and kissed me on both cheeks before doing the same to a surprised Beatrice. "I am so pleased! Oh, why didn't you warn me? We could have had food in and a nice meal waiting and… father!"

She screeched it so loud that dad and Bates rushed in. "Whatever is the matter?"

"Our Bill is going to marry this young lady, Beatrice."

Bless dad, he hugged Beatrice so hard I worried that she would break in two. "Well, that calls for a celebration!"

Mum looked crestfallen, "We've nowt in!"

"I'll nip up to the big house and have a word with our Sarah."

"Eeeh you can't, our Bill, that's proper cheeky."

I grabbed my greatcoat, "Shy bairns get nowt. Besides, you two can chat."

I ran to the house. I was ecstatic. I don't know why I was worried. I should have had more faith in mum and dad. I rang the bell and Cedric, our Sarah's husband, answered it. He smiled when he saw me. "Harry said that you were home. Good to see you." He saw my broken arm. "You've been in the wars I see."

I burst out laughing! "For the last two years!"

Our Sarah appeared, "Whatever is the… oh, Bill!" She hugged me. "Do you want his lordship? They have just sat down to dinner."

"No, it's mum she has no food in and I said I would cadge some off you!"

They both laughed, "Cheeky bugger. Come round to the back and I'll sort something out for you."

I went around the familiar path to the servants' entrance. Sarah arrived first and she opened the door. Come in and I'll get you a box."

The servants were eating around the table. Cedric and Sarah were the head servants but I knew all the others. They all shouted hello. Harry said, "I told you he was home. Wounded little soldier eh?"

"It's just a broken arm, Harry."

"Oh." Harry sounded disappointed.

Sarah had just returned with the box. "Yes, but you broke it escaping from the Germans and you nearly died!"

"It was nothing!"

Before it became even more embarrassing Lord Burscough came in. His right arm was in a sling. We both burst out laughing. "Well a fine pair we make, Bill and I can't even shake your hand."

Sarah looked embarrassed, "I was just getting Bill some food for…"

"Nonsense we have plenty let them eat here."

I shook my head, "Very kind your lordship but you know Mum. She will want to cook for me the first night back."

"Quite. Well, how about tomorrow? Harry tells me you have a pretty young lady with you and someone from your squadron."

"Yes sir, it is my fiancée and my manservant." I saw the reaction from the servants around the table. That moment marked the instant when I changed in their eyes, my sister included. I had left the world of service and become a gentleman.

"Well, bring them both. Her ladyship is looking forward to meeting her."

"She has met her already sir. She met her at the hospital in London. She was my nurse when I was wounded."

He shook his head. "Then it will be a fine tale at dinner!"

When I reached the cottage again there was no sign of Bates but mum and dad were busy chatting to Beatrice. "His lordship insisted on giving us a box of food. And it is cooked!" Lord Burscough had had Sarah make up plates of food from the dinner they were enjoying. There was more than enough and it would mean mum didn't have to cook.

Beatrice took it from me and said, "Get washed up then."

"Where's Bates?"

"John is upstairs warming and airing the beds." I looked in surprise at my dad. "He's a nice chap he is. You look after him!"

I was not certain that my father understood the way the Royal Flying Corps functioned but I nodded and went to get washed.

It was crowded around the little table with five of us but cosy. Bates, or John as everyone else was calling him, and Beatrice, or Beattie as my mum and dad called her, served up.

Mum glowed, "Eeeh this is lovely. It's like before the war when we had all the family around." She looked at me sharply, "And where is Alice I should like to know?"

I exchanged a knowing look with Beatrice. "We met her in London. She was at my friend's wedding but she had to work."

"I am still not happy about her being in London all by herself. It is a sinful place."

"She is doing well Mrs Harsker."

"I told you, it's Mary or Mother."

"Well, Mary, we saw some of her work and she designs beautiful dresses. The wedding dress she made for Mary Hewitt was exquisite." She looked at me. "I hope she will make me one."

Every head swivelled to look at me. Dad said, "Have you picked a date, son?"

I shook my head. "With the war and, its winter and…"

"And we haven't had time to talk about it yet." A twinkle came into Beatrice's eye as she said, "But we have a few days now to sort things out."

For some reason, that pleased my mother inordinately. "This one will sort you out, young Billy Harsker!"

Later, as Dad and I went to the pub, I discovered what impact Beatrice had made. Bates had declined a visit to the pub saying he would stay and do the dishes. Beatrice fought over the right to do that and I left a minor battle of wills between the three of them.

It was pleasant strolling to the pub with my dad. "She is a lovely lass, our Bill. Your mum and I can rest easy now." He took his pipe out to examine the bowl. "Your mum was so upset when you were reported missing. She still thinks of you and Albert as young kids."

"I know, Harry told me."

"Anyroad up your young lady has given us comfort."

We entered the pub and I saw the effect of the war. The ebullient welcome of my earlier leaves was now replaced by dour, sad faces. The village had lost many young men. They appreciated my visit and I think I cheered them up but it was a reminder of why we were fighting this war.

Chapter 5

Bates and I were the first ones to arrive at Victoria Station. It had been a sad parting for both of us. Beatrice had become quite close to my servant. As we had travelled south she had finally told ME that she preferred Beattie or Bea to Beatrice. I had asked why she hadn't said anything before and she told me she thought I liked to call her Beatrice and didn't want to upset me. It was then I resolved to speak my mind a little more. It would save misunderstandings. I had another poignant goodbye from the woman I loved. Victoria Station seemed just a little chillier than it had after she left us.

"Thank you for this little break, sir."

"What are you talking about, John? One handed I could not have managed without you!"

"And that is simply not true, sir. Miss Porter would have cared for you. She is a nurse after all."

"Well, I am glad you came. Mum and dad were quite taken with you."

"That's what I mean sir. I was in a family and I was welcomed. You can't imagine what that is like for me. I feel ten years younger and, well, happy, and I just wanted to thank you."

As I filled my pipe I wondered what kind of home life he must have had to make him the way he was.

Freddie and Johnny arrived next closely followed by Ted. They all seemed to have had a good time but Johnny was disappointed not to have had Christmas with his family.

Freddie tried to cheer his friend up. "It will be grand to have Christmas this year with just a few of us. We'll have the whole mess to ourselves. We can get some decent booze in Amiens. It will be great."

I was not certain if he was trying to talk it up for himself. I knew that this was as good a Christmas as I could have. Bea would be on duty all over Christmas anyway. We had celebrated Christmas twice; once with my family and once at the Big House with Lord Burscough.

Gordy arrived out of breath. Ted shook his head and pointed to the cigarette. "Too many gaspers me old mate! You'll have to cut down!"

He grinned, "I wanted the maximum time with Mary. I have had to run the last mile!" He looked around the half-circle. "Where's Charlie?"

"I don't know but he might miss the train if he doesn't get here soon. It leaves in two minutes. We had better get aboard!"

We managed to get a compartment to ourselves and while Bates arranged the bags on the luggage rack I stood by the open door watching for Charlie. I wondered where he could have got to. The guard came down the platform. "You'll have to board Captain. The train is due out."

I could not see him and I climbed in and then, as the guard slammed it shut, pulled the leather strap to open the window. I had just heard the whistle when I saw Charlie and Alice, hand in hand as they ran down the platform. The train gave the familiar judder as its wheels turned and struggled for grip. "Come on Charlie!" I saw that Alice held her shoes in her hands and was running in stockinged feet. I flung open the door. The train was barely moving and he would be able to jump on board. Then, to my amazement, he stopped and gave Alice a long lingering kiss.

The train began to move a little faster. "Lieutenant Sharp, get your arse on this train now!" Ted could still sound like a sergeant when he needed to.

Charlie turned, picked up his bag and began to run. The train had picked up speed. He hurled his bag on board and then threw himself into my arms. I dragged him on board and Gordy slammed the door shut.

Bates rolled his eyes as he picked up the bag and placed it on the luggage rack. Charlie could not take the grin off his face. Ted said, "If you had missed this train you would have missed the boat and then you would have been Absent Without Leave! What were you thinking?"

Gordy lit a cigarette and stretched out his legs. "I think our young flight commander wasn't thinking. He is in love. Am I right?"

He grinned and nodded, "I think I must be. Bill, er sir, your sister is wonderful."

I was worried and I asked, "And she feels the same?"

"Oh yes, sir. We have been together every night seeing shows and well, doing all sorts sir and she is wonderful!"

Ted said wryly, "I think we can take it as read that she is wonderful."

Johnny and Freddie laughed at Charlie's discomfort. I changed the subject to take the attention away from my former gunner who still looked as though he was on the station at Victoria. "I was talking to Lord Burscough. He flies the DH 2."

"I hear they are a nice little machine."

"Oh they are but they are as slow as our Gunbus. He and his squadron were badly knocked about by those new Albatros fighters with the twin machine guns. He said that the Germans just couldn't miss and they flew rings around his aeroplanes."

I began to fill my pipe.

"Are there any new aeroplanes on the cards for us?"

I lowered my voice as Lord Burscough had been in his cups when he had told me. "There are two: a Bristol with a synchronised machine gun and rear gunner and a nippy little single-seat number made by Sopwith. They call it a Pup and it has a synchronised machine gun."

"Just the one though."

"Just the one."

"Then the Hun still has the advantage."

The journey back was more sombre and there was less jollity and fewer jokes. We played cards or just closed our eyes and thought of the pleasant time we had all had in England.

The major had sent a truck for us. I think he and the others were keen for their leave to commence. As soon as I dismounted he said, "Go and see Doc Brennan. I want to know if you are fit to fly."

I turned to go and then asked, "Something up?"

"We lost Bertie Cole the other day."

"I thought we were staying on our side of the lines?"

"We were but the Germans decided to come over and play. They flew rings around us. Anyway, if you aren't fit then I shall have to stay."

When I reached the sickbay the doctor had just finished packing. He smiled when he saw me. "Is it still itching?"

In answer, I proffered the knitting needle I had borrowed from my mum. "If it wasn't for this I would have gone mad."

"That is a good sign it means it is healing. Jackson!"

His orderly came in, "Sir."

"Get me the cutters, we'll take off the plaster."

I sat in the chair. I was excited to be getting rid of the cumbersome plaster cast which had made me so reliant on others. I should have noticed that Jackson had his hands on my shoulders; it was a warning I missed. Doc Brennan went carefully but the cold steel did catch the tender point where the break had been and I winced. I was determined not to show pain for I wanted to be returned to active duty.

When the cast came off I felt the cold air on my bare and exceedingly hairy arm but I smiled. Doc Brennan laughed. "You should be on the stage Bill. That hurt like buggery I dare say." He examined the arm and was very careful not to hurt it. "A compression bandage, Jackson, and it will need changing every day. Make sure that Captain Harsker reports every morning or you have my permission to stop him flying!"

Jackson grinned, "It'll be a pleasure, sir!"

"Now you are fit for duty but for goodness sake take it easy with the arm. At least it is your left one so you are less likely to strain it." He went to his desk and brought out a rubber ball. "Every day I want you to squeeze this five hundred times in the morning and five hundred times at night. If you are bored during the day then use it as often as you can. It's called physiotherapy. All the rage apparently. And now I will bid you farewell and enjoy a decent leave with my wife and children."

"Thanks, Doc, you are a brick!"

"Be careful, Bill. You take too many risks and from what I hear you have a young lady now. Think of her."

I left the sickbay and returned to the office. The Major and the Captain were both there. I smiled, "He gave me the all-clear."

I saw the relief on Archie's face. It had been a long time since he had had a leave. "It should be quiet. Headquarters have told us that there will be no offensive in our sector over the Christmas period. Just tootle about and show the lads in brown we are still here but take no chances!"

Bearing in mind what Lord Burscough had said I had no intention of poking the sleeping dog. I would let it lie.

Flight Sergeant Hutton had had a shorter leave but he was pleased to see me. "I spent some time with Senior Flight Lowery We managed to get a few more revs out of the engine. From what I have seen we will need all the speed we can get and then some."

"We have been told to keep a low profile. I don't think there will be too much action over Christmas."

"How is the arm, sir?"

"A little tender but not too bad."

I asked Charlie to be adjutant for the next two weeks. It was mainly paperwork and it would help me to find out what really went on between him and Alice. I did not want to see him retreat back into his shell. And, in addition, it would make him a better pilot for he would see the bigger picture.

I sat with Gordy and Ted in the mess. Charlie was busy writing a letter to Alice and I needed to work out a strategy for the next two weeks which would keep us safe and yet watch over the men in the trenches.

"Well, if the weather stays the same as it is now then we won't be flying!"

Ted was right. There were gales and the remnants of an Atlantic hurricane. We would be safe for the next few days. "But once the storm passes then we know it will be calm. How should we approach this?"

"We only have six aeroplanes. We have too many chiefs and not enough Indians."

Gordy had hit the nail on the head. I looked at my two friends and came up with an idea. "Well, how about this? You two fly as one flight. Between you, there is more experience in the air than the rest of us put together. I will fly with Freddie. Charlie and Johnny can be another flight. We will fly a one-hour patrol so that we have all six aeroplanes in the air during one day. It will make the Hun think we have a full squadron at the field."

"You think they may try to take advantage?"

"Archie and Randolph told me that the new German squadron's aeroplanes are brightly coloured but one aeroplane, in particular, has a distinctive red livery. That sounds like someone trying to make a name for themselves. With the new aeroplanes, they have they know they can knock us out of the air anytime they like. If I was their squadron leader I would try to give us a bloody nose over Christmas so that in the New Year we will be nervous."

"I am bloody nervous already and no mistake. But I think you have made the best of a bad job. You are the boss. We will go with your idea... sir!"

"Ted, I prefer the miserable old sod! You are unnerving me with this optimism!"

Three days later I took Freddie on the first patrol. I have to admit that I, too, was nervous. I was not certain how my broken arm would cope with the rigours of a two-hour patrol. Although we would only be over the front for one hour it would take us thirty minutes to get there and thirty to get back. I think all of the ground crew were worried too for they fussed over the engine and the guns right until take off. I felt happy with Freddie behind me. He had developed into a sound pilot and he and his gunner had a good relationship. I climbed higher than normal. Perhaps it was nerves. Once we reached the Somme River I slowed the engine down and engaged in a simple patrol along our lines.

Lumpy had a camera, for headquarters wanted photographs of the front. We had been told to get as many as we could along the length of our patrol area. It did not take a genius to work out that there would be an offensive in the spring.

My decision was vindicated when we saw the three old Fokker IIs as they headed for our lines. I had dreaded running into the deadly Albatros D.III. The three had not seen us and were flying over our lines. I saw the men in the trenches popping away ineffectually with small arms.

I heard Lumpy's voice in my ear. "Well, sir, are we doing owt about them or are we going to let them photograph our positions?"

It was as near to a criticism as Hutton would go. "Point taken Flight Sergeant, let's go and discourage them.

A soon as I banked to cross their lines I knew that Freddie would follow. "Ready, Lumpy?"

"Oh aye, sir."

I watched as he cocked his Lewis. I cocked mine and regretted it immediately. I had a spasm of pain shoot up my left arm. I thanked God I would not have to do it again.

We came down and across the flight of three which was flying in an arrow formation. It gave us our best chance for Lumpy could spray all three of them. I had meant what I had said; I was in no mood for heroics. I merely wanted them discouraged.

Lumpy opened fire and I knew that we had caught them unawares. His bullets ripped through the fuselage of the first Fokker and into the tail and rudder of the second. Then his gun jammed. I was ready with my gun and I opened fire. Like Lumpy my bullet struck the fuselage and I saw it bank. I must have either hit the pilot or something vital. I began to climb. I did not want to lose the advantage of height. I heard Freddie's two guns. I swung to the west and saw that Freddie had downed the last of the Fokkers and the other two were heading east. One had smoke from his engine. It was as good an ending as I could have hoped.

We tootled around for another thirty minutes and then I led us home. Relieved but aching from my arm which was telling me I should not have flown.

The other four aeroplanes had uneventful flights. I sat in the office, smoked my pipe and did the paperwork which mounted up every day. Perhaps we could just send two aeroplanes a day up. It would save wear and tear on the pilots and buses. Charlie asked, "What are you thinking sir?"

I told him and he said, "We could always keep two aeroplanes ready to go in case we needed them."

He was right and I saw the advantage of an adjutant. Another brain was always handy. For the next ten days, whenever flying was possible we used the technique. We shot no more enemy aeroplanes down but we had no casualties either. I was changing in this long-drawn-out war.

Chapter 6

I would be lying if I said I was unhappy with the return of the others in January. I found the pressure of command just a little too much. Charlie had been an excellent adjutant and showed a real skill. He liaised with everyone from the quartermaster to the cooks to ensure that everything ran smoothly. His attitude and demeanour had changed dramatically following his meeting with Alice. He was a different man. He could go far in the Corps after the war.

I spent an hour with the major and Randolph and told them what we had done while they were on leave. "You've both done well. Do you think that Sharp is ready for promotion?"

"He does the same job as Gordy and Ted so I would say yes."

"Well, we are getting replacement pilots next week ready for whatever the brass hats have in mind for us in spring so I'll put the paperwork through." He smiled, "Despite your little spat with Captain Ebbs our credit with the General appears to be high. Don't tell him of his promotion yet in case it doesn't come through but you can tell Hutton that he has been awarded the M.M.." He laughed, "You are quite the double act; the only M.C. and M.M. in the whole squadron!"

When I told Lumpy he was suitably modest. "You should have got something. We would both have died if it weren't for you."

"Don't worry Flight, I am more than happy with my M.C."

The weather gods smiled on us for we were unable to fly for the next ten days. It allowed us to meet with our new pilots so that we could tell them what to do once we were in the air. They came directly from flying school and just wanted to get in the air and knock the Hun from the sky. They could fly but they could not fight.

Flight Sergeant Lowery had had a couple of his lads make models of German aeroplanes as well as our own so that we could show them, in the safety of the mess, the tactics and moves we would be performing. We were also able to tell them a little more about the enemy aeroplanes we would be meeting. They had to know how deadly the new Fokker and Albatros fighters were. Thankfully there only appeared to be a handful but with their twin guns, they were a danger to be feared.

Charlie was pleased about the promotion when it came through, but not as pleased as I had expected. "Don't get me, wrong, sir, I think it is marvellous and the extra money will come in very handy. The thing is I am not certain now that I will stay in after the war is over. I mean there is

Alice. You didn't want to drag Beatrice around the country following you, well I can't do that to Alice. She has a career."

I was taken aback. He had known her but a week. "You are thinking about marriage? Rushing things a little aren't you?"

"With respect sir, life is too short not to take the bull by the horns. We love each other and we want to be together. I haven't asked her yet but there is an understanding. Next time we get a leave I am going up to meet your parents and that might be a good time."

"We won't have another leave in Blighty now until much later in the year. You know that."

"I know sir. But I can plan."

I knew that I couldn't blame him but it all seemed a little hasty. I mentioned it to Bates that evening as he was laying out my clothes. "I know what you are saying, sir, but they do seem to be a lovely couple; much like yourself and Miss Porter. I envy you both. The other officers I served had had wives and enjoyed a brief family life. From what I can see Mr Sharp has had none of that. It would be cruel to deny him the opportunity. The war can't last forever."

"I know, Bates, but can we survive this war? It seems to me that the odds are now moving against us."

He had hung up my tunic and said, "Yes sir but you and the other chaps seem to have the knack of evening the odds, don't you?"

We now had four flights of five aeroplanes with Major Leach as a floating reserve. Having done his job for a few days I understood why he did not fly as much as the rest of us. The old Colonel had never flown at all. I had told him what Lord Burscough had said about the new German aeroplanes. As a result, we flew in two flights of ten aeroplanes. We needed protection in numbers. It was the middle of January when we began our patrols in earnest.

We were given the sector north of Cambrai. I was the one who had flown over here when we had fled the Germans in the autumn and I had ridden the land when in the cavalry. It looked to be a jungle of icy jarred spikes and water-filled craters. The winter had frozen the scene of death and destruction. Everything looked black, white or grey. Nothing seemed to move. When the weather eased and it became warmer I knew that it would be a morass of mud. I pitied the Tommies trying to hold that let alone advance across it.

The fact that we were patrolling meant that the Generals were planning a spring offensive. Our first patrol was just to acclimatise us to the new sector. It proved to be a baptism of fire.

We reached our sector and I led A and C flights north, in the general direction of Arras. Gordy led B and D flights south towards the Somme. Lumpy flashed signals to the ground to identify us. We would be liaising closely with them and it was important that the signallers on the ground and Lumpy got to know each other's signalling idiosyncrasies. There was low cloud that day. It made Lumpy's job easier but made our life more precarious. I was glad that it was Freddie who was at the rear of our line. Although I had the most experience flight we still needed everyone's attention on the grey clouds scudding in from the east.

"Righto, sir. We have established communication. They say it has been quiet over this sector for a while. We can carry on with the patrol."

"We'll go north for twenty minutes and then turn around. No point risking anything if this has been quiet."

It was almost peaceful as we chugged north-west along the front line and No-Man's Land. We could see tendrils of smoke as the footsloggers brewed up. We saw nothing of the enemy and I banked right to begin us on a reciprocal course. It was as we banked that I caught a flash of light. Some stray shaft of sunlight must have flickered off the small windscreen of a German aeroplane. There was a flight of six of them. They must have been doing the same as we were and had banked at the same time.

"Lumpy, eyes to port. Try to identify the Hun over there."

"Will do, Captain Harsker."

I began to climb. If they stayed on their side of the lines then I would leave well alone but if they were inclined to cross No-Man's Land then we would jump them.

"They look like the Halberstadt D.V. sir."

They were marginally faster than we were but they only had a single forward-firing machine gun. They had a greater ceiling but if we gained the height advantage then that would negate its effect. I waggled my wings to let the other aeroplanes know that I had seen the enemy.

"Looks like they are heading west sir." I looked and saw that he was right. This made no sense unless they had spotted something interesting. Lumpy's sharp eyes spotted it. "It looks like Captain Thomas is nursing one of the new lads back sir. His bus looks to be smoking."

The six Halberstadt aeroplanes had seen two easy victims and were ready for quick kills. "Right Lumpy let's go."

I armed my Lewis as Lumpy armed his. I pushed the stick forward as I banked left. It would bring us on to the rear quarter of the flight of six. The Gunbus was such a huge aeroplane that I knew they must have seen us. Their speed meant that they could outrun us unless we could cut them off.

I saw that they were closing rapidly with Ted who was taking his young pilot as low as he could. I could imagine the terror for the young lieutenant. This was his first patrol, he had a dodgy engine and there were six fast German aeroplanes on his tail. I watched as Ted's gunner stood and manned the rear-firing Lewis. I brought us around a little more to starboard. We were now less than a mile from them and they were so intent on their helpless victims that it appeared that they had not seen us. They were single-seaters and had no observer. I knew that my flight would know what to do and all Charlie's flight needed to do was copy us.

The rattle of German guns showed that they were in range. The single Lewis, which fired in reply, seemed inadequate somehow. I saw holes appear in the rudder of Ted's aeroplane. The six Germans were flying in two formations, line astern. "Lumpy, I am going to take the front two. You concentrate on the second two eh?"

"Yes, sir."

It was an advantage I would take. We could fire at two targets. Smoke was now pouring from Lieutenant Tinkler's aeroplane. He would be lucky to get home in one piece regardless of what the Germans did. I was forced to open fire earlier than I would have liked. I needed to distract them. The tracer arced towards the nearest Halberstadt. The bullets missed but he jerked his aeroplane around to face the new threat. I gave a longer burst at the second aeroplane as Hutton sprayed the next two. I heard the chatter of the Lewis guns of the buses behind me. They were dealing with the first German whom I had missed. I struck the engine of the second Halberstadt and I emptied the magazine. The propeller stopped turning and the doomed aeroplane began to dive towards the ground. I banked left to enable Lumpy to continue firing.

As I tried to change magazines my injured arm sent waves of pain and I had to stop. I could not fire. It was up to Lumpy now. I saw that he had managed to damage a second aeroplane. As I came around the first Halberstadt I had missed was tumbling to the ground and the remaining Germans were fleeing; they were outnumbered. There was little point in following for they had a greater speed than we did. I banked right and followed Ted and his wounded chick. It was fortunate that we had come upon the enemy unawares and that they only had a single machine gun. The newer fighters would have made mincemeat of us.

Lumpy took out the bugle he kept in the cockpit which he used to announce our departure. He blew the cavalry charge. I wondered what the men on the ground and the new pilots would make of the sound. It was good for my flight for we were the cavalry flight with all the connotations the word brought. My Gunbus had the rearing horse painted by Freddie. It was still new and sharply painted.

Lieutenant Tinkler was flying as well as he could and when I saw the airfield in the distance I knew that he would make it. Ted's flare told me that he had someone wounded. I hoped it was not him. We allowed the damaged craft to land first and then Ted. Finally, we landed in two lines. The airfield had been repaired since the German bombing raid. We parked the aeroplanes and the gunners and mechanics began to service both the guns and the aeroplanes. It was a handy routine and enabled the pilots to make their reports.

I saw that it was Ted's gunner who had been wounded. It looked as though he had had his hand mashed by a bullet. He would be invalided out now. Ted was smoking a cigarette when I wandered up to him.

"Thanks, Bill. It was getting a bit dicey up there."

"What happened?"

"Young Michael's engine started to smoke. It is a new aeroplane and he has not had a chance to put the hours in the air. It must be a Friday afternoon engine." It was probably unfair but when we had an occasional mistake in a new Rolls Royce engine we put it down to the last shift on a Friday.

"We were just fortunate that it was the old Halberstadt. The new German jobs would have had you both before we could have reached you."

"And don't I know it."

We went to make our report. I head Lieutenant Kay chuntering on at Charlie. "But sir, if we had chased them over their lines we could have got them all!"

I let Charlie answer. They were his flight and he needed to establish his authority over the new pilots. "First of all, you obey orders. Captain Harsker has shot down more German aeroplanes than you have had hours in a Gunbus. Secondly, we would have had to risk German anti-aircraft fire and, possibly, the new Albatros. Today was a good result. Our flight did not score any hits but the squadron did. This is a team, Sonny Jim. There is no room for prima donnas!"

"Sorry, sir. I didn't think."

"That's all right. Until you are a first lieutenant then we do the thinking for you." His men laughed and I knew his flight would be better after this. Perhaps Alice was good for him. He had far more confidence now than before Christmas.

It was frustrating because we were grounded the next day due to low cloud. I had wanted to build on the success of the previous day. We made up for it by going through the different German aeroplanes we would be meeting. Randolph had managed to acquire some pictures of some of them but not the two new ones. They looked remarkably similar to the old ones; the Albatros had a sharp nose and ugly radiator and the Fokkers all looked identical. As we went through the aeroplanes Gordy said, "The thing to watch out for is the two guns. If you see them then get into a circle or get out of there or it will be the Fokker Scourge all over again."

We took off the next day and I saw chastened pilots. The new ones had listened, over dinner, to the stories of the arrival of the new aeroplanes and their effect. We knew that we had not suffered as much as most but we were not complacent; our time would come.

It was one of the best days for flying we had had so far and visibility was clear. We could see clear to the rear of the German trenches. I took us up high. I saw a grey snake moving towards the front. It looked like German troops. "Flight Sergeant Hutton, can you see any Hun about?"

He did his job scrupulously. "No, sir."

"Signal the troops on the ground that there is a column of German soldiers marching to the front. Tell them we are going to attack them and then repeat to the others."

"Sir!"

I headed east. They would see us but we would be ten little dots high in the sky. I cocked my Lewis. I still could not change the magazine despite Doc Brennan's exercise ball. I was recovering far slower than I used to.

"All done, sir. Captain Sharp's gunner said A flight will climb above us."

Charlie was really on fire these days. By having his five aeroplanes above us we would have protection as well as the option of a second attack. I could see that it looked like a regiment below us. They had the new German helmet we had heard about. They were fresh troops. That, in itself, was ominous.

"Ready, Lumpy?"

"Sir!"

I pushed the stick forward and we dived. The engine being behind us seemed to make less noise than those with an engine in front and we dived a couple of thousand feet before the soldiers seemed to react. By then it was too late. They could make the ditches but that was all. I emptied the magazine down the ditch which ran along the side of the road. Lumpy fired obliquely at the other side. At that speed, we were over and through the thousand or so men and climbing as their small arms fire ineffectually tried to hit us.

I banked to starboard, partly to head home and partly to see the effect of the attack. I saw bodies littering the road. Had we had bombs then we could have destroyed the whole column, there was little point in using Hutton's Mills bombs; the Germans would have aeroplanes heading for us now.

I kept the two flights low as we ate up the ground back to the airfield. It was good practice for it kept you on edge and your reactions became faster. Fast reactions made for better pilots.

The men were elated when we landed and that elation lasted right until dinner. However, when Major Leach and Captain Marshall arrived late with very serious expressions on their faces then we knew that something was wrong.

"Gentlemen, there is a new German squadron at the front. They are all the new Albatros D.IIIs and they are brightly coloured. They all have red on them and their leader has a totally red aeroplane."

One of the new chaps shouted, "Well they should be easy to spot, what!"

"Tell that to the six pilots and crews of the FE 2Bs of 28 Squadron because they were all either shot down or forced to land behind enemy lines!"

Chapter 7

Our war changed the next day. We learned that the new squadron was Jasta 11. I have no idea how we discovered that save that there must have been British spies working behind the German lines. We also heard that the squadron leader was someone called Baron Manfred Von Richthofen. His name became increasingly familiar as the year went on. We gathered that he liked to publicise himself. Surprisingly we learned much about him through German newspapers for, unlike us, the Germans publicised their heroes. We liked to keep them hidden. Everyone knew the generals and their names but the likes of Lanoe Hawker and Albert Ball were only known within the small world of the RFC.

Major Leach held an emergency briefing. "From now on we patrol as a squadron. Until now the Gunbus has proved to be tougher than any other aeroplane we have. Six aeroplanes destroyed by six Albatros and no losses is a serious state of affairs. We cannot assume that our luck will hold"

"But sir how can we do our job?" Johnny Holt was always acutely aware of our responsibility to the troops on the ground. "The footsloggers have worse odds and take greater casualties than we do."

It was Captain Marshall who gave him the sad but brutal truth. "It takes longer to train a pilot than a footslogger and all he needs is a rifle. The Gunbus takes some time to manufacture. The fact of the matter is we can't afford to take so many casualties and to lose aeroplanes." He waved a hand at the squadron. "There is one pilot here from 1914 and only four more from 1915." He let that sink in. "There is no long-term life expectancy in the RFC so let us do what the major wants and not make it easy for Fritz eh?"

I knew the men were frustrated. It seemed cowardly somehow but until we had better aeroplanes then we would have to eat humble pie and travel mob-handed.

Bates was delighted. "Oh, this is much better, Captain Harsker. Look what happened when you only had two aeroplanes with you. You were shot down! No, I will sleep easier now."

The Major led us the next day while Lieutenant Kay's aeroplane was repaired. As I had seen German troops moving up towards Cambrai we patrolled that sector. We left early for there were reports of aeroplanes in the vicinity. As soon as we reached No-Man's Land we saw the two reconnaissance aeroplanes. They were obviously photographing our lines. That was normally the prelude for either a raid or an offensive. As soon as we began to climb they decided that discretion was the better part of valour and headed east.

Archie took us high above the front lines. We had four cameras amongst the squadron and the gunners photographed the German lines which would be assaulted. None of it would be a surprise. When our next offensive came we would have to patrol well behind the enemy lines and I did not relish the prospect.

Six Halberstadts appeared and I wondered if they would take us on. Lumpy's eyes picked out the squadron markings and he told me it was the same squadron we had knocked about a little. They were wary and when Archie took the squadron east, then they left. It was something of an anti-climax when we headed west. I was philosophical. We had suffered no casualties and stopped the observers from taking photographs.

I was lying in my bath when Bates burst in. I knew that something terrible had happened for it was not his usual style. His face was red and his eyes were wild.

"I am sorry to burst in, sir, but the captain just received a message. Lord Burscough and five of his pilots were shot down. He is dead!"

I was stunned. How could that be? Lord Burscough was the finest pilot I had ever known. I had been his gunner and he had taught me how to fly. He was like an imperious eagle and yet he was now dead. The DH 2 had been one of the few new aircraft which had shown promise. If his lordship had died flying one as well as half of his hand-picked squadron then what chance did the rest of us stand?

I was suddenly aware that John was weeping. He had enjoyed his time at the Big House. It had been his world and he had been enchanted with both his lordship and Lady Mary. They had fitted his mental picture of a perfect pair of aristocrats. The death of Lord Burscough would shatter his world and make him even more fearful for me.

"If you want to take the night off…"

He stiffened, "Oh no, sir. His lordship did his duty and I shall do mine."

As he dressed me I thought about the effect on mum and dad. They had known him since he had been a child it would be as bad as losing me or Bert. I hoped that they were strong enough to survive the shock.

That evening, after the loyal toast, Captain Marshall stood. There were just five of us left who had flown with Captain Burscough, as he had then been. "Gentleman can you raise your glasses in memory of a fine pilot, a courteous gentleman and one of the best officers to serve in this squadron: Lord Burscough."

We downed our drinks in one and there was a sombre, almost funereal atmosphere. It contrasted with the heady days in summer before I had been shot down when we had felt invincible. Now doubts were creeping in. Even when I had been shot down I had been convinced that we would survive. Now I was not certain. Perhaps Gordy had it right, and Charlie. Maybe I should live for the moment. Marrying Beattie as soon as possible was now a priority.

We knew things were serious when, after a week of storms where no flying was possible, we had a visit from the commander of the Royal Flying Corps in France, Major General Hugh Trenchard. I had seen him before but I was more familiar with General Henderson.

I thought he would just wish to speak with Archie but I was summoned to the office. There were just the three of us there. He gave me a wry look. "General Henderson has mentioned you more than once, Captain Harsker. You may not be the ace with the greatest number of kills but you are certainly the one that people talk about."

There was little I could say to that, "Well sir, I always try to do my duty."

"I don't doubt that for one moment and no criticism was implied. Smoke if you wish." The three of us filled our pipes. When his pipe was going he continued, "I wanted you here because I know that you like to go on the offensive whenever you can. I have heard of you taking on odds of four to one. That is what I like. Now I know that it may seem the wrong time to go on the offensive when the Germans had superior aeroplanes. I happen to believe that offence is the best form of defence."

I looked at Archie who said, "But General Trenchard, I agree that the FE 2 is a dependable aeroplane but it has seen its best days. Bill here is the best pilot in the squadron but he would stand no chance against this Von Richthofen and his red-painted Albatros."

"I am sorry, Major Leach, but this Baron is just one man, a man with one squadron. I know that we have more aeroplanes than the Germans. Are you telling me that our pilots aren't good enough?"

"No, I am saying, General Trenchard, that our aeroplanes aren't good enough."

"Hmn." He looked at me. "You are a bit quiet. Cat got your tongue?"

I smiled, he sounded like my dad. "No sir." I rose and went to the cupboard with the models of the aeroplanes. "You are a pilot sir so I know you will understand." I modelled to show him what I meant. "The Gunbus has fine defensive qualities. We have two guns at the front and one at the rear. But we are slow. When the Albatros comes at us it has two Spandau machine guns firing steel-jacketed bullets. They fire at a gunner with no protection." I smiled, "I was a gunner and I know how scary it is. They can kill the gunner on their first pass. They do the Immelmann turn and get behind us. From what I have heard this is easy in the new Albatros. We have no protection if the gunner is incapacitated. We used to be able to counteract the Immelmann when it was the Eindecker; they were slow. The Albatros is so fast and nippy that they can turn inside us, come up behind and we have a crashed Gunbus and a dead pilot. And that, sir, will happen no matter how good the pilot is."

"I see. Well explained. You see I thought the gunner in the front was the deterrent but you are saying that he is not."

"Not with two guns firing at him, sir. It is simple mathematics. The Hun has twice the chance of hitting us. The pilot is, in some ways, protected by the body of the gunner. We get through more gunners than pilots."

He was silent for a while. I learned that he was a thoughtful man. "I am glad I had this chat with you. Look, I will try to get you the new Sopwith Pup. It is a single-seater but it is nippy and it is fast. It has a synchronised Vickers machine gun. It's the best I can do until we can get the Bristols built." He looked at Archie, "Any malt, Major?"

"Aye, sir." He poured us three glasses and the general toasted us.

"However, I still want you to take the fight to the Germans. You have done it before. Fit bombs to your buses and harass their rear areas. If this Red Baron fellow turns up then you have my permission to run. You have shown here at 41 Squadron, that you have the ability to achieve more with the Gunbus than any other squadron on the Western Front. I want you to buy me a month to get the new aeroplanes out to the squadrons." He lowered his voice. "By March we will be preparing for a new offensive and you will be operating behind German lines. Hopefully, when we reach spring you should have three new aeroplanes, perhaps more."

We waved him off and then Archie shook his head. "I think yon general has just signed the death warrant for most of the young laddies in this squadron Bill."

"We'll just have to do our best then. We can use the old technique of two flights bombing and two escorting and watching out for fighters."

He laughed, "The glass is always half full with you, isn't it Bill?"

Surprisingly enough the general's surprise visit made us more optimistic. We knew that we were in trouble but the fact that we were considered so good gave us hope. The gossip permeated the whole squadron and evening saw us in high spirits. Part of it was due to the fact that the storms had not abated and we would not be flying the next day but the rest was down to the general.

Charlie also showed a different side to himself. He had really come out of his shell since meeting Alice. He had had a little too much to drink, but then we all had. He began to tell us about some of the shows he had seen in London with Alice.

"We saw this marvellous chap from the northeast, Mark Sheridan. He's getting on a little bit but he sang some wonderful songs."

Gordy winked at Ted, "Sing us one!"

"I haven't got a voice, I …"

Ted started clucking like a chicken and the young pilots began to chant, "Sing, Sing, Sing."

Red-faced he said, "Very well then." He took off his jacket and struck a pose. When he began to sing I couldn't believe what a good voice he had.

"Oh! I do like to be beside the seaside
I do like to be beside the sea!
I do like to stroll along the Prom, Prom, Prom!
Where the brass bands play:
"Tiddely-om-pom-pom!"
So just let me be beside the seaside
I'll be beside myself with glee
And there's lots of girls beside,
I should like to be beside
Beside the seaside!
Beside the sea!"

The mess exploded. It was like a release of tension and emotion. He had to perform it a second and a third time. Ted and Gordy disappeared during the third rendition and emerged with tea towels on their heads and aprons around their waists. They vamped it up as women next to Charlie and performed it a fourth and fifth time. I was laughing so hard that tears were streaming down my cheeks.

The rest of the evening was joyous. Archie took me to one side. "I think your sister has done more for morale than a hundred Christmas tins from the king."

The exuberant atmosphere continued into February. Partly that was because we had few missions to fly and the Red Baron and Jasta 11 could not slaughter anymore of our comrades. Two things happened quite quickly: the weather cleared and the first of the three Pups promised to us arrived.

Although I was keen to try the new beastie out, Flight Sergeant Lowery and Major Leach were adamant that the mechanics and armourer should examine them first now that they had finally arrived. Bearing in mind what had happened to Lieutenant Kay when he flew a factory-fresh fighter I concurred. It would only mean a delay of a day or two and then I would have to allocate Lumpy to another pilot. I knew that he would be unhappy. I immediately thought of Ted. They would make a good team. One was dour and one was ebullient. Nothing ever got Flight Sergeant Hutton down.

Chapter 8

We were up before dawn. We checked the guns and the buses twice. We needed no jammed guns this time. We fitted flights D and B with bombs. Charlie and I would act as aerial cover. The major joined us so that we had twenty-one aeroplanes. I had never flown such a large operation. Just before the engines started Lumpy sounded the bugle and the cavalry charge. There was a cheer over the airfield. I have no idea what Major General Trenchard would have made of it but it improved the morale of the squadron no end.

We headed across No-Man's Land. There was cloud cover but it was not low cover." The German fighters could fly at a much higher altitude than our Gunbuses. "Flight Sergeant, keep your eyes peeled."

"Sir."

"Have you got your Mills bombs handy?"

"Always sir. You know I will have to think of a job for after the war where I can throw something. I seem to have a knack for it."

"Don't worry, Hutton, you will do well after the war. You have the ability to adapt to any situation. I will probably end up working for you!"

"In which case I will make sure you are well paid, sir."

As we crossed No-Man's Land we both cocked our weapons. The Major and the bombing buses were a thousand feet below us. They would see the targets sooner than we would. I saw the line of water snaking north. It was the Canal De Saint Quentain. I watched as Archie banked. He had seen a target.

"What is the name of that village, Lumpy?"

"Masnières, sir."

"Mark it then. I think the Major is going to attack."

I banked, too, so that we were flying north to south. That way we could watch to the east. I glanced down as the Major led the buses down. It looked like barges had moored for the night. Even moving they would still be an easy target. They were confined to a narrow canal. I did not have the luxury to be an observer. I looked east. The secret was to move your head slowly and examine each piece of the sky. We heard the crump of the bombs as they struck. There was one loud explosion which sounded as though we had hit ammunition. Lumpy and I had to focus on the skies.

There was a lull below us as we turned at the end of the leg and headed north again. The Gunbuses would be beginning their second run.

I hoped they would only use two runs. We were pushing our luck as it was. Lumpy saw them as soon as I did. I recognised them as a mixture of Fokker D.III and D.II. The D.III had the twin machine guns. They were heading in two V formations directly for the Major and the rest of the squadron. We had the advantage of altitude. It was our only advantage and I was about to throw it away when we dived.

"Here we go. Usual procedure, Lumpy, I'll go for the Hun ahead and you enjoy yourself."

"Very kind of you sir."

I hoped that I would be able to change my magazine for I knew that we would need it. As we dived down I saw six Fokkers peel off and rise towards us. They formed two lines. The bad news was that these were D.III. We were in for a world of pain. I decided to burst through the middle of them. We were so big that we would break up their formation. It also meant that the two flights would be able to bring all our guns to bear. The leading pilot made the mistake of firing too soon. He barely missed us; one bullet pinged off the stanchion holding the rear-firing Lewis. You have to assume that the bullets will miss you. If you flinched you might be dead. I had to keep us as stable as possible. I opened fire as did Lumpy. I saw my bullets arc and I corrected our descent until I saw them strike his engine. I had no propeller in front of me.

They rose above us and the last of my magazine was emptied into his belly as he soared above me. I quickly tried to change the magazine as the next Fokker flight rose towards us. My arm had healed up but it seemed to take an age. Hutton was firing for he had changed his magazine already. I had just changed it when the Hun's bullets ripped into the front cockpit. I heard a scream as Hutton was hit. I opened fire and had the satisfaction of hitting the Fokker's engine.

I began to bank and head west. Below me, I saw two burning buses and the rest heading west. We could head home… if the Germans would allow us to. Suddenly I felt the thud of Parabellum rounds as they hit the engine. I needed Lumpy on the rear gun. "Hutton we have a German on our tail."

I heard a sob of pain and Flight Sergeant Hutton held up what remained of his left hand. It was a bloody stump. His hand and part of his wrist had been shattered. He had had the wit to fashion a tourniquet. He tried to turn towards me. "I am sorry…" His head slumped forward. I hoped his tourniquet was tight else he would bleed to death before I could land. I had no time to reflect on his wounds for more bullets struck the engine and I felt the loss of power. My bus was mortally wounded. I banked right in an effort to throw him off. The ground seemed to be coming at me rapidly… too rapidly and I pulled back on the stick. The old bus seemed sluggish. I was not certain I could land. "Come on old girl. Lift your nose."

What saved us was the huge expanse of wings. Ever so slowly the nose came up. I saw the roof of a half-destroyed house loom ahead of me. We barely cleared it but I think it must have thrown off the aim of the German behind because the bullets stopped.

"Well Lumpy, it's time to get home and get you seen to." There was an ominous silence from the front cockpit. I was too low to risk looking behind me and I was not certain how much power I had left. I would keep at a lower altitude in case we had to crash land. I reached down for the Very pistol. I risked lifting the nose a little when I was a mile from the field. I saw Gunbuses taxiing along the greensward as I fired my pistol. I could see huddles of men around the parked aeroplanes. The Major had suffered casualties too.

The engine gave a sickly cough as we cleared the hedgerow. We were landing but it was the Gunbuses' choice, not mine. There was an ugly crunch as the undercarriage hit the ground too hard and one wing dropped alarmingly to the ground. If we flipped then we were both dead. Luckily the lower wing bit into the ground and we slewed around. The tail lifted a little before crashing to the ground and we were down.

I scrambled out and ran to the cockpit. Doc Brennan and his orderlies, as well as the fire crews, were running towards us too. When I saw the front of the cockpit it looked like a colander. I dreaded what I would see. I put my hand on Hutton's neck and felt a pulse. He was still alive.

Doc Brennan reached me. "How are you, Bill?"

"Not a scratch but Lumpy has lost a hand."

"Right. Clear off then. You are only in the way."

It was brutally true and I stepped away from the wrecked aeroplane. My hands were shaking. I took my pipe out to fill it. I counted the aeroplanes as they landed. We had lost aeroplanes. I also saw slumped and bloodied gunners. The twin Spandau machine guns had decimated our squadron. Flight Sergeant Hutton was still, mercifully, unconscious as he was cut free from the cockpit and laid upon a stretcher. I wandered over.

Doc Brennan held something in his hand. "Your sergeant might lose his hand, possibly his arm, but he has been extremely lucky." He handed me the mangled bugle which had lain in his lap. "I think the bullets hit this and were deflected into his hand. If it weren't for the bugle then they would have gone through him and, I suspect, your legs too. You have both been lucky."

I did not feel lucky.

He followed the stretcher and I examined the bugle. A spent shell dropped out of it. It would never be played again but it had done a job I never imagined it performing. I took it with me. We would put it in the Sergeants' Mess as a reminder. Lumpy's war was over but I could not even begin to conceive of his one armed future. He might become one of the crippled beggars from the Boer War who lived on Liverpool's streets.

I saw both Freddie and Johnny. They, too, were distraught. The two corpses covered in blankets told their own stories. Their gunners had not had the luck that Lumpy had. Jack Laithwaite had been Lumpy's best friend and was almost his equal as a gunner. He too would never fly again. I knew that he had a wife and three children back in Blighty. Another family would have to learn to live without a breadwinner.

Charlie caught us up. "I am sorry, sir. I tried to get to you when Pete Harrington bought it but didn't make it in time. Sorry."

I shook my head, "It was an accident waiting to happen." I suddenly realised what it meant. I had lost one of my flight. I turned to look at the field.

Freddie said, "Piers Gerard bought it too."

"And I lost poor Lieutenant Kay. He had two missions and both ended badly. Connor and Morley didn't make it either."

We had lost five aeroplanes in one day. Archie had been right; the general's offensive strategy had cost us a quarter of our pilots and even more gunners.

When we reached the office Archie already had the whisky bottle out. "Well, we can tell the general that the mission was a great success. We destroyed ten barges! Of course, I, have fifteen letters to write to the families of the dead and the wounded but we sank the bloody barges!"

Randolph coughed, "Well Bill, while the major composes himself what kind of fighters were they?"

"It was a mixture of Fokker D.III and D.II. They can outfly, outrun, out climb and outgun us. Those twin machine guns make mincemeat out of us. The front of my bus had so many holes it looked like the mice had been at it." I held up the mangled bugle. "Lumpy is lucky. He has lost his hand but he could have been like Jack Laithwaite and lost his life. The steel-jacketed shells just cut through everything. With only one machine gun firing at us we had some sort of chance but two means that they can't miss. They aim their aeroplane at us and fire. I hit both the Fokkers that hit me but all I struck was the engine. One was damaged but the second was still flying."

"No, it wasn't Bill. I hit him. You can have half a kill!" Charlie was smiling.

"I don't want half a bloody kill! I want my gunner whole again! Can you fix that Charlie?"

He looked as though I had slapped him, "Sorry Bill I …"

Gordy put his arm around me, "Steady on Bill. It isn't Charlie's fault. Go and have a bath and a drink. I'm sure Bates is waiting." I turned and glared at him. I just wanted a fight with someone. There were no Germans around and my friends were bearing the brunt. Gordy smiled, "I remember when I was going off the rails and you set me straight. Let an old mate do the same for you eh?"

I knew he was right. "Sorry, Charlie, sorry chaps. You are right Gordy. I'll call back later with my report, Randolph."

"No hurry Bill. I am not certain we can manage to fly tomorrow anyway."

As I walked through the base I saw the sickbay. There was little point in trying to visit Lumpy. Doc would still be working on him as well as the other wounded. I realised that I still had the bugle in my hand. Bates was, as Gordy had said, waiting for me outside my room. There was a large whisky in his hand. He took the bugle from me and handed me the whisky. He reverently laid the mangled instrument on my bedside table.

"Here you are, sir. Have this one and then take your bath. It is lovely and hot." I swallowed the neat whisky in one. "That's the ticket, sir." He put the glass down and then took off my tunic. "The Mess Sergeant told me he has had a consignment of fresh meat today. I think you are in for a fine dinner. It looks like roast beef. Of course, I don't think his Yorkshire Puddings will be a patch on your mother's. They were the best I had ever eaten. I watched her make them but I don't think I could copy her. You are born with that kind of skill aren't you sir?"

I was aware that his senseless chatter was to make life normal for me. I saw the pain in his eyes. He understood what I was going through. I would be able to talk about it but not yet. "Thank you, John. You are a good fellow."

He smiled and seemed relieved, "Just doing my duty, Captain Harsker. Now off you go before the water gets cold." He held my tunic and my greatcoat. I saw that they both had blood and pieces of flesh on them. I had noticed neither in the battle nor since. "I'll get these cleaned up. It is a good job we bought that new tunic eh sir?"

Both Gordy and Bates were right. I did feel better when I had bathed and dressed. Lumpy had been lucky. He could be dead but he was alive. At least I hoped he was alive. As soon as I was dressed I ran to the sickbay. The Sick Bay Sergeant stopped me from entering the ward.

"Now then, Captain Harsker, where do you think you are going? Flight Sergeant Hutton has just come out of surgery and he will be out for the count until morning. Doctor Brennan did a fine job and he saved the arm below the elbow." I looked at him blankly. He smiled sympathetically, "They can fit him with a false hand, sir. So you see you can do nowt here, sir."

I had not even thought that far ahead. "Thank you, Sergeant. When he wakes tell him I was asking after him."

"Of course sir. You can visit in the morning. Now go and get some food inside you. You and the rest of the flight crews have been through a lot today." He shook his head, "Even the Doctor was shaken."

As I left I knew what the sergeant meant. The sickbay only had a few wounded but there were twelve dead men. That was a shock for us all.

There was no jollity in the mess that night and poor Freddie and Johnny looked to be at rock bottom. They had both been with their gunners almost as long as I had been with Lumpy and so I knew how they felt. I rose to speak with them but Gordy restrained me. "They won't thank you for it. Let them sleep on it. Tomorrow is time enough."

Archie was on the other side of me, "And I know you don't want to hear this either, Bill but you will need to face it. Tomorrow you and the two lads will need to check out those new Pups when they arrive. We might not want to fly but sure as shooting the Germans will. If we aren't in the air in the next couple of days then they will be over here." I looked at him in horror. He shook his head, "Remember what the General said about March? It is just a week away."

I swallowed the wine and held up my hand for the mess orderly. Archie's words sank in. "You want Freddie and Johnny in the new Pups?"

"After you went for your bath we had a chat, the three of us. We will reorganise the flights. We will distribute your old flight amongst the others and B Flight will be the Pups. Freddie and Johnny are good pilots and they have a good relationship with you. Gordy is right. Tomorrow is another day. Let's start fresh eh? You fly the Bristol tomorrow while the Pups are checked out."

Chapter 9

Bates brought me an early morning cup of tea accompanied by a concerned expression. "How are we today, sir?"

"Better thank you, John. And thank you for last night. You made it easier for me."

He seemed pleased, "That is my job, sir but I am delighted that you are feeling better."

As I stepped on to the cold floor I said, "I am not certain that '*better*' is the word I would have chosen but it is another day and I am still alive."

"That's the spirit, sir. *Nils Desperandum.*"

I suddenly felt as though someone had walked over my grave. That was what Lumpy had said when we were fleeing the Germans across Northern France.

As soon as I was dressed I went to the sickbay. It was still dark and the night staff was on duty. The sergeant grinned, "The doctor said you would be up before the larks, sir. You can go in but just to say hello, mind!"

"Thank you, sergeant."

The three patients were all asleep. Lumpy's hand was hidden beneath a mountain of white bandages. My broken arm of a few months ago now seemed insignificant. He looked to be breathing well enough and I turned to go.

"Hello, sir. You are up early."

I turned and saw his smiling face. It was a little paler than normal but the smile was there. "I just wanted to see how you were."

He nodded to his left arm. "A bit of a mess sir but the doctor said I was lucky. The bugle saved my life."

"And my legs." I sighed; there was no easy way to say what I was about to say. "Your war is over Lumpy, you know that."

"Aye, sir. But I am alive and that is more than can be said for poor Jack Laithwaite. He has a wife and three bairns. I am lucky. I have just meself and me mam and dad."

"What will you do?"

"Go back to Shildon. The Doc reckons I can have a dummy hand but it will take some time. I can't go back to the pits. A one armed collier is neither use nor ornament is he?"

"There must be jobs in the offices you could do. You can still write."

He brightened a little. "Aye, I suppose you are right."

"And I will be more than happy to write you a reference."

"Really sir? That would be just the job."

The sergeant came in. "That's it, sir. We need to see to these lads. Afternoon for visiting."

He stood with his arm out as though he was a shepherd herding sheep. He reminded me of Beattie's Matron. "I'll see you this afternoon then."

"Aye, sir and I'll write a letter to Jack's widow. I know as what he might have said to her."

As I went to breakfast, I realised that the likes of Lumpy Hutton were the backbone of Britain. The sad thing was it was the Lumpy Huttons and Jack Laithwaites who were dying. There was a generation who would either be crippled or dead.

It had done me good to talk with Lumpy. His positive attitude had rubbed off and I determined to be like him and make the best of things.

Holt and Carrick were in the mess, their uneaten breakfast before them. The cigarette butts showed that they had been there for some time. I sat opposite them. The orderly followed with a cup of tea and my breakfast. "Thank you Sarn't. Take these plates away and bring them some fresh food will you?"

"Yes, sir."

"I don't think I could eat anything, sir."

"Nonsense. Bring them two plates and they will eat it." I glared at them. "And that is an order."

"But sir, you don't understand, we both lost a gunner yesterday."

"And you are going to spend the rest of the war moaning about it and feeling sorry for yourself. In 1914 I lost a regiment and they were my best friends. Lumpy Hutton has lost a hand and he will have to work out how to live so you two are lucky. Yes, I am sad that your gunners died but we start again. And we start today."

The food was brought and I stared at them until they began to eat. When we had all finished I lit my pipe. Johnny said, somewhat sulkily, "I am not certain that I could face losing another gunner."

"Good, because you won't have to." They both stared at me. "We have a busy day. We have to find out what makes the Sopwith Pup tick. When the weather clears, probably tomorrow, B Flight, that is us three, will be in the air. We are going to be the guardian angels for the rest of the squadron. We will be the eagles soaring high in the sky." I saw the first hint of a smile. "So you can see why you needed to eat. Now come on. Get your overalls on and we will find Sergeant Lowery and Sergeant Richardson. I think we have much to learn and only one day to do it."

The three Pups had been kept away from the runway while they were checked over. They had an engine with which the mechanics were unfamiliar and the Vickers was not like the Lewis. In addition, it was a synchronised gun. They were waiting for the three of us. I saw the anticipation on their faces.

I shook my head, "Bloody hell Flight. They are a bit small aren't they?"

The two senior flight sergeants laughed. "Just a little sir. Would you like the tour?"

They took us around pointing out the differences. I could not get over the discrepancy in size. The wingspan was twenty-six and a half feet as opposed to almost forty-eight feet for the Gunbus. It was thirteen feet shorter and four feet lower. My first thought was that it was a smaller target for the Germans!

Percy Richardson took us to the gun. "This is a big difference, sir. There is no magazine. It is belt-fed. If you run out in the air then you can't reload." He smiled and looked at the two young lieutenants, "You two gentlemen will need to be as accurate as Captain Harsker here." I saw their faces fall. "The good news is that the ammunition comes in two hundred and fifty round boxes so that is more than twice the magazine of the Lewis."

I was happy about that but I worried about jamming. "How do we clear a jam?"

I liked Percy but he had a tendency to show off a little when it came to guns. "Sir, in August, last year the 100th Company of Machine Guns fired their ten guns for twelve hours continuously in a battle. They fired a million rounds and changed ten barrels for each gun but not one gun jammed in all that time. We will service them every time you land. I can guarantee, sir, that they will not jam!"

I smiled and patted him on the back. "And if you are wrong Senior Flight Sergeant, it is my ghost who will remind you of that promise."

He had the good grace to nod. "Mind you, sir, the other good news is that the effective range of this gun is over two thousand yards; the Lewis gun is eight hundred yards. The Lewis fires more bullets per minute, but not by much."

I looked at the two young pilots. The thought of that kind of firepower was awesome. I hoped that Flight Sergeant Lowery would give us good news about the engine.

"Now your engine isn't a Rolls Royce but the Le Rhone is a nice little engine. It has plenty of power and you can reach speeds of up to a hundred and five miles an hour. You have a ceiling of seventeen and a half thousand feet."

"That is almost twice as high as the Gunbus!"

Flight Sergeant Lowery frowned at Freddie's interruption. "You have the same endurance but a much faster rate of climb. The length of the body means you have a tiny turning circle. I haven't seen these new Hun aeroplanes but Captain Marshall says that the Pup here is six feet shorter. I reckon that gives you the edge. Finally, the three wheels of the Gunbus aren't necessary; you just have two but that means that you don't take off flat like the Gunbus. Until you get up to speed you are looking up. I think that will take some getting used to."

I saw what he meant. The Pup looked to have its nose in the air. "Right, lads let's get to grips with these three. Remember, tomorrow we fly."

With one brief stop for a sandwich, we worked through the morning. We sat in the new aeroplanes and had the engine started. It was strange to go back to a bus which had an engine in front. I wondered about the vision but then the Germans had the same problem and they had managed to shoot us down. We took them to the field to practice take off. The rest of the squadron gathered to see these new war machines. It was two o'clock when we were all satisfied. I saw a break in the weather and took an instant decision. "Right lads, we'll take them up and practice flying in formation. Get your gear."

I think Senior Flight Sergeant Lowery was worried we might damage his new toys but he was a good soldier and knew when to say, "Yes sir."

Archie wandered over when he saw us getting suited and booted. "Are you sure about this, Bill?"

"If we are ordered into the air tomorrow I don't want to have to learn about this Pup with Germans trying to kill me. We will just do a couple of laps of the field and test fire the guns."

"Very well."

When Freddie and Johnny returned I said, "I want to try a different formation for this new bus. I will fly in the centre. You two fly either side of me, level with my wing. That way you can both see my signals.

We'll take them up to cloud level." I could not wait for a clear day to see just how high they would go. "We'll try a take off in line. I think they are small enough."

The Gunbus had such a span that you could only have two aeroplanes take off at the same time.

"Righto, sir."

When we level off I will test-fire my gun. Then you two can as well." They nodded. "No point putting it off any more."

I climbed aboard. I had never flown alone before. There had always been a gunner. It would seem lonely. The first thing I noticed was the power. It was such a light aeroplane that we were in the air almost before I realised. This was no Gunbus. We climbed and our rate of ascent seemed to be twice that of the Gunbus. I levelled off before the clouds and took us in a lazy circle around the airfield. I practised waggling my wings to see the effect. I found the stick very responsive. I watched Johnny as he used too much stick and rose alarmingly quickly. He rejoined the formation and shrugged apologetically.

There was no putting it off, I had to test-fire the Vickers. I gripped the trigger and pulled. It sounded slower, to me, although that might have been my imagination. The spent shells flew to my left. As I watched the tracer bullets tear off into the distance I noticed that they flew straight. I stored that information in my head. The Lewis' shorter-range meant that at extreme range, they dipped and slowed down. I saw that the other two had test-fired. I motioned a roll. They gave me a thumbs up and I pulled back on the stick. It was, as the Flight Sergeant had said, a very tight turn. I was convinced that we could get inside an Albatros. For the first time in days, I felt a little more confident and I signalled for them to descend. We went down quicker than we had climbed. Our problem would be flying at the same speed as the Gunbus!

The other pilots crowded around us when we landed. The envy was written all over their faces; even Gordy and Ted. Charlie's eyes were alight. "The climb was phenomenal and your loop is tiny! When do we all get one?"

I laughed, "We were lucky to get three."

Archie caught my eye and shook his head. "I don't think, laddie that they will give them to us. The best replacement we can hope for is the new two-seater Bristol F2. That's a canny aeroplane. It has the same speed as the Pup but it has a rear gun too."

I could see that Charlie was still disappointed. After I had changed I went along to see Lumpy. "I hear you have a new single-seater sir?"

There were no secrets. I felt a little guilty. "Yes, we had them up this afternoon."

He waved me forward, "I am glad. It probably sounds daft but I would have been a little jealous if you had another gunner. We were a good team, weren't we sir?"

"Lumpy, we were the best. Without you in the front cockpit, I know I wouldn't have lasted this long."

"Very kind of you, sir. They are shipping us out tomorrow so could I shake your hand, sir."

"With pleasure."

He gripped my arm, "I have been honoured to serve with you Captain Harsker and I look forward to reading about your exploits as the war goes on. There'll be another medal for you before too long. Mark my words."

"Don't forget you have a little ceremony to get your M.M. That means Buckingham palace."

He brightened, "Really." He suddenly appeared to remember something and he reached into his bag. "Could you post this for me, sir? It's to Jack's wife. I am not certain when I will be able to."

"I will." I read the address, "Stockton on Tees, isn't that close to Shildon?"

"Aye, it is, sir. I might call and see her when I get home."

"I'll find out which hospital you are in." I smiled, "I know a nurse in London you know?"

He laughed, "We all know. Perhaps I will drop lucky too eh sir?"

Chapter 10

The wounded were taken to the railway line before dawn. German bombers had been bombing the railway lines and travelling during the hours of darkness was seen as the safest method. I wish I had had the opportunity to say goodbye to Lumpy properly. I resolved to see him on my next leave. The doctor had given me the address of the hospital where he would be recuperating and I would write to Beattie to see if she could visit. I had little opportunity to mope for we were ordered into the air. The German bombers which had raided the railway were also emulating us and driving deep into our rear areas and damaging our supply lines.

Freddie had completed his artwork on the three Pups. He and Johnny were keen to have the same design as me and so he painted a horse on each of our Pups. Mine was rearing and was white whilst they had a prancing horse each, one black and one chestnut. They looked good and mine, in particular, stood out against the brown fuselage.

We took off and flew due north. B Flight was the umbrella. We had much greater altitude and our speed meant we could come to the aid of the rest of the squadron quickly. We only had nine airworthy Gunbuses. The ground crews had been too busy with the Pups to repair the damaged Gunbuses.

As we headed north I checked that I had my Luger and my two Mills bombs. I had promised Lumpy that I would deliver his last two presents for him. I would keep my word.

Johnny spotted the Albatros CIIIs as they headed east. There were twelve of them and they had climbed to over ten thousand feet. That was a thousand feet above the ceiling for the Gunbus. We, however, could climb even higher. We ascended. It was a pity we had no means of communicating with the rest of the squadron. I just hoped that their gunners would alert them to our climb.

We banked to come east as we climbed. I was not certain if they had seen us but I was fairly certain that they would not have encountered a Pup in this sector. The fact that they did not deviate from their course suggested to me that our small size had hidden us. They were now below us. I daresay that their observers had seen the Gunbuses and would be watching for them. They were in for a shock.

They were flying in three lines of four. It made our life much easier. I armed my Vickers and signalled the attack. The Pup seemed alive as it leapt towards the Germans. It felt more like were an eagle hunting rather than a friendly little pup. This Pup had teeth. I opened fire at two hundred yards. I used just ten bullets. It was a greater range than I usually fired at but I was aware that my new Vickers had the ability to fire further. I saw the bullets tear into the rudder of the rearmost aeroplane. I lifted the nose a fraction and fired again. This time I gave a longer burst as I saw the bullets stitch a line through the observer and into the pilot. The doomed craft plummeted to the ground.

I heard the sound of two heavy Vickers machine guns from port and starboard. My wingmen were in action too. I closed with the second Albatros. I had quickly adjusted to the huge propeller in front of me and I saw just the German aeroplane. I put myself below the arc of the Spandau in the rear of the Albatros and then I gave a long burst which tore into the belly of the German aeroplane. Smoke began to pour from the engine as it spiralled down to attempt a landing. He would probably save his aeroplane. We were like foxes in the henhouse. The Germans panicked as we zoomed around them. We were just too fast and nimble. It must have been like trying to swat an annoying fly.

I brought the Pup under the tail of the flight leader and opened fire. I shredded his tail. I knew what that felt like. It began to descend rapidly and that was the signal for the whole squadron to dive and reach as low an altitude as possible to rejoin the Gunbuses.

I had overtaken all of the Germans and I banked to bring the Pup behind them again. I was at least ten miles an hour faster. I used my speed to follow an undamaged Albatros as it tried to make it across No-Man's Land before I caught it. He made a brave attempt and took his Albatros almost down to the barbed wire. His gunner wasted drum after drum as I jinked from side to side. I fired a burst which hit his fuselage. The shock of the strike made the pilot lose concentration for a second and the nose pitched down and into the German trenches. I barely escaped the concussion as the Albatros struck some ammunition.

I banked and climbed as the angry bullets from soldiers on the ground zinged around me. I realised I was alone and I hedge-hopped home. The rest of the squadron had landed and were anxiously looking east for my return.

I jumped out of the aeroplane and began to check for damage. The way the bullets had been zinging around me I was convinced that there must be some holes. I found just one or two in the fuselage. I patted the wing. "You'll do for me you little beauty."

I had a grin from ear to ear. Gordy smiled, "That was impressive!"

"They were only the CIII."

"You managed to turn them inside out. That is three more kills for you and your new wingmen got three between them. I think that calls for a celebration tonight."

We swung from trough-like lows to ecstatic highs in the squadron. I suppose it was the nature of the beast. Life at five thousand feet was precarious. If you survived then you partied.

Charlie sat next to me when the party was at its height. Gordy on Ted's back pretending to be knights and fighting Johnny and Freddie with pillows. The younger pilots were egging them on.

"You know sir," I glared at him, "I'm sorry, Bill. The thing is I have never felt as alive as right now. And that is down to Alice. I have a future after the war but I am scared of being shot down. I didn't used to be. I had nothing to live for but five pilots killed and all those gunners too, well, it has set me to thinking. I now have something worth living for in my life."

"That's the worst thing to do."

"What? Thinking?"

I nodded. "You are a damned good pilot and a damned good gunner. It is a good combination: ask Ted and Gordy. You just need to trust your instincts. I know exactly what you are going through. Beattie and I want to get married too but the war is in the way. We can't do anything about that but I know that if I worry too much then I am more likely to get killed or wounded. Lumpy's life was saved by a cheap bugle. You never know what will come to your aid. Keep doing what you do Charlie and stop worrying. It can do no good. When I am in the air I empty my mind of everything except for flying and shooting down Huns."

Even as I told him that and he nodded I felt like a hypocrite for his feelings were exactly the same as mine. I needed to convince myself. We had three days of inaction as we patrolled and saw nothing. That suited me for I grew to know the Pup a little more with every hour in the air. I listened to the engine and knew what each irregular beat meant. I was annoyed when we followed the three days of no Germans with four days of no flying because of atrocious weather. The more hours in the air the more likely that the aeroplane and the pilot would become as one.

On the fourth day, a motorcycle messenger brought us sealed orders. When Archie opened them he flung them on to the desk and opened the malt. Randolph read them out to the four Flight Commanders gathered in the office. "The squadron is to patrol deep behind enemy lines and take photographs. There is an offensive in the pipeline."

I sat back and lit my pipe. "That means that every German aeroplane for miles will be able to get to us and have a field day."

Archie nodded. "We will need to change our tactics. Your new flight works well but there are only three of you."

"Did General Trenchard say when the new Bristol fighters would be arriving? Their extra speed might make all the difference."

Captain Marshall held up a handful of letters. "I write to them every couple of days and I am told that we have to wait."

I had my pipe going and, as usual, that had helped me to gather my thoughts. "I think we are all missing the point here, sir. We can't go in as a squadron. They will want photographs over a large area. We will be spread out. That makes us even more vulnerable."

I saw Charlie's face drop as he realised that there would be no Pup umbrella above him. The best we can hope for is that we can use each flight to photograph one area and, at the first sign of trouble they head west. I could have my flight spread out to help whoever was in trouble.

"That still means we are going to take losses."

I nodded. "And until we get the Bristols that will remain the case. We are going to be sending a lot of letters home."

Nature, in the form of inclement weather, came to our aid again and we were spared having to venture into No-Man's Land. What we did discover was the identity of the area we were to photograph. It was the area east of Arras and Cambrai. We knew the southern sector quite well but we also knew that it was the hunting ground of the Red Baron, and his Flying Circus as the newspapers had dubbed them. Jasta 11 was steadily building up a reputation as a squadron of efficient and deadly killers. The nature of the weather in northern France meant that while we might not be able to fly, someone sixty miles away on the battlefield could. General Trenchard had sent a letter to every squadron telling them to only send patrols out in numbers which were able to defend themselves. It was not enough.

I studied the map of the area we were likely to be flying over. We had a rough idea where some of the German airfields were and I marked them on my own copy of the map. We would have to learn the skill of flying, reading a map, observing and flying our guns. My new flight had no observer who could do that for us. I made certain that both Freddie and Johnny were familiar with the area.

"The thing is, chaps, that we are more than likely going to have to separate. We have a whole squadron to watch out for. We will not have the luxury of watching each other's backs. We will be watching the squadron's back. I have asked Flight Sergeant Lowery to fit a small mirror on the top wing so that we will have an idea of what is behind us. I am afraid that each of us will be the last aeroplane to leave the German lines."

Johnny nodded, "It is like being the scrumhalf at rugger." He grinned. "Until I was in the fourth form I was only little and I was the scrum-half. Well everyone was bigger than me so I learned to be sneaky. I twisted and turned and used my small size to evade tackles. That is us in the Pup. We have to dodge, weave and stop them getting hold of us."

Freddie became animated, "It might seem daft sir but if we are in trouble then we should get closer to them. Remember the other week when we were still flying the buses you made two German aeroplanes crash into each other. We are a good six feet shorter than anything we will come up against. If we get amongst them they won't be able to fire for fear of hitting each other and there will be a danger that they crash into each other. It would buy time for the squadron to escape."

"It is worth a try. Well done you two. Keep coming up with ideas like that and you get an invite to the wedding."

Johnny became quite excited, "You have picked a date then sir?"

I grinned, "Of course, when the war has ended! So we all need to stay alive until then."

The best news we had was a delivery of letters from home. I had three. When I returned to my room after our planning meeting I saw Bates grinning from ear to ear. "We have letters from home, sir."

I saw mine on my dresser. "We, John?"

He looked a little embarrassed, "Well sir, I took the liberty of writing to your mother to thank her for her hospitality and to Miss Porter to… well, she asked me to write to her, sir and let her know how things were with you."

I adopted a mock-serious expression, "So, Bates, you are a spy!"

"Oh no sir, it's just that…"

I put my hand on his shoulder. "I am just teasing, John. I think it is wonderful. I am sure that your letters will be far better written than mine."

"Anyway sir, I have drawn your bath and your whisky is there. Enjoy your letters."

I laid the letters out in the order I would read them. Sarah's first, then mam's and Beattie's last. It was the way I ate my Sunday dinner; vegetables first, then the meat and finally the roast potatoes. I always saved the best until last.

Sarah's letter was full of the sadness over Lord Burscough. As I had expected, it would have had a devastating effect on the whole house. Sadly there was worse to come for the death duties meant that Lady Burscough would struggle to maintain the estate. Sarah was worried that parts would have to be sold off. She didn't say so but I knew that my parent's cottage might be one of the things that would have to be sold. Where would they go? They had lived in the cottage their whole married life.

I opened my mother's letter more worried than before. Thankfully she appeared to have not had any idea about the possible problems to come. Her letter was obviously written not long after we had left and before the news of Lord Burscough had reached them.

December 1916
My Dearest Son, Bill,
It was lovely to see you and your young lady before Christmas. It was a wonderful surprise. And your manservant, John, is a lovely man. He fitted in really well and your dad said that Cedric and the other servants at the Big House liked him too. You look after him! Good servants are hard to find.

Have you and Beattie set a date yet? Your sister Kath shows no sign of giving me, grandchildren. Don't let the war make you delay, son. Poor John and Tom went before they could leave a mark on this world. You have done a great deal already but marry her! We are not getting any younger! Your dad and I couldn't be happier about your choice. She is the first girl you have brought home and, in our eyes, she is perfect.

Our Alice came home for Christmas and she seemed changed. She looked older but she is happy. I thought she would hate London but she seems to love her job. She didn't say anything but I think she must have met someone down there. It is typical of the little madam that she hasn't brought him home for us to meet. She is not as thoughtful as you. But at least she is happy. And our Bert doesn't write or visit often enough.

Keep your letters coming. We read them over and over.

I remember you and Bert each night in my prayers and I pray that God spares you. Your dad and I are so proud of you Bill I can't tell you properly. God speed and we love you.

Mum xxx

I read the letter twice and poured myself a second whisky. I hoped that Lady Burscough could do something for them. I hated to think of them on the street or even in the workhouse. That would kill my mother for sure. I would make certain that didn't happen.

I sniffed Beattie's letter. She must have used a few drops of her perfume when she had written it. If I closed my eyes I could imagine her next to me.

January 1917
Dearest Bill,

I am sorry I have not written until now. You would think that Christmas would be a quiet time but we had huge numbers of wounded officers from the Somme Offensive. I had to work double shifts. Luckily the other nurses are back from Christmas leave now and life is a little easier.

It is heart-breaking to see some of the maimed officers who come through our doors. I worry that their lives have almost ended and many are barely 20!

Your ears must have been burning last week. We had a Colonel McCartney of the 17th Liverpool Battalion. He had lost a leg. We were chatting and I mentioned your name and he knew you! What a small world eh Bill? He couldn't stop singing your praises. He said if we had more pilots like you and the others then they would have taken fewer casualties. He asked me to remember him to you. I am always proud of you but when I heard that it made me realise what a difference you make. Take care of yourself! I want to be Mrs Harsker and I don't suit black!"

I have only seen your Alice once in the last few weeks but she is very taken with your Captain Sharp. He seems a nice chap and they looked good together. I know your mum worries about her but tell her that Alice has an old head on those young shoulders. She needn't worry about her.

1917 Eagles Fall

I will need to finish now, my love. My eyes are closing. I love you and pray each night that you are safe. I hope that Lumpy and John are well. Tell them that I remember them in my prayers too but all my love is reserved for you.

Beattie (now that you have finally started to use it)
xxx

I was still reading it, for the tenth time, when the gong went for dinner. I put the letters in my drawer. I had to stay alive for all of them.

Chapter 11

We managed just one patrol before we were given our specific orders for photographs. The squadron headed east. We had not received our replacements yet. It was not the pilots who were causing the problem but the gunners. We heard that a request had been sent to the Machine Gun Battalions for volunteers to transfer. We headed towards Cambrai. Archie had been ordered to fly a patrol along our lines to Arras. It was a relatively safe assignment. We immediately saw more activity behind the British lines. There were horse-drawn vehicles and guns being moved and brown snakes moving into support trenches behind the front lines.

The German aeroplanes were also curious. We were higher than the Gunbuses and we saw eighteen dots in the distance. I waggled my wings to attract the attention of the others. I pointed up. We needed height. I knew that eventually, the Germans would cotton on to our tactic but it was early days and we might just get away with it. Once again I thanked the designers who had made such a small aeroplane and yet one which had so much power.

Archie had the squadron in one long line. It gave maximum protection and made the move into our defensive circle much easier. When we were three thousand feet above the Gunbuses I took us into a lazy circle. If the Germans had any sense they would turn back rather than risk a mauling. Of course, if they were the new German fighters then they would relish the opportunity of giving us the mauling. The trouble was the only difference in the shape of the fighters, old and new was the extra Spandau. By the time you saw the armament, your gunner could be dead.

The fact that the Germans came on told me that they were confident and they hadn't seen us. I watched as Archie led the fifteen aeroplanes into the defensive circle. I saw that Peter Dunston was now the last pilot in Charlie's flight and his gunner stood on the rear Lewis. He was the one responsible for closing the stable door. Archie had done all that he could. If the Germans were going to observe our movements they would have to come through us.

When I was certain that they had not seen us I led my three aeroplanes in a steep dive to pass along their line. These were the old Fokkers with a single machine gun and no observer. They were faster than the Gunbus but we had their measure. The trouble was there were just three of us.

The gunners of the squadron sent a wall of lead towards the advancing Germans. The limited effective range of the Lewis meant that little damage was done and the Germans split into two flights to try to attack the rear of the Gunbuses. It was as they were banking that the three of us hit them. I waited until I was just four hundred yards away. I had perfected the technique of firing five bullets to show me how close I was and then a burst of twenty or thirty bullets once I was certain I could hit them.

The Fokker in my sights jerked his nose up as I fired my longer burst but it just meant that I shredded his tail. It made his Fokker unstable and I watched as he dived from the fight to head east. I saw the footsloggers as they peppered him with ground fire. I banked to port and took a snap shot as a Fokker came across my guns. I stitched a line from his engine along to his fuselage and he too began to smoke and headed east.

I felt the thud of bullets strike me and I looked in my mirror. It worked; I could see a Fokker on my tail. I pulled hard and went into a loop. The Sopwith had a wonderfully small turning circle and the Fokker could not compete. As I came around he was still on the way up and his aeroplane was a perfect cross in my sights. I gave a ten-second burst. I hit the pilot and his fuel tank. They exploded before my eyes. I flew through the debris and, when I emerged on the other side I saw I was in clear skies.

I checked my mirror. There was no one behind me. I banked to port and saw that the Germans were heading east. There were still a couple of dogfights ahead of me. Freddie and Johnny were fighting three Fokkers. I began to climb. I fired at a thousand yards. Far too long for a Lewis but the Vickers sent a trail of bullets towards the rearmost Fokker. I hit his fuselage. There was little damage but it must have worried him for the pilot banked the Fokker to starboard. I fired again as I followed him around. I was aware of Johnny and Freddie both looping at the same time. I could concentrate on the last German. My bullets struck him and I saw the Fokker judder. He banked to port to head east. I followed his line. I was catching him. I fired another burst and hit his tail. He began to descend. I was aware of ground fire. He had tried to lure me over the German lines. I banked to port and, as I did so, pulled the pin on one of Hutton's Mills Bombs and hurled it over the side.

As I climbed I saw, in my new mirror, the grenade explode some fifty feet in the air. It would shower the German gunners with shrapnel. "That one was for you, Lumpy."

I saw the two Fokkers who had been attacking Freddie and Johnny. They were spiralling to earth. I checked my fuel. I was getting low. I turned to port and headed west. We had survived another day.

As I came in to the field I counted only fourteen aeroplanes. Someone had not made it back. I saw in my mirror the two Pups following me and I breathed a sigh of relief.

The mechanics raced to my bus as soon as I stopped. They went to the rudder. As I climbed out I noticed the holes from the Fokker which had caught me napping. I chastised myself. I needed to get used to looking in my mirror. "I think you lads are going to have to do a lot of repairs over the next month or so."

"At least if we are repairing them, sir, it means you have returned."

"Who didn't make it?"

"Lieutenant Dunston."

He had been one of my flight and was one of the more experienced pilots in the squadron. I wondered if this was a taste of things to come.

When I reached the office the others were all there. "Good show today, Bill. Your three little Pups made all the difference."

I was more cautious. "These weren't the new German buses. These only had one Spandau. Wait until we meet the new boys!"

Randolph held up the map. "Here are the areas we need to photograph. It is a place called Vimy Ridge. We will be working alongside a couple of other squadrons. They want complete aerial photographs, a picture of everything from here," he pointed to the map, "Vimy, to here, Fleuchy. When we have those we will have to photograph further east. And we have to fly low to get as much detail as we can. You will have to endure ground fire."

"That means that they will be ready for us. They will have time to observe our strategies."

"I know, Gordy, but we have our orders."

"And think about the poor sods who will need to attack across the mud."

Archie held up his hand. "There is no point in debating this, we have our orders. What is the time scale?"

"We need everything photographed by the middle of March."

That gave us less than two weeks. Archie looked at me. "We are getting no replacements. It is up to your guardian angels to watch our backs."

"You might try Lumpy's old trick of a couple of Mills Bombs too. It makes the Hun a little more nervous if he thinks you are going to drop a grenade or two. And I used the new mirrors we had fitted the other day. They work a treat. So long as you remember to look at them. You might need it if your gunner is photographing."

"Good idea. I hate having a stiff neck."

Ironically the death of Peter and his gunner did not induce a sombre feel to dinner, rather the squadron focussed on the success of the Pups. They had all had a front-row seat to the show. After dinner, Gordy got up and began to tell the young pilots of the time I had been a gunner and a pilot had tried a loop. It raised a chuckle and then Charlie said, "And of course, the best thing was Captain Harsker had his own song." Emboldened by his earlier success he began to sing. Gordy and Ted stood on either side and harmonised with him.

"He'd fly through the air with the greatest of ease,
That daring young man on the flying trapeze.
His movements were graceful, all girls he could please
And my love he purloined away.
Once I was happy, but now I'm forlorn
Like an old coat that is tattered and torn;
Left on this world to fret and to mourn,
Betrayed by a maid in her teens.
The girl that I loved she was handsome;
I tried all I knew her to please
But I could not please her one quarter so well
As the man upon the trapeze.
He'd fly through the air with the greatest of ease,
That daring young man on the flying trapeze.
His movements were graceful, all girls he could please
And my love he purloined away.
This young man by name was Signor Bona Slang,
Tall, big and handsome, as well made as Chang.
Where 'er he appeared the hall loudly rang
With ovation from all people there.
He'd smile from the bar on the people below
And one night he smiled on my love.
She winked back at him and she shouted "Bravo,"
As he hung by his nose up above.
Her father and mother were both on my side

And very hard tried to make her my bride;
Her father he sighed, and her mother she cried,
To see her throw herself away.
One night I as usual went to her dear home,
Found there her father and mother alone.
I asked for my love, and soon they made known,
To my horror that she'd run away.
She'd fly through the air with the greatest of ease,
You'd think her the man young man on the flying trapeze.
Her movements were graceful, all girls she could please,
And that was the end of my love.

The young pilots thought it was hilarious and soon the whole of the squadron was singing it. Archie leaned over, "They don't mean any harm you know Bill. It is just a bit of banter."

"I know and I am quite happy about it. I just can't get over the change in shy, Charlie Sharp. He is like a different person."

"That must be down to your sister. His flight can't sing his praises high enough. A lot of that is down to you. He models himself on you. I think it is good for the squadron."

"It is good for me too." They all finished singing and were congratulating themselves. I stood and bowed. They applauded as though I had sung. That was a happy night. There were not many more of them in the next month.

Chapter 12

We headed northeast on the 5th of March. I had a bad feeling as we took off. We had been lucky the last time we had been attacked; we had been very close to our lines. This time we would be twenty miles behind enemy lines. We would have both ground fire and enemy aeroplanes to contend with.

I had spent some time talking to Freddie and Johnny about the mirror, the Vickers and our tactics. We were all learning so much each time we went up. I was in love again and this time it was with metal and canvas. The Pup seemed to be an extension of me. I missed Lumpy but I did not miss the responsibility of knowing that I could be the cause of another's death. Now I just had my own soul on my conscience.

We let the squadron take off and then we climbed high to be above them and use the superior ceiling of the Pup. We saw the Gunbuses below us. I felt for them. The gunner had canvas and wood to protect him and the Gunbus was so slow and big that the Germans could not miss them. Having flown a few missions in my Pup I could not believe how long I had survived in a Gunbus. They were such a huge target, how did the Germans miss them? We crossed the lines and after we had passed the main German defences, the squadron dropped to an altitude where they could photograph the ground. Only a quarter of the aeroplanes had cameras. The rest were watching for the Germans.

We managed fifteen minutes before the black crosses appeared in the distance. I waggled my wings, armed my Vickers and then began my slow dive to attack from above. We needed to conserve fuel. The Pup only had an endurance of two and a half hours. I saw that there were at least two Jastas. They were a mixture of Halberstadts and Fokkers. I guessed that they only had one machine gun. We had a chance; only a slight one but some of the squadron might survive and give the generals their precious photographs. I knew I was being unfair. The intelligence we would gather would save the lives of many Tommies but I was thinking about my squadron.

I knew that we would have to try our new tactic of flying as close to the enemy as we could. Their formation could wreak havoc on the Gunbuses. They had seen us this time and six of them were angling up towards us. The word had got out about the new nimble little fighter. The puffs of smoke from the ground fire were alarming but, in reality, they were not even close. They stopped as the Halberstadts closed with us. I opened fire at a thousand yards. It was a comfortable range and our tracer rounds were a good way to see how close I was. I saw that I was aiming high and so I dipped the nose marginally. It was hardly a movement at all but the next burst struck the propeller. That was how quickly we closed. The leading Halberstadt peeled off as the power dropped. I moved the stick to starboard and hit another burst. The Germans were now firing too, my move had taken me from the sights of the Halberstadt. My rounds were striking too low and I pulled the nose up a little. This time the German moved and bullets struck his wing.

    I passed him so closely I could see that he had a waxed moustache! I pulled hard on the stick and banked to come up on his tail. It was like turning on a sixpence! The Pup was so responsive that I was able to fire a burst as he wiggled out of my sights. I hit his rudder and I could see him becoming more sluggish. I glanced in my mirror and it was empty. I was so close to him now that I felt I could reach out and grab his tail. I fired another burst and the bullets tore through the fuselage and into the pilot. As he slumped backwards the Halberstadt rose into the air as his dead hands pulled on the stick. It was dead along with its pilot. It would loop until it either ran out of fuel or the controls I had damaged broke. Either way, I chose my next target.

    I banked left and began to dive. My first responsibility was to the Gunbuses below. As I passed a black cross I snap fired. I had no idea if I hit him or not but I was so close I felt as though I must have.

    Below me I watched the other Halberstadts swarming around the Gunbuses. I saw that Ted had four around him and his wingman. I aimed the Pup at them and gave a burst at a thousand yards. I wanted them nervous. I only fired twenty bullets but the effect was instantaneous. The rear Fokker banked into my sights. I fired a long burst and saw his tail shredded. His dive became terminal. He was too close to the ground to avoid it. The concussion threw the other Germans and Ted's craft into the air. I fired again and saw my bullets hit the Fokker in the engine. It dropped close to the ground, smoke pouring from a damaged engine. The other two climbed east. I fired again and heard the click of an empty chamber. I was out of bullets.

    I scanned the skies and saw that there was just Ted and me left. High in the sky to the west, I saw the two Pups as they fought with the last Fokkers. We headed home.

As we landed I saw the medical teams around the Gunbuses and counted the aeroplanes. I did not see Lieutenants Tinkler and Chapel from Ted's flight. We had paid a high price for the photographs.

I stood and watched as Freddie and Johnny landed. I knew that they were flying on fumes. The bullet holes in their Pups were a testament to the combat. However, they both climbed safely from the tiny yet formidable fighters. I could see the grins on their faces. "It works sir. If you get in amongst them and mix it up they can't hit you."

"But, my God, is it scary?"

The photographs were sent off. Randolph had a message from Headquarters that we were stood down for the next day and another squadron would risk the German fighters.

We needed the time to repair our buses. I knew I had been profligate when firing. I would have to revert back to the system I had used with Lumpy. I would fire short bursts when I was close to the enemy. We were three aeroplanes against squadrons. We had to be better shots. We now had only eight Gunbuses and three Pups. Ted was down to a flight of two. The Major would have to join us now.

Out first replacements were due at the end of the week. After we had repaired our Pups I sat in the office smoking my pipe and drinking some whisky that Randolph had managed to acquire. "Will we have a squadron by the time the replacements arrive though, sir?"

"A moot point; I hope so. Believe it or not, we have done damn well." He pointed to Randolph. "Randolph here tells me that 36 Squadron, who were on camera duty today, lost eight aeroplanes; three of them when the new pilots reacted badly and crashed."

Gordy put down his whisky glass and stubbed out his cigarette. "I am guessing here that you do not want to throw the new pilots in at the deep end."

"You know Gordy you could get a job at the end of Blackpool pier as a fortune teller!" Archie downed his whisky and poured us all another. "What is the point of letting them go up under-trained and watching them die?" He pointed to me, "Look at Bill. He nurtured and mollycoddled his two young pilots. The result is that Carrick and Holt saved the squadron today. Looking after young pilots is an investment in the future. I am not sending up the young lads until we have given them time to find their feet."

There was silence. Ted and Gordy had been brought up the hard way; they had been sergeant gunners. Charlie sighed, "Look Gordy, the C.O.

is right. The four of us in this room were all gunners first and we learned how to fight in the air with someone else ferrying us around. How many gunners could become pilots now? The poor buggers are lucky to survive twenty hours in the air. This isn't 1915 anymore. The Eindecker was a pussycat compared with the D.III."

I smiled at Charlie. He would make a good brother-in-law. I had liked him as a gunner. As a friend and a pilot, there was none better.

We were given a sector further south and east for our next reconnaissance flight. Although we had further to fly into enemy territory the flight there and back would be shorter. Sadly we only had nine aeroplanes to use for the photographs. Archie was getting more time in the air than he wanted.

That was the day we worked out that the Germans must have used forward observers with a telephone link to the airfields for we were jumped before we even reached the German area we were to photograph. It was a mixed squadron of Albatros D.III and D.II. I had discussed this eventuality with Freddie and Johnny; we would have to mix it up with the deadly D.III and hope that the Gunbuses could handle the D.II.

The one advantage we had that day was that we had the advantage of height. The Gunbuses had not descended to a lower altitude and the German airfield was close to the front and they were still climbing. This was when I missed Lumpy's bugle. When he sounded the cavalry charge it stirred my blood.

Our three Pups plunged down like hunting birds. As we neared the Albatros fighters I raised my nose a little. It was a risk. I was inviting a shot at a bigger target but the nippy little Sopwith was so responsive that I knew I could react quicker than the German. When we were in firing range I dipped my nose and fired at the same time. The tracer arced towards the target as I adjusted my descent. The German bullets whizzed into the air above my head striking the space I had just occupied while mine struck the German. The pilot was protected by both his radiator and his guns. I hit both and he peeled away. He was not downed but he was out of the dogfight.

I saw bullet holes appear in my wings. Glancing in my mirror I saw that there was no one behind me. I banked blindly left and then right to throw off the aim of my attacker. I saw him. He was below me. I went into a steep climb. I almost crashed into Carrick as he dived after his target. Had we not been flying such small craft then we would both have perished. I heard the twin Spandaus from behind me but no holes appeared. I could feel the force of the turn as I completed my loop and began my descent. My opponent had tried to match my loop but he had only reached three o'clock. I brought the nose of the Pup up and pulled the trigger. I hit his tail and his controls. The Albatros side-slipped out of my sights and headed towards the ground. I suspected he would be able to land and, as we were behind German lines, his aeroplane would live to fight us another day.

As I sought another foe I saw the pilot, somehow, regain control and he hedge-hopped east. Johnny was on the tail of an Albatros but another, with the Austrian Edelweiss painted on the side, was descending to hit him in his blind spot. I checked that I had no one behind me and then I climbed. I had only fired a third of my ammunition and I risked a long shot. I hit him and watched as he looked around for his attacker. He saw me and turned to fly directly at me. He had the advantage of height and speed. He had two guns. I braced myself for the strike of his rounds.

I dipped my nose slightly; inviting the shot and then I dipped my wings to port. They were small adjustments but I knew that he would not have the killing shot he wanted. He would wait until he was closer. As I straightened up I fired. The bullets sparked from the side of his radiator and I dipped my wings to starboard while lifting the nose slightly. The German disappeared from view. I heard the twin guns as I dipped the nose. I fired as the German's engine appeared just ninety feet in front of me. I pushed the stick forward as I gave him a last burst. I shot his undercarriage to pieces. It was fortunate that I did. I was so close to him that I would have struck it with my top wing.

I started to pull another loop to come up on his other side but he headed east. Instead of completing the loop, I banked to starboard to level out. I checked my mirror and it was empty. I saw the other two Pups. They were heading west. There was no sign of the Gunbuses. I climbed and headed west. I watched the ground as I did so. It appeared that neither side had lost an aeroplane but I knew at least three which would need repairs. There were three D.IIIs which would not attack our reconnaissance aeroplanes the next day. Our mission had not been a total failure.

The stretchers on the field told their own story as I landed on the greensward. Lieutenants Swan and Walker's aeroplanes looked to have suffered damage. Johnny walked over to me his flying helmet in his hand. "They both lost a gunner sir and Jack Swan took a round in the leg."

"That means two more buses down. Things are getting tight."

"Thanks for coming to my aid, sir, although I thought you were going to crash into him."

"Yes, the Pup is nippy but you live on your nerves. We didn't destroy any of them then?"

He shook his head. "We damaged a couple and you hit three of them but no kills."

Randolph was on the telephone to Headquarters when I entered. He continued talking and pushed the whisky bottle towards me. "No sir, we didn't manage to get any photographs today. The squadron was attacked by superior numbers before we could reach the German lines but we did damage a number of aeroplanes. Whichever squadron goes up tomorrow will have an easier time." There was a pause and I saw the captain's eyes look up at the ceiling. "But sir we have only ten aeroplanes… yes sir. I understand." He slammed the telephone down. "We go up again tomorrow." He nodded towards the telephone. "Apparently our losses were the lowest on the whole front today."

Everyone's heads were down. Charlie said brightly, "How about taking off in the dark? If we fly high then the observers on the ground won't be able to get a fix on our course."

Ted shook his head, "Flying in the dark…"

I thought it was a good idea, "Think about it, Ted, all of our pilots are experienced. Tomorrow the five senior pilots will all be flying. We have to do it so let us give ourselves a chance. I think it is worth the risk. If we get the mechanics to line the airfield with torches then we should be able to take off and we will be landing in the daylight anyway."

Archie nodded, "We'll do it and if it fails… well, we had a good run for our money eh lads?"

In theory, there was no difference in taking off in the dark as opposed to daylight but we weren't used to it. The three Pups took off first. I wanted us in position before the Gunbuses arrived. Even if we only took a few photographs it would be worth it. As we lifted off and began to climb I saw that the land below was completely black. I would have to use all my navigational skills to get us to our target. Ironically it was the Germans themselves who helped me to fix our position. As we crossed their lines some of their machine guns opened fire. As we were over four thousand feet above them they were wasted bullets but they marked the German trenches for us.

I used our airspeed to determine roughly where our new sector was. Once there we flew lazy spiralling loops to gain altitude while we watched the sun rise in the east. Once the first rays lit the ground I was able to see that we were too far to the north and I led us south. The Gunbuses would take their position from us. We flew in line astern to maximise our chances of seeing any German fighters. I alternated looking east to glancing west. I saw the Gunbuses as they lumbered towards me. I hadn't realised how big they were. It was fortunate they had no fuselage to speak of or they would be easy to knock from the skies.

As soon as they saw us Archie led the long line to a lower altitude. There were few guns and our only danger was the Hun. Each Gunbus was fifty feet from the wingtip of its neighbour. Archie was making sure we took some photographs, in detail, of a large area. If we took enough photographs then they wouldn't need to send us out again.

We watched to the east. As we banked at the end of each circuit I breathed a sigh of relief. This could not last. The Germans must know what we were up to and, sure enough, ten minutes after the Gunbuses arrived I saw the black dots in the distance. I waggled my wings as a signal for Archie. Someone must have seen me for the Gunbuses began to bank and climb west. I took my three Pups even higher before we headed west. I saw the slower Gunbuses ahead of us. They were at five thousand feet and just a mile or so ahead. We were still spiralling gently up so that, while we headed west, we could still keep an eye on the ten fighters desperately climbing to reach the Gunbuses.

The German front line was fully awake and ready. The guns began to pop at the Gunbuses. Suddenly I saw Ted's bus take a hit and smoke poured from his engine. The German gunners renewed their efforts. The fighters would struggle to catch our aeroplanes and I levelled out and took us west. To my horror, I saw a line of six fighters approaching the Gunbuses from the north. As I banked to starboard I pushed the stick forward. I would attack this new threat obliquely from the side and hoped that the first Jasta would give up.

The bark of the machine guns told me that they were the new fighters. Smoke poured from Harry Dodds' aeroplane; that meant two wounded birds. There was little point in saving ammunition and I wanted to distract the fighters. I fired at a thousand yards. The tracer rounds told me that I was close. The rear Fokkers veered to starboard and away from the Gunbuses. I saw that these fighters had a green tail. I stored that information for my report and then banked to port to attack the leader of this Jasta.

At five hundred yards I gave a long burst. I struck the fuselage and tail. As I edged to port I fired a second burst and struck the engine. Johnny and Freddie added their fire and the second fighter was also hit. The ground fire from the British lines was the final straw and the Jasta headed east.

As we crossed the British lines I saw the Tommies cheering. I waved back. I had been in the trenches and knew how they appreciated such gestures. Just beyond the trenches, I saw Ted's bus. He was dragging a wounded gunner from the cockpit as flames began to take hold of the wings. I looped around to watch. To my relief, he managed to pull him to safety just before the whole thing exploded. He waved to show he was safe and I waggled my wings. He was close enough to the field for medical help to reach him within the hour.

As usual, we were the last to land. As we approached the field I saw a lorry heading east. I assumed it was for Ted. Harry's gunner looked to be in a bad way and Harry looked shaken up.

Gordy ran to me, "What about Ted?"

"He walked away from this one but I am not certain about his gunner. His camera would be ruined."

"We got plenty. I think you were right to call this one. But I would not want to do it too many times."

I reported the markings on the Jasta we had seen. It was not the Flying Circus. Randolph filed the information and then put a large circle on the map to the north of where they had been seen. He wrote on the map, *'Green-tailed new Fokker Jasta'*. It built up a picture of who we faced. So far we had been able to avoid the Red Baron. We wondered how long it would last.

Ted and his gunner arrived back. His gunner was badly wounded and we were now desperately short of both aeroplanes and gunners. That was the day, March 12th, when we received two pieces of good news. Our replacements would be here within a couple of days and we had two new Bristol two-seater fighters delivered.

Just as with the Pups, there was a great deal of excitement as every pilot swarmed over them. We knew that one would go to Ted but we were not certain who would get the second. Senior Flight Sergeant Lowery made that decision. "It will have to be Mr Dodds, sir. His bus is a right off. It is only fit for spares."

The two pilots both looked happy about that but they had no gunners and the new buses needed checking. We discovered that they had the same speed as the Pup and the same synchronised machine gun. The rear Lewis was the one we were used to. However, it was much longer and wider than the Pup. We were still far more manoeuvrable. Our joy was complete when we discovered that a weather front prevented us from flying for the next three days. Other squadrons would have to risk death alley and photograph the German lines.

Chapter 13

That turned out to be our last reconnaissance flight for the Battle of Arras began on March 20th with a creeping bombardment. It went on until April 8th which was supposed to be Zero Hour. We had more than enough to do making sure the new pilots knew how to fly the Gunbus and working with the gunners, especially the replacements. Ted and Harry also had to become familiar with the Bristol.

Maddeningly we had three days where we could not fly. When we could get aloft Major Leach watched from the ground to identify weaknesses in the four new pilots. Of course, we had to reorganise the flights. Harry and his Bristol joined Ted while three new pilots and David Garrick joined Charlie. It did not make for neat flights but it was efficient. The Bristols could go as fast as we could in the Pups. We were all much happier with the five newer machines. General Trenchard had been as good as his word. If we could survive this offensive then we would be given another ten Bristols. That would make all the difference.

After three days of the creeping barrage, we did not even notice it any more. It went on during the night and I dreaded to think of the effect on the trenches. I heard later that they expended almost three million shells. The Somme Offensive had not achieved all that it could when they ran out of shells. That would not happen this time.

The letters from home arrived in the last week of March. Inevitably there was some overlap. My mother's letter told me of the death of Lord Burscough and the worry over the death duties. However John's letter had lifted her spirits and, once again, she urged me to look after him!

Sarah's letter was grim reading. She and Cedric were now the only servants left in the Big House. Chunks of fine farmland had had to be sold off to pay the death duties and the children had had to come home from boarding school. She could not afford the fees. The one bright spot in the whole thing was that Lady Burscough had said the last thing to be sold would be the cottages.

I was pleased that I had saved Beattie's letter until last. I was about to start to read it when Charlie knocked on my door. "Er, Bill, I have a letter for you."

"For me?"

He gave me a shy smile. "Yes sir, Alice wrote to me and enclosed a note for you. I haven't read it."

"Thank you, Charlie."

He hesitated at the door and then said, "I'll leave you to read it then."
As he left I said, "If it relates to you I will tell you."
I saw the relief on his face. "Thank you, Bill."

He could have read it. It was just a brief note. It explained that the premises where they made their dresses had been damaged in a Zeppelin bombing raid and that they had had the idea of relocating to Lady Burscough's estate until the war was over and it was safe to return to the city. I was relieved. It solved many problems which I had envisaged. Alice would be back at home and mum and dad would not be evicted. It would be good for lady Burscough too. Her home would not be taken from her. There would be hard times ahead but there was hope. I looked forward to reading Beattie's letter even more. There was a black cloud but I had glimpsed a silver lining.

February 1917
Dearest Bill,

I saw your gunner today! I liked him when I met him the first time; he gives me hope for the future for even with one hand he is positive about his life. I am not certain I could be so cheerful. He idolises you. That makes two of us. He left hospital today, which is why I am writing this letter now. He is going north, back to Durham. He says he will visit with Jack Laithwaite's widow so that he can give her Jack's possessions. The men had a collection for his widow and Lumpy is going to give it to her. It will help her. He is kind. I have his address and I promised that I will write. I know that you might want to but you don't have the time. I do.

Life is a little more hazardous here in the capital at the moment. We have bombs being dropped on us. It isn't every night but they appear so random. The Zeppelins are silent. None has been close to us yet but we are close enough to the palace for us to worry.

I know I am rambling on and you have far more to worry about but I didn't want you hearing about the dangers from someone else. I will always tell you the truth. I am telling you not to worry, no matter what you hear or read about in the newspapers. Your life is far more precarious. Talking to Lumpy has shown me that.

Take care, my love. You are ever in my prayers and thoughts. We will survive this war and we will be together. We just need to have faith and believe.
Your love
Beattie xxx

I was glad that she and Lumpy got on. The first brief meeting when I was in the hospital was over before it began. I was happy that he had a future. I had no idea what it would entail but he was resilient and he would make the best of it. In a way, I was pleased that he had lost his hand for it meant he would survive the war. Over fifty pilots and gunners from our squadron would never have a future.

As April drew closer we received our orders. We were to patrol the lines south of the creeping barrage and discourage Germans from either bombing or spotting. We knew that we would soon be spotting for our artillery. It was a necessary but unpopular job. However, we knew that the new German fighters would not be wasted spotting. They would be the hunters preying on our slow-moving reconnaissance aeroplanes and outdated fighters. At the same time, we heard horror stories about the new Jastas wiping out six and seven aeroplanes at a time. We had been lucky but I knew that our luck would run out soon. It had to.

On the last day of March, we prepared to patrol the lines. Archie had given us our orders. The five buses of B and C flight would be the high cover while the ten remaining Gunbuses would fly at a lower altitude. Anyone spotting for German guns would need to be low but any German hunters would be high. Ted and Harry were keen to use the new Vickers. We had extolled its virtues for the past month. It was an overcast day when we took off and it was hardly the best conditions in which to fly for the cloud cover was low.

I decided to take us up and keep just inside the lower clouds. It might hide us and we could emerge to check the skies. The barrage to the north was deafening for we were much closer to it. If there were any Germans left on Vimy Ridge then they would be in no condition to defend their lines. I wondered if the brass hats had got it right for once. The German technique of hiding whilst being bombarded and emerging once it stopped would not work in this Arras Offensive.

As we descended from the clouds to get our bearings I saw a Jasta as they headed for the Gunbuses below us. I waggled my wings and dived. I could see that amongst the Fokker and Albatros aeroplanes, there were a couple of LVGs. They were a two-seater reconnaissance aeroplane. They would be spotting for the German artillery. I would let the Gunbuses deal with those. Our priority was the eighteen fighters escorting them.

I signalled with my arm to indicate that Freddie and Johnny should flank me. Ted and Harry would add their firepower behind us. We fell upon them like five hunting eagles. The rear gunner on the LVG spotted us and I saw his arm waving as he tried to attract the attention of the fighters. The Fokkers were diving toward the Gunbuses. I opened fire at five hundred feet. I caught the pilot of an Albatros unawares and he looked around in panic for this unseen attacker. The other aeroplanes all began to climb to meet this new threat. The two LVG headed east as fast as their aeroplanes would take them. No matter what happened now we had prevented them from spotting.

These were the Albatros D.III or at least some of them were. I saw the twin Spandaus. I gritted my teeth as I fired at the Albatros which was still wiggling like an insect on a pin. He must have been new. He was flying too straight. I kept raising and lowering my nose and banking to port and starboard. A fighter pilot needed lightning reflexes. I fired a third burst and saw the bullets as they struck the pilot and the cockpit. The Albatros went into a steep dive. I glanced in my mirror and saw Ted and Harry diving too. I banked to port. Flying in a straight line when Albatros D.III fighters were around was foolish. Bullets whizzed past my head. I had taken evasive action just in time. I put the stick over the other way and, as an aeroplane came into my sights, I fired my Vickers. The green-tailed aeroplane was gone before I could fire another burst.

I pushed the stick down and then looped. As I came up I saw the same aeroplane. He was trying to loop inside me. The Pup could turn on a sixpence and I gradually began to get the upper hand. The Le Rhone engine was screaming but it pulled the tiny fuselage around and when I saw his tail in my sights I fired a long burst. I was so close I could not miss and his green rudder and the top of his tail disappeared. He was a good pilot and he straightened up and headed east while I was finishing my loop.

I followed him. He was faster than me but I was still close enough to fire. My bullets struck his fuselage and he dipped the nose to escape across the German lines. As soon as the German machine guns on the ground began to fire I started to climb. I had damaged him enough to keep him out of the air for a day or two. I headed west. My fuel gauges told me to get back to the field.

Despite our plans and our best efforts two new pilots and buses had been shot down by the Hun. We had stopped them spotting and I had managed to shoot down a new Albatros but we were losing the war in the air. The four flight commanders trudged wearily into the office. I don't know what the others were thinking but I was thinking that this was the first day of our Arras Offensive. The ground attack had not started. The Somme offensive had lasted months. At this rate, the squadron would cease to exist by the middle of April!

Randolph put the bottle of whisky on the table as we gave our reports. I asked, "What happened to Jameson and Murphy?"

Charlie and Gordy looked at each other and shook their heads. Archie poured himself a glass of whisky. "They panicked and crashed into each other."

"They weren't even shot down?"

"No. We were just getting into the circle and their wings touched." He downed the whisky. "I know, it happens all the time and we don't crash but they both turned the wrong way."

Ted rolled his eyes. "I don't want to worry you, sir, but when we get the Bristol fighter for everyone then there is still going to be a problem. They are almost as big as the Gunbus but they are faster and the engine is at the front. I know Bill mentioned it but it takes some getting used to a propeller in front of you when you are used to a Gunbus."

"The Pup is only small but we have had some close calls and Freddie and Johnny are really experienced. Sir, we need to make sure that the pilots know what they are doing before they go up."

Before he could speak Randolph said, "We have to patrol and the other squadrons are suffering more than we are."

"Then why not just patrol with the new aeroplanes? At the moment the Gunbuses are just bait. When the next batch of Fokker fodder arrives spend a couple of days flying as many hours as you can over our own lines. Technically we are still patrolling. Ted and I have the newer buses; we hold the fort."

Randolph went to the map. "He might have something, sir. Look at today. We were here." He pointed to a spot on the map. "That was just over our lines and the Hun came to us. They are getting more aggressive. Having the Gunbuses a little further back might actually help and, at the moment, we are not needed for spotting. We just need to stop them spotting and the five new buses are the best equipped for that."

Archie looked at me. "Well Bill, how do you feel about that?"

"It was my idea. I think it will work and I would rather have a full squadron later in the offensive." I turned to Randolph. "And you need to keep on at Headquarters to get us the new Bristols."

He shook his head, sadly, "I do, Bill, every day."

I told my young lads what we would be about. They were surprisingly sanguine about the whole thing. "It's only fair, sir. We have the best and newest aeroplanes so we should take on theirs."

"The trouble is Johnny, their aeroplanes are better than the Pup. They are faster, better armed and have a better rate of climb."

"I know sir but we are small enough to be annoying. We have watched you, sir. You fly like a scrum-half wriggling through tackles. The big boys are grabbing at fresh air. Staying close to them works."

Ted was listening to us. "Well we don't have the same advantage but at least I have a sting in my tail." He actually smiled, "I don't worry about the Hun in the sun so much these days."

I laughed, "Ted Thomas is becoming an optimist. You never know there may be some hope left for us after all."

The five of us left first, the next day. We were well wrapped up because we were flying high and there seemed to be a cold front coming in. The air felt too cold for April. We flew at five thousand feet to give ourselves plenty of room. We had no Gunbuses to worry about. I realised I missed chatting to Lumpy as we flew along the lines looking east for the enemy. I nearly missed them for they were flying high. They had adopted our technique of a high approach and then dropping down to a lower altitude to spot. I waggled my wings and we began to climb. I cocked my Vickers and tried to identify them. They had two of the LVGs they had used the previous day. Each one was protected by five Fokker D.IIs. I frowned. They had had more the previous day. Had we damaged them or was this a trap? Sometimes you could overthink.

We were more evenly matched this time. As we had a slightly faster rate of climb than Ted I headed for the southernmost Huns. The LVG bravely assumed its position while the protecting fighters headed for us. I knew that the LVG would relay its information back quickly but we had to destroy or at least discourage the Fokkers.

They had the advantage of speed as they roared down towards us. I raised my nose and then dipped it. I feinted to port and then to starboard. I wanted to make myself as difficult to hit as possible. One advantage I had was that there were five of them and Johnny and Freddie were far enough away for me to have air room. I side slipped to starboard as the first Fokker fired and then I jinked to port so that I attacked him from the side. He could not fire at me and his neighbour had to turn. I waited until I was two hundred feet away and as the Fokker tried to turn to meet me I gave a ten-second burst. The .303 struck him along the cockpit and he slumped dead. His aeroplane was undamaged and it continued its turn to port. I banked and climbed to my left.

The second Fokker which had tried to turn to follow me suddenly smacked into the pilotless bird. They exploded in a fiery ball. I banked to starboard. I would leave the three Fokkers who remained for Freddie and Johnny. I dived after the LVG. His observer saw me and the Spandau began to bark. Perhaps he was lucky or I was careless but he struck my propeller. I noticed the change in pitch. I fired a long burst at him as he fled east. I hit his fuselage and, when I saw his gunner slump in his seat I knew that they would take no more photographs.

I turned west. There was little point in going on with a damaged propeller. Although still flying the little Pup did not feel right and I was relieved to see the empty airfield. For once I was the first to return.

Flight Sergeant Lowery raced over. He knew our buses better than we did. "There's something wrong with her sir. Have you been hit?"

"Yes, Flight Sergeant Lowery. The propeller."

He walked to the front as I descended. There was a hole on one side and an ugly crack along its length. As he touched it a whole piece fell from it. He shook his head. "You are lucky sir. Well, that means you won't be flying for a couple of days. We will have to send for a spare."

For some reason, that did not please me. I liked to share the dangers with my pilots and I hated the inactivity of just watching.

Chapter 14

Randolph was philosophical when he heard about my damaged propeller. "It is a reasonable trade-off, Bill. You destroyed one aeroplane and stopped their spotting. You will be out of the war for one perhaps two days at the most. It also works out for we needed a pilot to go to the front. General Trenchard wants one of us to make a courtesy visit and jolly the troops up at the front."

I was confused, "But why?"

"For some reason, we are seen as the positive side of the war. I know that we see the Hun winning but, by and large, the lads on the ground see us winning. It will just be one day."

I remembered when the Colonel and I had visited the Liverpool Pals battalion. It had seemed to make a difference to morale. I just felt like a cheat. I swanned in, shook a few hands and then swanned back to a comfortable billet. The poor Tommies had lice, mud and rats to contend with.

"Very well, Randolph."

"Take Bates with you."

"Why?"

"If you go on your own then it looks like you have been sent because you have nothing better to do. If you take Bates it looks planned. He can be your driver. It will look more official."

"But I am going because I am a spare part."

He shrugged, "They don't need to know that do they? You can take the major's car. I'll get the directions for you later."

I was the only casualty from the morning's patrol and the rest of the squadron were in high spirits. That evening, as we sat in the mess, Freddie looked at me nervously. "Come on Freddie, spit it out."

"Well, sir, Johnny and I had a suggestion for Captain Thomas but it seemed impertinent to mention it."

I saw Ted's eyes flicker as he heard his name mentioned. "I am sure Captain Thomas would take any advice; especially as you have now shot down more Huns than he has."

I said that loud enough for him to hear and he chuckled as he said, "Cheeky bugger! It's only because I spend all my time running a kindergarten. Come on then what is this idea?"

"Well, sir, your Bristol is as fast as our Pup but you were flying it today as though it was a Gunbus." I saw Ted's eyes narrow. "No sir, what I mean is you can climb faster than a Gunbus and throw it around in the air. It isn't as though the gunner can fall out of the front like they can in a Gunbus is it sir? And I think it will bank and turn far better than a Gunbus. In addition, you have a good machine gun. Don't just get into a position for the gunner to get a good shot. He is there to watch your back. The Bristol is made for fighting. It's worth a try isn't it sir?"

"You are talking as though it is a fighter!"

Charlie smiled, "Actually Ted, it is a two-seater fighter. In many ways, it is better than a Pup as it has rear protection."

"You've been doing your homework, Charlie."

"I can't wait to get one. It will be good to have something which can hold its own against an Albatros. I am fed up with being target practice."

He really had matured over the past months. I didn't recognise him as the shy and nervous gunner I had first met. He would make a good Flight Commander when we did get our Bristols.

"Anyway let me know how it goes. I shall be in the trenches tomorrow."

Ted shook his head, "I'd rather be in the air. I tell you what, young Carrick, I will give it a go tomorrow. You two will be flying on my wing anyway. We might as well use the same tactics. Just remember the Bristol is a wee bit bigger than those toys of yours."

They had taken off by the time that Bates and I headed up to Arras. Bates drove and he chattered away like a budgie all the way north. The town of Arras was full of military vehicles. There were columns of men marching north. I heard the throb of Rolls Royce engines above and saw a squadron of Gunbuses preventing Germans from bombing the busy town. I followed the directions and found myself at a checkpoint where a Redcap held up his hand. "This is as far as you can take a car, sir. It's on foot from now on."

"Thank you, sergeant. Where can we leave it where it won't be in the way?"

"Just over there sir, against the side of that building."

The building he pointed to was a wall. The rest had been destroyed by artillery. I hoped I would not come back and find a car shrouded in rubble! I had been to the trenches before and Bates and I donned our tin lids. As we headed along a support trench I sensed the nervousness from Bates. "You can stay in the car if you like, John. I know that this must be difficult for you."

"No sir. I have to get back on the horse. Besides this is just a visit. It isn't as though I have to sleep in a mud tomb is it?"

That brought home to me what the Tommies had to endure. They dug their own graves and then had to sleep in them. We were to meet with a Colonel Roger DeVere who was keen to meet some fliers. When we met him I discovered why. He had his own ideas about flying and aerial warfare.

"Jolly glad to meet you." He pointed to my medals. "M.C. eh? How many of the Boche have you shot down then?"

I hated this game of numbers but whatever answer I gave it could be taken the wrong way. "Oh, thirty or so."

"Jolly good. That makes you an ace." He turned to the other officers in the dugout. They all looked hollow-eyed and grey and the assault had not even started. "This is an ace chaps." He shook my hand, "You know I would love to be a pilot."

"You ought to train then sir. We are always short of them."

He took my arm and led me down the trenches. "The thing is there is a tradition in my family of serving in the Army. The old chap was colonel of this regiment before me. Still, after the war, I think I'll learn. It isn't hard is it?"

"A little harder than it looks but, yes sir, you could learn."

That seemed to satisfy him. "Good. Now I wanted someone from the Royal Flying Corps to gee up morale. As you probably know Zero Hour is in a few days and if they see a hero." He tapped my tunic, "Well it helps them."

He kept stopping to introduce me to huddles of soldiers. I tried to be as cheerful and optimistic as I could despite the fact that I knew we were outgunned in the skies. We now had as much chance of dying as these young men who would have to march across mud, through machine guns and over barbed wire.

He stopped at what I thought was another bunker. "We'll have to stop here. The Engineers are in there."

Just then two Engineers came out of the tunnel. One of them said, "Captain Harsker! You haven't joined the infantry have you, sir?"

I vaguely recognised him as a comrade of Bert's but I couldn't have named him. I shook his hand, "No, just a visit. How is Bert?"

"I'll go and get him." Like the White Rabbit, he disappeared down the hole.

"Sorry about this, sir. My little brother is a sergeant in the Tunnellers."

He smiled, "Don't apologise. They have done sterling work and they will save lives. I wouldn't like to do what they do." He shuddered, "I hate confined spaces."

"Then you would not like my aeroplane, sir. It is very cramped and hard to get in and out of."

Bert came out looking like a coal miner. He grinned and his teeth looked shockingly white. "Nice to see you, Bill!"

The colonel laughed for Bert was now very broad; digging had built up his muscles. "He is your little brother?"

"He was until he started digging your tunnels."

"I'll go back to headquarters. Get some tea or something on. You can find your own way can you?"

Bert saluted, "I'll bring him, sir. I am due a half-hour off anyway."

I saw him looking at a bemused Bates. "This is Airman Bates, my servant."

Bert raised his eyebrows but made no comment. "What are you doing here then? Checking up on me?"

"No, although mam did wonder why she hasn't heard from you lately."

"I never seem to have the time besides it is you they all want to write to. You are the hero."

"Don't you start too! I just do my job."

"I am not having a go. All the lads are envious of me having an ace for a brother."

I shook my head. "Have you had a leave lately?"

"Nah. We have been here since October. Us and the New Zealanders. They are such nice chaps. They are tough too. I think I would like to go there after the war. It seems a place where you can make something of yourself."

"Speaking of that, our Alice is doing really well. She designs dresses." I suddenly realised he might not know the news. "Did you hear about Lord Burscough?"

"No. What is it?"

"He was shot down a few weeks ago. He was killed and the estate is crippled by death duties."

"I liked Lord Burscough. He was a genuine bloke." I saw the concern on his face as he took in the import of the death. "What about the cottage?"

Well, our little sister has persuaded her boss to relocate to the estate and I think everything will be all right."

"I hope so. At their age…"

"Quite." We had reached the main headquarters trench. "The colonel reckons it is dangerous in the tunnels."

"Well, the Hun has started trying to dig underneath us. We now go armed but, as I said, those New Zealand boys are hard lads. We give as good as we get." He looked at his watch. "Well, I had best get back." He held out his hand for Bates. "Nice to have met you."

"And you sir."

He laughed, "Nah, just a sergeant!" he grasped my hand firmly. "And you watch yourself but keep doing what you are doing. The lads love it. Every time there is a newspaper story about one of you flyboys they dig a bit harder."

"But why?"

He shrugged, "We are in the same army, we are brothers… I don't know the reasons. I just dig tunnels but I know that morale goes up every time we hear of a Hun being shot down."

I nodded, "And you, write home!"

"I will." He turned and strode confidently back to his hole in the ground.

"Sir, you didn't mention Miss Porter and your engagement."

"No Bates…" I shrugged, "I have enough to live up to as it is. It will be a nice surprise for him."

I knew that Bates was not convinced but Bert had enough to live with. I didn't want something else for him to envy.

Chapter 15

I was quiet on the journey back. Bert had not lightened my load, he had added to it. He had also added worries for me. He was in more danger than I was. He seemed so confident and yet he was like a mole beneath the ground. There could not be a greater contrast. I soared like an eagle high in the sky; he burrowed beneath the ground out of sight of light. It did not seem fair.

The squadron had survived another day without casualties and they were in the mood for a celebration. When we had passed through Arras I had stopped and bought some decent wine, chosen by Bates, and some good cheese. It made me feel less guilty about having the day off. I also found some tobacco I knew that Archie would like. The wine, cheese and tobacco seemed like the perfect accompaniment for the celebration.

I also felt more like celebrating. My propeller had arrived and I could fly in the morning. Ted slapped me on the back. "Your lads came up with a good idea. The Bristol is a good fighter. She can't turn like your Pups but you just aim and fire. You don't have to worry about shooting your gunner's head off and you have two hundred and fifty bullets! And the range…"

"I wish you two would just shut up about your wonderful new aeroplanes. Some of us have to make do with the old Gunbus. Charlie is right. You do feel like an Aunt Sally up there. It is a good job that they are so solid and reliable."

"You'll soon get yours, Gordy. I heard that 48 Squadron were equipped with the new Bristols yesterday. They are the first squadron to be fitted out with them. It is only a matter of time."

"They have that Captain Leefe Robinson, don't they? He's the chap who got the V.C. for shooting down a Zeppelin over London."

"Well Charlie, we have Captain Bill Harsker who should have had a V.C."

"That's all right, Ted. I am happy with my M.C."

Ted and Gordy took to arguing about the Bristol and the Gunbus. Charlie and I went to the bar for a brandy to finish off the night. "I wish I had been with you today."

"Why is that Charlie?"

"I am keen to meet all of your family and to get to know them better. I wish we could have come with you when you went to Burscough. Your whole family seem so interesting. I have no brothers and sisters. There is just me and mum and dad and we, well, we are just ordinary."

"Trust me no one is more ordinary than us."

"You can't believe that sir. I mean, look at what you and Alice have done. You are both successes."

"Lucky."

"Then look at Bert. He joined young and yet he is a sergeant already. You didn't expect that did you, sir?"

"Well if that is your yardstick you have made even greater strides. You are a captain."

He toasted me with his brandy. "And I would not be but for you so, cheers, Captain Harsker."

The mood changed the next morning when we were given our orders; it was not the mission we wanted. We were to photograph the German lines near Vimy and to ascertain the success of the creeping barrage. They were going to halt the guns for one hour while we flew over and photographed the ridge. It would be touch and go. Once we reached the British lines then they would cease fire and one hour later they would begin again. In theory, we would have plenty of time but I knew that there could be small delays; the weather and wind could change; we could be attacked by the Hun.

Although the five newer aeroplanes took off first we waited for the Gunbuses to catch us up. All of the Gunbuses were fitted with cameras. We had to ensure the maximum photographs. The wind was still a cold wind from the east. That, in itself, was a problem. It would slow down the Gunbuses even more. We would escape quicker but any Germans sent to intercept us would be able to do so easily.

We headed across the front in two lines. The five angels were three thousand feet above the Gunbuses. I did not envy the Gunbuses. The German anti-aircraft fire and the soldiers in the trenches would be desperate to strike back at a foe. The Gunbuses were an enormous target. We would be the first to reach the ridge. The British artillery stopped by the time we had reached the forward trenches. I pictured Bert beavering away below the ground and the Colonel pointing proudly at us. It was good to know that, just by flying east, we were helping us get closer to victory.

The anti-aircraft fire began while we were over No-Man's Land. Jack Swan's bus caught one and I saw him peel off with smoke coming from his engine as he headed west. The other eight continued on. The next to be hit was Archie Leach. I saw holes appear in his wings and his rudder. He slowly descended. He was an old hand and he knew that he needed to be close to the ground in case he lost power.

I had little time to observe for black dots appeared in the distance. We had just reached the area we were to photograph and we had just forty minutes to take them and return home before the barrage began again.

We had to do our job now. I led the others east. I recognised the shape of the Albatros. The question was, would they have one Spandau or two? The fact that they headed for the Gunbuses told me that they were desperate for us not to know the effect of the bombing. It also gave us a slim chance. If we could hurt them first they might be discouraged. They were rapidly closing with the slow-moving Gunbuses. We were still a thousand or so yards from them. We could fire but it would be a waste of bullets and it would warn them. The double chatter from the first Albatros gave us the bad news. They were the Albatros D.III.

Gordy's aeroplane was hit and his gunner stopped firing. I saw his bus jerk in the air and then he banked to head home. As the first Albatros banked, a second opened fire at Dicky Walker's bus. His gunner managed to hit the Albatros and smoke poured from its engine. Even as it pulled away, a third raked Dicky's undercarriage and it too poured smoke. Out of the corner of my eye, I saw Archie's bus as it juddered from the strike of a pair of Spandau machine guns. It was like flying into a hailstorm of bullets.

Luckily we were now less than five hundred yards from the Germans. I opened fire at the Albatros which had just struck Walker's bus. I stitched a line across the wings. I lifted the nose and fired, almost blindly at the first Albatros which had banked around. Perhaps I was lucky for I managed to hit the radiator and engine from above and the Albatros juddered.

I was now at the end of the line and I began to bank. I glanced in my mirror and saw that I had made the manoeuvre in the nick of time. A Hun was just lining up on me and my sudden move threw him. I knew that I could turn inside him. I pulled back as hard as I could on the stick. As I came up I saw a black cross and I squeezed the trigger. I had no idea if I hit it for I found myself coming down towards my pursuer. He was less than fifty yards from me. I fired again and saw my bullets miss. He jinked to the side. The Pup is so responsive that I was able to replicate his move and fire again. This time I struck his rudder. He tried to dive down towards the ground. I gambled and banked starboard and then to port. He may not have had a mirror for he turned to starboard. I imagine he had a real shock when my tiny Pup appeared on his port side. I fired again and struck his engine. He was mine for the taking. Then my ammunition ran out. I banked to port and, as I passed him I waved. He saluted me. He had been lucky.

I looked up and saw Johnny and Freddie descending to join me. My flight had all made it. I looked at my watch. We had fifteen minutes to cross No-Man's land or risk being struck by our own artillery. We had just seen our barbed wire when I heard the first of the guns as they fired. I stopped breathing. When we passed our trenches I began to breathe again. That had been close.

Even the new buses had been badly shot up. I saw mechanics swarming all over the damaged aeroplanes and the medical orderlies dressing the wounds. We knew we had been in a battle but I did not count any losses. That was how we measured success in 1917; small gains and no losses.

Archie was in his office his arm in a sling. It was his right arm. He slumped into his seat, having had the cut dressed by Doc Brennan and he picked up the whisky. He downed it in one. We were still giving our oral reports to Randolph. It was grim. Dicky Walker and Gordy both had aeroplanes which needed a great deal of work. Archie, obviously could not fly and the new aeroplanes needed repairs.

I watched as Archie tried to fill his pipe one-handed. "Here sir." I reached over and filled it for him.

"Thanks, Bill. I forgot that you had to learn to do things one-handed when you were wounded. It is annoying."

I handed it to him. He put it in his mouth and I struck a match. When it was going he tamped it down and nodded. "Thanks. Well, that was a bit of a bugger. I hope they appreciate those photographs."

Charlie seemed quite upbeat. "We lost no aeroplanes sir and we chased them off. I saw Bill here wing a couple and their engines smoked. They might not get up tomorrow either."

"If I hadn't run out of bullets I would have had that last one."

The telephone rang. Randolph nodded and then spoke. He gave our report. He listened again. "Yes sir, I'll have the film sent over immediately. Thank you, sir."

"Well, the good news is we don't have to fly tomorrow. 45 Squadron is up and running and they are keen to try their new Bristols out. They will cover the reconnaissance aeroplanes. We are stood down until the sixth. We may not be needed again until the seventh."

Gordy slammed the desk in joy. "That is the best news I have had in a long time. If 45 Squadron have a good show tomorrow with the new bus then we will get ours that much quicker. I have had enough of being a target in a Gunbus."

Ted wagged his finger. "They might be better than the Gunbus but they still only have the one forward-firing gun. The Hun has more powerful engines."

Charlie smiled as he poured himself another whisky, "We just have to outfly them. We have the best pilots here. We just keep on being the best."

Archie raised his glass, "Lads let's celebrate the fact that we have had no losses. 41 Squadron!"

"41 squadron!"

Bates handed me a letter when I reached my quarters. "I don't think it is from your family sir. I don't recognise the handwriting."

I didn't either. I opened it. "It is from Lumpy Hutton."

Bates smiled, "I liked him sir and I miss his happy, smiling face. I hope he is coping."

"So do I."

19 Hind Street
Stockton on Tees
County Durham

February 1917
Captain Harsker,
I thought I would drop you a quick line to let you know how things are going. I met your young lady again. She is lovely and you are a lucky man, sir. I was a little down sir but she gave me some good advice and cheered me up no end. Tell the doc that he did a grand job with the amputation. Your young lady looked at it and said it was the neatest job she had ever seen.

I met with Jack's widow. She was in a bad way. It wasn't just the loss of Jack, she and the bairns hadn't been well. There was no one to look after them. I took a room in a lodging house nearby and I have looked after them for a while. I am still receiving Flying Corps pay and I can help out. The collection from the lads helped out too.

I have managed to get a job as a clerk in an engineering firm in Stockton, Wrightson's. The pay is not too grand but they were short of someone who could read and write and knew how machines worked. The boss lost a son at the Somme and when he saw my record he was keen. It's something, sir.

This will be my address for the time being.

I am getting used to the one hand. Of course, I sometimes try to use it. It's daft, sir, but sometimes I could swear I still have it. It itches all the time. I can almost feel my fingers. It's stupid I know.

Tell the lads to take care of themselves and you too, sir. This country will need blokes like you when this is all over. I have seen that for myself. It's sad, sir, that decent lads like Jack get killed. Most of the blokes I have seen, since I came home, look shifty. They haven't been to war. I don't bother with them. I drink with the ex-servicemen in a little pub overlooking the river. We joke that between us we have one whole body. We are a close-knit bunch. It feels like the Sergeant's Mess.

You take care,

I remember you, each night, in my prayers. Your young lady says that you worry about me. Don't. Worry about yourself. I will be fine.

Yours,

Lumpy Hutton

I was happy that things were going well for him and that he had found friends. My worry had been that such a gregarious fellow would pine away. I should have known better. Lumpy was like the other servicemen he had found. He was the salt of the earth. We were a tough and hardy lot in the north. Even Lady Burscough had bounced back from the edge of disaster.

Chapter 16

I went to check on the repairs to my Pup's wings the next day and saw the Senior Flight Sergeant with the fuel bowser and cans of fuel. I was intrigued. "What are you and your boys doing Mr Lowery? It doesn't look like a normal service."

He smiled, "No it isn't. It's Mr Sharp's idea and it is a good one. He wondered if we could filter the fuel before we put it into the aeroplanes." I had a puzzled look. "It's not a bad idea. He noticed that sometimes there must be dirt or something in the fuel for the engine occasionally misfires and slows, especially when climbing. He said that he knew we all checked the filters on the engine and that we serviced them. The only thing he could think of was dirt in the fuel. Here, Joe, show Mr Harsker the first filter we used." The mechanic showed me the fine metal filter. It looked like they had stolen it from the kitchens. I saw in the bottom tiny pieces of dirt and other foreign bodies. "He's a bright lad is Mr Sharp. A piece like that could cause a blockage and..."

"You are right Sarn't, carry on." Charlie was growing day by day. He could have saved lives by his suggestion.

A day off was never really a day off. The bus needed many small jobs doing; making sure the cockpit would be right for the next flight. Ensuring that I had everything I needed in the cockpit; checking the compass and gauges. The mechanics would do all of that but they didn't have to fly at nine thousand feet. Once that was done I had all the paperwork to do for the flight. Surprisingly I did not mind. I had never been a good student while at school. I had always wanted to be off with the horses. My handwriting had been atrocious. All of the girls in our class had been much neater than I was and I hated having to practise on the blackboard in front of the whole class. Now I could take my time and I had no one to judge me.

Randolph put the telephone down. "Well, that is good news."

"What's that Randolph?"

"They are sending two Bristols over tomorrow. It means we can give one to Gordy and one to Archie. Half of the squadron will have a decent bus."

"I can remember when the FE 2 was a good bus."

"Times change. Look at these, what do you call them, tanks? They will revolutionise the face of war. Machine gun bullets can't penetrate them. They ride over any obstacles and I am not even certain that they could be bombed."

"Didn't I hear that they broke down on the Somme when they first used them?"

"Teething troubles. And mark my words they will have aeroplanes which can go much faster than the Pup soon."

As I went back to my reports I thought about that. War killed but it also brought about changes. They were now talking about building huge airships to travel to America and Australia. I was certain that would not have happened if the Germans hadn't built them for the war.

Randolph hummed happily to himself. He was like the mother hen of the squadron. He didn't fly himself but he watched us as we took off every day. He kept the records of life and death, success and failure. He would be more than happy if we had an aeroplane which gave us a chance in the air.

That evening, at dinner, he was late. It was not like him. When he finally arrived his face looked drawn. He sat between Archie and me. "A large whisky Sarn't."

He said nothing until it arrived and then he downed it in one. Archie asked, quietly, "A problem Captain?"

"That was headquarters on the telephone. Number 48 squadron had a patrol on our side of the lines. The Red Baron and his squadron jumped them. Four were shot down and the other two barely made it home. One of the missing is the VC, Captain Robinson." He held up his glass for a refill. "They were flying the new Bristol!"

It was as though the heavens had opened and rain had poured down. The high spirits evaporated. We ate in silence. It was broken by Charlie, "They might not have flown them properly."

Gordy shook his head, "How can you fly them badly? The man was a V.C."

"Freddie here said it, you need to fly the Bristol like a Pup and not a Gunbus." He waved his arm around the assembled pilots. "If we take Bill out of the equation then most of us flew, or in my case, fly, the Gunbus for the benefit of a gunner. You don't loop, you keep a stable platform and you get your gunner into a position where he can fire. The Bristol is like the Pup. You can throw it around and the gunner won't fall out. The gunner just defends and it is the pilot who attacks. With the Gunbus we are chauffeurs and with the Bristol, we are a fighter."

The mood lightened, especially when the others discovered that we would be getting two Bristols the next day.

We were just two days away from Zero Hour and, the next day we launched our smallest patrol yet. There were just nine of us. Charlie had three Gunbuses with him and Ted and I had our five new fighters. Our mission was to prevent any Germans from flying over our lines. Bearing in mind what had happened the previous day there were nine very nervous pilots.

The guns were still blasting away. I wondered how they had managed to manufacture so many shells. It seemed unlikely that the Germans would risk flying through the artillery barrage. I found that I was right; they flew around the barrage and they approached from the south. It was Ted's rear gunner who saw them. He flashed his mirror to attract my attention as he headed south to engage them. There were eight of them. They were far faster and more manoeuvrable than the Gunbuses of Charlie's flight. Before we had set off we had decided that Charlie would watch our back unless we were seriously outnumbered.

The five of us would take the war to the Germans and get as close to them as we could. Once amongst them then the Bristols would come into their own. The rear gunner could cause havoc. He could fire to both sides and above him.

I decided not to be as profligate with my ammunition. I would not run out again. They were above us and we went towards them in a line. We both had the same rate of climb. I cocked the Vickers and decided which one I would attack. These looked to be the Albatros D.II. They had a bulkier radiator than the D.III. To my horror, I saw that they, too, had twin Spandau machine guns and these were a faster aeroplane than the D.III. It was too late to back out now. We would have to take our medicine and hope for the best.

I tried my usual gambit. I lowered my nose as though I was going to fly beneath him and when the leading pilot corrected I came up and opened fire. It worked and the double machine guns spattered above my head. They were alarming but they missed. At a hundred and fifty yards I fired. I just brought the nose up and squeezed gently. The bullets struck the bottom of the propeller and, as I came up, his engine. I took my finger off the trigger and moved slightly to port. He had moved to starboard and my next burst struck his fuselage, close to the cockpit. My earlier bullets had damaged both his propeller and his engine. My last burst must have hit some cables. He lost power and began an irreversible dive to his death.

I caught a glimpse of an Albatros in my rearview mirror. I banked to port and put the Pup on its side. Already a small target, it would become almost invisible to the German. His bullets whizzed into the space I had just vacated. I pulled hard to bring myself round close to my pursuer. No matter how hard he tried he could not match my turn. I snap-fired at his fuselage and saw my bullets stitch a line along it. I threw the Pup on to the other wing and banked in the opposite direction. I was acutely aware that we had left Charlie and his Gunbuses unprotected. I saw them above me and four of the Huns were trying to get around to their vulnerable rear.

I straightened up and began to climb. I checked in my mirror. I had managed to lose my last pursuer. He had either gone after someone else or one of my colleagues had attacked him. The four Albatros were so intent on attacking the huge and slow-moving Gunbuses that they neglected to watch for me. I raised my nose to climb as near vertically as I could manage and then I dipped it to fly the length of the four Albatros. I fired in short bursts when I was close to each Hun. I didn't want my bullets to pass through and hit my fellows. My sudden attack caused panic amongst them and one of them flew directly in front of Charlie and his gunner. The Albatros was torn apart by the two Lewis guns firing at ridiculously short range.

I followed an Albatros which had a yellow wavy line running its length. It was faster than I was and would eventually outrun me but I kept after him as long as I could. My bullets continued to clatter into him no matter how much he jinked, banked and climbed. I was stuck to him like glue and the range of my Vickers meant that even while he was getting away from me I was still hitting him. Eventually, he went to the ground and landed behind our lines close to the spot where I had met Bert. As I roared over the trenches I saw the guns from the Tommies waving in the air in celebration. I wondered how many of them would be alive a few days from now.

I glanced up and saw the Gunbuses ponderously heading west. One or two were smoking but they were all there. I could not see the Pups and the Bristols. We fought our own fight. The Gunbuses relied on each other for protection.

I landed at the same time as Ted and Harry. As I taxied I heard the two Pups as they landed. When Ted got out he shook his head, "That's all we needed" The buggers have fitted a second Spandau to the D.II."

"I know. It is not as good an aeroplane as the D.III but it is faster and they have squadrons of them. How did you get on?"

He grinned, "We managed to down one and damage two more."

"It looks like we did better than the boys yesterday then."

Gordy and Archie were already in the office. Both looked like little boys who had seen early Christmas presents. "We will be with you tomorrow in our Bristols! We took them up for a spin this afternoon. They are a joy!"

Gordy was just full of it but Archie asked the more pertinent question. "How did you get on?"

"We lost none and shot down at least four but," I paused for effect, "they have armed their older Albatros with twin Spandaus. It is not going to be easy."

Charlie came in. "Thanks for that, Bill. I think we would have been a goner but for you. As it is we only have two Gunbuses fit for tomorrow."

"Then that decides it. We will just fly the Bristols and the Pups tomorrow. We will need the Gunbuses for Zero Hour the day after."

"I won't deny that I will be glad for the rest but will you be able to manage with just seven aeroplanes? Remember what happened to Number 48 Squadron."

Archie spread his arms. "We have no choice; we are running out of aeroplanes. If the Germans see the preparation for the offensive they will be ready and thousands of our lads could die. It is a risk we will have to take. But at least we know that there is no barbed wire in No-Man's Land. In fact, I doubt if there is a single German left alive within a mile of the front."

Our flights across the front had shown the effect of the barrage which had crept further west as the days had gone on. Having seen what Bert and our lads had done I knew that there would be Germans who were living underground however what their nerves would be like was something else entirely.

As it turned out there was a hiatus. We went up and patrolled but we saw only a few distant reconnaissance aeroplanes which turned tail at the sight of us. We used it as an exercise in seeing how to fly in formation with the two different types of bus. Gordy was disappointed when we landed. "I was looking forward to having a pop with my new gun, and flying something which can actually climb and turn." It became even worse when we were told that Zero Hour would be delayed by one day. One of Randolph's friends at headquarters told him it was because the French weren't ready. All squadrons were told to ready themselves for the 9th of April. This time we were convinced that the Germans would be prepared.

I don't think many of us got much sleep the next day. The Germans would know that an attack was imminent as soon as the barrage stopped. It had gone on for days and days. The men in the trenches might be in no condition to fight but the artillery and air force would. We would have to stop them from s from spotting and bombing.

I was up before dawn. Bates must have heard me for he scurried along in his dressing gown. "Sir, is there a problem? You are up early."

"I couldn't sleep. Go back to bed and I will see to myself."

"Sir! Do not even think that! I will get dressed."

"I'll just go outside for a smoke then."

I put my dressing gown on and picked up my pipe, tobacco and matches. As I opened the door I could not believe my eyes. It was the 9th of April and it was snowing. There would be no attack that morning and we would not be flying either.

I sat with Charlie in the mess. Gordy and Ted were busy out on the field talking about the new fighters. I knew that Charlie wanted to ask me something. He was smoking very nervously; lighting a cigarette and half smoking it before lighting another. I smiled and waited for him to get around to it.

"Bill, are you going to marry Beattie?"

"Of course you know that already."

"Yes, of course, I do, no what I meant was how did you ask her? Did you build up to it or did it come just out of the blue?"

I sipped my whisky. "That is a good question. I suppose we both knew that we wanted to be together. Besides you were there, at the Ritz when I actually proposed."

"That was your proposal? I thought you would have got on one knee. "He seemed relieved somehow.

"We both understood that we wanted to be married and Beattie, she needed me to say it out loud. Women are different from men, Charlie. They need reassurance. I thought it was taken for granted that we would marry because we got on so well together but she needed it saying." I think I knew then where he was leading with this but I let him get there in his own time.

"I am going to ask Alice if we can get married on my next leave." He smiled as though I would be delighted.

"Now steady on, Charlie. You have missed out a stage."

He looked confused, "It's just like you and Beattie."

"No, it isn't. It is one thing to say you will wed but to name a date is something else. What about Alice's mum and dad?"

"You mean they might not like me?" He looked appalled.

"Don't be daft, of course, they will like you. But Alice isn't twenty-one yet. They need to be asked for permission and even if she was twenty-one, well, they deserve to be asked."

"Oh," he looked crestfallen, "I just wanted to write and tell her."

"Then write to her and say that you would like to visit with mum and dad to ask their permission. But remember you have to have the banns read. It's not like going into a post office and buying a postal order, is it? You need to do some planning. Our Alice will want to invite people and to get a nice dress... talk to Gordy. It took Mary a couple of months to organise theirs and that didn't involve any parents."

I waved the orderly over and pointed to the glasses.

Charlie stared at the table. Then he brightened. "Of course you are right. Your way is just as good. After the offensive, I will put in for a leave. We can go to Burscough and then Alice can do like Mary did and organise the wedding. She will enjoy that."

"That's the ticket. Now you are thinking straight. Women enjoy planning and anticipating." I hated deceiving Charlie but there would be no leave for a long time. We would be lucky to see Blighty before October at the earliest. I did not regret the deception, not then anyway, for he looked happy once more.

Chapter 17

We were ready to fly before dawn. The weather people had told us it might be clear and we waited in the dark to see if the snow would come, having breakfasted early in anticipation. The attack was not signalled by a barrage but a hurricane. It was five minutes of the most intense noise I had ever heard. Every gun fired for five minutes and then, at five-thirty the attack began.

We were helpless. The snow still fell. As the morning drew on we became increasingly frustrated. Finally, at eleven, it stopped. "Archie, let me take the Pups up and see how the attack is going."

He pointed to the field, it was covered in snow. "How can you take off in that? You'll never get up."

"The Pup is the lightest fighter we have and needs the shortest runway. It is worth a shot. Then you can clear the field of snow."

I could see the debate going on in the Scotsman's head. If the attack had started then we needed eyes in the sky to watch for the Hun. "Right but you try it first and if you think you can't get up then abort. I won't risk all three of you."

"You are a brick. Freddie, Johnny, let's go."

I never had any doubt that I would get up but as the Pup skidded a little when I increased the power I began to wonder. I had to coax her up but she rose and, once in the air seemed to shake herself as though she was pleased to be free from the earthly shackles. Soon Freddie and Johnny joined me. I led them towards the Arras, Cambrai road. We knew it as a major target for the offensive.

The brown Tommies stood out against the white of the ground. I could see that they were well on their way east and the village of Fleuchy was close to being taken. I was about to lead the Pups down to strafe the village when I caught sight of six crosses in the distance. The white clouds made them stand out clearly. They were Germans.

I banked to starboard and Freddie and Jonny followed. As we drew closer to them I saw that they were two old AEG bombers escorted by the Albatros D.II. This time we would not be taken by surprise. I pointed to Johnny and signalled for him to attack the bombers. Freddie and I would attack the fighters. We might be outnumbered but we could not afford for the Tommies to be bombed having made such impressive gains.

Luckily we were flying high and we had the advantage of altitude. The fighters saw us and were drawn to us like moths to a flame. Johnny had learned to be cunning and he stayed with us until the German fighters were committed to the climb and then he banked and dived towards the two lumbering AEG bombers. They were well-armed but Johnny could run rings around them.

I did not worry about Johnny. Freddie and I would have four machine guns against each of us. I opened fire, with a short burst, at a thousand yards. I wanted them to think I was a novice and become overconfident. I edged away from Freddie. I wanted a gap so that I could use the manoeuvrability of the Pup to dive between them and make them hesitate. If we were close then they might not fire for fear of hitting one of their own. They held their fire. They outnumbered us. They were flying in two lines banked above each other. I kept edging to starboard while Freddie flew straight. I was drawing the two columns apart.

I made as though I was going to bank to starboard and flee west. It was a severe manoeuvre which I quickly reversed as two Albatros fighters turned to follow me. As I roared towards them I snap fired at both of them. I fired four short bursts. My turn meant I had them briefly in my sights and I managed to strike both of them. If I had caused damage then that would be a bonus for I wanted Freddie and I to be able to fire at the other two.

Freddie had already fired at both of them and was looping. They were climbing to try to hit him when I opened fire at the first Albatros. My bullets struck his wheels first, then his lower wing and finally his engine. I saw oil and smoke and he began to descend. The second tried to bank in my direction. As he did so Freddie completed his loop and fired a long burst into the cockpit. I was close enough to see the pilot die and the Albatros tumble from the sky. We let the wounded bird limp home while I banked. There were two Albatros fighters coming for us.

Freddie fired at the two of them while I side slipped out of their cone of fire. I twisted and climbed to get above them. When I began to turn I saw that Freddie was looping again and Johnny having seen off the bombers was climbing to come to our aid. Freddie distracted them with his loop and I screamed down towards them both. I fired at four hundred yards and made it a longer burst. Freddie fired too and we both hit one of the Albatros fighters. The second struck Freddie and I saw smoke begin to come from his engine. I fired again and the Albatros we had both struck spiralled to earth. The last fighter had Freddie dead to rights.

Johnny's Vickers fired from a thousand yards and his bullets smashed into the rudder of the Hun. He fled east.

I did not want to risk losing Freddie. Johnny and I escorted him back across our lines to our field. I breathed a sigh of relief when I saw that it was free from snow. Archie had had it cleared. I had no idea how much damage Freddie had suffered.

When Freddie had safely landed Johnny and I followed him down. Senior Flight Sergeant Lowery and the mechanics crowded around the Pup. He shook his head as I approached. "I'm sorry gentlemen but this one will not be flying tomorrow or the day after. We will either have to get a new engine or rebuild this one. Either way, it will take at least two days."

Freddie was downcast. "Sorry, sir."

"Don't be silly it was not your fault."

Archie and Gordy strode over to me. "Well?"

"The troops have made great strides but there were German aeroplanes trying to bomb them. Johnny here drove off the bombers and we scattered the fighters."

Archie nodded, "Then it is a good job you went up. We will have to get as many up tomorrow as we can."

"Unless the state of the field improves, sir, then the Gunbuses will not get up."

"Dammit! Headquarters must get their finger out and deliver those Bristols. The new pilots and gunners arrived today. I hope to God they don't send replacement Gunbuses. They might as well send the young lads a coffin. It means the same."

When we were in the office and after I had finished my report. "I have one piece of good news though, sir."

Archie looked up, "And I could do with some."

"The two young lads and I had been working on some tactics and they seemed to work. I am not certain if they would work with the Bristol but the Pup is so manoeuvrable you can pull the Germans out of position and concentrate your fire on one of them."

Randolph nodded, "The old Napoleonic strategy."

"What? An idea from a hundred years ago on the ground works in the air?" Archie was incredulous.

I nodded. Randolph continued, "If Napoleon could he split his army in two to divide the enemy. He would move one half to draw the enemy forces in one direction and then use his speed to attack a smaller half of his enemy."

"Except in our case we were evenly matched but I was able to attack them on their side. Freddie held their fire and I had a clean shot. If we had had three aeroplanes Freddie might not have been damaged."

Gordy looked at the models of the Gunbus and the Pup on Archie's desk. "So why couldn't we try that with the Gunbuses and the Pups."

"How do you mean?"

"Have the Gunbuses and the Pups fly one way to draw off the Germans and when half follow them the Pups return to join the Bristols."

"That would leave the Gunbuses exposed."

"They use the rear gunners and head back over our lines. The ground fire has got really fierce and they might get lucky."

We decided that the next time we flew with the Gunbuses, we would try the new tactic. Charlie and Ted seemed quite happy about the idea when we told them. "Besides," added Charlie, cheerfully, "we will soon have our new fighters anyway."

We took just six aeroplanes up the next day. Harry Dodds and Johnny were chuckling as we walked to our buses. "What is amusing you two?"

"Well, sir we have four chiefs and just two Indians. We just thought it was funny."

"Aye laddie well just you two watch us older ones. You may learn something."

We had left earlier than usual in light of our experience. We wanted to be on hand in case the Germans decided to catch the early worm. We flew in two uneven columns. I took the Pups to starboard of the major and the formidably armed Bristols. We flew high. It was only when flying in formation with the Gunbuses that we needed to be lower. We could see that Fleuchy had been captured but it looked as though the attack was struggling to take the fortified village of Neuville-Vitasse.

We flew south to north and then turned. Had we had bombs we could have aided the Tommies who were trying to take the village house by house. However, if we had had bombers then I think there would have been Germans to shoot them down. It looked as though the Germans were in another sector although I could not fathom out why. Then I saw the ten Germans as they approached from the east. Archie pointed towards them. I waved acknowledgement. I began to draw away from the Bristols to tempt the Germans to do the same. Johnny had been told by Freddie of our manoeuvre the previous day and I was confident we could pull it off with two of us. He was fifty yards behind me. That was close in a Gunbus but there was plenty of room for the tiny Pup.

We had now learned that the firepower of most of the Germans was the same. They all had two machine guns. It was just that we seemed to be able to hold our own with the D.II models. I also knew that we had not yet come up against the Flying Circus. They were the true test of our skills.

We were approaching at a collective speed of over two hundred miles an hour. You needed quick reactions. I saw that the Germans had split their Jasta too. Four headed for us while the other six climbed towards Archie. Either way, they outnumbered us. At a thousand yards, I sent a hopeful burst east and when it missed I banked as though we were fleeing west. I hoped this was a different Jasta who had not compared notes with yesterday's pilots.

They, too, began to turn and, as they did so, I pulled the Pup around again on its side and headed in the reverse direction. We caught them by surprise and, as we passed their line, we both gave each German a burst as we passed them. They were too busy trying to readjust to our change of direction and failed to fire in return. The last aeroplane began to smoke as Johnny fired.

Up ahead I could see the four Bristols engaged with the Albatros and Fokker fighters. The rear gunner was proving to be a nuisance and I saw my comrades throwing their fighters around to keep close to the Germans. I glanced in my mirror and saw that the three Germans who were undamaged had reformed and were trying to climb to catch us. I dived towards the rearmost Fokker and gave a short burst. As my bullets hit his tail he banked to starboard and I followed him around. In my mirror, I saw Johnny peel off to attack the next Fokker. I had no wingman now.

My nippy Pup straightened up quickly and I fired another burst which struck the Hun. He jinked to port and I was able to adjust quickly and this time I hit him in the fuselage. He banked to starboard. I noticed that he was always heading east. He was desperate to escape. I fired again and this time I banked to port before he did. He came right across my sights. I gave a long burst and hit the pilot and the engine. The doomed pair fell from the skies.

As I glanced in my mirror I saw that I had the first three fighters on my tail. I pulled back on the stick just as the first one fired. I felt the bullets as they hit my tail. When I reached the top of the loop I turned the

Pup on its side as I headed west. It made for a difficult target. Then I swung south, straightened up and flew directly towards the side of the flight of three who were still trying to work out where I had gone. I opened fire as I came at them unexpectedly. I heard the chatter of a machine gun behind me. I recognised the sound of Johnny's Vickers as he joined me. It proved enough for the three Huns who turned east.

I began to turn north again to find the Bristols. They too were heading towards us. The Huns had had enough. I saw them in the distance with smoke coming from two of them. Our ploy had paid off.

Charlie joined us in the office, eager to hear of our patrol. "That worked out well, Bill. Gordy here managed to bag an Albatros and we damaged two others. Perhaps the tide is turning."

Randolph put the telephone down. "I would not get too excited, sir that was James at HQ. We have lost in the past four days. We are the only squadron to have shot down any fighters since April the 4th!"

"Bloody hell!"

I tapped out my pipe on the ashtray. Of course, sir, for the last few days we have not flown the Gunbuses and you can bet that most of a hundred and thirty-one aeroplanes were the older aeroplanes."

"And tactics, Bill! Your tactic, today, worked a treat. If we can repeat that…"

I was dubious. "The Germans are quick learners, sir. When they work that out then we will be in trouble."

There was a knock on the door. It was Senior Flight Sergeant Lowery. "We have all of the aeroplanes ready for tomorrow sir. You can have four Bristols, three Pups and five Gunbuses."

"Thank you, Flight." After he had gone Archie looked at Charlie. "I think I will fly with your flight tomorrow Charlie and watch your rear. That will be one flight of six. Bill, you lead the three Pups and Ted you lead the other three Bristols. We will keep the Gunbuses in the centre. The tactic we used to today might work even better if we have two flights taking the Germans off on a wild goose chase."

The telephone rang. We listed as Randolph spoke to Headquarters. "Excellent news, thanks, James!"

He turned to us. Charlie said, "What's the news, Randolph? The Germans given up?"

"Not quite but the new Bristols will be here in a few days. We only have a couple more days to fly the Gunbus!"

Charlie looked excited. "And about time too!"

We went back to our rooms to prepare for the next day. I wrote letters home. I was mindful of my words to Bert. I could not be a hypocrite and I wrote five letters. I know our Kath had not written to me very much but she was my sister after all. Charlie came along as I was finishing my last letter.

"Still writing Bill?" I held up the four letters I had already sealed. He laughed. "I just have two: one to mum and dad and one to Alice." He held them up and I could see how bulky the one to Alice was. "I'll pop them in the post. See you in the mess."

I finished my letter to Beattie. I had so much to tell her. I knew that she would worry especially as there would be the Arras casualties arriving now. There was no getting around this. We were luckier than most. Since Tom and John had gone in the early days of the war we had had no telegraphs for the family. Even the squadron had been spared, recently, the decimation of its pilots and gunners.

The conversation after dinner that night was the performance of the Bristols. The new pilots and the Gunbus pilots were excited about the prospect of flying a real fighter. Our only bugbear was the lack of a second Vickers. Poor Percy Richardson had been inundated with requests from the Bristol pilots for a second Vickers. He had pleaded with Archie, "The problem we have, Major Leach, is the interrupter gear. It works for the one gun but the boffins haven't made it work for two. We'll have to wait until someone back in England devises one."

We had discussed mounting a second on top of the wing but that would not have helped. The pilot could only fire one at a time and the compass on the Bristol would be affected. We would have to continue with the one gun.

Chapter 18

We were lucky the next morning. We took off on an airfield which was still hard from a late frost. The Gunbuses lumbered up the field. The fighters, circling in above watched the east. We had heard rumours of the bold Germans attacking airfields. As Charlie and his flight took formation below us I wondered if this would be the last time they would do so. If the Bristols arrived then we could match the Germans in the area and wrest back some degree of airpower.

When we neared our patrol area we started to climb. Charlie waved at me cheerfully. He and his Gunbuses would be the rock on which we hoped the Germans would break. I watched the crews as they cocked their Lewis guns. I wondered if they all carried Mills bombs as Lumpy had.

I checked my mirror and Freddie and Johnny were both in position. We were a small flight but we worked as a team and I could not ask for a better pair of wingmen. I looked below and saw that the land below me was being reclaimed by British and Canadian troops. It confirmed that our soldiers had achieved their objectives. We now had to protect them so that it would not have been in vain.

We headed to the Arras to Cambrai road. The offensive had moved east of there and we could expect to find German fighters, bombers and reconnaissance aeroplanes in that vicinity. It was a dull grey day which made it difficult to see approaching aeroplanes. The visibility was not helped by smoke swirling across the battlefield.

We met the Germans closer to Cambrai than Arras. There appeared to be twelve in the formation and they were high. They were far closer to us than I would have liked. Our two sets of fighters began to move away from the Gunbuses as we had planned and, sure enough, the Germans copied so that they formed three lines of six. It meant that the Pups had odds of two to one but it would not be for long. We were steadily ascending to meet them although the Gunbuses were a little slower to rise.

As we drew closer I saw that they were the Albatros D.III. They had more power and more guns. However, we had drubbed the Albatros D.II without loss and now had more aeroplanes and experience. We went steadfastly on. There was a noticeable gap opening up now between the three uneven columns and, worryingly we were leaving the FE 2s behind and below us. I was happy that Major Leach was guarding the rear of the

Gunbuses. There was none better. With him at the rear and Charlie at the front, the young pilots in between had a chance.

At a thousand yards, I fired and then banked to starboard as though we were fleeing. It had worked well twice before. I noticed that the Albatros I fired at had a red propeller. It made a clear target. Although my bullets missed I hoped they would have alarmed the pilot. Freddie and Johnny fired as they approached. As soon as I heard Johnny fire I began to bank to port. I levelled out and I expected to see the six Albatros flying parallel to us. To my horror, there was clear sky. There was no target for us. Even worse, as we turned I saw the whole Jasta, all eighteen of them converging on the Gunbuses. Ted's column was, like me, out of position and too far away to give immediate support to the Gunbuses. The lumbering beasts didn't stand a chance.

Charlie and his gunner were struck by the two Spandau machine guns of the first two Albatros. They could not miss the unprotected cockpit. I saw it all unfolding before me. The first shock of bullets hit the gunner and he looked like he had St.Vitus' Dance. I saw Charlie hit as he tried to turn. Then he was hit by the force of a total of eighteen hundred bullets a minute. In ten seconds his body was riddled by three hundred steel jacketed 9mm bullets. They tore through Charlie and into the Rolls Royce engine. The Gunbus simply fell from the sky. Charlie, my old shy and industrious gunner Charlie, and the love of my sister's life would have known little about it. They would have been killed instantly. The two flanking columns converged and, by the time we were in range, five Gunbuses were falling to earth their crews dead. We had the living to worry about for the Huns were targeting Archie. He began to pull a loop as I opened fire on the rear Albatros. I was lucky, his rudder disintegrated and he began to drop to a lower altitude to escape us.

We had no time to finish them off for we had to get to Archie. Freddie and Johnny had banked inside me and we were flying towards the unprotected side of the formation as a line of three. We could not miss. We all opened fire without return. The three of them were all hit and they pulled out of formation. It took the pressure off Archie but the remaining, vengeful Germans banked to come directly at us. They were flying head-on at the three of us. The double Spandau spat a wall of bullets directly at me. I jinked left and right and waited for my shot. Bullets whizzed by me but I seemed to bear a charmed life. As the propeller came into my sights I fired one long burst. I shredded his propeller and hit his engine. His nose began to dip and I fired another burst directly at the pilot. I saw his head disintegrate like a ripe plum. That had been pure revenge for Charlie. I could have let the pilot live for his aeroplane was already doomed.

I glanced in my mirror and saw two Albatros behind me. They were closing rapidly side by side. If I tried to turn one of them would have me. I threw the Pup into a loop. When I reached the top I banked to port to take me closer to one of the Albatros. Frighteningly he had anticipated my move and he and I were on a collision course. Unless one of us blinked we would crash into each other. I knew that if I moved his wingman would have me and I resolved not to blink. I only had one choice, fly straight and hope he moved. I held down the trigger and poured the .303 into the Hun. His bullets smacked into my engine and my undercarriage but we flew on. He had missed everything vital. He blinked and, as he raised the nose of his aeroplane to fly over me my bullets struck his belly. He dropped from the sky like a stone. I knew that I had few bullets left and I jinked the other way just as more bullets thudded into my fuselage. The Pup suddenly felt sluggish.

I levelled out and looked in my mirror. The sky behind was clear. I looked ahead and realised that I was flying east and the Huns were coming west. I banked as quickly as the damaged Pup would allow. Coming carefully around I saw the remnants of the squadron heading west. I was alone except for the German aeroplanes which had my wounded Pup at their mercy.

I dropped the nose and headed for the ground. If I had to crash land I wanted to be as close to the earth as I could. In my mirror, I could see the faster Albatros fighters hurtling after me. My manoeuvrability had gone. I could no longer wriggle. I could barely rise and fall. They would catch me and shoot me down. It was inevitable. I would have been a goner had I not flown over a support trench close to Fleuchy, the Tommies and Canadians there opened up with every machine gun and rifle as I zoomed over them. In my mirror, I saw one Albatros pouring smoke and the others climbing to avoid the hornet's nest they had disturbed.

I had survived but I had no idea which of my fellows had. It had been a disaster. My plans had gone awry and been neatly unpicked by the Germans. It had cost Charlie his life and my sister her happiness. I saw a cluster of medical orderlies around Archie's Bristol. Freddie and Johnny both appeared to be safe and they waved to me as I landed.

They both rushed to me, "I say, sir, a bit of a sorry mess eh?"

Freddie looked really upset. "Poor Captain Sharp. They didn't stand a chance... any of them."

I nodded. "A whole flight gone in the blink of an eye. Ten of our comrades. What a waste!"

I saw that Ted had his arm in a sling while Gordy had a bandage around his head. Ted shook his head, "Lucky Bill again!"

I pointed to my bullet-riddled Pup. "You think so? If it hadn't been for the footsloggers I would be lying out there with Charlie and the others." I pointed to Archie. "How is he?"

"His gunner is fine but he took a couple of slugs in the shoulder. They are having the devil's own job to get him out."

Senior Flight Sergeant Lowery walked over and his face was drawn. "Is it true sir, about Mr Sharp?"

"I am afraid so Flight. The only consolation is he wouldn't have felt a thing."

He gave me a sad look, "I am not sure I would take that as consolation. He was telling me about his young lady, your sister, and the plans they had made for the future. I shall miss him. He was, begging your pardon sir, the nicest officer in the squadron. He always had a cheerful word and a smile. He had so much to live for. "

"I think, Flight, that the future is a luxury we can't afford."

As I trudged to the office I wondered how to tell her. She was not next of kin and would not receive a telegram. I would have to write to her. I suddenly remembered the letters Charlie had written and I ran to the office. Freddie and Johnny stared after me in amazement. "Has the mail gone, Flight?"

"Yes sir, sorry, did you want a letter to go?"

"No, Flight, I wanted to stop a letter. I was trying to ease some pain." I could see that he had no idea what I was talking about. I looked up as Randolph appeared. "I'll do my report later, Randolph. I have an important letter to write."

He nodded, "I understand. Take all the time in the world." He hesitated, "I am terribly sorry about this Bill. I knew you were close and ... well, y, our sister...."

I looked at him, bleakly, "That is the letter I have to write."

Bates was waiting for me. "Your bath is drawn, sir. There is a drink on the dresser."

I shook my head, "I have a letter to write to my sister."

"The letter can wait, sir, until you have had a bath and a drink. The letter to your sister needs thought and right now, well I can see how upset you are." He put his arm around me. "Come along sir, I'll help you." He suddenly looked old, "I have done this before."

He was right; I would not even be able to write a letter which would be coherent. I needed to get the emotion from my head. I lay in the bath sipping the whisky. Charlie was dead and it was my stupid fault. It had been my clever plan to trick the Germans; Charlie and the others had paid the price. I found myself sobbing. I had no idea why; I couldn't remember the last time I had cried but I was so angry and frustrated and full of self-loathing that it just erupted from me.

When I stepped from the bath Bates was there with a warm towel. His words told me that he had guarded the door while I had bathed. "The body works in funny ways, sir. Those tears will help to clear your mind now."

"Aye, they have done that all right and shown me that the entire disaster is my fault. I came up with the plan of attack and Charlie Sharp is dead."

He stood in front of me and wagged his finger like an admonishing schoolmaster. "Now listen here, sir. Mr Sharp thought the world of you and he thought your plan was a brilliant one. It went wrong. If it had gone right would that have made the plan different? No, it would just have meant it succeeded. If every plan of battle worked then wars would be over in days and not years. Plans go wrong. You are a clever man, sir. Come up with another."

And that telling off put everything in perspective. I nodded and, after dressing, we composed a thoughtful letter to Alice. John knew the right words and he changed my mawkish sentimentality for something which would make Alice feel better. I doubted that she would ever be happy but John had managed to elicit from me the memories which Alice could cherish.

By the time I reached the office, it was getting on towards late afternoon. Ted and Gordy were seated with Randolph and the whisky was open. I suddenly remembered Archie. "How is Archie?"

"Doc has gone with him to the hospital at Arras. He will make it but it will take a good surgeon to save his arm. Doc Brennan said something about the nerves being affected."

"But he will live."

Gordy nodded, "I think so Bill." He handed me a whisky.

Randolph looked at the other two and said, "Which makes you, for the time being at least, the Squadron Leader of Number 41 Squadron."

Chapter 19

Gordy and Ted looked at each other. Ted poured me another drink as Gordy said, "We'll help out if we can."

"Have we even got a squadron Randolph? My bus is damaged. We have no Gunbuses. Ted here is wounded."

"I can still fly, Bill. Remember you did and this is just a scratch."

"And you can fly Archie's Bristol. He still has his gunner."

I listened to Ted and Gordy. I knew they were trying to jolly me along but it wasn't working. Randolph handed me a manila file. "And this is your bedtime reading Bill. These are the service and training records of the six crews who are ready to begin flying their Bristols when they arrive tomorrow."

"Tomorrow? I thought it would be the end of the week."

"General Trenchard lit a fire under them. He thought he was doing us a favour."

"Some favour."

Ted said quietly, "Charlie thought so. He couldn't wait to fly a Bristol."

And he was right. Randolph gave it to me straight, "If Charlie was here Bill you know he would be right behind you and encouraging you to lead the new boys. He would be suggesting how to train them and volunteering to help."

"I know! And he is not here!"

Gordy raised his glass and looked at the ceiling, "Then let us imagine he is here in spirit. Here's to you, Charlie, you were one of the best."

"Charlie."

That was the point at which I nearly broke but if I had then I would have been letting down my gunner. I needed to be a good squadron leader, if only for Charlie.

"And the other thing is, well, the letters to the families of the dead crews."

My heart sank. Ted came to my rescue. "That's not fair, Randolph. We will divide them up. Otherwise, our new leader will be in no condition tomorrow to lead us up into the wild blue yonder."

And so we drank, smoked and wrote the ten letters which almost broke my heart. It was Airman Bates who stopped us. He knocked on the door. "Gentlemen, the mess is waiting for dinner. There may not be many of them left but those young men are hurting just as much as you are. Whatever you are doing may I suggest that you leave it until tomorrow?"

He might have been the lowest-ranked soldier in the room but we all obeyed. We trudged before him to the mess. There were just three pilots there and then the new boys. All of them looked as though they had suffered. They had a drawn look about them and Freddie and Johnny looked to be on the verge of tears. I stood at Archie's seat. "Gentlemen sit." As they did so I said, "I apologise for the delay. Major Leach will be away for a while and I will be in temporary command. As you can imagine there is much to do and I hope that you will all help me." I was gratified to see nods.

"We will fly as one flight in the morning. I shall fly the Major's bus. You young pilots need to familiarise yourselves with your new fighters; they will be arriving tomorrow. We fly as a squadron the day after."

Again, there were more nods. I waved over the mess orderlies. "You can serve the food but first make sure everyone has a drink."

Every glass was charged.

"Gentlemen, be upstanding." They all stood. "The King, the Squadron and absent friends; may we never forget them!" It was an emotional toast and a silence descended as soon as we had all emptied our glasses. I nodded and sat.

I said little during the meal and I barely tasted the food. I had so much running through my mind. I had the emotion of the deaths of so many men I had flown with and that seemed to run into the mundane as I tried to work out how to reorganise the flights. By the time the meal was over, I felt a wreck and yet I knew I still had some letters to finish and that I had to commit my thoughts on the flights to paper.

Gordy and Ted had drunk a great deal. Harry, Johnny and Freddie saw them to bed. I went to the office and lit my pipe. Randolph appeared. "You should be in bed, Bill, you will be flying tomorrow."

"I will do no one any good if this is on my mind. I will get them finished."

"I'll give you a hand then." With two of us working we managed to finish the letters in an hour.

As we sealed the last envelope Randolph rose. I took a clean sheet of paper. "What now?"

"The new flights and flight commanders; they need to be done too."

He took off his tunic again and sat down. "Right, what are your thoughts?"

"Freddie and Harry seem to me the best two to be Flight Commanders. I can still fly the Pup once it is repaired and Harry seems competent enough in the Bristol. We'll make Ted the second in command in the air."

"Not Gordy? I thought he was your best friend?"

"And he is but I want the best second in command. That is Ted. He knows the Bristol and he has changed in the last year."

"I agree. I was just surprised."

"And they will all have an equal number of new pilots. That is also fair. But I want to spend an hour a day, at least, working with the new pilots. Use your influence at HQ to cut us some slack."

"I am not sure that there is any slack to be cut but I will try."

The door opened, without a knock, and Bates stood there like a house mother in a public school. He pointed to the officers' quarters. "Bed now! Both of you!"

We were both so taken aback that we laughed and then followed his orders, marching off to bed. He said nothing more until I was in bed and he closed the door saying, "I promised your mother I would take care of you. But you don't make it easy! Good night, sir."

My sleep was troubled with bad dreams and seemed to be far too short. I wolfed my breakfast down and raced out to the Bristol. After the Pup, it seemed enormous. Airman David Speight was already there checking over the guns and the rigging. "Morning sir. I wasn't certain if we would be flying this morning but I thought I would be ready anyway."

"Good man. Yes, until my bus is repaired I shall be flying Major Leach's. I'll try not to bend it!"

He laughed, "I don't think there will be any danger of that sir."

He seemed to have more faith in me than I did. The rest of the depleted squadron soon joined me. Randolph came out with the orders and the maps. "We are to stop the Hun photographing the ground we recently took. I think the brass is worried that the Huns are preparing a counterattack."

"Thanks." That was not so bad. We would be over our own lines and the Hun would have to endure ground fire too. "Right gentlemen, we'll have the Pups above us." It seemed ridiculous to have to issue orders. There were just four of us. Until the doctor gave Gordy and Ted the all-clear I would not risk them in the air. Their accusing looks told me that they were not happy to be grounded.

The Bristol was faster than I thought but the Pup did not need as much airfield in which to take off. Unlike the Gunbus I needed no speaking tube as Speight was right behind me. "Are the Pups in position, Speight?" I also noticed that there was no mirror on this fighter. I had to rely on my rear gunner.

"Yes, sir. Just above and behind."

"And Mr Dodds?"

"On station sir. You needn't worry about him, sir. He sticks to the bus in front like glue."

As we headed north I noticed another squadron coming from the west. There was a brief moment of alarm until I recognised them as Gunbuses. We had company. I hoped they would not run into the same squadron we had.

The Bristol's powerful engine had twice the horsepower of the Pup. The configuration of the wings was, however similar, and the gun was in exactly the same place. I soon felt at home in the roomier cockpit. I gradually took us higher. I knew that Carrick and Holt would match my moves. I wanted to be as high as I could get. With just four buses we could not afford to get jumped. I realised that we did not have the constraint of the Gunbuses to tie us to the earth. A sad result of the previous day's losses was that the remaining aeroplanes had more freedom.

As we headed closer to the area around Vimy Ridge we saw lines of reinforcements heading east. The footsloggers had made remarkable gains in the first two days but now the offensive looked to have stalled somewhat.

We heard the sound of German artillery and it alerted us to the fact that they must have had aeroplanes spotting. I led us east over No-Man's Land and towards the German lines. There appeared to be four or five of the slow-moving two-seaters, above them were six fighters. As we approached they began to descend to meet us. Once again we were outnumbered. Freddie and Johnny would be on their own.

"Right David. Things will get hot in a moment. There are six fighters. We will have to get rid of them before we can attack the spotters."

"Righto, sir." I heard him cock the Lewis.

The Huns came at us in two lines of three. One flight would take out the Pups while the others came after us. I wondered if they thought we would fly them defensively. If so they were in for a shock. There would be no sneaky tactics this time. We would just get in amongst them and cause havoc! They would learn that this fighter had a sting in the tail!

The Bristol was fast but was also a bigger target than the Pup. We were heading towards each other at a combined speed of two hundred and ten miles an hour. I knew that I would have a short time to react. I lowered my nose slightly. It prompted the Hun to fire, thinking I was trying some tricky manoeuvre. As I pulled up the nose and fired his bullets clattered into my top wing. My bullets hit his radiator. I saw a jet of steam erupt from the front. I fired again and then moved to starboard a little so that I could bring my bus in at an oblique angle.

The second Albatros tried to turn. I heard Speight's Lewis as he finished off the first German and I fired at the second. His change of direction meant I only hit his undercarriage while his bullets struck my fuselage. "Are you all right?"

"Yes sir, he didn't get close and I finished off the first one sir!"

"Good man." The second Hun had dived below me. "You had better watch for one coming from below us." I glanced to starboard and saw Harry Dodds firing at the spotters. I was on my own.

The third German came straight at me. We both fired at the same time. Although I hit him, I appeared to cause little, if any damage. As he came over me I knew what he intended; the Immelmann turn. If I had been flying the Gunbus then that might have caused me a problem. The Bristol was a different matter. "Hang on Speight!" I threw the Bristol on to its side and pulled a hard turn to port. He could not know what I had planned and he must have had a shock when he turned to attack out tail; we were not there. I levelled out, "Ready Speight?"

"Sir!"

As we passed my gunner emptied a magazine into the side of the surprised German who tumbled to the earth. I banked again and saw that the sky was free of German aeroplanes. The two Pups were heading towards us and Harry was climbing, having destroyed a spotter.

"Time to go home! Well done Speight."

"They were my first two kills, sir! Lumpy was right about you sir. He reckoned he only shot down as many Huns as he did because of the way that you fly. I see what he means. It isn't half exciting!"

I smiled. His enthusiasm was infectious. Whoever had him as a gunner would be lucky.

When we landed Gordy and Ted came to greet me. They both had relieved looks on their faces. "Were you worried, boys?"

"Not really, Bill, but it is a pleasant surprise to have four aeroplanes return without damage and with their crews intact."

As Speight clambered out I said, "And my gunner here bagged two Albatros D.IIs!"

As ex-gunners themselves, they knew the feeling and they both slapped him on the back. "Good man! A celebration in the mess tonight then?"

"Yes, sir!"

I went directly to the office without waiting to talk to the other pilots. I no longer had that luxury. I was C.O. now and that meant paperwork.

"Well Randolph, we are back safe and sound. What about the replacements?"

"Glad that you are safe, Bill. I would be lying if I said I wasn't worried. What was the new Bristol like?"

"It is an excellent machine. I can't understand how 48 Squadron lost four in one day. They must have been flying them the wrong way."

"Our new buses will be flown in tomorrow. The crews will be with them."

"Is that wise? I remember a couple of new pilots getting lost."

"Apparently the replacement for Captain Robinson is going to lead them over with their replacements too. They should make it."

"Right."

The other three pilots came into the office. Their looks told me that they had all had kills. "It looks like our luck has changed eh sir?"

I nodded to Harry however I was feeling anything but lucky. I would swap all the kills of that morning for Charlie not to be dead. As I had come in to land with the ebullient Speight chattering away behind me I thought of Charlie and Lumpy. Both had been my gunners; one was crippled for life and the other was now dead. I was anything but lucky.

After they had gone Randolph said, diplomatically, "When will you tell Harry and Freddie about the new arrangements?"

"I should have done it then, shouldn't I?"

"You have a lot on your plate at the moment and you are new to this. Why not have a briefing in the morning before the new pilots arrive."

"What about our patrol?"

"HQ said we could stand down." He shrugged, "I don't think they realised that we were down to four aeroplanes."

There was a knock on the door and Doc Brennan came in. "Just thought I would give our new leader an update." He was grinning as he said it. "I think Gordy and Ted need another day to recuperate."

"That is not a problem we aren't flying tomorrow."

"Good, head wounds can be tricky. And I heard from the hospital that Archie pulled through and he won't lose his arm. However, I, think it will take months, rather than weeks for him to fully recover." He patted me on the back as he left. "So it looks as though we have you to say yes sir, no sir, three bags full sir, for the foreseeable future."

I spent the rest of the afternoon with Randolph arranging the new rotas and signing the mountain of forms which had accumulated in the last day. I was ready for my whisky and bath by the time we had finished.

Chapter 20

I held the briefing in the mess. I had the mess orderlies make a pot of coffee for I wanted a relaxed atmosphere. I did not want the strained days of Hamilton-Grant to return.

"Right gentlemen, as you know Archie will be laid up for some months to come. I have spoken to General Trenchard and he is happy for us to continue working as a squadron without drafting in new senior officers." I saw the relief on the faces of Ted and Gordy. This would be music to their ears. "However we are getting new aeroplanes and new pilots today so we will need to rearrange and reorganise the flights."

"Freddie, Johnny and Harry I am making all three of you up to First Lieutenant. I know that Archie would have got around to it eventually. Freddie and Harry, I want the two of you to be temporary Flight Commanders. I will still be flying but we may need to use smaller flights from time to time and I need the flexibility to be able to delegate."

I saw Johnny congratulate both of his friends. I would find time to talk to him about it later. "Ted I want you to be second in command." I looked anxiously at Gordy. His face was non-committal. As with Johnny, I would need to find the time to talk to him. "We are getting nine new aeroplanes, ten pilots and nine gunners. I will be reverting to the Pup. Don't get me wrong I like the Bristol but having the three Pups gives us an advantage over most other squadrons. We will all need to train the new boys. Each of you can work with two pilots. That includes you, Johnny. I want them to survive more than most pilots in the RFC."

I finished off my coffee. "The average number of hours a pilot has before he is killed or shot down is down to eighteen hours. All of you have more hours than that by a huge margin. We need to pass that knowledge on to the young pilots. They need to fly our way and not the way they were taught in flying school. We know that our way works. Any questions?"

There appeared to be none. "Randolph here has the details of the new pilots in your flights. You need to get to know them before they get here. I want this team to be the best in France."

They all found a table and began to read their dossiers. "Gordy, could I have a word with you outside, please?"

When I was outside Gordy just said, "If this is about why you chose Ted over me then don't worry about it."

"You aren't annoyed?"

"I assume there is no more money involved, "I shook my head, "And I don't need the responsibility." He lit a cigarette. "I'll be honest with you, Bill. Since I married Mary my priorities have changed. If you add to that Charlie's death then all I want is to get out of this war alive. If you want a word of advice I would ask for a new Squadron Leader as soon as you can. Lord Burscough, Major Brack and now Archie; it seems the job is hazardous."

"But someone has to do it."

"Then let someone do it who has nothing to live for. Beattie would not suit widow's weeds."

He stubbed out his cigarette and went back inside. I knew what he was saying but I could not abdicate responsibility. I would be letting down Lord Burscough, Colonel Pemberton-Smythe, everyone, if I did what he was suggesting. But he was right. The odds of me surviving the war had now become longer.

I put my head in the door. "Johnny, could I have a word please?"

He looked worried when he came out, "I haven't done something wrong have I, sir?"

"No, of course not. I just wanted to explain why I picked Freddie over you."

He grinned, "No need to, sir. I would have been amazed had you picked me over him. He is a more natural leader anyway. He is my best friend and I am delighted for him."

I felt as though a weight had been lifted from my shoulders. "Well thank you for being so understanding."

He gave me a puzzled look, "Sir, the other pilots and I would do anything for you. I hope you know that. We are all delighted to be serving under you."

We had just had lunch when we heard the drone of Rolls Royce engines and our new pilots arrived. We went out to watch them land. Every one of my officers would judge them on their landing. Surprisingly enough most were satisfactory. Two of them bounced like Australian kangaroos and I saw Senior Flight Sergeant Lowery wince. He would have two sets of undercarriage to check over. One pilot, Lieutenant Alldardyce, had come over in the gunner's seat. He would be flying Archie's bus now that my Pup had been repaired.

They lined up next to their aeroplanes looking at the field that would be their new home for the next few months. I stood before them, "I am Captain Harsker and I am the acting commander of this squadron. As you can see we have had a difficult time of it lately and I do not anticipate it getting any easier. If you think your training was finished then think again. None of you will be allowed to fly combat until you have proved to my Flight Commanders that you can survive in the skies. Your training will start this afternoon."

I waved to my Flight commanders. They stood behind me. "Lieutenant Alldardyce."

He stepped forward, "Go with Lieutenants Carrick and Holt." They led him off.

"Lieutenant Duffy, Lieutenant Ellis, Lieutenant Sanderson, go with First Lieutenant Dodds." I watched their faces as the new young pilots followed a very nervous-looking Harry Dodds.

"Lieutenant Ferry, Lieutenant Hanson, Lieutenant Short, follow Captain Thomas." Ted actually tried to smile and look cheerful. Perhaps he, too, like the rest of us was changing.

Lieutenant Hargreaves, Lieutenant Foster, Lieutenant Simkins, you will be in D Flight with Captain Hewitt."

Once they had gone I walked over to where the mechanics were checking the new buses. "Well Flight, when can we have our first operation?"

"These will be ready in the morning sir, but will the pilots?"

I laughed, "No, I am afraid not. Are these easier or harder to work on than the Gunbus?"

"Hard to say, sir. We were used to the Gunbus. I shall miss them. These are a much better machine though."

"You are right there. Carry on."

"Sir!"

Pilots were everywhere as Gordy and the others took them through the theory of actual combat flying. I heard the stories my pilots were telling them. They pulled no punches and the faces of the young pilots reflected that. I returned to the office to check with Randolph about our next operations. His face did not look full of joy when I entered. He was on the telephone and listening more than he was talking, "Well thank you, James. At least we know what the situation is now."

"Problems?"

He nodded, "It looks like the Germans have started to counter-attack. They have retaken some of our early gains. And that is not all. The German pilots have become bolder and they are flying deeper into our territory. I will have to make sure that our air defences are ready."

That was always one of our nightmares. Our aeroplanes were at their most vulnerable when on the ground.

"And I take it they would like us in the air, if possible?"

He nodded, "I told them that we had too many new pilots but they want a presence tomorrow."

"Very well. I will take C flight. We will leave Lieutenant Alldardyce with Gordy. The Pups are versatile enough to cause problems for the Hun." I turned to the orderly sergeant, "Flight, go and ask Mr Lowery if he will make sure the Pups are in tip-top condition. We fly tomorrow." After he had gone I said, "And I want every pilot in the air tomorrow practising flying in formation. It is bad enough being shot down but I heard that we have lost many pilots through collisions. I will not have that."

After we had finished all the paperwork for the new pilots and gunners I left the office. As I walked back to my quarters I realised that I sounded nothing like the nervous young sergeant who had joined the RFC with Lord Burscough. The steel in my voice had frightened me a little. Bates saw me coming. I saw he had a worried look on his face.

"You are flying tomorrow, sir?"

It sounded like an accusation. I smiled, "Yes, John. Is that a problem?"

"It might be, sir, if you are only taking three aeroplanes up."

"The sad fact is that if I take up the young boys tomorrow then half of them will not come back. My mother might have asked you to take care of me but I have to take care of them."

He sniffed, "I hope they appreciate you, sir!"

"Oh, I dare say they will come to hate me but I am not here to be liked." I entered my quarters and took off my tunic. "I think my hair could do with a trim, Bates eh? And then I shall write a couple of letters."

I had much to tell Beattie.

I took the opportunity, at dinner, to ask Gordy and Ted about the day. I knew that Freddie and Harry would tell me that it had gone well but Ted and Gordy had done this before. They both had an eye for potential weaknesses.

"They are still training them badly in Blighty, Bill. They all think you fly in a straight line and keep the same altitude. It is a good job they have a gunner in the rear of the Bristols. I think if they were flying your Pup they wouldn't last a week."

Ted nodded and took another swallow of whisky. "And no one seems to tell them about the German buses! They think they are all the same. I spent an hour with the models and the drawings explaining the differences."

After they had gone through their individual pilots I asked, "Will they be ready for the day after tomorrow?"

"Possibly, it depends on what we get through tomorrow."

"Well, you will need to have Alldardyce with you. Freddie and Johnny are coming up with me. We have to mount a patrol."

They were both shocked. "Three of you? That is suicide! We haven't seen less than six Huns in the past two weeks. They will outnumber you two to one."

"I know but orders are orders." I could see that both of them were unhappy with the patrol. "The thing is the Huns are counter-attacking. Our lads on the ground have done wonderfully well. I know we are only three aeroplanes but we might be the difference between holding on to those gains and being back where we started. That is why you must impress on your young pilots that they have to become better pilots as quickly as possible."

Ted emptied his glass, "Then we will have them ready for the day after tomorrow. I promise you that!"

I was up well before dawn. I had decided to be on station as the sun was coming up and to use the altitude to our advantage. I also wanted us in the dark when the sun came up so that we would see the Germans whilst being invisible to them. Bates handed me my goggles and helmet as I left for a quick breakfast.

"There is a letter for Miss Porter on the dresser, would you see it gets in the post?"

He frowned, "You could do it when you came back, sir?"

I knew what he was thinking. "It is not a goodbye letter, John, it is just my regular letter to her."

He relaxed, "Well that is different, sir. You watch out up there. I know Mr Holt and Mr Carrick are fine boys but there are only three of you."

As I ate my scrambled eggs on toast I wondered how we could use that to our advantage. Everyone seemed worried that we were just three aeroplanes. We were, however, very small, well-armed and almost as fast as the enemy. If we used our manoeuvrability and agility we might disrupt their formations. I felt more confident knowing that they could not fire as easily when we were in amongst them as we had predicted. They were afraid of hitting their own aeroplanes. The large formations were a danger when they came at you or were pursuing you.

I was waiting at the Pup for my two wingmen. "We are not going to be defensive today. We are going to hunt the enemy."

Johnny looked shocked. "But there are just three of us!"

"That is correct. I intend to jump the first Jasta that we see. I want you two to fly on my port and starboard when I dive. We will get amongst them. When they are disrupted we head west. If we use altitude they will not see us."

Freddie clapped Johnny about the shoulders. "Come on Johnny! This will be fun! Fritz will not be expecting this. Whoever heard of three Pups attacking a whole Jasta?"

"That's the spirit, but first we have to find them. Let's go!"

The mechanics lined the airfield with lanterns. They would all be in the mess by the time we were in the air, tucking into a hot breakfast. We would be in the chill April air heading towards a deadly encounter.

Chapter 21

I kept climbing until we reached ten thousand feet. I would have gone higher but there was cloud cover just above us. I just used my compass to take us east and estimated our position from the flight time. The wind was coming a little from the north and it did not affect us that much. Once I thought that we were behind the enemy lines I took us up into the clouds. It was a dangerous tactic for we risked crashing but I trusted my two wingmen.

When I saw the first lightening of the sky I took us down into the thinner lower parts. I suddenly had an idea. When we landed I would have the lower wing and the bottom of the fuselage painted a pale blue. It would make us harder to see. That way we could use altitude to hide us. I was not certain if it would work with the larger wingspan of the Bristol but the Pup was just small enough that it might work.

We only had another forty minutes before we would need to head back and I worried that we might have arrived too early. Dawn broke to the east and I led us on a north-to-south course. I peered to the east hoping that we were still hidden in the dark of the west.

I saw the black crosses appear in the distance and I turned east and began to climb back into the clouds. This would take timing, a little good judgment and a huge amount of luck. I estimated that they were four or five miles ahead of us. After three or four minutes I descended. As we emerged from the clouds I scanned to the east and south to see them. They were a thousand feet below us and to the west of us. It was perfect. We could attack from their blind spot. I banked and waved my arm to signal the other two to assume their positions on my wing. I noticed as a shaft of sunlight illuminated one of them, that they were the squadron with the green rudder. We had fought these before.

I made my dive shallower so that I could rake three aeroplanes before I needed to turn. There were twelve aeroplanes but their guns were all facing the wrong way. We would not have to run the gauntlet of death to reach them. I decided I would wait until I was just a hundred feet from them before I fired. That way I could not miss. Johnny opened fire just a little too early when we were almost two hundred feet from them. I had to fire too.

Our dive meant that we were travelling faster than they were and we were overtaking them. I fired when the wings and the pilot came into the centre of my sights. I watched the bullets thud into the pilot and his body juddered. I lifted the nose slightly and headed towards the next Albatros. The pilot I had shot would be dead even if his Albatros continued to fly in a straight line. I fired at the next Albatros. He was trying to turn and face the new danger. My bullets smacked into his engine which poured smoke and he began to spiral towards the earth. He might not be doomed but he was too badly damaged to continue the fight.

The leader was the next in my sights and I anticipated a turn. I banked to port and, my luck held, he also turned to port. I felt bullets whizzing around my bus and I looked in the mirror. One of those to my right was firing at me but he was so far away he was wasting his bullets. However, it was a reminder that I needed to strike and flee.

I matched the German's turn. I still had more airspeed for I was above him. I dipped my nose to get a little more power and then gave a burst as he turned into my sights. I hit his engine and his fuselage. He must have been fully laden with fuel and his tank exploded. I flew through a maelstrom of metal and wood. I heard a ripping sound from my wings as debris struck me. I banked hard to port and put my bus on to a vertical axis. The Huns were not expecting that and the bullets of the ones following whizzed into fresh air. As I turned I gave every Albatros a short burst as I passed them. My manoeuvre took them by surprise and they took evasive action. It meant that they could not fire at the tiny insect which had buzzed into their world. As I came around I saw clear sky before me. I looked in my mirror and saw Freddie heading west while Johnny was busily defending against two Albatros.

I looped my aeroplane. Johnny tried to turn west too but his two opponents were very close to him. At five hundred feet, as I came out of my loop underneath one of the Albatros, I fired into his belly. He peeled off. I banked to starboard and took a snapshot at the other. I hit his rudder. As I climbed above Johnny I waved to the west. He nodded. I noticed that he had taken some damage to his bus.

As I levelled out I saw that we had totally disrupted their formation. The survivors were too busy trying to reform to worry about us. Freddie was almost a dot in the distance while Johnny's uneven throb told me that his engine was not well. I climbed to be his guardian angel. When I reached the clouds I levelled out.

I breathed a sigh of relief when I saw the British lines approach. Then I heard the double chatter of two German Spandau machine guns. I saw Johnny take evasive action. I dived and banked. The brave Albatros pilot had no idea I was there. He had thought he had a wounded bird to finish off. I screamed down, almost vertically and emptied my magazine into him. My bullets smashed into his guns and his engine. I pulled to port as soon as my gun clicked empty. I saw the German as he turned to head east, his engine smoking and the British ground troops firing futile bullets into the sky. My ploy had worked…just.

I watched as Johnny finally made the field. The mechanics and fire crews had seen the smoke and they ran to see to him. I waited until they had moved his wounded bird from the field and then I landed. Gordy, Ted and the other senior pilots watched me as I landed. They ran over along with Senior Flight Sergeant Lowery. I climbed down. I watched Freddie as he landed his Pup.

"How is Holt's bus?"

Sergeant Lowery took off his hat and scratched his head. "Sir, never mind Mr Holt, what about you?" He pointed to my Pup.

I turned and saw that the debris from the exploding German had torn holes not only in my wings but also in my fuselage. There were holes big enough for me to put my hand in. "Oh, it was an Albatros which exploded in front of me. I didn't notice any difference when I was flying."

I left the mechanics and riggers to start the repairs. "How did the training and flying go this morning?"

"A mess, if I am honest. We are having the aeroplanes refuelled and then we will take them out again this afternoon. They need all the hours they can get. We daren't have them test firing their weapons; they are just as likely to blow the tail off the bus in front."

I noticed that it had been Ted who had answered. He had slipped into the mantle of second in command effortlessly. It had been a good decision to give him that responsibility.

Johnny and Freddie joined me. "Thanks, sir! I nearly bought it that time."

Freddie said, "You should have turned west sooner. We had done enough."

"How did you do?"

"Shot one down and damaged a second."

"Johnny?"

"Shot down one and winged a couple."

Gordy whistled. "Impressive! And you Bill?"

"I managed to get a couple. I would have had a third if I hadn't run out of bullets."

"A great return."

"The trouble is we can't repeat it. The weather was perfect and we were able to hide in the clouds. We know that Fritz is a quick learner. He will be ready tomorrow."

We entered the office. "What is the forecast for tomorrow, Randolph?"

"About the same."

"Ted, you will need to lead the squadron tomorrow. You can have Freddie as your guardian angel. I can't see our two birds being ready. And I would be on your toes; the Hun doesn't like to be bested."

After we had given our reports the others left. "Bill, you can't keep taking chances like this. You are like a cat, I know, but how many lives have you left?"

"The Pup saved me today."

"I heard from James that some of them have proved to be a little unstable in steep dives. Two pilots were killed when their wings were torn off."

"If you ask your friend I think that you will discover that they were young pilots. You can feel the stress and the pressure on the bus when you dive. You listen to your aeroplane and adjust your flying. I wouldn't want a squadron of them, not unless they let me pick my pilots."

"Strange you should say that. Intelligence reports that this Red Baron has done just that. So far his Jasta has not lost an aeroplane and they are downing five or six of ours every day, not to mention the ones he has damaged."

"Then we are lucky we haven't crossed his path."

"And I heard, on the grapevine, that there will be an improved Sopwith coming out in a month or so."

"Really?" He nodded. "Find out where General Trenchard is tomorrow. I'll go and see him. What is the point of being an ace if you can't ask for favours? Get me an up-to-date record of how many kills we have made since this offensive started and I will take that with me."

I went to my quarters where Bates was waiting. He smiled when he saw me. "Well done sir! Mr Carrick told me what you have done. Congratulations. And you won't be able to fly tomorrow either!"

"You sound pleased, John."

"I am sir, someone else can take chances." He took my goggles and helmet. "I have your bath drawn sir and the cooks have saved some lunch for the three of you. I posted your letter too." He wandered off humming happily. His world was a small one and it did not take much to upset the equilibrium.

I felt better after my bath and I joined Freddie and Johnny in the empty mess. There was a mountain of food for me. I looked up at the Sergeant cook. "Do I need feeding up Sergeant Oliver?"

"Your man was quite insistent that we give you a hearty lunch. He can be quite forceful at times!"

I began to plough my way through the food. The other two had finished and I listened as they talked.

"You need to fly less straight, you know Johnny. Keep looking in your mirror. I think that was how those two got on your tail. The Pup is nimble enough to nip around in the air and make it a harder target."

"I know, Freddie. The trouble is that I wanted to make sure the Hun I had hit stayed hit."

I stopped chewing and pointed with my knife. "Then don't. I am not bothered if I don't destroy an aeroplane. If we are outnumbered then we do not have the luxury of making sure every damaged aeroplane is finished. You just need to get them out of the air."

"Is that why you fly the way you do sir?"

I looked at Freddie, "How do you mean?"

"Well sir, you always look as though you are trying to hit every single German. You hit one and then move your bus to hit another. You turn and spin and fire when you see a third. It is frightening to watch."

"I was brought up in the cavalry. I had a good horse that I could ride with just my knees and Caesar became an extension of me. I just do that with the Pup. I couldn't do that with the Gunbus. It was too ponderous and I had to worry about Lumpy in the front. This is more like being in the cavalry. I never fell from my horse once. I never fear making a mistake in the air."

"But your reactions sir, they are like lightning."

"That was the cavalry. All you had was a sword and if you had two or three chaps coming at you then you learned to use all of your senses and to duck, dodge and weave." I put my knife and fork on my plate and wiped my mouth. "You two are the best combat pilots in the squadron. You have great instincts. Just use them."

They both looked surprised at the compliment. "Freddie you are going up tomorrow without us. You need to be the guardian angel. Fly high and use the Pup to break up any enemy formations. You will have freedom for you will not be in formation. Lieutenant Alldardyce can fly with Ted tomorrow."

"What about me, sir?"

"You can come with me when we visit General Trenchard so wear your number ones. I want to impress him. Let's use that public school education to our advantage eh?"

I watched, with some trepidation, as the squadron took off. I would not be there with them. I trusted Ted, Gordy and Freddie but I felt that if I were not there then something untoward might happen. As they disappeared east I went to the car where a smart-looking Johnny awaited me.

"But why do you want me to come with you, sir?"

As we headed towards Amiens I explained, "I know, Johnny, that you have a better education and have an upper-class voice. Now some of those on the General's staff might look down their nose at me because of my background but they see you as one of them."

He was appalled, "But sir, that is ridiculous. You have the M.C., and you have shot down forty Germans; you are a hero."

I laughed, "Trust me, Johnny, that means nothing to some people. It is breeding which counts."

He was silent for a while. "I remember some of the chaps at Officer Training were like that. I thought they were unusual."

"No, Johnny, believe me, there are lots of them. What is unusual is the fact that our squadron has three sergeants who have been promoted from the ranks. Before your time we had a Major who did not like that. We all had a hard time so if you see anyone you know when we are there, we need to cultivate them."

"Why are we going, sir?"

"Because I want the new Sopwith when it becomes available and if I have to sweet talk the General then I will do so."

Chapter 22

Randolph had discovered where the general would be and his contact, James, would meet us there.

There were a huge number of military vehicles in Amiens and I virtually abandoned the staff car on a pavement. The sentry at the building carefully examined our papers. When we were admitted a sergeant directed us to Randolph's friend's office. James Ogilvy was older than I expected. He was a captain like me but he had flecks of grey in his moustache and a world-weary look on his face. I later learned that he found it hard to send so many young men to their deaths while he sat behind a desk. He smiled broadly when he greeted me.

"I have been looking forward to this for a long time, Captain Harsker. My cousin has told me much about you and I have heard your name mentioned many times by the general. If you don't mind me saying so you are much younger than I expected."

I had no answer to that, "This is Lieutenant John Holt, one of my pilots."

"Pleased to meet you both. I am afraid that the general is busy until lunchtime but I told him that you were coming and he wants to have lunch with the three of us." he shrugged apologetically, "It was the best I could manage."

"I don't need long. Thank you for arranging this."

"My pleasure; as I said I wanted to meet with you anyway. Now listen, there's no point in hanging around here. Lunch is at 12.30. Pop around town for a while and meet me back here at 12.00 how is that?"

"Spot on. Thank you very much."

As we left Johnny said. "He seemed a nice chap."

"He did. I can see now how Captain Marshall gets his information so quickly."

We used the hour in Amiens to buy some supplies for the mess. Tobacco was always in short supply. I did not manage to get any whisky; that was as rare as hen's teeth but I did get a case of brandy quite cheaply and some red wine. After we had put the purchases in the car we headed back to James' office.

We chatted for a while and then we heard a buzz of noise coming from the room down the hall. "That will be the General. Come along you two. He hates to waste time.

He had a gaggle of officers with red trim; staff officers from the Army. Johnny and I stood to attention. Our hats were under our arms and no salute was necessary. An overweight and podgy-faced major gave me a funny look. I vaguely recognised him but dismissed him from my mind as the general said, "Good to see you Harsker. Let's go to lunch I am starving and I suspect you have been up since dawn eh? Watching your young lads take off?"

"Yes, sir."

We went to his private dining room where his orderlies laid out the food. We chit-chatted about the new pilots and he asked Johnny about his background. I was pleased I had taken Johnny for the General knew his family and the conversation was much easier and relaxed.

When the plates had been cleared and we were sipping the brandy he lit his pipe and asked, "Now I do not think for one moment that you came here for a free lunch did you, Harsker? So what do you want of me now?"

"Well sir, we are really happy about the new Bristols and they are working out well."

He nodded, "Yes after poor Robinson and his flight went west we were worried but your chaps seem to know how to handle them. Do you want some more?"

"No, sir. The three Pups you sent us have worked out really well. Lieutenant Holt here shot down a D.III yesterday and damaged a second."

"Good show! Your people will be pleased."

"Thank you, sir."

"But we have heard that there is a newer version, the Camel, coming out soon."

The General flashed an irritated look at the captain. Then he shook his head and smiled at me. "And you would like one."

"No sir, I would like three."

He burst out laughing. "I admire your cheek, captain. But why should I let you have them?"

"Because, sir, I imagine that they will be delivered in dribs and drabs. We are in a perfect position to take small numbers and put them to good use. We are also quite good at shooting down German aeroplanes and we could evaluate them far better than any other squadron."

"You think highly of your squadron, Captain."

"They are the, best sir." I paused, "And I think you agree with me."

He inclined his head, "Perhaps. We are training a new squadron in England with them. Once they reach the front then we will see."

I pushed my luck. "Well, sir we have two damaged Pups at the moment. What happens if they need major repairs? I would imagine that Sopwiths will be ceasing production of spares soon. With this offensive, it means we cannot be as effective as we would like to be."

He shook his head again, "You are like a dog with a bone. Very well I will arrange for three to be sent over but they won't be here until the middle of May, you do realise that?"

"Thank you, sir and we will do you proud."

"I know you will." He smiled, "And you may not have heard but as of the 5th of April the Americans are in the war. It will take them some time to get over here but they have a rather nifty air force themselves. We may get some relief sooner rather than later." He looked at his watch, "and now I have to get to another meeting." He shook our hands, "Listen, Captain, the offensive is not going as well as it should and I think we can expect Germans counterattacks soon. You and your squadron are the front line. Things will get much worse. This April has been catastrophic for the Corps. I am just damned grateful that so many young men like Holt here wish to volunteer. I will do all that I can to send you replacement aeroplanes and pilots but we both know that it is experience that we need and not young Fokker Fodder. Keep your pilots alive. You and your young men need to be careful. Our country can't afford to lose the likes of you. The war will end one day and then you will be needed to pick up the pieces from our shattered country."

James waved us goodbye and we donned our hats and left. It had been a good meeting. We had what we wanted and I actually felt appreciated. As we left the building I saw the rotund major. He stepped towards us and we both saluted.

"It's Harsker isn't it?"

There was something in his voice which was familiar but I could not place his round face and pencil moustache. "Yes, sir. Do I know you, sir?"

"The last time I saw you, you were in the cavalry and you were a corporal."

I suddenly remembered him. Lieutenant Ramsden who had nearly got me killed more often than enough. It did not surprise me that he had a staff job. He liked the idea of action in others but not in himself. "Major Ramsden."

He nodded and sneered, "How on earth did you get promoted? They must give them away in the Flying Corps."

I heard the intake of breath from Johnny but it did not surprise me. He had always had a superior attitude. I smiled, "We have both done well, sir; a Major on the staff at Headquarters. Well done, sir." I paused, "I miss those days in the cavalry, sir, do you?"

I knew he did not but I enjoyed his discomfort as he coloured slightly. "Yes, well the cavalry are a thing of the past now. Tanks. They are the future." He smiled and warmed to the subject, "I was the chap who used them on the Somme! We showed the Germans there."

I frowned and looked at Johnny, "Didn't they break down at the Somme, Lieutenant Holt?"

"I believe they did."

"They probably had the likes of you driving them!" He poked me in the chest as he said that. His finger rested on my medal ribbons and I looked down at his carefully manicured nail. He seemed to see the M.C. for the first time. He withdrew his finger. "Are you entitled to wear that ribbon?"

"I wear nothing that I not entitled to. That includes ribbons and pips. Anyway, sir, I have to get back to my squadron."

"Ah, skiving off are you?"

"No, sir, my bus was badly shot up yesterday and I was here to meet with the general. Don't worry sir, tomorrow I will be over German lines again, leading my squadron."

"You, command a squadron? But you are just a captain!"

I shrugged, "It is only temporary but I will be happy to stand down again when our Squadron Leader returns. There are high casualties in the air, sir. It is a very dangerous place. It is much safer here in Amiens." I saluted and we both turned.

When we were out of earshot, Johnny said, "I see what you mean sir about some officers who think they are better than others. He was a dreadful man."

"Between you and me he was a dreadful leader too and I fear that he will get more crews of those tanks of his killed before someone realises how bad he is. I shall put him from my mind. He won't bother us again."

Of course, I was wrong.

I drove back far too quickly. I was anxious to see how the squadron had fared. Gordy and the other flight commanders were with Randolph. They looked up guiltily when I entered.

I deliberately took out my pipe and sat in Archie's chair. "Carry on, chaps, don't mind me."

Ted looked as though he was going to say something but he closed his mouth and nodded to Harry who carried on with his report. I knew something had happened. I forced myself not to react. I couldn't be there with them all of the time. Randolph went to the map and placed a pin in it. It marked another Jasta. He asked, "How did it go with General Trenchard, Bill?"

"Fine, he is giving us three Camels as soon as they are available."

"Good show!"

"Your cousin sends his best too."

"He is a good egg isn't he?"

"Now do you want to tell me who we lost this morning?"

Ted stubbed his cigarette out. "We lost Simkins and Ellis' gunner was killed. Some of the Bristols were badly shot up. Sorry, Bill."

"It is war and these kinds of things will happen. We will have more cover tomorrow with the three Pups. How did it happen?

"They jumped us on our side of the lines. They had altitude and the sun behind them. Simkins just seemed to panic. He flew straight on when the rest followed Gordy and banked."

I tapped the loose ash from my pipe. "Perhaps the others will learn a lesson then. Drill into them the need to stay calm and follow orders." I took out my reamer to clean the bowl of the briar. "I heard today that 43 Squadron lost thirty-five gunners and pilots flying the Sopwith Strutter. They ceased to exist as a fighting unit." I allowed the figures to sink in. "I think, from what General Trenchard said that today is just a forerunner of what is going to come. We will no longer be fighting over their lines. They know their machines are better than ours. Once they defeat us then their artillery will pound our positions to dust and the gains we have made will be for nothing."

I filled my pipe. Ted shook his head ruefully, "And they say I am the miserable bugger."

"I think you deserve the truth but if you ask me if I think we can win and I will say yes. But it will not be easy. And so I want us in the air before dawn tomorrow. I want us to be as high as we can. Randolph, I need you to have the defence on the field beefed up. Get sandbags. I want fire crews ready to douse any fires and keep the fuel well away from everything else. Have the cooks ready to help. We can have something simple tomorrow."

"You think they are coming?"

"I have no crystal ball, Harry, I am just planning on the worst that could happen. That would be a raid by bombers and escorted by Baron Von Richthofen. If that happens then we will be prepared."

"And if that doesn't happen?"

"Then, Gordy, we will have an easy day and a cold dinner." I stood, "I can live with that option, can't you?"

I poured a large brandy when I reached my room. Ten of the bottles had gone to the mess but two were in my room. The meeting with Major Ramsden had stirred memories I had long hidden. Ramsden had been the only one of my comrades whom I did not miss and now there was just Robbie McGlashan and George Armstrong who were left. Lord Burscough had gone and Charlie too. I felt like the last man at a party. They had all gone and left me alone. When this war was over would there be any whole men left? Would it be a Britain populated by those like Lumpy with visible wounds and the rest of us who had our wounds deep inside? I swallowed the brandy in one. It made the emptiness recede a little and I poured myself a second.

When Bates came to lay out my clothes he looked at the brandy bottle which was a little over half full. "I want to be up well before dawn tomorrow John."

"Yes, sir." He brushed a speck of dust from my tunic. "The cooks were saying it may be rough rations tomorrow." I nodded, "Is it likely to be dangerous here?"

I remembered that Bates had transferred from the infantry to be away from the horrors of the trenches. "Yes John, but it will not be like the trenches. If they do come it will be over before you even know it."

"I wasn't worried about me, sir. I was thinking of those new pilots. They are so young."

"I know and that frightens me too. They come straight from school and into the meat grinder. If they do survive I wonder what they will be like? What will I be like?"

He brightened at that. "Oh don't worry Captain Harsker, you will be fine. You have a lovely young lady and you have your head screwed on." He picked up the brandy bottle and put it in the cupboard. "You just need to keep the top screwed on the bottle too."

I nodded as he left. Gordy had dived into a bottle once and it had cost the squadron dear. I needed to be stronger. I resolved to drink my brandy one small glass at a time from now on.

Chapter 23

The Pup looked tiny standing next to the two-seater Bristol. Speight saluted me, as he went past me to the machine we had flown together. Young Lieutenant Alldardyce looked nervous. Speight looked as though he wanted to speak and so I gave him an opening. "Now you look after Mr Alldardyce as well as you looked after me and you will come back with another couple of kills under your belt."

He grinned, "Too right, sir. I have Lumpy's record in my sights. We have a pool you know, sir. Half a crown in each! There's six quid now! That'll make a nice little wedge at Christmas when the competition is over."

The Lieutenant asked, "Who is Lumpy?"

"He was the captain's gunner. They were a legend the two of them, sir..." he led the Lieutenant off to their bus telling him of our exploits. It would do them good and make them a better team.

Johnny walked towards his aeroplane. "I will try to remember what Freddie told me, sir. I won't let you down."

"I know Johnny."

I saw Freddie having a word with Lieutenant Alldardyce. His job would be to watch our backs as we engaged the enemy. I saw the young pilot nod earnestly. I remembered that it was not that long ago that Freddie had been our earnest young pilot desperate to please.

Before he mounted his Pup he came over to me, "I told him that if there were spotters or bombers then he should take them on. If you are right sir then I reckon the rest of us will have our hands full with their fighters."

"Good idea, Freddie, I should have thought of it myself."

"You have enough on your plate, sir."

We were the first flight off and we spiralled into the skies. I wanted us higher before dawn. I saw now that my early morning attack had come back to haunt us. The Hun had seen the benefits too. I could not see the rest of the squadron for it was too dark but I knew that a collision was unlikely until we levelled out. Once we reached ten thousand feet I began to circle. I saw the rest of the squadron arrive. Once I was certain that we were all in position I led the four columns east.

That morning the cloud cover would be too high for anyone to hide in its cotton wool fluffiness. I was pleased that we had had the lower wings painted pale blue but I did not think we would reap the benefit that day.

The horizon showed the first crack of sunlight and I cocked my Vickers. I stared up and ahead for the dark shadow of an enemy aeroplane. I saw none. The lack of clouds meant that the sun suddenly erupted in the east highlighting the six bombers and ten fighters which emerged ominously from the darkness. We were roughly at the same altitude. The Germans, however, had twice the firepower. I signalled to the other flights that I had seen them. Had we not left before dawn we would have been preparing to leave our airfield just as the bombers arrived. The squadron would have ceased to exist. I had got one thing right, at least.

The Pups would be responsible for getting amongst the Albatros fighters. This time we would not be able to surprise them and we would have to brave their twin machine guns to get close. Freddie and Johnny closed up with me. The other three flights had spread out to try to outflank the Germans; that way we could use the rear gunner to add to our firepower.

I saw that these Albatros fighters had their noses painted in four different colours. They were obviously to identify the different flights. I stored that information for Randolph.

As we approached I raised my nose a little to tempt the German into firing but he did not take the bait. It did not matter for I then lowered my nose and, as his yellow propeller came into view I opened fire. He moved at the same time as I fired and my bullets struck his wing. He had to turn again to fire at me and I gave him a second burst. This time I struck his engine. The two machine guns spat their 9mm bullets towards me. The tracer in them told me that they were going to hit. I pushed the stick down and the rounds hit my top wing. I heard one of the stays as it was severed. Remembering what I had been told about the dangers of the airframe I resisted the temptation for a violent move. Instead, I dived beneath the Albatros and banked at the same time.

I saw a second Albatros firing at Ted. He was beam on to me. I ignored the bullets coming from starboard and began to climb towards the Albatros. At fifty feet I opened fire. He was a huge target at that range and my bullets hit him behind the cockpit. He banked to the right and I turned with him, firing as I did so. My bullets hit his tail and he began to descend. I remembered my advice to Johnny and I banked to starboard. The Albatros which had fired at me was flying a parallel course. I suddenly remembered my Luger and I drew it and fired at the German who was a hundred yards away. He banked to starboard in surprise. I holstered my gun and banked after him.

It had been a cheap trick but it meant I gained the advantage by being on his tail and not the other way around. My turn was smaller than his and, as his tail came into view, I fired again. I hit his rudder and he juddered. Some of the controls had been hit. I banked to port and anticipated his next move. We had been heading south and he would want to head east. As he drifted into my sights I fired again and hit him behind the cockpit. He began to lose height. I checked my mirror and there was no one there. I glanced to left and right and the sky was clear. I had just decided to follow him and end this when I heard the explosions from behind me. The bombers had got through.

I banked hard. I could see that there were just three bombers but they could do a great deal of damage. Lieutenant Alldardyce was coming from the south to help me but I would reach them first. The Pup fairly zipped through the early morning air. I had gained airspeed by diving down to the same altitude as the bombers. I caught them when they were making their turn at the end of the field. The machine guns on the ground were firing but it is hard to hit a moving aeroplane. I opened fire at a thousand feet. I used short bursts. The bombers had no forward armament; they were just a two-seater. The first one exploded in the air. It must have been a lucky shot which detonated the bomb. The concussion threw the second AEG into the air slightly and my bullets ploughed into its belly. It veered to starboard and plummeted into the field next to the cookhouse. The third bomber took off north. I saw Lieutenant Alldardyce hurtling after it.

I banked and began to climb back to join the dogfights in the sky. They were quite high up as each pilot strove to gain altitude. I never reached them for the Germans decided to head on home. Their superior speed meant that the Bristols and Pups would not catch them. I returned to the field and landed.

Senior Flight Sergeant Lowery was directing operations as the holes in the field were repaired. "What's the damage, Flight?"

"Not as bad as it could have been. They made a few holes in the grass and the windows in the Sergeants' Mess were broken but no casualties. We were ready, sir, thanks to you."

I shrugged, "I guessed lucky."

He shook his head, "Mind you, sir, the broken windows were down to that bomber you blew up."

"Oh that reminds me, there is a second bomber in the field yonder. Best to send someone and see if there are any survivors and if there is anything worth salvaging."

"Righto, sir."

I took off my helmet and goggles and jammed them into my greatcoat pocket. I watched the Bristols and Pups land as I filled my pipe. There was one missing. It looked to be Lieutenant Ellis. I had hoped to avoid any losses. I strode over to Harry when he landed; Ellis had been in his flight.

"What happened to Ellis?"

"His engine began to smoke and he crash-landed in a field to the north of us. I'll take a lorry and some mechanics. We might be able to repair it."

"Good man." He jogged off shouting to a group of mechanics and riggers to join him. He was growing into his role. He did not wait for orders he just got on with things. I headed to the office. There were a couple of windows blown out and a little damage in the office itself. I saw a medical orderly dealing with some cuts to Randolph's face. I laughed.

"It's all very well for you to laugh! I am supposed to be safe on the ground. I shall have to start wearing a tin lid!"

The orderly chuckled as he left us.

"That's not such a daft idea, Randolph. Until this sort of thing stops we might be as well to make sure that the ground crews are protected."

"You think this will happen again?"

"The Germans are on the offensive now. They do not want us spotting for our guns. I have learned that they are an efficient bunch. The Teutonic mind must realise that by getting rid of us first they can do pretty much as they please. I am going to take the squadron up again this afternoon. Find out where the Huns have attacked and we will see if we can help out. Get Lowery to refuel and rearm the buses."

"Right, Bill."

I went to the cookhouse where the cooks were clearing up. The senior sergeant leaned against his broom. "It is a good job we were not cooking, sir, or we might have had more damage and casualties."

"Well, we won't need a hot meal. I am taking the squadron out soon so just get some sandwiches for the men. We will have a hot meal this evening."

"Will they be back sir?"

"I doubt that they will return today but they might repeat this again."

"In that case, I'll put some tape over the windows. We can't be having flying glass in the kitchen. The blokes moan enough as it is but finding a piece of glass in a stew would mean they would have my guts for garters!"

When I reached the office the others were already there. "You want us out again this afternoon, Bill?"

"Just C and D Flights. Ted and Harry can keep an eye out in case the Hun comes back."

"Do you think they might?"

"It is a possibility. They must be desperate if they are resorting to using the old AEG."

Randolph put the telephone down. "The Germans are attacking the Australians at Lagnicourt."

"Then that is where we will go. Gordy, have your gunner take his signalling lamp with him in case we can direct the artillery."

Ted looked around, "Where is Harry?"

"Collecting Ellis and his broken bus." He nodded. "I have arranged for sandwiches. We eat now and as soon as the buses are refuelled and rearmed we will take off." I nodded to Freddie and Gordy, "Come with me and we will eat on the hoof."

I led them to the cookhouse where half of the cooks were still clearing up while the other half was preparing sandwiches and tea. I grabbed a handful and a mug of hot sweet tea and went outside. Freddie followed me.

I bit into the cheese and pickle sandwich and pointed towards the buses. "I want you and Johnny to be our umbrella this afternoon. I'll have Alldardyce as my wingman." I pointed to Gordy's buses, "You and I will ground attack."

"Do you want us to bomb?"

I shook my head, "We haven't got time to fit the racks. I suppose we could take a couple of Mills Bombs."

Gordy laughed, "Give them a Lumpy special eh?"

"Something like that. You can liaise with the artillery. If you have to spot then I will lead your flight in."

"I can always get one of the others to spot."

"They haven't done it yet. You know how to do it and do it right."

He saw the sense in it. "Right. I'll go and get Randolph to telephone the artillery and find out what the call sign is."

After he had gone I finished my tea and lit my pipe. "Freddie, you may need to split up if we get jumped. Make sure that Johnny doesn't get carried away with a pursuit. We can't afford to lose experienced pilots."

"He seems a little better these days. He stayed right on station this morning and managed to damage a couple. He resisted the temptation to follow them back to Germany."

I laughed, "Well that is an improvement anyway."

Gordy ran back. "We had better get there quickly, Bill. The Huns have overrun the Australian guns. There is a danger of a breakthrough."

Right! Let's go!"

Freddie ran into the mess and brought out the pilots and gunners. I saw Senior Flight Sergeant Lowery. "Are we good to go?"

"All ready, sir and I have the German's effects. Their bodies are being buried this evening."

"Good. Give them to me." He handed me two bundles. There were two helmets secured by the goggles. Inside were the papers, identity tags and watches as well as wallets. I noticed that they were both bloody. I dropped them into the bottom of the Pup's cockpit. "Lieutenant Alldardyce you are my wingman today. Stick to me like glue."

"Yes, sir!" I smiled. I could imagine his fear of falling foul of his commanding officer. Speight would keep him straight.

I led the two flights high into the sky. I looked in my mirror and saw Freddie leading Johnny high towards the thin wispy clouds above us. I doubted that Gordy would need to signal the ground forces for if the Germans had overrun the guns the artillery would have no target.

It took us twenty minutes to reach the village which was at the southern end of the line. I saw the grey lines as they swarmed forwards towards our forward trenches. The Australians were doggedly resisting but I could see that they were being forced back. I swung around so that I could fly along their lines. The Pup was a really small aeroplane and I was able to descend to treetop height. I was not certain that Alldardyce would be able to get as low. I began firing my machine gun. There were so many Germans I could not miss. They dropped to the ground searching for somewhere to hide but the only place was behind their dead comrades. As I zipped across at a hundred and five miles an hour the German bullets were striking where I had been and not where I was.

When there were no more Huns I lifted the nose and banked to starboard. As I did so I glanced aloft. I saw the two Pups but they appeared to be alone. We had caught the Jastas napping or, perhaps, licking their wounds.

As I descended again I saw knots of fresh Germans kneeling and firing into the air. The Vickers cracked away and scythed them down. I glanced in my mirror and saw Alldardyce doing the same while Speight was spraying any who emerged from behind. I clicked on empty. I lifted the nose and surveyed the scene below. The Australians had stopped retreating. I saw them digging in. I was not certain if the others had any bullets left but our very presence would halt the attack. I descended again. I suddenly remembered Lumpy's grenades. I still had one in my greatcoat pocket. Flying as low as I dared I dropped the bomb close to a huddle of machine gunners who were trying to set up a Spandau.

The sharp crack of the grenade which exploded just above their heads showered them with shrapnel. I saw them in my mirror. The gun would never fire again. Alldardyce did not fire this time. He was out of ammunition too. I saw Gordy leading his flight to continue the attack. We had slowed down the German advance and allowed the Aussies time to dig in.

I climbed to a reasonable height. I signalled for him to come alongside. When he did so I pointed to the north-west and mouthed, 'Home!' He nodded and turned the Bristol. Speight gave me a cheery wave. I turned east. I had another task to complete.

I kept my Pup low and headed east. I knew there were four of five German airfields close by. I reached down to pick up the bloody helmets and goggles and placed them on my lap.

As I sped across the French countryside I saw lines of grey heading west towards the battle. They raised their rifles to fire but I was gone before they could aim. I knew I was close when I saw the windsock ahead. I raised the nose a little. I saw lines of Fokkers on the green field and grey uniforms running to man their guns. As I flew down the centre of the parked aeroplanes I hurled the two helmets over the side and then banked to starboard. As I returned down the field I saw two men lift the helmets and then wave at me. I waggled my wings. They would know what had happened to their comrades.

Chapter 23

I was, of course, the last to land. The others were anxiously watching for me. As I stepped out and they crowded around me I said, "I returned the effects of the dead bomber crew."

"You might have told us what you were going to do." My old friend had an angry, almost petulant look on his face.

I smiled at Gordy, "I thought Bates was my mother?" he laughed. "Any losses or damage?"

Freddie shook his head, "No. It was a bit of an anti-climax really. We watched you stop their attack and then followed the Bristols home."

"That suits me. Every hour in the air for the new pilots means they have a better chance of surviving. Did Ellis get back?"

"Yes, although his bus might not be ready for tomorrow."

"Ted and Harry come to the office while I give you tomorrow's orders."

Randolph was already compiling his report. "The Australians were grateful to us for this morning and they want us to spot for their artillery tomorrow so that they can consolidate the ground."

I turned to Ted and Harry. "Then that is your mission. You will need to work with your new gunners to tell them what to do. I think you might find the Germans try to discourage you tomorrow."

"Aye, I reckon you are right. What will you and Gordy be doing?"

"We will patrol the field in case the Albatros Jasta returns and then we will take over from you in the afternoon."

Ted nodded to Harry, "Right then Lieutenant Dodds, we have our work cut out. Let's go."

After they left Randolph held up a sheet of paper. I ordered more Vickers and Lewis machine guns. I also requested more soldiers to defend the field."

"Until then draft in the cooks, orderlies and anyone else who can hold a gun. If we dig slit trenches close to the sandbags then they can shelter from the bombers and fire at them with their rifles."

"Will they hit anything?"

"I doubt it but it makes nervous pilots even more nervous and nervous pilots make mistakes."

In the event, we had no visitors to the field. I led the two flights to Lagnicourt in the afternoon and we covered D flight as they directed the artillery to clear the Germans from their newly acquired gains. I had time to observe the Australians making new defences. They were not bothered by the Huns.

We had had two days without damage or losses and the squadron was in high spirits. I had time to complete all the overdue paperwork. "Randolph, just find out what the Germans are up to. If they aren't bothering us then someone must be getting it."

I worked through the late afternoon while Randolph telephoned to Intelligence.

"It seems there is a battle going on at Vimy Ridge and the Canadians are getting a hammering. The Albatros D.III squadrons have been decimating the fellows up there."

"Do they need us?"

"No, they want us to help the Australians to consolidate the ground they recaptured. And they are sending us three more Bristols and crews tomorrow."

"Good. Give two to Gordy and one to Ted. I want those two flights to be the strongest. Harry and Freddie need to grow into their jobs." I leaned back and filled my pipe. "Any news of Archie?"

"The doc said he heard they sent him to your young lady's hospital."

"Then he is in safe hands. They have good people there and I don't just mean Beattie!"

He laughed, "I assumed she wasn't running the place single-handed."

The next few days were the most peaceful days of war we had experienced. The Germans did not bother us and, by the end of the week, the Australians no longer needed us to spot and we were asked to help out further north. The time had been well spent and the three new crews assimilated into the squadron. On the 26th of April, we were given new orders. We were to fly north and support the British and Canadian attack at Arleux. Our holiday was over. This was the area where the Red Baron ruled. We would finally meet this vaunted Jasta of elite pilots.

We left as dawn was breaking. The new machine guns had arrived and we had sandbagged trenches should the German bombers return. Quartermaster Doyle was trying to acquire some barrage balloons which could be raised over the field in the case of an attack. I had no doubt that the resourceful Scouser would manage that. He had more contacts in France than anyone I knew.

I flew with C Flight above the other three flights. Our job would be to deter any fighters while Gordy would attack any ground targets which presented themselves. It was a day of high cloud and I made sure that we were at ten thousand feet. It was a comfortable height and would enable us to avoid any ground fire. The Hun arrived within fifteen minutes of us. They must have had good intelligence from the front alerting them to our presence. There were twelve of them and their colourful livery told me that it was Baron Manfred Von Richthofen and his Flying Circus. I saw that they were climbing to reach us and I led C Flight higher. They flew in three formations of four. They were echeloned so that there was one extra aeroplane on the starboard side. I was using a line astern. It meant that while I would be the target for two Spandau machine guns we would have four chances to down the leader and Speight, at the rear, would be able to cause some damage.

One of the flights detached itself to attack us. I hoped that our smaller profile might make us harder to hit. Once we had passed through them then it would be every man for himself. I fired at four hundred feet. I had not worked out yet the size of the German's magazines but I wanted to make him fire and waste his bullets.

He was good and the twin machine guns rattled into my wings. The recent repairs were undone as the Albatros closed with me. I had managed to strike his radiator before I had to bank to starboard. His wingman fired and I felt the Pup judder as his bullets hit my undercarriage. I used the Pup's agility to turn to port and I saw Freddie's bullets strike the Albatros leader causing smoke to come from his engine. I pulled hard and saw the fourth Albatros come into my sights. Flying at a strange angle I snap fired and my bullets traced a line from his tail to his cockpit. He pulled up to avoid me and, behind me in Alldardyce's Bristol, Speight poured bullets into his belly. I continued my bank and fired at the second Albatros. I managed to hit his undercarriage and I raised my nose a little to continue firing into his wings, stays and struts. I began to climb so that I could swoop down again. As I did so I saw that the Germans were fleeing east. In the distance, I could see the rest of the Jasta and the Bristols engaged in dogfights.

Freddie and Alldardyce were diving to join the fray but, to my horror, Johnny Holt was heading east following a smoking Albatros. He was half a mile away and they were both going at full power. I had to follow. He kept firing at the Albatros whenever the German pilot's concentration lapsed and they gradually went lower. I knew what the German's plan was; he was luring Johnny towards the guns on the ground. Sure enough, when they were at five hundred feet Johnny's Pup was hit by shells from the ground. It might have been a lucky shot but it did for Johnny. A huge hole appeared in both his upper and lower starboard wings. He began to plummet to Earth. The Pup is a tough little aeroplane but the strain was beginning to tell. I saw wires snapping as his Pup started to fall apart. He was saved by his low altitude. He managed to crash land a mile or so from the nearest Germans. I dived down and machine-gunned the eager Huns who began to run towards the burning Pup. I flew over Johnny and saw him stagger from his Pup. He was alive. I banked and flew back towards the Germans. I fired once more and then turned. I would try to land.

In any other aeroplane, I would have been doomed to failure but the Pup could almost land in a living room. It was not the best landing and it was only when I heard a creak from below that I remembered that I had suffered damage to it. There was little I could do about it. I turned into the wind and shouted, "Johnny! Get over here!"

He staggered toward me. I saw that his face was covered in blood.

"Grab my hand and climb up behind!"

In the distance, I could see Germans as they ran towards us. Holt's Pup was now an inferno and the smoke from it drifted in front of us disguising our position.

"Lie down on the fuselage. Spread your legs as though you are riding a horse and hang on to my seat belt and cockpit."

"I am sorry sir. You should leave me."

"You just hang on." I was not certain if the Pup would get off the ground but one thing was certain if I did not then it would be a quick death for both of us. I gunned the engine and we screamed through the smoke. The hedge, the end of the field and the Germans were all approaching rapidly. I pulled back on the stick and we started to rise. I heard the chatter of bullets and then there was a huge crack. As the undercarriage hit the top of the branches part of it fell off and we rose over the hedgerow. We were in the air.

I dared not risk any tricky manoeuvres. Holt was clinging on for dear life. I kept us as low as I could and we zoomed over the front at a height of fifty feet. We were travelling so fast that we were gone before anyone else could fire at us. I saw the fuel gauge as it drifted towards empty. We would be landing on fumes. At least that would mean there was less chance of a fiery death.

"How are you doing, Johnny?" I had to shout because of the noise of the creaking bus and the wind in the wires.

"Still hanging on, sir. Just don't climb though, sir. I'll slide off if you do."

"Don't worry, we are going back as level as I can manage." I reached down for the Very pistol. When we crossed our lines I knew that we had barely ten miles before the field would be in sight. As soon as I saw the derelict barn a mile from the end of the runway I fired the pistol and watched the flare arc.

"We have no wheels, Johnny, so this will be a little bumpy." That would be an understatement for I had no idea how much of the undercarriage remained. The last thing I needed was for a spar to dig in the ground and cartwheel Johnny to his death. Thankfully the runway was empty. The engine began to cough and splutter, "Come on old girl, just a few more yards!"

The ground seemed to race towards us. "Stand by Johnny!" I lifted the nose slightly and heard the intake of breath from Holt as his arms took the strain. The propeller stopped and we were gliding. We hit the ground hard but there was no cartwheel. The lack of any undercarriage meant that we slid just thirty yards or so and then slewed around. As we did so Johnny rolled off the Pup and hit the ground.

I was out in an instant and ran back to him. I put my hand on his neck and he was still alive. Doc Brennan was there almost as soon as I stood up. He shook his head, "I don't think much of your taxi service." He then rolled Johnny over as his orderlies joined him.

Freddie and Gordy arrived. "How on earth did you get him back and land it?" Gordy pointed to the Pup. It was a wreck.

"I have no idea but I guess someone was watching out for us."

Flight Sergeant Lowery wandered over. "I think this is a right off, sir. It will need a complete rebuild."

I nodded. "Do the best you can Flight. Did we lose anyone today?"

"Two of the new boys, Grant and Wright. Freddie managed to get one of the Albatros fighters."

"Well done Freddie."

He shook his head, "I have failed you, sir. I thought I had made it clear to Johnny that we didn't follow wounded birds east."

"You have nothing to reproach yourself about. You have vindicated my choice of Flight Commander. You could just as easily say that it was my fault. You cannot fly for another pilot. But I think that he has learned a lesson today."

"Will he be alright sir?"

"He is shaken up, that is all. The bump on his head looks worse than it is. He was talking to me on the way back. Of course, I am no doctor but…"

We had reached the office. Gordy said, "We might have been bloodied by this Red Baron but we weren't battered. Our young lads did fine. They were fighting the best they had. I counted at least five damaged birds. We will do better next time."

Randolph looked concerned. "You had us worried there, Bill."

"I had me worried."

"General Trenchard heard about the show today and he sends his congratulations." I gave him a puzzled look. "It is the first time anyone has managed to bring down one of Jasta 11. He said your Camels will be here in the next fortnight."

"Well, we will need them!"

Chapter 24

We were stood down the next day as a storm closed in our field. It was a late spring soaking for all of us but it allowed the mechanics to repair the damage to the Bristols and for Johnny to recover a little.

I had him in my office as soon as he left the sickbay. I did not want this hanging over him. He knew what was coming and he had a hangdog expression on his face. I lit my pipe and watched him. He had a bandage on his head but Doc Brennan had said that he could fly by the end of the week. Of course, we had no bus for him to fly anyway but no matter what I said the loss of his Pup would be the greatest punishment. I needed to know if he had learned his lesson.

"I know that you are a good pilot, Johnny. I have told you before that you and Freddie are the best in the squadron but the difference is that Freddie has self-control and you do not."

"I know sir and I…"

"Let me finish. You were lucky the other day. If I hadn't followed you then you would be behind German bars by now and we would have lost a damned good pilot."

"It won't happen again, sir." There was an earnest tone in his voice.

I nodded, "I know because if you ever do anything like this again then I will ground you and give you a desk job."

He looked up; horror was written all over his face. "I promise sir. I have learned my lesson. Get me back in the air and I will show you."

"I am afraid, Johnny, that, like me, you will have to wait until the new aeroplanes arrive before we can test your resolve."

"I know sir. But thank you for the chance."

The next morning Johnny and I watched the squadron as they left without us. The field seemed empty somehow. Bates was delighted that I was grounded. He whistled cheerfully as he tidied my room. I went to the office to catch up on some overdue paperwork.

Randolph was in a chatty mood. "Did you hear about the Yanks coming in to the war?"

"Yes, General Trenchard mentioned them."

"That will make a difference. They will have fresh troops and machines."

"Hopefully they will use them in different way."

He leaned back, "How do you mean, Bill?"

"If they come in and try to fight the war the way that we have then things will not change. We need a whole new approach. I hope the Yanks can bring it."

I fiddled around until it was nearly noon and then I watched for the return of the squadron. I knew that I would rather be up there than waiting like the father of a girl out with her young man and worrying about what was happening. The uneven sound of engines told me that the squadron had hit trouble. Two smoking and sickly Bristols returned first. They were the new pilots and it was to be expected. I breathed a sigh of relief when Gordy, Ted and Harry returned. I noticed that there were at least two Bristols missing. When Lieutenant Alldardyce landed, somewhat shakily then I knew that there was just one missing and I realised that it was Freddie.

I heard the Pup which seemed to be approaching the field like a crab, sideways. I turned to the fire crews. "Get out there; Mr Carrick is in trouble. You had better fetch the doctor too."

I ran to the field. Freddie was in trouble, I could see that. When the Pup rolled to a halt I ran to the cockpit. Freddie was out for the count. I did not know how he had managed to land the Pup. Miraculously the Pup appeared to be undamaged and I wondered what injury he had suffered. I saw that there was blood close to his helmet. I took off his goggles and his helmet. A bullet had scored a line along the side of his cheek and his head.

"Let me see him, Bill."

Doc Brennan leapt up to the cockpit and I stepped down. Gordy and Ted ran from their Bristols. "He and Alldardyce covered us when we were jumped. I didn't see any damage to his bus and I assumed he was fine."

Doc Brennan stepped down as his orderlies manhandled Freddie from the cockpit. "His head has been creased by a bullet and he has concussion. He won't be able to fly for a few days."

"That's not a problem. I can replace an aeroplane but not a fine pilot."

When Ted and Gordy had finished their report I could see that the Germans had determined to get revenge for their loss the previous day. Once again we had lost a couple of pilots but we were suffering fewer casualties than the other squadrons. Somehow that seemed like cold comfort. Our young pilots were still bleeding for Britain. I knew that the human body had eight pints of blood coursing through it. How many pints of pilots did Britain have?

I looked up at Randolph. "How long until those Camels get here?"

"I told you, Bill, it could be a fortnight."

"Well until then we have one Pup and just four experienced pilots. We need a miracle."

Although we were suffering casualties others had to endure wholesale losses. Pilots in training from England were rushed too early to the front with the direst of consequences. "We are ordered up to Vimy again. We are supporting 56 Squadron. They have a new bus, the SE5, which can fly at a hundred and thirty-five miles an hour. Perhaps their presence will be of some help."

"If it can fly at that speed it might be but it really needs two guns. We shall see."

Inside I was quite hopeful. The Bristol had been an improvement and if the SE 5 was as good then perhaps we could turn the tide.

I led the squadron up the next day. The stubborn little Pup had stood up to the rigours of war well but it was the last of the three. They had all done remarkably well for such a small aeroplane. I had Alldardyce behind me and I felt slightly lonely five hundred feet above the rest of the squadron. Below me, I could see the new roads which the engineers had built to supply the newly dug trenches. We must have outstripped the underground bunkers and roads which Bert had been building. I wondered where he and his moles had been sent now. There could not be a bigger contrast between our worlds. He was in the dark and with not enough room to swing. I had the skies above me and fresh air too.

I saw the eight SE 5 coming from the north. They were the size of the Bristol but without the rear gunner. As we converged on them I saw that they had a second Lewis mounted over the wing. It was still not what we wanted but the extra speed might help. They were fast and as they sped east the leader gave me a cheery wave. I took a position to the south of them. Their extra speed gradually took them away from us. Not by much but they were ahead.

The Jasta swooped down from above and emerged from the thin cloud cover to the north. The SE 5s had not seen them but they reacted quickly enough. They quickly climbed to meet the Albatros squadron. I banked and led my squadron to add our firepower. Although the new fighters were powerful they were not as agile as us and, unfortunately for them, they were not as agile as the Germans. Their speed saved them and the two converging forces exchanged fire and then began to turn.

The Germans had not seen us. Gordy and Ted were climbing to reach us and it was just Alldardyce and me who were close enough to them. We hit their rear buses. I fired a long burst at five hundred feet and struck the tail of an Albatros with a green rudder. As I banked to fire at the next Alldardyce fired a burst at the green rudder and he struck it in the middle of the fuselage. The Albatros pilot turned the wrong way and he flew into the rest of Alldardyce's bullets. He began to spiral to earth. Our sudden appearance had disrupted and disorientated the Germans. I was in my element and the Pup began to squirm amongst the bright green rudders of the Albatros squadron. I fired when I saw a target. I knew that Gordy and Ted would add their firepower soon and my job was to be like a Jack Russell terrier and worry them.

It took nerves of steel to fly so close to the Albatros but the Pup never let me down. I found myself in clear air and I banked to starboard. I saw the Albatros leader had had enough and was trying to run east. The SE 5 came into its own and they began to overhaul the slower Albatros. It was only the skill of the pilots and the agility of the Albatros which limited their losses but two more fell to earth. I descended to join the rest of the squadron. 56 Squadron pursued the Germans east while I led my Bristols to ground attack behind the German lines.

This was a rare opportunity. We knew that there would be no German fighters and we were safely behind their anti-aircraft guns. The main road west was thronged with German troops marching towards Vimy. As soon as I dived down the lines of grey fled the road and headed for the hedgerows and ditches. It availed them little for we just had to move our guns a little to the left and right. There were vehicles on the road. I could not bring myself to fire at the horses and I deliberately stopped firing when they came into my sights. It meant I was able to fire for longer and we travelled four or five miles down the road disrupting the German's attempt to reinforce their men attacking the Canadians.

When I ran out of ammunition I climbed. The others would continue to attack until they had run out of ammunition too. I took the opportunity of studying the land. I could see that the ridge over which the Canadians and Germans were fighting was a vital one. Whoever held it could control the land hereabouts. I knew that the Canadians had taken many casualties but if they could hold it then the sacrifice would not have been in vain. As the squadron joined me and we headed west I reflected that we had managed to achieve something like success. Although we had only destroyed one German aeroplane we had killed many soldiers heading to the front. It would also demoralise them for this was the first time since Bloody April that we had managed to penetrate their front line. It was a good measure of our success.

As soon as we had landed I went to the sickbay. I had not seen Freddie since he had been pulled from his bus. The doctor had wanted him to rest. When I went in to his room he was sat up in bed with a bandage around his head.

"How do you feel then?"

"A bit of a headache sir and I am a little dizzy but otherwise fine."

"The doctor said you might suffer for a few days. I am flying your Pup anyway so you might as well recover completely. Until we get the new Camels there will be no bus for you to fly."

"How is she?"

"A nifty little number. Alldardyce bagged an Albatros today. He is improving."

"Good. I now see what you mean about nurturing young pilots." He hesitated, "Sir, did we lose any today?"

"No Freddie. We flew with 56 Squadron. They have a really fast new fighter, the SE 5. They saw off the Albatros fighters the Germans sent after us. Hopefully, it is a sign of things to come. Anyway, you, need your rest. I just wanted to stop by and make sure that you were all right."

"Thank you, sir."

Randolph was in good spirits too. The rest of the squadron had made their reports. "Good show today, eh Bill?"

"Yes, Randolph I have just said to Freddie that we might have turned the corner. Are we scheduled for the same run tomorrow too?"

He shook his head. "We have been ordered south close to Lagnicourt. We are trying to take Bullecourt and the Germans are resisting. They want us to escort some bombers who are going to disrupt the supply lines."

"What kind of bombers?"

"The Sopwith $1^{1/2}$ Strutter. They have been withdrawn as fighters as they were getting knocked about a bit too much by the Germans. There will be eight of them." He handed me a piece of paper with the map coordinates. "You rendezvous at 6 a.m."

I nodded. The Pup had been developed from the older, two-seater Strutter. "Very well. Any sign of replacements?"

He shook his head, "Our losses have been so light that they are filling up the other squadrons who have suffered far more casualties."

As I headed back to my quarters I wondered about that. We had lost two of the latest batch of pilots and had three more wounded. If they were light casualties then I dreaded to think of the losses from other squadrons.

Bates' face told me that I had letters from home. He positively bobbed up and down. "Here is your brandy, sir and I have drawn a bath for you. He gestured towards the dresser. "And there are letters from home. Your mother, Miss Porter and, I believe, your sister Sarah." He tapped his tunic pocket. "I have one from your mother too."

I left the letters until I had had my bath. I needed to feel clean when I read them. I would also enjoy the brandy far more. How Bates managed to get the water to the perfect temperature I would never know. The tin bath was not the best in the world but it was a luxury I have become used to. As I washed myself I felt as though I was washing away the war.

Mother's letter and Sarah's were difficult to read for they were filled with sadness. Alice had received my letter and both letters told of the effect on Alice. They were from different perspectives. Mum couldn't understand how Alice had become so close to Charlie in such a short time while Sarah told me of how Alice had opened her heart and told my sister of their plans. I had known about them and I understood my sister's loss. The only good news in the letter was that Lady Burscough had become a working woman and was helping Alice with the design of the dresses. That would be good for Alice; Lady Mary had suffered a loss herself and would be the one person who would truly understand. Both women would have a life without the men they loved. What would become of Beattie if I fell? Would she find another love in her life?

I finished my brandy and poured another. I sniffed Beattie's letter before I opened it. By closing my eyes I could picture her in the room. As I took out the letter a lock of her hair fell from it. It felt like Christmas! I laid the lock of hair on my dresser as though it was a precious jewel.

April 1917
Dearest Bill,
I hope this letter finds you safe. We have had so many casualties through the doors lately that I dread you being one again.
I have met your Major and he is a dear! What a lovely gentleman he is. Even Matron is quite taken by him. He speaks so highly of you that I am even prouder of you than I was before. He can't wait to

get back but the doctors are being careful with him. He nearly lost his arm, you know.

Lumpy also wrote to me. He seems quite happy in the North East with his new job. He also seems to be taken with Jack Laithwaite's widow. He is a kind chap. It was he who suggested the lock of hair. He said it would bring you comfort in the air. He is thoughtful. I think Mrs Laithwaite could do much worse than him.

I am not sure that either Alice or Lady Burscough will be lucky enough to find someone as easily. I know that your mother can't understand her feelings after such a short time. (Alice told me of her words in a letter). But I can. I fell for you so quickly that I immediately knew I wanted to spend the rest of my life with you. Alice and Charlie were both equally smitten. It is a tragedy that they will never be together. I am just happy that the business is going well and your sister has work to keep her mind off her loss.

Write to her, Bill! You are her hero and her big brother. More than that you were Charlie's friend and hero. Anything that you write will be a comfort to her.

I pray each night that you will be safe and this awful war will be over soon but in the meantime please take care of yourself. There are many of us in England who care deeply for you. Come home safe.

Your fiancée
Beattie
xxx

I read and re-read the letter five or six times. Then I replaced the lock of hair into the envelope. I would need to find something to keep it safe and about my person.

The mess was buzzing that night. Our success and the ease with which the Germans had been seen off made everyone more hopeful about a successful outcome to the war. It was Ted who injected the first note of caution. "They were not the Flying Circus today. We have given these lads a good hiding before now. We outnumbered them and we surprised them. Let's not count our chickens."

I nodded at the wisdom of his words but the younger pilots carried on with their high jinks as though the war was coming to an end.

Gordy had been quiet and somewhat distracted. "Something wrong Gordy?"

He gave a shy smile, "I had a letter from home today."

"Me too. Nothing wrong is there?"

He sipped his brandy, "Oh no, of course not, in fact just the opposite. Mary is going to have a baby! I am going to be a dad."

I toasted him, "Well done! But why the long face?"

"What if something happens to me? Mary will be even worse off than she was before I met her. She would be alone and have a baby to look after."

"We have talked of this before. You can't think that way. You have to believe you will survive."

"But Charlie…"

"Charlie was not flying a Bristol he was flying an outdated Gunbus! You know yourself that once you start to have doubts then you don't fly as well."

He nodded and finished off his brandy, "But how long before I can see him?"

"You know it will be a he?"

He laughed, "I don't mind but I can't call him it can I?"

"Well the baby isn't here yet so when will the birth be?"

"Some time in August."

"Well, you never know. You might get some leave in September or October. November is definitely a possibility. The first month or so they are asleep most of the time. By the time you get to see him, he will be able to appreciate his hero dad!"

"Hero?"

I waved a hand around the mess. "If the men in this room aren't heroes then I don't know what a hero is."

Chapter 25

As Bates helped me to dress in the hour before dawn I wondered about Gordy. I hoped that he would not lose concentration and focus. I knew that I forced Beattie from my mind once I was in the air. One lapse of concentration when you were in a dogfight could easily result in your death. Thinking of Beattie I remembered the hair.

"John, Miss Porter has sent me a lock of hair. Can you think of anything that I could use to keep it close to me?"

He scratched his head, "Your pocket watch, sir."

"Of course." I took it from my pocket and opened it. I took out the lock of hair and placed it within. It seemed to fit but it was hardly secure. "I am worried that it might fall out."

He shook his head, "You leave that with me, sir. I will see one of the riggers. I am certain we could fashion something out of thin wire to hold it in place. It will be ready when you return home tonight."

"Thank you, John, I don't know what I would do without you."

"You don't have to sir and it is my pleasure to serve you. Let's get you finished." He fastened my Sam Brown around my waist and handed me the Webley service revolver. "There it is nicely polished up now, sir. I have cleaned the Webley, and reloaded it." He handed me the Luger. "I cleaned the Luger too. However, you only have twenty rounds left for that one sir."

As usual, I tucked it into the top of my flying boot. I had grown used to it and it was easy to reach when I was flying. "I should have asked the infantry for some when we visited them. Remind me to get some."

"I will do, sir."

I strode out to the Pup. Hopefully, this would be a milk run, the same as yesterday. When we had last been in the area around Lagnicourt it had been quiet. We would be flying barely five miles away from there. The squadron was all ready and we headed east for the rendezvous.

We reached the coordinates and I flew the squadron in a box pattern until the bombers arrived. The Strutters were late. It shouldn't have bothered me but it did. I was always early for any meeting. The sun was up by the time they reached us. Their commander waved to us and I acknowledged it. I led my squadron high above them as they headed for the cluster of villages the Second Division and the Australians were trying to capture. We would be the eagles hunting in the sky. They could operate safely beneath our canopy of guns.

The Strutters were much lower and I left the decision of the actual target to them. I could see, even from five thousand feet, where the front line was. Their bombs could be dropped with pinpoint accuracy to destroy gun emplacements without risk to the advancing troops.

I stared intently towards the east. Sometimes you imagined that you saw something and you have to look away and then look back. I did that. The twelve crosses rapidly heading our way told me that the Germans had been alerted to our presence. I waggled my wings to let the others know that the Hun was in the sun but I knew that their sharp eyes would have picked out the enemy as quickly as I had. I began to climb. You could never have too much height when fighting the faster Albatros fighter. We outnumbered them but that meant nothing. We had an advantage of one! Realistically that was not an advantage unless the German pilots were novices like most of our squadron. As we drew closer I saw, to my horror, that they were brightly painted. It was the Flying Circus.

I heard the bombs and the explosions as the Strutters dropped them and they struck the ground. I watched as three Albatros fighters detached themselves from the main formation and headed for the six Strutters. I waved to Lieutenant Alldardyce to support the Strutters. I hoped that seven to three might be odds on our favour. The Strutters had the same engine as the Pup and Alldardyce had the redoubtable Speight with his Lewis. They had a chance.

Having gained the height I now used it and I dived towards the red Albatros which was leading the Jasta. It was all red; it was the Red Baron himself. Knowing that it was the leading German ace made me concentrate even more. I now had no wingman and I would need to look after myself. He had shot down many of our aces already. What made me think I could hurt him? He opened fire first and his double column of bullets tore into my Pup. I felt it judder as they hit my engine and propeller. I feinted to starboard with a flick of the stick and, as he began to turn to match me, I gave him a short burst with the Vickers. Miraculously I managed to hit him. I banked inside him and fired again. I hit his wing and saw one of the struts as it cracked into two. He started to climb. He was no fool. He had structural damage to his aeroplane and it was a superior aeroplane to the Pup. The Albatros could out climb the Sopwith. I fired a longer burst and hit his tail. I saw that he was leading me east. That was not a direction I wished to take. I was about to turn and I checked my mirror. I saw that I had two more brightly painted

Albatros fighters on my tail. If I turned then I was dead. One or the other would have a clear shot and they were so close that they could not miss.

I decide to wiggle and wriggle my way out of the trap and then head west as soon as I could manage it. I put the nose down to try to throw them. The agile little Pup lost one of them but the second gave me a long burst and I felt the bullets hit my rudder. At the same time, I saw oil and smoke coming from the engine. The Red Baron's first bullets must have caused some damage to the engine although it had not lost any power. This was serious and potentially fatal. What was happening inside my engine? The oil was a worry for I did not want the engine to seize up. As I watched I saw that it was just a trickle but, even as I watched, more began to run down the side of the engine. Oil was the lifeblood of the engine and it was there for a purpose. My Pup was dying.

I banked to starboard to take me back over our lines. West was my only salvation. I had no idea how far to the east I had been drawn and dragged. I flew directly into the other Albatros, the one I thought I had lost. Its steel-jacketed bullets thudded and smashed into my already damaged engine and this time I did feel the loss of power as it was struck a mortal blow.

I would have to get down and try to land my stricken Pup. If the engine seized in mid-air it could be a disaster. The dying Pup helped me by gradually losing power so that I began to glide to earth. In my rearview mirror, I saw two Bristols as they opened fire on my pursuers. The rain of lead stopped as they turned to deal with their attackers. I could see a field ahead. There were now flames coming from the engine. Suddenly the propeller stopped and the nose dipped alarmingly. I pulled back on the stick and managed to lift the nose a fraction. It saved my life. Had I not done so then the nose would have hit the ground first. The wheels hit first; it was a heavy hit. They rolled for a few yards. They hit something in the field and, as I bumped up and down again, they broke and the bus slewed and spun around. The front of the Pup was now a raging blaze and I could feel the wall of heat getting closer as the wind fanned the flames. A spark hit the starboard wing and that caught fire too. I undid my seat belt and, even as we slewed around like a spinning top I threw myself from the cockpit. As I hit the ground flat I winded myself but the fact that I was lying prone on the ground saved my life as the Pup exploded.

When the smoke had cleared I stood. I saw Lieutenant Alldardyce's Bristol as he came east towards the pyre to see if I had survived. I waved to Speight who waved back. Then an Albatros zoomed down and fired at him. Speight fired at the German and Lieutenant Alldardyce turned the Bristol around and headed west. I was behind enemy lines again but this time there was no Lumpy to help me. At least this time, if my wingman reached base, they would know that I had survived the crash; that would be something. There might not be a telegram to Burscough.

My country upbringing came to my aid. I knew how to hide in farmland and woods. I had spent hours as a child playing hide and seek in such places. I ran from the burning aeroplane and headed for the west side of the field. I was less than twenty miles from a very fluid front. The trenches were still being established. I had my best chance to slip across to the British lines.

I heard a shout from behind me. There were German infantry flooding into the field. I threw myself through the hedge. Brambles and hawthorn tugged at my leather coat but I made it. I was glad I had left my goggles and helmet on my head; they saved my eyes and face from too much damage. I emerged in a lane which ran north to south. I remembered crossing it in the Pup. I saw a gate and ran towards it. I hurtled across the field; I kept heading west.

I heard the crack of a rifle as I reached halfway and saw the Germans aiming their rifles at me. I headed towards the gate in the field. This time I hurled myself over it and turned left to run towards a large and semi-derelict barn. I threw myself through the entrance and rolled behind an old rotting stack of hay. I lay there panting and trying to catch my breath. I could see, through a crack in the decaying wooden walls, the Germans as they entered the field. They did not turn left as I had but ran west following my original course.

I decided that I would wait until the hue and cry had died down before I left my sanctuary. I realised just how thirsty I was. I glanced around but there was no water to be seen. The barn itself had another exit behind me. It had had a gate once but it was no longer there. Beyond it, I saw that the land began to descend to the first road I had crossed. That would be my escape route.

I heard voices and I froze as the Germans returned across the field. They had shouldered their arms and I hoped that they had given up. Then I saw a non commissioned officer point towards the barn and four soldiers unslung their weapons and walked towards me. I slid down behind the hay and drew my Webley. I wondered if I could surprise them. I lifted my head a little and saw that the other soldiers had left the field. I had four Germans to dispose of and then I could head through the other door. I covered myself with the rotting and smelly hay and moved back into the shelter of a broken cow byre.

I made myself as small as I possibly could. I heard them shout something in German. Then they began to talk. Suddenly a long vicious bayonet stabbed through the hay. It missed my head and my eye by inches only.

I heard more German spoken and this time the voices began to recede as the searchers left. I lay there until all was silent. I didn't realise until I tried to stand, that I had hurt myself when I had been thrown to the ground. I was stiff. I put my Webley back in my holster. I did not want to trip and fire accidentally. I decided to head out of the other door. I moved towards it, peering down, across the field, to the road. It appeared to be silent. I had no watch but I thought it was late afternoon. As I was about to step out I heard the sound of a vehicle and I ducked back inside the barn and pressed my back against the wooden wall.

The engine drew closer and then stopped. After a few moments, it began to move again and I breathed a sigh of relief. I waited until I had counted five hundred in my head. Then I left the security of the barn and moved down the field to the gate which stood between two imposing walls which were the height of me. I suspected the farmhouse would be further down and was attached to the wall. I glanced left and saw, a hundred yards away, the burnt-out shell of the farmhouse. That proved that there were no people close by. With the Germans gone, I had the chance to head west. As I neared the gate I worked out that I would probably reach the German lines at dark and that would be my best chance to escape.

On reaching the gate I waited and listened. I saw that the gate was secured by a piece of rope. I unloosed it from the post but did not open the gate. I listened. The road, which appeared to be narrow, was, once more, silent. I slowly opened the gate and eased myself through it. I glanced to my right and the road was empty. I turned my head to the left and found myself looking down the barrel of a German rifle.

The German officer standing behind the soldier said something in German. I did not understand what he said and I heard the bolt on the rifle click ominously. The officer gestured with his Luger and I raised my hands. He smiled and said something which sounded like 'Good.' He took my Webley and pointed up the road, to the left. There was the vehicle I had heard and there were six German soldiers standing nearby with their rifles pointed at me.

As I trudged up the road I visualised the prospect of spending the rest of the war in a prisoner-of-war camp. I smiled to myself. At least I could keep my promise to Beattie and survive the war.

Chapter 26

I was placed in the back of the German lorry. Four of the occupants kept their guns trained on me. I hoped they had their safety catches on otherwise one bump might be fatal. I expected a long drive to somewhere in the east; a large headquarters perhaps but we drove for no more than seven or eight minutes. When I was helped from the back I saw that I was at an airfield. There was a mixture of aeroplanes lined up. I recognised the AEG, the Fokker E 1 and a couple of Halberstadts. A young officer strolled over towards us. He had a guard with him but the guard's rifle was slung over his shoulder.

He said something in German to my captors who saluted him and then climbed back aboard the lorry and drove through the sentries at the gate. He held out his hand and said, in quite good English, "I am Lieutenant Josef Jacobs of Jasta 22. You are now our prisoner." I shook his hand. "But I hope we can be civilised and treat you as a guest. You are, after all, a fellow flier."

"I am Captain Bill Harsker of 41 Squadron."

"Good, pleased to meet you." He shrugged apologetically and lifted the flap on my holster. He saw that my service revolver had gone. "Just checking. Please follow me." I saw the glow from the open door and I heard the boisterous noise of pilots who were celebrating. I was being taken to the mess.

The guard took my greatcoat, helmet and goggles; I took the pipe and tobacco from the pocket and entered. He remained outside. The room went silent as I entered. It was similar to ours and there were roughly the same number of officers. White coated orderlies stood around the side and I saw that I had arrived at mealtime. An older officer came up to me and he held out his hand. My escort said, "This is Staffelführer Rudolph Windisch, the commanding officer of this Jasta," He shook my hand and said something.

"Captain Bill Harsker."

My interpreter led me to the head of the table and I was seated between the Staffelführer and the lieutenant. I noticed that the Staffelführer was younger than me.

The orderlies brought food and wine. I was starving but I knew enough about the protocol to wait until everyone else ate. The Staffelführer said something and everyone stood with their glass in their hand. They all turned to face the photograph of the Kaiser and said something before drinking. I raised my glass and drank. The Staffelführer nodded his approval.

We sat and they began to eat. I ate as slowly as I could manage despite the fact that I was ravenous. I could see the young officers staring at me but everyone ate in silence. That was a difference with our mess where chatter and banter were the order of the day. We finished, not with cheese, as we did in our mess but with a many-layered chocolate cake covered in cream. It was delicious but I could not imagine eating it too often. It would have been too sickly.

After the plates had been cleared we were given a clear spirit which I knew to be Schnapps. I had enough sense to drink this carefully. They all looked at me expectantly. The lieutenant asked me questions which he translated from the others.

"Are you the pilot who flies the small Sopwith with the picture of the horse on the side?"

I nodded, "I am."

When he translated the answer I received a round of applause. I looked at Josef questioningly. He smiled, "You were the one who returned the effects of the dead bomber crew. We respect that and your aeroplane is known to us. You are a fine pilot."

"Thank you." I took out my pipe, "May I?"

"Of course."

I got the pipe going and he asked, "The Staffelführer wants to know why the horse? Is it a family name perhaps?"

I shook my head, "No, I began the war in the cavalry."

When that was translated I received a second round of applause. The Staffelführer clapped me on the back and said something.

"He says you are a true knight. He, too, was in the cavalry briefly and that you are brothers beneath the skin."

The evening turned out to be far more pleasant than the one I had expected. I was careful not to drink too much and to tell them nothing which might be considered a secret. To be honest they were more interested in the Pup and how it flew. It seems our three Pups in this sector had caused something of a stir.

I wondered how long I would be there. When the Staffelführer went to the bathroom I asked Josef, for we were on first-name terms, about my future, "What happens now?"

He looked at me sadly, "The day after tomorrow you will be taken to a prisoner of war camp." He shrugged apologetically and then brightened, "However tomorrow evening we will be honoured by a visit of Baron Manfred Von Richthofen, our greatest ace. He is keen to meet for you managed to drive him from the skies today and that is rare."

"I thought I recognised his red Albatros."

"He is a great ace. He is an inspiration to us all." Once again he gave me an apologetic look. "I am afraid that we will have to put an armed guard outside your room but…"

"I understand."

For the remainder of the evening, I was formulating my escape plan. There was little point in trying to get out at night; not without knowing the layout of the field. I would be able to see that the next day and then escape after the evening meal. I had had no hope when I had been taken prisoner but now I had some.

"Come, I will escort you to your room."

The mess all stood and saluted as I left. It was bizarre. We fought and died in the air as enemies and yet I had just been treated as a cousin visiting a relative abroad.

Although not a cell, the room they had given me had no window and was crudely furnished. I did not mind. As my dad might have said, *'Where there is life there is hope'*. I would make the best of any opportunities which came my way. I chuckled when I remembered Lumpy's words too, "Nils Desperandum'.

After I had washed and put on the pyjamas they had provided I examined the room for any weapon. They had not searched me nor had they asked for my word that I would not escape. I think they assumed that, as a gentleman, I would not try. I still had my Luger in my boot and I had put them beneath the bed in case the guard came into my room during the night. As a precaution, I placed the chair close to the door so that it would make a noise if anyone tried to enter. I was finally ready for sleep. I closed my eyes and tried to find a way to escape back to the British lines.

The German bugle awoke me the next morning and I smiled as I remembered Lumpy. I dressed quickly so that I would have my boots on when the guard came in. As it turned out they were in no hurry for me to leave the room. I heard the sound of aeroplane engines roaring down the airfield and wondered where they had gone. It was Josef who came for me. He apologised, "The squadron has taken off for a mission and the Staffelführer thought it would be insensitive for you to have to watch them."

They didn't know me! It would not have worried me in the least. After breakfast, Josef and our guard took me on a tour of the airfield. "Why are you not flying today, Josef?"

He looked a little embarrassed. "I damaged my aeroplane when landing the other day and we are waiting for spares. My gunner is not happy about it. Come I will show you my aeroplane."

I saw the mechanics around a two-seater. It was an LVG and the engine was in bits. He would not be flying soon. He spoke briefly with the mechanics and then shrugged as we walked away. "They say three more days." He shook his head, sadly, "I will be sorry to see you go."

"Why?"

"Because tomorrow, after you leave I have to fly that!" He pointed to an old Aviatik. I had not seen one in the air for a year or so. "And I hate spotting. I would be like you, a fighter pilot!"

"It looks as though it has not flown for a while."

"No, we use it to train fresh pilots. The mechanics will be working on it today. When it is ready we will test the engine and take it for a test flight" He had given me too much information. If he was flying the Aviatik then he was spotting for artillery. That was valuable intelligence.

We wandered the base for a couple of hours. I saw that they had a similar defensive arrangement as we did but they appeared to have specially trained gunners on the machine guns with their own officers. We returned to the mess for coffee and some more of the chocolate cake. Josef look sadly at the coffee pot. "Coffee will have to be rationed soon. With America in the war, w,e only get it from our allies, the Turks. I will miss my coffee."

I discovered much about young Josef. He came from Stuttgart and his father had been a soldier in the Franco-Prussian War. He had been a cavalryman. Josef asked me many questions about my time in the cavalry. I felt more comfortable answering those questions as they could not compromise our war efforts. The cavalry were no longer a fighting force, sadly.

I asked him about his English. "We had a governess for the family and she was English. My father had admired your Queen Victoria, who was a relative of the Kaiser. I grew up speaking English before I could speak German."

"It is excellent."

"If the war had not come along I would have gone to Oxford to study. I would have liked that."

"You still can."

"Perhaps." He did not look convinced. I wondered at the similarities in the pilots I had met here and those at home. Freddie and Johnny would have fitted right in with the German pilots.

"Tell me, Captain Harsker, when you were in the cavalry did you kill?"

"Yes."

"You see, in the air, we rarely see who we kill do we?"

"Sometimes you do but you are right it is rare."

"My father said that when you use a sword to kill a man it is hard but once you have done it then every other death becomes easier. Is that true?"

I remembered the last Germans I had killed in close combat in old Albert's house in Belgium. "Never easier but you lose the hesitation. Often it is his life or yours. You do what you must to survive."

"I understand. I now know why you have shot down so many of our aeroplanes. You are like the Baron, you have the killer instinct."

We heard the drone of engines and walked to the window to watch the mixed formation land. I could see that they had lost an aeroplane. The slumped shoulders of the younger pilots spoke volumes. I said, "I will go to my room, Josef. It would be awkward to be here when you have lost a pilot."

He nodded, "You are a gentleman. Franz here will go with you."

The guard, Franz, spoke no English but he smiled more now and seemed quite happy to follow us around. His gun was always over his shoulder. I had another reason for returning to my room, I wanted to work out my escape plan. It had been brewing in my head all morning. Josef's chatter had stopped me from clarifying it. I sat in the chair and smoked my pipe. By the time the tobacco was all gone, I knew what I would have to do. I felt guilty that Josef would be hurt by my action but I was an officer and it was my duty to escape. If I did not leave in the next eighteen hours then I would never leave. The car which was coming to take me away would here by noon the next day.

Franz knocked on my door, "Please, come."

He looked inordinately pleased with his new English. I smiled at the young soldier. "Thank you, Franz, good!"

He beamed and I was led to the mess where they were preparing for lunch.

The Staffelführer bombarded me with more questions. This time, however, it was questions about England and my background. He seemed surprised to discover that my family had been servants. Josef asked, "The Staffelführer wants to know is this usual?"

"In most squadrons, no, but in ours, there are a number of us who have come from the ranks."

"The Staffelführer says you are a natural pilot. He knows that his friend, the Baron, is impressed with you."

"When will he be arriving?" The question was reasonable but it would affect my escape plans.

"He will be here for dinner. We are honoured to have him and the Staffelführer has arranged for a fine meal. It will be a banquet to celebrate the Baron's recent victories." He looked embarrassed, "Sorry. They were your comrades."

I shrugged, "It is war."

During the afternoon I went with Josef and Franz when he went to look at the Aviatik. He was annoyed that there was just one mechanic working on it. There was an exchange of words. He turned to me, red-faced and angry. "This fool says he cannot see what the fault is."

"I thought you did not wish to fly this old aeroplane?"

He looked offended, "I do not want to but it is my duty and besides if I survive in this then the Staffelführer has promised me a chance in a fighter."

I laughed and took off my tunic. "Then, in that case, I had better give him a hand."

"You are a mechanic?"

I shook my head, "No, but I know my way around an engine."

He was right, the mechanic was not very good but he made a good assistant. I quite enjoyed getting my hands dirty and oily again. It had been some time since I had been allowed to do this. I stood back. I fiddled around and found the fault. It was a loose lead. "Right Josef, I think we can give it a go. Hop in."

He climbed in. Franz and I stepped back. The mechanic spun the propeller and it coughed, spluttered, spun around a couple of times and then stopped. "Hang on, I think I know what it is." I took a screwdriver and turned a screw two notches. "Try that!"

This time it coughed, spluttered and caught. Josef was delighted. He shouted down, "Climb up and we will take her up."

I climbed into the front seat. "We will have to wait for a few moments. It takes time for this old engine to warm up." After a few minutes, he seemed happy and he tapped me on the shoulder, "Now we fly."

The young pilot took us down the airfield and we climbed into the sky. He did a loop of the field. It was a slow beast after the Pup and I found the huge engine in front of me a distraction. Had the arrangement been the other way around I could have forced Josef to fly me over our lines. He was, however, behind me and I could not use my Luger. I just had to enjoy the flight and get a view of the land around the airfield.

We landed and the Staffelführer came over. He snapped angrily at Josef who coloured and then rattled out his answer. The Staffelführer stopped scowling and started to smile. Josef looked relieved, "He asks how you learned about engines."

"I learned about them when I learned to drive." I smiled, "Tell him it is a handy skill to have."

When my answer was translated Josef said, "The Staffelführer agrees with you." he pointed to my hands. "We had better get you cleaned up before the Baron arrives."

I found myself becoming excited about meeting the infamous Red Baron. I took especial care with my toilet and I made sure that my moustache was trimmed and I had a close shave. They did not trust me with a razor but Franz proved quite adept with a blade. I was brought to the mess before the famous ace arrived and we waited for his car to pull up.

I was surprised, when he walked in, for he looked to be younger than I had expected. He was my age. He was, however, a very gregarious and pleasant chap. I saw the reaction of the squadron and saw that this was hero worship. Surprisingly it did not seem to affect him. He was led directly to me. "So you are the English pilot who nearly shot me down."

I watched his face as his words were translated. He was weighing me up and my reaction. "Yes, sir, I think I would have done if it were not for your comrades."

There was a silence and then he laughed, he nudged the Staffelführer and said something. They both laughed. "He said that it cost him a bottle of schnapps for Ernst Udet, his rescuer."

I would be lying if I said that it was an unpleasant evening. It was not. Richthofen was courteous and amusing. He told me that he was a Freiherr and although this also meant Baron all the male members of his family were allowed the title. His younger brother Lothar was also accorded the title. It told me much about this German. He was more like Lord Burscough than me. He had noble blood. He was complimentary about the Pup which he admired.

I found myself enjoying the conversation. I asked him about his brightly coloured aeroplanes. He told me that it helped to identify his pilots in the air. I was flattered that they had noticed my three Pups with the pictures of the horses. "You see you do it too," he had smiled, "in an understated English way."

Like the Staffelführer he was fascinated by my rise in fortunes. "You are a gentleman. Your behaviour with the dead crews' effects proved that and yet you were born a servant, a groom?"

"I suppose I had good teachers."

He pointed at my medals. "What is this one?"

"The Military Cross."

"Is the V.C. higher than that?" I nodded, "And I see you have the highest French honour. That is unusual. Tell me how you won that."

I told him and he seemed happy with the story, despite the fact that I had shot down Germans. I pointed to one on his own chest I had not seen on any of the other fliers, "And what is this one?"

He seemed proud of it. "This is our highest honour. Pour le Mérite, the Blue Max." He went on to tell me how he had won it. "You and I are the same and yet I come from a noble family and you are the son of a servant. War is the great leveller is it not? It is skill in the air which counts and not breeding. I am glad that I have met you."

He rose after he had smoked his cigar and drunk his brandy. He looked sadly at me as he shook my hand. Josef translated for us, "I am sorry that you will go to camp. You are a flier, a knight and you should die in the air and have glory."

I was not certain that I would like that particular end but I nodded politely. "Farewell horseman!"

The Staffelführer insisted on having a final schnapps of the night. He was a little drunk and, like Richthofen, he was sad that I could not be returned to my squadron. I nearly told him that it would be easy; he could just fly me there but I had learned that they had a set of rules and they adhered closely to them.

As I lay in bed that night I knew that I might only have one chance the next day but I would need to take it.

Chapter 27

The pilots all shook my hand before they took off for their sortie. I hoped they would all return for they had been such pleasant and affable chaps but I also hoped that they would not kill any British or Commonwealth soldiers. My life had suddenly become complicated. I had breakfast and Josef joined me. He looked sad.

"You will be gone when I return from my test flight."

"When do you take off?"

"In an hour or so."

"Are you waiting for your gunner?"

He shook his head. "He is with the Jasta, I am going up alone." He smiled, "Come with me while I check the engine. You can watch me take off and see what a fine flier I am. Your car will be sometime this morning."

"Do you mind if I get my coat then?"

"Of course." He sent Franz off to get the coat. I realised then how trusting this young pilot was and I felt guilty about what I was about to do.

Franz came running back and held out the greatcoat for me to don. We walked across to the aeroplane. There was no mechanic. Josef looked irritably at his watch. "Where is the fool?"

"Perhaps I could start it for you?"

"If you wouldn't mind?"

He climbed in and I spun the propeller. After a couple of coughs and splutters, it started. As Franz watched the propeller spin I put my hand into my boot, pulled out the Luger and slipped it into my greatcoat pocket. He climbed down while the engine throbbed unevenly. He was waiting for it to run regularly. He held out his hand, "This is goodbye I think."

"Goodbye Josef and thank you for your kindness."

I had the Luger in my left-hand pocket and, as I held out my hand to Franz I pulled the Luger out. They were both facing me and looked shocked. "Tell Franz to drop the gun and lie on the floor."

"You will not shoot us. You are a gentleman."

I shifted the gun to my right hand. "The German I took this from was a gentleman too until I killed him. I told you, Josef, I am a killer. Now I can just shoot you both in the kneecap and cripple you for life but I don't want to. You have been kind. Now stop me from shooting Franz and order him to lie down."

I saw the indecision on his face and I lowered the gun to point at the soldier's knee. I saw him bunch his fists. He was ten feet away and would be dead before he could strike me. Josef's shoulders slumped and he shouted something to Franz who lay down.

"Good, Now you."

"I will shoot you down for this Englishman."

"I would expect nothing less. My aeroplane will have the white horse on the side of the cockpit; remember that." He nodded. "Now on the floor."

As he did so I leapt into the cockpit. I could see soldiers running from the main building. I fired four random shots towards them and they leapt to the ground. I did not bother with the helmet and goggles which were lying on the floor I headed down the airfield as fast as the old bus would manage. As I lifted off I heard the crack of rifles. They missed. I knew that the Aviatik was a slow aeroplane. I would be lucky to make sixty miles an hour. That meant it would be almost an hour before I reached the airfield. I had to run the gauntlet of German and British fighters and German and British guns. I had no doubt that the airfield would be letting all and sundry know that they had lost an aeroplane and a prisoner.

I began to climb. As I recalled, from conversations with Franz, the ceiling was about ten thousand feet. I would need all of that. I was just grateful that it was a stable machine. I still did not like the radiator sticking up in front of me although my vision was not as impaired as it had been in the gunner's seat.

I managed to reach the German trenches before I hit trouble. The trouble came in the form of a couple of BE 2s. They were brave souls for they were classic Fokker fodder. They saw me and realised they had an easy kill. I did the only thing I could, I flew directly at them. Their gun was rear-facing and in the front cockpit. They would try to go on either side of me and rake me with both guns at the same time. As I approached them I lifted the nose slightly to make them think I was climbing. They would be wondering why I was not heading east. They were just fifteen miles an hour faster than me and I needed to open a gap between us.

When we were just fifty yards apart and closing rapidly I pushed the stick forward and went into a steep dive. I had no mirror to see what they were doing but I had an idea. I would make it impossible for them to fire at me. Their guns could not depress and they were forced to bank. The very act of banking would put one behind the other. They were a big aeroplane with a wide turning circle and I had an idea that I could gain more than half a mile on them by my manoeuvre. Of course, I would then have to brave the British trenches in a slow-moving German aeroplane but I had to cross one bridge at a time. The dive had given me extra speed and I zoomed over the British lines at a thousand feet. I saw holes from the small arms fire appear in my wings. So long as the engine ran I would still be able to fly. Out of the corner of my eye, I saw, not the BE 2 but a pair of Bristols. They were well to the north but at their speed, they would be over me like fleas on a dog.

Having passed the trenches I dropped the nose to hedgehop. I was less than ten minutes from my home field. I estimated that the Bristols would be on me in eight! I saw the burnt-out farmhouse which marked the outer marker for the airfield. I looked down into the cockpit but there was no Very pistol. That might have saved me. The Bristols were out of sight and I assumed they were lining up behind their leader to take turns at shooting a sitting duck. I recognised the heavy sound of the Vickers and then felt the judder as the bullets hit my tail and fuselage. I literally clipped the hedges as I lowered the nose. As the bullets thundered in to me I saw the windsock in the field fluttering away. I thought I was going to make it when a long burst from a Vickers tore through my right upper wing and it crumpled. My German saviour dipped and the lower wing caught the ground. As it dug in the whole aeroplane began to slew and spin around. The seat belt broke and I was thrown from the aeroplane. Everything went black as I hit the ground.

"Hands Hoch Fritz. Come on!"

I recognised the voice. I tasted the grass and soil. I was face down. I raised my head slightly. "Flight Sergeant Richardson, that is no way to talk to your commanding officer!" Suddenly hands turned me over and I looked up into the barrels of four Lee Enfields. I pushed them away. "Not strictly necessary eh, Percy?"

He helped me to my feet. "Sorry sir, we saw the Hun and we thought.... sorry sir."

I tried to move my arm and my chest hurt as though I had had a ton weight on it. I winced.

"Get a stretcher for Captain Harsker! Here sir. You lie down. You are hurt."

"I am fine."

He put his hand to my head and it came away bloody. I tried to say something but my legs would not support me and everything went black again.

I heard the voices and the conversation in my dark and comfortable world. "How is he Doc?"

"Archie, he has just been brought in but at the moment I would say he has a slight concussion." He pushed into my ribs and I gave a yelp. "And I guess broken ribs too." I opened my eyes and saw Archie, the Doc and Randolph staring down at me. "And he is awake! Welcome back to the war, Bill."

I could see the relief on their faces. "Archie, aren't you supposed to be recuperating in Blighty?"

I saw he had a bandage on."Aye, laddie, I was but when Randolph here rang your young lady, what a peach she is, by the way, to tell her you were behind enemy lines then I discharged myself and hitched a lift over here."

"You had us worried but how on earth did you manage to steal an aeroplane?"

Doc Brennan held up his hand. "He's awake. You can tell everyone that he will live and I will sort him out. Questions later!"

As they left Randolph chuckled. "I will have to ask Cecil Alldardyce if he still wants to claim the Aviatik bearing in mind it was the squadron's leading ace who was flying it."

I closed my eyes as the doctor and his orderlies saw to me. I had escaped so why did I feel so bad? I should feel elated that I had cheated both death and the Germans but it was the thought of poor Josef and Franz getting into trouble on my account. I felt like I had been, in some way, dishonourable. I had never given my word not to escape and it was their fault for not searching me closely. Even so, it did not sit well with me.

"There, all done." I opened my eyes and sat up. The orderly began to dress me. "No flying for a few days." He chuckled, "Not that you can. Your flight does not have an aeroplane between you. Your young lieutenants are climbing the walls waiting for those Camels of yours. They were so bored they took the car and went into Amiens to buy more tobacco and brandy. They will be sorry to have missed you." I stood up and winced. "I can give you some painkillers for the ribs. I am afraid they will just set in their own time."

I nodded, "I know, I was in the cavalry. This happened every time you fell off. You learned not to fall off. I won't bother with the pain killers. I still have some brandy left."

I left the sickbay and headed towards the office. Bates ran across to me, his face filled with joy. "I heard you had returned sir. Shall I run you a bath? You will want one I dare say."

"Not today. I have bandages on my ribs. Perhaps tomorrow?"

"Righto, sir." He looked disapprovingly at my soiled tunic. There was a mixture of blood, dirt and oil on it. "And the tunic?"

"I'll call in at the office and then you can make me respectable again." That seemed to satisfy him and he went off to my quarters. I had no doubt there was not a speck of dust anywhere but I knew that he would make sure.

Archie and Randolph were in the office. "I'll shift my stuff out of your office Archie."

"No rush. I don't think I will be doing any flying for a long time. I have the use of my arm but it is far from perfect. Doc Brennan reckons six months or so." He shrugged, "I can't sit on my arse for that length of time while you blokes are doing my work. I will become a desk-bound commanding officer for a while. By the way, General Trenchard is sending a car for you tomorrow. He wants you debriefed by Intelligence." The displeasure must have shown on my face. "I am afraid it goes with the territory besides the Camels aren't here yet. Perhaps you could mention them to the General?"

I looked around, "Where are the rest of the squadron?"

"There was just Alldardyce and Ellis around when you returned. Both had engine trouble. Ted and Gordy are on patrol."

"Well, the Germans are sending up spotters and bombers. The Jasta who captured me had a mixture of bombers and spotters and the Flying Circus was not far away."

"How do you know?"

"I met the Red Baron."

They both stopped their work and started at me. The orderly sergeant did too. The newspapers had been full of the man who shot down Lanoe Hawker. "Really?"

I nodded and began to fill my pipe. "Yes, and it might surprise you but you would like him if you met him. He is just like us."

"But the showy colours on his buses?"

"It helps with identification and he reckons it creates good esprit de corps. I think there is something in it. He said he had seen the horses painted on our buses and knew that I was a kindred spirit."

"Sounds like you got quite chummy."

"I had dinner with him. I think they relaxed around me and that helped me to escape."

"Sarn't, go and get a pot of tea while Bill tells us all."

I spent the next thirty minutes telling them all that had happened. They were so engrossed that they failed to hear the Bristols returning.

Gordy and Ted entered the office and their mouths fell open. Gordy suddenly began to laugh, "That Aviatik in the field- is that yours?"

"Yes, Lieutenant Alldardyce is getting better at shooting down Germans."

"Tell us all!"

Archie shook his head, "There will be time enough for that. Your reports please."

Ted shook his head, "We jumped a squadron of bombers. We shot a couple down and then the Red Baron and his lads arrived. We lost Short and Gilfoyle."

"Did you shoot any of theirs down?"

"Just one." Something in my voice must have told Ted that I was interested. "Why?"

"I had dinner with the Red Baron last night and if the squadron had green rudders then I was their guest for the last two days."

Ted shook his head and laughed, "Yours will be a short life my son but by hell, it will be interesting!"

As I left the office Archie reached into his pocket, "By the way, this is for you. Your young lady scribbled it as I left." He handed me the note.

"Thank you, sir."

I resisted the temptation to read it in front of the others in case I could not contain myself. Once outside I opened it eagerly.

Bill,

I don't know if you will ever read this. Your Major has told me that you were shot down behind the enemy lines. You are alive and, although you will be a prisoner you are alive!

I want you to know that I will wait for you, no matter how long this war lasts. I promise you that. You are the only man in my life and the only one I want.

I love you,

1917 Eagles Fall

Beattie xxx
I don't know why but that note made me feel ten feet tall.

Chapter 28

The General's car arrived bright and early the next day. I was whisked to Amiens where the General and four senior officers awaited me along with an Intelligence officer, Captain Fleming.

They noted my bandaged head. It was like the scene from the painting, *'Where is your father?'* The six of them peered at me like vultures about to devour a carcass.

The General waved his arm in my direction. "Gentlemen may I introduce Captain Bill Harsker. As you can see he has a few medals, one of them from the French. He has crashed twice; the first time he escaped across the Channel and the second time he stole a German aeroplane and was shot down by his own men. He has forty kills to his name and he has met, apparently, the Red Baron. He has also landed behind the enemy lines to rescue one of his pilots on the back of a Sopwith Pup! I think this should be illuminating for us all."

If I did not have their attention before I certainly did now. I was grilled, again, by all of them but the most pertinent questions came from Captain Fleming. Whilst the senior officers wished to know about the Red Baron and such the Captain seemed preoccupied with the minutiae of the Jasta. I could see why. He wanted to know what made the organisations tick. Heroes came and went but the structures remained.

At the end of an hour, I was finished. The senior officers left. Captain Fleming shook my hand as he left. "Do you mind if I come by your field and see you again? I think there may be more hidden inside your head than you know."

"I think I am just lucky. I don't know much."

"You are doing yourself a disservice. I know of spies who have spent less time behind German lines than you. I think we could write a pamphlet to give pilots in case they are shot down behind enemy lines."

I shrugged, "Perhaps."

"I think it is a damned good idea. See to it, Fleming."

"Sir."

Once alone he took out his pipe and filled it. "We were all worried when you were shot down you know. Ball and Hawker were both shot down. There are a couple of Canadians, Bishop and Collinshaw who are doing quite well but you are the leading RFC ace. It is important for recruitment that you stay alive. There are lads in England who want to be like you. I have no idea how long this war will continue but we will need more pilots than enough."

"Are we still haemorrhaging pilots, sir?"

He nodded, "The youth of our country are being sacrificed almost daily." He pushed a piece of paper over to me. "You are being rewarded for your efforts. You are being given the acting rank of major. I wanted it permanent but it seems you have enemies in high places." I must have shown my puzzlement for he added, "Major Ramsden."

"Ah, I see. Thank you anyway, sir."

"It will just make life easier for you should you have to command again, and of course," he chuckled, "it makes you the same rank as Ramsden."

I smiled, "Thank you, sir, that is handy. He seems to think I do not have the class to be an officer."

"I think that when this war is over we will stop worrying so much about class and judge a man by his actions. And the other thing is that you have been recommended for the V.C. for rescuing Holt. That was damned foolish but damned brave. I am not certain I would have risked it in a Pup."

"The Red Baron seems to appreciate them."

"Does he really? Well your Camels will be here by the end of the week but we have another Sopwith which will be ready by the end of the month; a tri-plane. Interested?"

"No, sir. From what I have heard the Camel is a better version of the Pup and I have never flown a tri-plane."

"Well the Camel is a better platform and," he leaned back and smiled, "it has two synchronised Vickers. Let's see what you can do with those."

As I left the Headquarters building I bumped into Major Ramsden, quite literally. He didn't see who I was and he just said, "Fool! Watch where you are going!"

When he looked up and saw me he scowled, "I might have known it would be you. No manners at all. Well? Where is your salute and sir!"

I smiled, "I am sorry major, I have only been a major for ten minutes I was not certain of the protocol."

His mouth opened and closed like a fish. "What but I..."

"It is only temporary but still...."

I turned and walked towards the General's car. It was a small victory but worth savouring. As I was driven back I decided that it was not worth mentioning the V.C. to the others. It would sound like bragging and besides, it might not come through. I had been disappointed once before and I would not get my hopes up.

The sad faces back at the field told me that we had lost crews again. This time it was Lieutenant Ellis. Two gunners had also been wounded. The good news, from Ted, was that they had managed to knock out a D.III. It was a better sign but we were still frustrated by the fact that the Camels had not arrived.

My senior colleagues were delighted by my promotion. "Well deserved, Billy boy. We'll have a wee dram to celebrate!"

"It's only temporary. They can always take it away."

"Only if the war ends next week and I can't see any sign of that, can you?"

Poor Lieutenant Alldardyce did not know where to look at dinner. He just looked embarrassed throughout the whole meal. His discomfort was not helped by the ribbing he received from everyone except for Freddie. His head drooped lower and lower as he endured the sarcastic comments.

When we retired to the lounge I sought him out. He began to apologise again and I held up my hand. "Despite what those jokers said you did the right thing in shooting me down. You could have had no idea it was me and suppose it had been a German bomber; what then? It might have done some serious damage to the base. You were right to shoot me down!"

"I don't know about that, sir."

"Well I do and I have told Captain Marshall to award you the kill. It was a damned fine shot. And if those jokers say anything you tell them I said you did the right thing."

"Thank you, sir. You know Airman Speight thinks very highly of you. All of the gunners do. You are a legend. You began life as a gunner and now you are the leading ace in the squadron. If I had killed you then I don't know if I could have gone on."

I laughed, "Captain Hewitt will tell you that I am a tough old bugger. It takes a lot to kill me!"

We realised that the Arras Offensive had petered out. The last actions over the next few days would be in bloody Bullecourt where our soldiers fought for inches to drive the Germans from the village. We had gained ground. It was not as much ground as we had held after the first few days but we were moving east. Ted, at dinner, took out a piece of paper and a pencil and did some calculations. "Well, that's alright then. Gordy, your son will be twenty-eight by the time we reach Berlin!"

We had two days of rain before the new buses and replacement pilots arrived. The doc cleared all three of us for active duty. For Freddie and Johnnie, it had been days of hell! When the Camels landed we winced as they were bumped across the field by their ferry pilots. Flight Sergeant Lowery stormed over to the pilots. I saw him gesticulating at the undercarriage and ranting at them. They disappeared as soon as they could. We waited until the five Bristols had landed before we went over. The flying skills of these pilots was more important to us than ferry pilots.

The three of them were even worse than the ferry pilots. Ted shook his head, "They are dead men flying."

I pointed to the Camels as we walked over. "We have those now. They have two Vickers and are more than eleven miles an hour quicker. The SE 5 is a faster bus but it is not a better one. The three of us will have to work twice as hard until these lads are bedded in."

"Or buried!" said Ted ominously. He nodded to us, "You go and check your Camels out. We'll have a word with our young eagles here!"

Gordy and Harry followed him. They knew how to turn poor pilots with a life expectancy of hours into the likes of Harry Dodds. I was not worried. Flight Sergeant Lowery was almost caressing the Camel. "Bloody ferry pilots! They really annoy me they..."

"Give you the hump?"

"Yes, sir they... oh very funny sir, hilarious! Laugh? I thought my pants would never dry!" He wandered off chuntering.

I had the specifications in my hand. "It is shorter and lower than the Pup but it has an extra one foot six of wingspan. It can climb two thousand feet higher and has a top speed of a hundred and seventeen miles an hour."

"Which means that Fritz can't run away any more when we start winning!"

I liked the new aeroplane before it had even been flown. It was roughly the same size as the Pup with far more power and twice the guns. I shouted to the Senior Flight Sergeant, "Don't forget to fit a rearview mirror." He waved. "When will they be ready?"

He considered a witty answer and then said, "Tomorrow afternoon, Major." He smiled and saluted, "Congratulations sir. It is well deserved."

We spent another hour checking the new buses on the ground and then I joined Gordy and Ted putting the new pilots through their paces. We had the advantage that the recently trained pilots who had survived also put in their two pennorth! With just one in each of the other three flights, there would be a more experienced pilot to perch on their shoulders.

Doc Brennan called me over as I walked to lunch. "Come to sickbay while I check you over."

No matter what he said I would be flying as soon as the new bus was ready.

After fifteen minutes he said. "Just take it easy but I will pass you fit." He shook his head, "It will stop you disobeying your doctor's orders."

After lunch, we allocated the pilots and prepared for the mission the next day. "I have a feeling that, if we are over Bullecourt then we may run into Richthofen. It is his hunting ground and I believe he will be looking for me."

Gordy cocked an eyebrow, "Really?"

"I am not being big-headed Gordy. He sees this as some sort of medieval contest between knights on chargers. We just use aeroplanes. I think that is the real reason he used the fancy paintwork. It is like heraldry. I am a challenge to him. Believe me, he is revered by the other pilots. There was a silence when he walked in the mess. It was like a church on a Sunday! They had their best silver for him and so much food we could have fed the squadron for a week. Do not underestimate him. The last time we tangled he outran the Pup and I was isolated. I won't be on my own this time and he will not be able to run."

"It sounds like you are ready for this?"

"Let's just say, Archie, that I am fed up with our young pilots becoming marks on the side of the aeroplanes. It is time for a little payback. The Bristol is a good aeroplane but the Camel is better. If these new pilots can last a week then I think we can rule the skies."

Archie laughed as he poured us all a whisky, "General Trenchard certainly lit a fire under you, Bill. Here's to the squadron!"

When I reached my quarters Bates had just finished sewing my crowns on to my epaulettes. "That might be a waste of time, John. This might only be temporary."

He snorted, "Even the brass hats can't be that stupid." He proffered the tunic. "Let's see what it looks like on."

I put it on and he stood back. "There, very smart. I'll have the other two finished for tomorrow, sir."

After I had written a letter to Beattie I walked back out to the field with my pipe. I wanted to look at the Camels again. I saw that Freddie and Johnnie were talking with Senior Flight Sergeant Lowery.

They turned as I approached. "Any problems, Flight?"

"No, Major, for once they have come ready to fly and those ferry boys didn't actually do any damage."

"Excellent." I winked at Freddie, "We can take them up for a test flight now then can't we?"

His mouth opened and closed and then he said, warily, "Yes sir. I'll get a couple of the lads."

He went off shouting for some mechanics to start them. I turned to the two of them. "We might as well see how high they can go. We'll take them up and then do a few loops. I think they will loop as well as the Pup."

"Me too, sir, and I was thinking of trying that loop of yours where you put the bus on its side. It always seems to throw the Germans off."

"Right, we will have an hour's practice and then land. When I come down you come."

"Yes sir!" they chorused.

The take off was just as quick as that in a Pup and the climb was exquisitely quick. I took them in as steep a climb as we could. I was amazed. We rose a thousand feet a minute! That was fast. I realised as we levelled out, that I should have brought my greatcoat. I was freezing. I waved to the other two and put the Camel into a dive. It was frighteningly fast. The loops we performed were just as tight as those in the Pups. As we came in to land I looked at the twin Vickers; this was firepower. This could make the difference! We landed and the three of us were full of praise for the Camel.

We were eager to be in the air and in action again the next morning. The battle of Bullecourt was still going on and our orders took us there. The bomber squadrons had taken a recent hammering and we were there merely to stop the Germans from observing our movements and attacking any ground targets. With Archie back in command, I could concentrate on leading the squadron.

The night before I had decided on a new plan of attack. C Flight would lead with me in the middle, Freddie to port and Johnny to starboard. Alldardyce would tuck in behind me. We would fly above and in front of the other three flights. Ted would fly in the middle with Gordy to his right and Harry to his left. They would fly the same formation as my flight. I had reasoned that it gave us the maximum firepower in the middle while giving flexibility and a reserve. The rear aeroplane in each formation could deal with any attacks from the rear.

As we approached the front I saw the explosions from small arms and grenades as the Tommies and the Aussies tried to establish some sort of control. It had been a brutal six weeks but, mercifully, it had not cost as many casualties nor had it dragged on as long.

I was not expecting too many German aeroplanes; they had been in constant action over the past weeks. I knew from my conversations with Josef that they suffered wear and tear just as much as we did. I was, therefore, surprised when I saw a formation of eight bombers being escorted by ten fighters. It looked as though they were heading for our guns.

We were at the same altitude and so I began to climb. I only needed to take us a thousand feet or so higher and that would give us a greater attack speed. I looked in my mirror and saw that Alldardyce was struggling. The powerful Camels ate up the sky. I levelled out as the Germans saw us. Our smaller profile made us harder to see. Richthofen had told me that. It gave us a few seconds advantage. It was the main reason I had chosen to fly ahead of the main formation.

The fighters climbed towards us. Again, our talk had enabled us to come up with a strategy for this situation. Harry would lead his flight down to engage with the bombers. He would be outnumbered but he would have a superior bus. We would, hopefully, outnumber the Germans.

I still could see their colours for they were head-on but I could see that they were the Albatros D.III. I hoped they would only see a flight of Pups. They were in for a shock when the twin Vickers opened up on them. We were closing rapidly as we dived to meet them. The combined speed was approaching two hundred and forty miles an hour- a frightening speed which needed the quickest of reactions. I took in the fact that they did not appear to be the Flying Circus and then put the Red Baron from my mind. I aimed the Camel at the leading Albatros. I saw a pennant fluttering from the rudder. That was new but I suspected it meant a Staffelführer.

At two hundred yards, I gave a short burst. I was slightly off but the beauty of the two Vickers meant that my bullets still hit him. My smaller size and my speed meant that his bullets zipped harmlessly above the top wing. That sometimes happened when you were firing at an enemy above you. The sound of the six Vickers as they ripped the air before us was breathtaking. The German pilots were not expecting the torrent of bullets. As we approached them they tried to climb above us. I pulled hard on the stick. Behind me, I heard the Vickers of Alldardyce and Speight's Lewis as the German I had hit was ripped apart by their bullets.

As I came around I saw the first Albatros tumbling to earth. I found myself on the tail of a surprised Albatros. I fired again and my bullets stitched a wicked trail from the rudder along the fuselage. The double line of bullets made a sizeable hole in the Albatros. I took my fingers from the triggers and began to bank to starboard. I had hurt the German and he would have to run for home soon. He had no support. Sure enough he, too, turned to starboard. The fact that I had kept up with him must have shocked him but when I opened fire as he crossed before me his shock ended. His body juddered as the .303 smashed into him and ended his young life.

I reversed my turn to see if there were any more Albatros fighters around. I did not need to follow him down. He was dead. As I completed my turn I saw that C Flight was alone in the sky. Below us, the Bristols were still engaged with the rest of the Jasta and the bombers. I began to descend to join them. I knew that the rest of my flight would take station on me.

As we drew closer I saw that the Germans, who had survived, were heading east. This time they would not outrun us. We had more power and more speed. I banked to port and followed the Jasta. I was gaining on the rearmost fighter which twisted and turned to avoid me. I fired very short bursts. I was hitting him but not doing as much damage as I would have liked. I decided to try a trick. I dropped my nose so that he could no longer see me. I came up from beneath him. Although my manoeuvre had allowed him to increase his lead I was still just two hundred yards behind him and he was no longer jinking. I waited until his aeroplane formed a cross in my sights and I fired a long burst. The bullets tore into him and he began to descend, it was gentle at first but as his dead hands lost control it became a steep dive and it crashed into the ground.

Ahead I saw the airfield from which I had escaped. As the Germans were landing I flew along its length machine-gunning the aeroplanes which were taxiing. I had no idea what damage I caused but then I ran out of ammunition and I banked and headed west. I saw that I was alone. I had outrun my flight. This time my journey back took just twenty minutes such was the difference in the Aviatik and the Camel.

My euphoria at the success of the mission was tempered when I saw the white coats around two of the Bristols. We had taken casualties. I also saw Senior Flight Sergeant Lowery and his mechanics with a Bristol whose engine still smoked. We might have bested the fighters but they had left their mark.

Freddie and Johnny walked over to me when I climbed from the cockpit. "A wonderful aeroplane sir. Very responsive."

"It certainly is Freddie. I think it helps that we flew the Pup first. Apparently, some pilots flying the Sopwith Camel have crashed during training. It is why they have delayed their use. I don't think it is as easy to fly as the Bristol."

"You have flown both sir, which one is the better?"

"No argument there, the Camel."

Cecil Alldardyce and David Speight walked over to us having checked over their bus. "Any problems Lieutenant?"

"The Albatros we downed caught the propeller with some of those 9 mm. We will need to get it replaced." That was not a problem, we had two spares from the Pups. He coughed, "Er sir, do you want to claim half of the Albatros? I mean it was badly shot up when Speight and I downed it."

"Of course not. That was a damned fine kill." I saw the relief on both of their faces. "We all had one; well done chaps."

"Er didn't you down the one you chased over their lines, sir?" Freddie had a cheeky look on his face.

"Oh yes. I forgot about that one."

We joined Gordy and Ted who were smoking on their way to the office. "Harry did well. They downed three of the bombers."

"Yes, I think the Germans had a bloody nose there."

Randolph and Archie were delighted with the result; just a couple of damaged Bristols and a couple of flesh wounds. Not a bad return. Well done chaps."

Bates was also pleased that I had returned unscathed and he had my two uniforms with the crowns sewn on. "I posted your letter to Miss Porter, too sir." He hummed as he tidied my room. "The war is going a little better now eh sir? The young officers are full of high jinks. It is good to see."

It was good to see and the mess was, once again, a jolly place. I was the one who celebrated the least. I knew that we had shot down many of the men who I had dined with and who had been so courteous to me. I felt guilty. My crash landing behind the lines had changed my perspective on the war. I would still shoot down the enemy but I had seen their faces and that made a difference.

Chapter 29

Even as we were celebrating the war was changing. The French Army mutinied. We had been on the brink of a breakthrough but the poor conditions endured by the French had led them to mutiny. And the French stopped fighting. In Russia, an activist called Lenin had begun to stir up the Russian soldiers and the pressure in the east lessened. Just when we might have gained the upper hand in the skies we found German reinforcements who were moved from the eastern front. The only resistance would be from the British and Commonwealth troops until the Americans made their way across the Atlantic and the French quelled their mutiny.

Luckily it took a few days for the news and the reinforcements to have an effect and we had a week of easy patrols across a front where the dying had ended, albeit temporarily. It enabled us to get the squadron up to strength with three more replacements and all of the Bristols repaired.

At the start of June, I heard news of Bert. It was not confirmed news but when a huge hill was detonated at Messines and ten thousand Germans killed after a year-long excavation beneath the German lines, I knew that our Bert had to have been involved. My brother was still serving his country and I felt bad about his lack of recognition. There was nothing glamorous about digging tunnels but he and his comrades had killed ten thousand men without loss. That, to me, was worthy of note.

We found that the Germans had been reinforced at the end of the first week in June. We were patrolling close to Cambrai. We had been given that sector as soon as the Arras Offensive had ended. Our new formation worked and we flew the same route; a north to south and east to west box. We now flew staggered formations which looked like a ladder. C Flight was the top rung and A Flight the bottom. It worked because Harry's gunners prevented us being surprised from beneath and our three faster aeroplanes would see an enemy first and be able to react aggressively and effectively.

We had just turned east to begin another leg of the patrol when I saw the ominous black crosses on the horizon. This time, however, there were twenty-four of them. We had met the first of the Jagdgeschwader which were the brainchild of Manfred Von Richthofen. Four Jasta were put together to rid the skies of the RFC and we were the first target.

1917 Eagles Fall

I immediately turned south-east and began to climb. It gave us an advantage and it allowed me to see the formation the Germans were using. It appeared to be a variation on ours except that they had five in each formation. It meant they had symmetry in their attack. I would use that to our advantage. If we kept our formation then I could take us between two of their flights. The Bristols below had the ability to fight off an attack from the side; the Germans did not.

I looked for the red Albatros of Richthofen himself but I did not see it. I knew that he would not allow another to lead an attack. That gave me some hope that we might hold our own. This might not be Jasta 11 I knew that I could have led the squadron back home but the Australians and Canadians below us were watching. How would it look to them if we fled without firing a shot? They had marched through mud and wire not to mention bullets to reach their enemies. The least that we could do was the same.

I cocked the Vickers and dipped the nose. I lined my bus up on the Albatros at the end of one of the flights. I had to run the gauntlet of the other members of the flight but they only had the briefest sight of me as I twisted and turned towards the line of German fighters and I bore a charmed life. Their twin columns of death missed me. I opened fire at the same time as Freddie and Johnny. My target turned slightly to starboard to protect his wingman. My bullets hit his struts and his wing. His starboard wing dipped allowing Johnny to strike the underside of his engine. It began to smoke. I banked to port. The turning circle of the Camel was as good as that of the Pup and I saw an Albatros on my left. He was desperately trying to turn too but my guns were slowly coming around onto his tail. Speight gave him a burst with his Lewis from behind and I heard the bullets clank off the radiator. It also made him flick to starboard and that brought him into my sights. I fired a burst and was rewarded by the sight of a shredded rudder.

He was a good pilot and he didn't panic. Turns would be slower and so he tried a loop. I pulled back on the stick to mirror him. I had the advantage that I could turn easily at the top of the loop. He would be able to turn too but it would be slower. What I had to do was to guess correctly. The problem was that there were many aeroplanes in a small part of the sky. I dreaded to think of the problems that Ted and the Bristols would be having.

Rather than looping, my German opponent kept climbing. He was in for a shock if he thought that he could out climb a Camel. I realised that we were well above sixteen thousand feet when he decided to descend. I was in a perfect position. I guessed he would head east. It was a familiar German tactic. I also began to turn so that he came into my sights. I had kept pace with him all the way up and he was not far ahead of me. As he turned I gave him a short burst to test the guns at such an altitude. They were unaffected and my bullets hit his fuselage. He tried to twist away from me as we descended but his damaged rudder gave me an advantage. I kept turning with him and firing as he came into my sights. His Albatros was a tough aeroplane to destroy. What came to my aid was the extra weight of my machine. The Camel is heavier than the Albatros and I began to gain on him as gravity came to my assistance. As I slid to port I fired at no more than fifty yards and the .303 rounds sliced through his fuselage and cut off his tail. He began to spiral out of control as he plunged to earth.

I saved my bullets and circled around the doomed aeroplane. I saw the pilot struggling with something. He pulled out a bag and slipped two straps over his shoulders. He jumped from the doomed aeroplane! I wondered why he had chosen to die this way when I saw that it was something I had heard about, a parachute. As it billowed open I saw that it was like a giant umbrella and the pilot slowed as the canvas caught in the air. The pilot waved to me and I suddenly recognised him, it was Josef! I waved back and then pushed the stick forward to rejoin the war.

I could see dogfights below me but there were fewer aeroplanes. I had no idea how much ammunition I had left and so I conserved the little I had. I saw two Albatros on Gordy's tail. He was twisting and turning but the Albatros was a lighter, nimbler aeroplane. His gunner was doing a sterling job and keeping them at bay but I saw that one of them was trying to get beneath him.

I was descending like a stone and I pulled back on the stick to bring me closer to the lower Albatros. I saw the effect of his bullets as they thudded into the belly of the Bristol. I opened fire at a hundred yards and then brought my nose up slightly. I fired again. My first bullets hit his tail, doing little damage but my second burst struck the fuselage and must have severed a control for it began to sideslip. I pulled up the nose again and fired my last ammunition into the belly of the Albatros. With fire from two directions, the pilot banked and headed east. Had I had more ammunition I could have finished both of them but as it was I had to join the rest of the squadron and head west. We had met the new formations and survived. I did not know how many of us had done so but I counted at least eight aeroplanes heading west.

As we flew west I saw some of the downed aeroplanes. Lieutenants Hopkins and Dawson's aeroplanes were wrecks and I counted four Albatros. I knew that would not tell the whole story and there would be more casualties waiting at home.

This time most of the aeroplanes had suffered damage. Some of it was minor and would not require much attention but there were Bristols which had suffered serious damage to their engines. Senior Flight Sergeant Lowery took me to look at Lieutenant Ferry's bus. "You see sir these steel jacketed jobs, they are being fired head-on at the engine and the propeller. It is bad enough when they just fire one gun but two of them, especially if they both hit the same place are causing mayhem with the engines."

"Thanks, Flight. I know you will do your best."

I joined Archie and Randolph in the office. "I think I know why we are suffering so much damage to the Bristols, Archie. The pilots fly too straight when they attack the Albatros and the Fokker. They are trying to keep a stable platform; I can see that but it means that they are giving the Germans the best shot at their engine. It works the other way too. I have managed to damage the engine and radiators of lots of their aeroplanes."

"Well, what is the solution?"

"Don't fly head-on! The Camels can because the three of us have worked out a technique to flick the nose up at the last moment. The Camel is like the Pup; it is a nimble little bugger and is very responsive. I have flown the Bristol and it is more sluggish. If we fly obliquely, as though the gunner is going to fire at them, and then turn at the last minute we can still hit them and not risk having our engines damaged."

Archie took out the models we had and he gave them to me. "Show me! I see pictures easier than hear words. I can visualise it better this way." I showed him with the model aeroplanes. "I get you now." He took out his pipe and filled it. "Right, how do we do this? We both know that if we fly towards the Germans they will make it a head-on attack."

"Then we use the Camels as camouflage. We use our ladder formation and when the Germans are committed then Gordy and Ted take their flights away from the centre so that they can turn and attack from the side."

"That puts all of the pressure on you and Harry. I know you can walk on water, Bill and you have the Camels but Harry flies the Bristol. He will be flying head-on."

"And he dives when the Germans fire and then loops. Senior Flight Sergeant Lowery told me it is the bullets coming directly into the engine that is the problem. They almost bore a hole in the engine. Coming from above they are unlikely to strike the same place twice and they won't hit the propeller as easily either."

"Get Gordy, Harry and Ted in here. Explain your plan and we will try it tomorrow."

Gordy nodded and mouthed his thanks as they came in. I could see that they were both shaken up. Ted lit a cigarette and I saw that his hands were shaking. The loss of his pilots had upset him. "Two young lads, Bill. They were bairns. I am not even certain that young Roger Hopkins had even started shaving."

I began to clean out the bowl of my pipe. "We were against two Jastas of Albatros aeroplanes. If it is anyone's fault it is mine. If we had run away from them then none would have died."

Gordy nodded, "But that isn't why we are here is it? If we all ran away then we would lose the war and all the sacrifices so far would have been in vain."

Archie poured us all a whisky. "Let's take the positives out of this. We knocked down Albatros aeroplanes today. They did not have the best of it and we lost fewer pilots than any other squadron. I reckon that is cause for celebration."

"I can't celebrate losing two young pilots, sir."

"You are right, Ted, and I phrased it badly. Listen to Bill. He has some ideas about how we can minimise damage to the Bristols and casualties."

Ted actually smiled. "Then I am all ears!"

I took the three of them through what I had just told Archie and Randolph. Because they had been flying more recently than Archie they had far more questions for me and they helped me to think things through a little better.

When I had satisfied them all Harry asked, "Where does this leave Cecil Alldardyce?"

"How do you mean?"

"The rest of us will not have to fly directly at the Hun but he will because he will be following you and he is not as agile as a Camel."

"That is a good point. He can join one of the other flights." I turned to Archie, "But I reckon we need a full flight of Camels. Six Camels could do some serious damage to the German formations."

"You are right. I'll get on to the General," he chuckled, "although you are the flavour of the month at the moment, Bill. Perhaps you should ring him."

The following morning when we reached our patrol area there was an anti-climax. There were no Germans in the air. We used the time wisely and our new pilots were assimilated into our formations.

After I had given my report I said, "I don't like this. If the Hun weren't close to Cambrai where were they? When I was their prisoner they went out each day. Their work ethic won't allow them to take time off. Where were they?"

The answer came when Randolph telephoned his cousin, James. The German formations had attacked a French airfield further south and destroyed ten Spads. Another of the Jagdgeschwader had attacked a mixed squadron of Gunbuses and Bristols further north and shot down or damaged six of them.

"We could have stopped them."

"Bill, you can't do it all on your own. We are just one squadron. What would you do? Fly up and down the front until you met them? Take this as a compliment. They are attacking easier targets and that isn't us!"

However, we were fated not to meet with the Jagdgeschwader of Richthofen that month. In the second week of June, we were moved north to be closer to the Ypres sector. We were told to leave a skeleton crew at the airfield for we would be returning there in August or September. As we packed our bags Bates worked out the reason.

"It will be another offensive, sir. Remember that news we heard about the hill at Messines? I know that is close to Ypres. I served there in 1915. That will be the prelude to an attack. What this squadron has shown is that it knows how to support infantry even when the enemy are superior. I am afraid 41 Squadron will be the little boy with his finger in the dyke."

Bates was a thoughtful man. He would have made a good officer in Intelligence had he chosen that route. Instead, he was content to be a gentleman's gentleman.

Chapter 30

The bad news was that we were back in tents. We were in a field close to Loker just to the south-west of Ypres. I knew that it had been chosen because it was so close to the front. The aeroplanes arrived the day after Quartermaster Doyle and the others had left to set up the tents and the field kitchens. We knew it would only be for a month at the most but we had been comfortable at our old airfield. Poor Bates was most unhappy at the bathing arrangements. "But sir? Where are the baths?"

I pointed to the tents being erected by the airmen. "It will be cold showers for a while I am afraid, Bates."

He had wandered off chuntering. We had more pressing problems. There were no air defences here at the new field. We were also closer to the front than we had been. If the Germans found out where we were they could make life very unpleasant for us. When Archie called us to the mess tent for a briefing I had a head full of questions and suggestions.

"We are here to stop the Germans spotting what we are up to. There will be an offensive and our job is to stop the Germans realising that. We have been brought in because we are a new factor. The Germans do not know where this field is and they do not know that we are here. They mainly have the BE 2 and Gunbus up here so, hopefully, your aeroplanes should come as a shock to them." Randolph wandered around handing out maps. "Here are the maps of the area northeast of Ypres where we will be patrolling. Passchendaele will be the area we are trying to take and so we need to have a perfect picture of the land around there." He paused and took out his pipe. "Any questions?"

"Should we see if we can spot the German fields; unless someone has already done that?"

Archie and Randolph looked at each other, "That may tip the enemy that we are around."

"Begging your pardon, Major, but if we are flying over Passchendaele then they are going to know that they have new neighbours. I was just thinking of finding out where their fields are and then we would be less likely to be surprised."

I could see the two of them were struggling for an argument against that. "I could just take the Camels over for a look-see. We are fast, we can fly high and they may take us for Pups."

He had no argument for that. "Very well, Bill and Ted can take the rest of the squadron over the land to the northeast of Ypres and photograph it."

I took Freddie and Johnny to the corner of the airfield so that we could pore over the maps in relative peace. "When Lumpy and I escaped through northern France last year we passed to the east of here. We saw airfields between us and Ypres. I think that means that they will be as close to Ypres as we are."

Freddie nodded. "If we come from the south then they may think that we are from a different sector. If we come from the west they will look for our airfield."

"That's a good idea. We have two and a half hours endurance. If we fly south for fifteen minutes to gain altitude and then cross east and head north we should be able to reach sixteen thousand feet and just be dots in the sky."

"How will we see the airfield then?"

"Simple Johnny. There will either be parked aeroplanes or buildings and tents with a runway between them. Basically, we look for green!"

The three Camels left before dawn. I had no doubt that there would be German listening posts along the front and they would report aeroplane engines heading south. I used the compass and my watch, now replete with a secured lock of Beattie's hair, to navigate. After fifteen minutes I turned east and flew for two minutes. We had managed to climb to the correct height and the guns which fired at the sounds from the German trenches were ineffectual. I suppose it made them feel better having shot at an enemy.

We turned north and I saw a faint glimmer in the east. It was dawn. There was little point in peering beneath us for it was still too dark to see. Our height gave us protection but also hid the ground from our eyes. Had we been a regular observation flight we would have been a failure but we were not. We were looking for one target and I estimated that it lay five or ten minutes ahead.

At this time of year, dawn came quickly and, as I glanced down, I saw that I could see the fields and buildings which lay to the south and east of Ypres. I risked descending a little. The other two were behind me a little and to my left and right to give us the best opportunity of spotting any fields. On my lap, I had a map and a pencil was jammed into my helmet. As soon as I saw something below which corresponded with the map I put a dot on the map. I knew that the other two would be doing the same.

I could see, to the west, Ypres. The ground below had nothing big enough for an airfield. Then the houses began to thin quite quickly and I saw an open space. We were too high to make it out and we had to descend. I had hoped to make the sighting from altitude but the light was too poor for that. I took out my watch as we descended; we had been on this course for sixteen minutes. We were north of our field. I smiled when my fingers brushed the lock of hair. Somehow it made me feel safer. It was silly I know but it helped.

When we reached three thousand feet I saw that it was, indeed, an airfield. There were huts and there were aeroplanes. It looked to be a double Jasta. I marked it with a double X. I raised the nose and continued north. I intended to see what there was further north. If the new German organisation had been put in place here then there should be another double Jasta. Three minutes later we saw it. It was much easier to spot because we were lower. Another double X went on the map. I knew we probably wouldn't see another field but I continued north for ten minutes. It was more a ploy to deceive the Germans. After I had reached that leg I turned west and towards the coast for five minutes before I was able to turn south and head for the field.

After we had landed I went to the tent which Randolph was using. I had the three precious maps. By cross-referencing all three of them, we were able to place the position of the two German fields and the four Jastas accurately. Archie shook his head, "I don't like that one bit, Bill. Four to one are not good odds."

"There are four more squadrons of our own close by."

Archie shook his head, "They are either reconnaissance aeroplanes or Gunbuses. The Germans will have them on toast."

"Then we will have to be the eagles and hunt them. The Germans did that with us. Let's turn the tables."

Archie began to fill his pipe. "Go on."

"If Randolph can find out the targets for the observers then we can wait closer to the German airfields and attack them before they attack us."

"We have to escort the spotters."

"We use A Flight for that and the other three flights are hunters."

"You are still talking about odds of four to one."

"No, because there are just two Jastas on each field. That is two to one. Add in the altitude advantage and the nimble Camel and we might just cause them trouble. They like to get into formation before they launch their attack; they will be over their own lines. Add that together and it means we can cause some damage. They are Teutonic and like to do things in an organised way. We use that as a weapon against them and strike before they are ready. We would be limiting their ability to get into the air the next day. We have the edge over the Albatros. All that we need is for the Gunbus to hold its own. We did that didn't we?"

Archie was convinced. "Randolph and I will go to Headquarters. I don't think we can manage a sortie today. Besides the senior warrant officers are still organising the camp."

"I would put up a flight as an umbrella, Archie. If the Germans decide to investigate where we came from they may come over here."

"Good idea. Organise it."

I sent Harry and his flight up first. After they had taken off I said, "Gordy, you go up when he lands and then you, Ted. Let's try to keep our presence disguised."

I went for breakfast with Freddie and Johnny. Johnny pointed to the canvas walls of our new mess. "I don't like this."

"It is only a couple of weeks."

"Why just a couple of weeks?"

"I am guessing that the High Command wanted to draw some Germans away from the French sector. The troops around Arras and the Somme have had a tough time of it. This has been a quiet sector for a while and they did blow that hill up and kill ten thousand Germans. It might convince them that this is a major offensive."

Even Freddie was shocked, "You mean that British soldiers will die and it is for no good purpose?"

I put down my knife and fork and took out my pipe. "The generals are different folk from us. They don't see their fellows having their heads blown off or suffering crippling wounds like Lumpy. They see the bigger picture. It's like when you were kids playing with your lead soldiers. It didn't matter how many fell so long as you won. You picked them up after the battle and started all over again."

"But that is lead soldiers!"

"I know Johnny but the families at home continue to make lead soldiers and the lead soldiers keep volunteering. The generals will keep on using them."

"God, that is depressing!"

"However the good news is that we make a difference. Not a huge one in the scheme of things but I have visited the chaps in the trenches twice now and I can tell you that their morale goes up when we fight above them and shoot down the German aeroplanes." I struck a match and drew on my pipe. "It is why I didn't run when those two Jasta appeared. Always remember when you fight in the air; you have an audience and they are on your side." I pointed with the stem of my pipe at Johnny, "It is like when you played for the first eleven with the whole school watching."

He nodded, seriously, "Then I shall make sure I have a damned good innings."

"Good, just one thing though."

"Sir?"

"Make it '*not out*' eh?"

I sought out Flight Sergeant Lowery. "We are a little exposed here Flight. Have the mechanics push the buses closer to the hedgerows and the trees. Let's try to hide them."

"Good idea sir. I'll get Mr Doyle to get some canvas netting to cover them too."

We wandered over to the resourceful Quartermaster who, like a magician pulled back the flap of a tent and said, "Voila!"

"Where did you get it from?"

He tapped the side of his nose. We had some spare bully beef and I swapped it with some engineers. I thought it might come in handy."

"Brilliant!"

I watched the mechanics and riggers as they pushed the Bristols out of sight and began to cover them with the netting. "Don't cover the Camels yet. My flight is cover in case anyone comes over."

Senior Flight Sergeant Lowery shook his head, "We would have to be extremely unlucky for that to happen. We only arrived yesterday!"

After I had written a couple of letters home I went out to the field to watch Harry land. He had no sooner landed than Gordy and his flight took off.

I strode over to meet him, "See anything?"

"A couple of spotters started west but turned back when they saw us."

I nodded, "Then we can expect visitors. Get some food."

"Do you think they will come over?"

"I hope not. We have no defences yet but I think they will need to find us first. It is why I wanted you up in the air. But for you, those spotters would have been over here and we would have company."

I found Ted and told him the news. "Then we had better be ready to get up quickly."

"It wouldn't hurt."

He summoned his pilots and they lined their aeroplanes up on the field ready to take off. I ordered the mechanics to stand by. We could expect Gordy back in two hours. I decided I would send Ted up fifteen minutes before that.

The sound of the squadron car made me turn. Randolph and Archie came towards me. "It seems we are to patrol the Passchendaele area. The Gunbus squadron will also act as fighter cover." Archie smiled at me, "They did not know that there were four Jastas so close to the front. Well done, Bill"

I shrugged, "If they had sent Gunbuses over to find them then they would have all perished. We know that." I told them Harry's news. "Ted will take off in an hour. We should be safe then until morning."

"The camera buses will be leaving at dawn tomorrow."

"Then we will need to leave before dawn. I'll get the cooks to do an early breakfast."

"And we have been promised another four Camels."

That news actually made me smile, "Great news sir. I think we should use the best pilots for those. The experienced gunners can help out the replacement pilots."

"Why?"

"The camel has a few idiosyncrasies and we don't want new pilots crashing our best buses do we?"

"He's right Archie. We have lost too many Camels due to pilot error. One of the chums I met at HQ told me that. Most squadrons want the SE 5. It is more stable."

"Very well. We will ask the others who they recommend."

We turned quickly as we heard gunfire in the air. I could see a dogfight some three miles away. I heard Ted and his flight start their engines. "Freddie, Johnny, get your flying gear!"

I only had my tunic on but my goggles and helmet were in the Camel. I hoped that they had been rearmed and refuelled. Senior Flight Sergeant Lowery was there himself. "I thought you might want to go up, sir. She's all ready."

"Thanks." By the time I was kitted out Ted and his flight were airborne. "Contact!"

"Contact!"

She fired first time and I roared down the airfield. The other two would need to catch me when they could. I could see that Gordy and his flight were surrounded by swarms of German aeroplanes. Ted and his flight were climbing to their aid. I decided to keep low and gain ground as quickly as I could. I soon found myself below B Flight which was still a mile or so away from contact. I began my climb. I saw a Bristol with flames pouring from its engine as it tried to evade two Albatros. I headed for them. The two Germans were below the Bristol and the gunner did not have a shot. The Bristols were neither as nimble nor as agile as an Albatros and this one was like a fish wriggling on a line.

I was nimble and I was faster than both of them. I opened fire at two hundred yards. I fired a long burst which tracked along the fuselage of first one and then the second Albatros. I saw them peel apart to come after me. They were trying to flank me. I had no doubt they had seen the horse and wished to bag an ace. As I began a loop I saw the wounded Bristol descend and limp back to the airfield.

My two opponents were trying to outflank me and were coming from my port and starboard. When I reached the top of the loop I banked to port and screamed down at one of the Albatros fighters. My extra speed and my small profile made me harder to hit. I side slipped across his front and gave a long burst. I hit his lower wing, then his engine and finally his undercarriage. I continued my turn. He, too, tried to turn towards me but I must have damaged his engine for he had little power.

The second German was heading directly for me. I had one Albatros to my port rear and one directly ahead of me. I started to turn to starboard. The Albatros corrected himself to match me. I flicked the Camel to port and opened fire when he came across my front. He was not expecting that and when he fired it was into empty sky. I felt bullets from the damaged Albatros hit my fuselage and I banked to starboard. The other fighter turned and came at me. I raised the nose and started to climb as he fired. His bullets missed me but ploughed into his colleague. The Albatros fell from the sky.

As I flew over the Albatros I gave a half turn and my airspeed dropped dramatically. The stall speed of the Camel was forty-nine miles an hour. I prayed that I was above it as I attempted my first Immelmann turn. It worked and I found myself directly behind and above the Albatros. I was but forty yards from his tail and catching him rapidly. I gave a burst which went from his rudder to his engine. Some of the bullets must have caught him in his back. He slumped forward and the stick sent the aeroplane into a terminal dive.

As I scanned the skies I could see Ted and his flight chasing the remnants of the raid east. I turned the Camel around and headed home.

Chapter 31

Another of Gordy's pilots had been shot down. It was on our side of the lines and so we recovered the bodies and the aeroplanes. Jim Jenson had not been with us for long but Gordy had had high hopes for him. However, two Albatros were more than enough for a seasoned pilot let alone someone with just twenty-five hours flying time. We had wounded pilots too as well as damaged aeroplanes. As Archie said, when we had all landed safely, "If they had bombed the buses on the ground then we could have lost everything."

"Gordy, do you think that they saw the airfield?"

He shook his head. All that you could see was a field with white tents around. I couldn't see any buses."

"Then the camouflage worked. I think we can expect a hot reception tomorrow." I turned to Randolph. "How long until the offensive begins?"

"Zero Hour is 3.45 on the 31st of July."

Archie unrolled a map he had under his arm. He pointed to a spot on the map. "Apparently the offensive began here at Messines Ridge on the 7th of June. It has been consolidated. Now they are going to push here towards Passchendaele. Our job is to stop Germans snooping too close."

Ted shook his head, "Easier said than done. Today they had two squadrons up... what about tomorrow?"

He was right and we all had an early night to prepare for what we knew would be a hard day. We would need to be on station before the spotters arrived. I had no doubt that the Germans would be there too. We would have to try out my new theory. I just prayed that it would work.

As we took off the following morning I was acutely aware that we did not know this area well. The landmarks we would use were unfamiliar. We had to learn quickly- it was merely days to the offensive. We circled above Ypres while we waited for the two flights of RE 8 aeroplanes which would take the photographs. Although a newer aeroplane than the hapless BE 2 it was still very slow and did not manoeuvre well. As dawn broke, the two-seaters arrived. Their leader gave a cheery wave. He was a braver man than I was. If the Germans broke our defensive umbrella then he had little hope of survival. He could try to flee but the Albatros and Fokker fighters we had seen would soon catch him.

My squadron began to climb to a better altitude. There were some annoying clumps of cloud ahead. They made wonderful hiding places for aeroplanes. We had our new formation and Harry and his flight were behind and below us. Behind them were the spotters. So long as they were quick then they might be able to take the photographs the brass wanted. Surprisingly we reached Passchendaele without being attacked and I began to fly a loop above the camera buses. I had taken photographs and I knew how long it could take to satisfy Headquarters. If you did not take the right ones then they sent you back out. You took them until you were chased off.

I saw them to the left as the two Jastas headed purposefully for us. I banked to port. My flight followed me. This time we would have to bear the brunt of their bullets. If it saved the Bristols from damage then it would be worth it. This was the first time we had not had Alldardyce watching our tail. I felt as though there was a hole in my trousers!

Now that we knew where their fields were we also knew that they would be struggling to gain the height they needed for superiority. They were close to the front. We had the high ground and I was determined to use it. I kept at the same altitude, while the mixed squadrons climbed to reach us. When we were just half a mile from them I put the stick forward and began to dive. Without looking I knew that Gordy and Ted were angling their flights away from me. There would be a gap opening in the middle of their line.

This time I went for the leader. His nose was painted yellow but the lack of any red that I could see told me that it was not Richthofen! He would still be in the Arras area. At a hundred yards I fired. He did so at the same time. As soon as I had stopped firing I dipped my nose. I felt the bullets strike my top wing and fuselage. There was another flight directly behind the first. I left Lieutenant Dodds' flight to deal with the ones we had fired at and I dived towards these four Fokkers who were racing towards us.

I glanced to my right and saw that Freddie was on station. However, when I looked to the left Johnny was not there. I prayed that he had not bought it. This time I might have to endure the fire from two Fokkers. I edged my Camel to port and raised the nose, inviting the shot. I quickly dipped it again and bullets zipped above me. As my nose came down I saw the side of the cockpit of the first aeroplane which was turning to get a better position. I snap fired a short burst and banked to port. I followed his turn and I fired again. As I did so I felt bullets thudding into me as another of the flight snatched his chance. I ignored the hits. I needed to finish this one off. I made it a longer burst and was rewarded by a column of smoke from his engine. It suddenly coughed and lost power. It went into a nosedive.

I pulled hard on my stick. As I did so I saw Freddie to my right finish off one Fokker. I had looped none too soon for bullets filled the space I had just occupied. I mentally chastised myself. I had forgotten to look in the mirror. As I completed the loop I did so and saw that the sky behind me was empty. When I looked up I saw why. I was heading west into a dozen dogfights. Some of the RE 8s were heading west but a couple were gamely battling the superior German fighters. The machine which had fired at me drifted in front of my sights as it tried to get into a shooting position on Freddie. I fired a long burst and the bullets hit the lower wing and the bottom half of the cockpit. I was close enough to see the pilot spasm. He had been hit but he had enough control to bank to starboard out of shot. I let him go. He was out of the battle and heading home.

I dived to go to the aid of one of the spotters. His gunner was spraying the attackers with his Lewis but they were dodging from side to side. They were making him waste his ammunition. Once he changed his magazine then they would attack him. If we were the eagles then they were the vultures. At two hundred yards, I fired a burst. I wondered how I had ever managed with just one Vickers. The twin shower of .303 rounds seemed to be drawn to the Fokker's tail. The rudder and tail disappeared. The Albatros became almost impossible to fly and he started to lose altitude and to turn east. I saw the gunner in the RE 8 clutch his shoulder. The second Albatros stopped dodging as he lined up for his coup de grace. I lifted my nose slightly and then lowered it as I fired. My bullets hit his top wing and, I assume, went through to his engine and radiator. Smoke, steam and oil began to pour from it and he too banked and dived, simply to avoid smashing into the slow-moving RE 8.

As I banked to starboard too the gunner waved his good arm as the pilot headed home.

I began to climb. The Germans, too, were trying to head home. I started to follow and then realised that they had too much of a lead on me. It would be a dangerous waste of time and fuel. I turned and joined the rest of our battered squadron as I headed west.

When I came into land I saw the field was filled with mechanics and medical staff. We had suffered. I did not manage to count the aeroplanes to see who was missing but I saw Johnny's Camel and Freddie's was in my rearview mirror.

1917 Eagles Fall

I taxied close to the fence to give the mechanics an easier job. I clambered down and Johnny rushed over to me. "Sorry sir, I was hit in the first pass and I lost power. I barely kept it in the air."

"Thank God you are alive. I was worried you might have been hit."

"Oh no, sir! Just my engine. Flight says he can have it repaired by tomorrow." He looked worried. "I promise that the engine was hit, sir. I would not take the easy way out. I shan't let you down."

I put my arm around the earnest young man. "Johnny you could never let me down. " I laughed. "We are like eagles, remember, and we rule the skies. You will be fine."

He saw a stretcher with a blanket covering a body as it went by. "That's Harry's gunner. He's pretty shaken up by it."

I knew that he would be. I had had two gunners wounded and it haunted me both times. I blamed myself. "Have we lost any buses?"

"Two of the RE 8s were downed and Lieutenant Stokes isn't back yet."

I looked at an empty sky to the east. "Then he isn't coming back."

In the office tent, I gave my report. Ted and Gordy seemed remarkably upbeat. "The tactics worked, Bill. Our buses suffered less damage than they normally do."

"It didn't help us. If it hadn't been for Alldardyce and his gunner Speight they would have had more than my gunner and poor Dick Stokes." Harry was visibly shaken.

I put my hand on his shoulder. "Cecil is used to taking that position. I am sorry. The only solution that I can see is if your flight divides in two when you attack and then converges."

Archie shook his head, "That is fine for experienced pilots but Harry has some of the younger pilots."

"It is probably my fault sir. Don't worry. I'll do better tomorrow."

In the event, we had a day off for the weather closed in and we had a stormy July day. One of the mechanics wondered if it was St. Swithins' day. Senior Flight Sergeant Lowery snipped, "What did they teach you at Sunday school, Loach? St. Swithins' day was almost two weeks ago!"

We were all grateful for the chance to repair aeroplanes and bodies. Harry received his new gunner and we were ready to escort the spotter aeroplanes. "This lot will be a mixture, Bill. They are running out of reconnaissance aeroplanes. Some are the old BE 2 and the rest are the RE 8s you escorted the other day." He smiled. "I don't know if it helps but their adjutant telephoned; they were grateful for our cover the other day."

"Harry, I want you and your flight to cover the spotters."

"Don't worry, sir, I can stay behind you again."

"I am not worried about me or you. I am worried that the mission will be a waste of all of our time if we don't get the photographs back. We are going back out because they shot down some of the aeroplanes with cameras. I want all of them to survive this time. Then we shan't have to do this again!"

A chastened Dodds nodded and said, "Sir! We won't let anyone get through."

"That's the ticket."

As we climbed into the sky I knew that this day would be harder. They would know where we were going. They might even be waiting. Of course, we had no choice over the time. The cameras needed light and that meant the Germans could be there before us. I hated it when I was right! The German fighters were in position as we arrived. They would not brave our guns on the ground. They would just stop us taking photographs. In addition, they had the altitude.

This time we climbed to meet them. They would be able to turn quicker and attack us from beneath. We would be struggling to turn. This could be a bloodbath.

I saw that these were a mixture of Fokker and Albatros, DII and DIII. We had hurt them and they were now cobbling together different types of aeroplane. It was a glimmer of hope; nothing more.

My slower climb and the Fokker's swifter descent meant that he fired before I did. He struck my wings and I saw wood fly from a spar. I held my nerve and moved to port a fraction. I fired as I did so. I only hit his undercarriage. I side slipped to starboard and his next bullets went into fresh air and he was hurtling past me. This time I fired as soon as the next Fokker came into sight. I saw the tracer as it arced towards his engine. There were sparks and then I saw steam as I punctured the radiator. It must have blinded him for a moment or two for he did not change direction. I moved my nose slightly down and fired. This time the bullets tore two tunnels deep into the engine. I pressed again and then jerked the Camel up and right as he came straight at me. I caught sight of him as I flew over him. His stomach was a bloody mess. My bullets had gone through the engine and into him.

I banked. To my horror, I saw twelve German fighters flocking and mobbing Harry and the spotters. Five of the spotters were heading west and Harry and the remnants of his flight were trying to take on the vultures that were desperate to pick at the corpses of the Bristols. Even as I descended I could see an old BE 2 bus gliding down to land with its engine on fire and a slumped gunner in the rear cockpit.

Harry managed to damage one of his attackers. I saw Harry's gunner spasm as he was hit. I fired from long range and missed. I was closing but I did not know if I would be in time. I glanced to my right and saw Freddie on my wing. Together we stood a chance. At five hundred feet we both fired. Our bullets tore into the fuselage of two Fokkers which had to abandon their attack. We both banked after them and fired again. I was about to follow the Fokker south when I saw that Harry was still being attacked from beneath by an Albatros. I banked to starboard. The normally nimble and agile Camel seemed to take an age to turn. I had to watch as Harry's body juddered and shook as the 9mm steel-jacketed bullets ripped up and into him. As he fell forward his Bristol began to spiral down to earth. Another eagle had fallen.

The Albatros appeared in my sights. He was less than a hundred feet away having been hidden by Harry's bus. I let rip and watched as the bullets tore him to shreds. His fuel tank exploded and I was thrown high into the sky by the concussion. I had to fight to control the Camel and I was not sure where I was. I looked to my right and saw Freddie give me a wave. The sky was empty and we headed west.

I saw burning aeroplanes as we began our descent. It was hard to tell if they were ours or theirs. There were three of them. Even worse, when we came in to land I saw a crowd of people around Johnny's aeroplane. It was quite obvious that he had suffered damage. One of the wheels had broken and it lay at an untidy angle. It took longer to reach him for we had to park our aeroplanes where they could be camouflaged. By the time we had run across the field, he was being carried on a stretcher. I saw that his face, although covered in dressings was a bloody mess.

I caught up with Doc Brennan. "How is he?"

He reassuringly smiled, "He will live. It looks far worse than it is but it is a serious wound." He stopped smiling. "He has lost his right eye and his face will be scarred for life. But he will live."

"What happened, how…?"

He opened his blood-stained hand. There was a small piece of silver metal the size of a farthing. "A bullet must have struck the engine and this piece ricocheted, with others and hit his face. He was lucky it did not penetrate his skull. If it had he would be dead. As it is he will be up and about in a week or so."

"But he lost an eye!"

"His body will adjust."

"Can he still fly?"

"No reason why not. Whether he wants to or not is another matter." I opened my mouth and he said, "You can see him tomorrow. The body is in shock and he will need rest." He put his arm around my shoulder. "And that will be good medicine for you too."

Archie and Randolph looked at me. I could see the concern on their faces. "A rough one?"

I nodded, "We lost Harry and Ben Sanderson. Johnny has lost an eye."

Ted and Gordy walked in. "Well, that was a bit of a bugger."

"Did you lose any pilots or buses?" I could hear the concern in Archie's voice.

"No, but we can only manage one flight between us tomorrow. They meant business today."

Cecil Alldardyce came to the tent and peered in. "Sir, do you want the report of A Flight?"

I could hear the catch in his voice. "Of course, come in and thank you for having the presence of mind to ask."

He nodded and gathered himself. "The Lieutenant led us to protect the spotters but they outnumbered us by two to one. They got Ben and they hit Joe Duffy." He looked at me and shrugged, "It is why I am reporting. I am the only one left, sir."

"You are doing well, carry on."

"We would both have been shot down but Major Harsker here came to our rescue. If he hadn't...."

"I am sorry that I took so long. What about the spotters?"

He shook his head, "They didn't get them. Well, they did hit one but it landed and I saw them carry the camera off. They did their job."

"And so did you. Off you go and, well done. Tell David he did well too."

He smiled, "He now has more kills than Lumpy! He is pleased with himself."

"As he should be, Lumpy was a legend."

Ted said, "If they come again tomorrow, what do we do? Throw paper aeroplanes at them?"

Archie leaned back as he puffed on his pipe. He took it out to point to the east. "If the photographs are what the brass hats want, then we will just have to stop the Hun coming over our lines. That may be our only salvation."

Randolph asked, "Bill you have Freddie left, then there is Alldardyce." I nodded as I filled my pipe. "Ted?"

"There is me and Gordy, Dave Ferry, Tony Hanson and Brian Hargreaves."

Randolph looked up from the list he was compiling. "That makes eight aeroplanes."

Archie nodded, "There are just three days until Zero Hour. We will just have to see what wonders Mr Lowery can perform."

Bates had the nervous look he had first adopted when he arrived at the squadron. He shook his head, "Dear me sir, so many young men. And poor Mr Dodds. He had a young lady at home, did you know?"

"No, I didn't John. How do you know so much about them all?"

"They see me as someone they can confide in. No offence meant to the reverend gentleman but the padre is not the sympathetic type. I must just be a good listener."

"Perhaps I should make you the morale officer eh John?"

"I don't think so." He peered at me, "Will the squadron be up again tomorrow?"

"What there is left of it, yes."

"Then I had better get your uniform ready."

That evening was sombre. There were too many empty places and all of us knew that the ones who remained might not be there much longer. The tent walls and dirt floor did not help but were surrounded by ghosts. Moving from Arras had been an unmitigated disaster.

Chapter 32

As we climbed, before dawn this time, I tried to be positive about the patrol. We had hit them harder than they had hit us. Their hastily assembled aeroplanes were testament to that. We also knew that other RFC squadrons had been knocked about worse than us. That did not make me feel any better. We were just two flights and we patrolled a north-south route over Ypres and the front line. The Tommies cheerily waved at us and we waved back whilst keeping a weather eye to the east and the Hun in the sun.

It was almost an anti-climax when no German fighters appeared. Of course, we had not ventured over their lines but I felt that they had declined to engage us. Perhaps we had hurt them more than they had hurt us.

When I landed I did not report to Randolph. I went to see Johnny. His head looked enormous. It was as though he had a turban on. He smiled when I entered, "How did it go today sir?"

"The Huns did not come. You scared them off!"

He laughed and winced, "I forget that there are muscles on my face." He pointed to his cheek. "I have many scars apparently."

I remembered talking to Beattie about such wounds. "You would be amazed how quickly they heal. Within a month or so you will hardly notice them."

"What about my eye though, sir? Will that heal?"

"Now Lieutenant Holt, you know that it will not. What do you want? Sympathy? If I give you sympathy will that give you back your eye?"

"No, sir."

"The doc says you can fly with one eye. In fact, it will hardly impair you. Think about poor Lumpy with one arm. He did not let it get him down. And we both know that Charlie Sharp would trade places with you in a heartbeat. So if you want sympathy ask for the padre."

"I am sorry sir. You are right. Is it true? Can I fly again?"

"As far as I am concerned you can. The question is do you think you can? If the answer is yes then you need to get better as soon as you can."

"Thank you, sir, and good luck tomorrow."

"You just get well and leave the flying to us for the time being."

I did not sleep well that night. I dreamt of my dead comrades in the cavalry, Lord Burscough, Charlie and poor Lumpy. I just saw them being killed or wounded over and over and I could do nothing about it. I was not refreshed when Bates woke me for the dawn patrol.

None of the damaged aeroplanes were ready nor were their crews and the eight of us took off on that fateful day in late July. We followed the same pattern as the day before. We were not worried that the Germans would be waiting for us. We had left too early for that. We reached the front shortly after dawn and peered east. The clouds were a little lower than we might have liked but they were acceptable conditions.

It would have been a pleasant patrol but for one thing; the Germans. Ten specks appeared on the horizon and then ventured west. The ground troops popped away ineffectually for they were too high. They were flying just below the cloud cover. Six of them were the new Albatros D.IIs but four of them were the Albatros C.III and they carried bombs. They were after our field. I led the squadron to meet them.

The odds were slightly in our favour. The C.III was much slower than any of us and our two Camels could outfly them all. C Flight was ahead and our newly combined Flight led by Ted followed us. As we neared them they began to dive towards us and we adjusted our climb. I had just fired at a D.II when I saw six Albatros D.IIIs pounce from the clouds. It was a trap and it was too late for us to escape. We had not walked we had galloped into it. As we climbed I realised that we could not escape. We could turn and outrun the enemy but if we did so then the Germans would bomb our airfield and our friends would die. If we died now, we could save our friends. There was no argument. I clutched the watch containing Beattie's hair and said, "I love you, Beattie!" She would never hear it but it was there floating around in the air and I was content.

I knew that Freddie and I would have to destroy the bombers. We had the best chance. I turned and shouted, "The bombers!"

I repeated it and he nodded. There were two Albatros D.IIs in our way. I dipped my nose and raised it before giving the first one both Vickers. The pilot panicked and he jerked his stick to loop. I ignored him and pressed on. I could not watch anyone else now. I was on my own. I knew that the other Albatros D.IIs would do all in their power to stop me. I had to be as efficient as I could with my ammunition. The brave bomber pilots kept heading west. I made my trajectory low and I fired at the first bomber. I was below his nose and his rear gunner could not depress his gun. Two Vickers' machine guns can do serious damage and I hit both the engine and pilot. They were dead and I aimed my Camel at the second bomber. I ignored the bullets hitting my wings; the Camel was a tough aeroplane. I repeated my shot and had the same result. The remaining four bombers, for Freddie, had hit one too, took evasive action. I think that saved my life for we were able to get closer to them and the fighters could not fire at us for fear of hitting their own bombers.

I seemed to bear a charmed life. I heard bullets zipping around and hitting my fuselage but none did any serious damage. I determined to stay below them. That way their gunners had no target. I banked to port to follow the bomber which tried to climb away. I was almost thirty miles an hour faster and had a much faster rate of climb. Had he dived he would have had more chance. I had no fear for I knew that I would be shot down eventually. Every bullet I fired was a bonus. My twin Vickers tore into his engine and he began to leak smoke. He banked and turned to the east.

Ahead of me was the open sky. Behind me, I saw an Albatros D.II. I looped. I knew that I could out climb him. I watched as he disappeared from my mirror. I came around and I saw his tail less than thirty feet from my propeller. I just fired. The bullets shredded his tail and he was forced to descend. There was nothing left in my mirror but ahead I could see one bomber which had evaded Freddie and me. It was heading for the field. All that I could think of was poor Johnny lying in the hospital. Suppose the bomb hit there. I headed for him. I was fast enough to be able to reel him in despite the fact that he was almost half a mile ahead.

I saw the field; it was three miles or so away. There were no guns and no balloons to stop him. In my mirror behind me, I saw the furious fights in the sky. I put them from my mind. I had one target and he was drawing closer. My problem was ammunition. How much had I used? I would have one shot and one shot only. I dipped my nose to approach from below. His gunner might get lucky and hit me. The field was a mile away and he was less than a third of a mile away. I could fire and hit him but I had to make sure.

I saw the gunner reach out and hold his first bomb. I was now two hundred yards away. I took a sudden decision. I pulled my Luger and fired nine shots in his direction. He ducked. It bought me enough time to get a little closer. At one hundred yards I had no choice. He was over the field and the gunner had the bomb ready. I pulled the triggers until they clicked empty. Someone was watching over me that day for I managed to hit the bomb. The brave pilot and gunner exploded over the airfield. My friends were safe.

I banked and looked east. The survivors from the squadron were landing. I suspect the loss of their bombers had discouraged the Germans. I turned again and landed.

None of the landings were good. I watched from my Camel. Freddie's had been badly shot up. Tony Hanson was missing and the wings of the rest of the buses looked like Swiss cheese.

I climbed out and made my weary way over to them. When I saw Doc Brennan running to Freddie I found new energy and ran myself. I saw blood and that Freddie was not conscious. Doc Brennan waved me away as he followed his stretcher-bearers to the hospital. Freddie's Camel was badly damaged. Ted's Bristol was the next to land and its left front wheel suddenly collapsed and it stopped at a bizarre angle. Gordy's was on fire as he landed. He and his gunner leapt from his bus and ran before the whole aeroplane caught fire.

The rest of the flight all landed and shell shocked crews walked from them. Dave Ferry looked in a daze, "He just blew up! He just bloody blew up!"

"Who, Dave?"

"Tony Hanson."

The crews staggered off and I walked around their buses. None of them would fly the next day. We had a stalemate. We had stopped the Germans but we could not go up again. The offensive would begin the day after tomorrow and we were like a newborn baby.

Senior Flight Sergeant Lowery confirmed the bad news. "We have one bus for tomorrow, Major Harsker. Yours! That's all. I can have three Bristols ready for the 31st and that is it!"

Doc Brennan also gave us bad news. "Freddie Carrick has a bad wound to the leg. He will be out for months."

"But he will live?"

"Oh aye. The bullet went through the muscle."

Archie leaned back. "That makes this nice and easy, we can't fly tomorrow."

Everyone, remarkably, seemed to relax. The telephone when it went made us all start. Randolph answered it. "Yes, sir?" He nodded and wrote some information down. "But sir we only have one aeroplane fit to fly." There was another silence. "Major Harsker…. Very well sir. I will tell him."

Everyone looked at me. I poured another whisky. "I take it I am flying tomorrow?"

The others looked incredulously at Randolph. "That is ridiculous! The laddie canna do it alone."

Randolph downed his whisky in one, "I am sorry Major but they want every bus which can fly in the air tomorrow. The attack begins the day after and they don't want the Hun to know our dispositions."

Ted stood, "I'll go and have a word with Lowery. He might be able to work a miracle."

"I'll join you, Ted."

After Gordy and Ted had left I asked. "So how will it work? I pop up on my own?"

"No, Bill. There will be two squadrons up there; a mixed squadron of DH 2s and Gunbuses and a BE 2 squadron."

My mouth opened and closed at the lunacy of that. "Those poor buggers won't stand a chance."

Randolph nodded, "Hence the seriousness of the situation."

"Right sir. I had better go and get ready."

The riggers and mechanics had finished with my bus. I saw a huddle of mechanics busy with Cecil's bus. I wandered over and Senior Flight Sergeant Lowery said, "This is the only one we have a chance of fixing sir." He spread his arms apologetically. "Most of our spares are down in the south of the line at the field. "

"I know Raymond, just do your best."

I found an excited Cecil and Speight. "Is it true sir, are we coming up with you tomorrow?"

"If the lads can repair your bus then yes."

Speight punched the air, "Then I have a great chance of increasing my lead against the other gunners!"

I shook my head. "We will be going up against overwhelming odds."

Cecil nodded seriously, "Yes sir, but we will be with you. How can we fail?"

Bates fussed over me as soon as I reached my tent. "You will be careful won't you Major Harsker? Don't be too heroic."

"I never try to be heroic, Bates. I just do my duty."

He gave me a sceptical look. "Well, I will be glad when the squadron is stood down. We have lost too many fine young men lately and I can't see that we have gained much."

Bates was right. Although we had shot down more than our fair share of German aeroplanes in terms of the ground gained it was negligible. We could see, from the air, how little we had advanced. I hoped that the offensive of 31st of July would make all the difference. However, a little voice inside my head told me that it would not.

It was dark when the three of us ate our breakfasts. They say a condemned man is given a hearty meal before the last walk. It felt like that to me. Archie, Randolph, Gordy and Ted all joined me and Cecil as we boarded our buses. Randolph handed me the map. "I have marked the rendezvous there. You and Cecil will be between the other two squadrons. The BE 2s will be to starboard."

"Thank you. Ready Cecil?"

"Rather!"

The noise of the engines seemed inordinately loud on that chilly July morning. We rose into the sky and I circled to gain altitude. Today, of all days, we would need it. As I was levelling out I heard the Bristol's engine begin to cough and splutter. Cecil tried to bring it back to life but there was no power. He waved in the direction of the field and I nodded. As he left I know that he thought I would return with him but I didn't. Those pilots and gunners in the BE 2s might not be in my squadron but they were British and I owed it to them to do all that I could.

In one way it was a relief. I would not have to worry about Cecil and he and Speight would survive. He might live to survive the war! I reached the rendezvous early and I circled as I waited for the other two squadrons to arrive. I had time to reflect that if we had not been sent from Arras then the Germans would have had free rein and there would probably be no British aeroplanes left to oppose them. We had paid a high price but we had done what was asked of us. The brass could ask no more.

Dawn was breaking when I heard the drone of the BE 2s as they arrived. Their squadron leader waved to me. I could not see his face but I was betting that it would be a mixture of amazement and shock that there was but one aeroplane from 41 Squadron. They set off in a loop south and then north. I followed. When we reached the start point the DH 2s and the Gunbuses had arrived. The new squadron looked strange with their pusher engines. The Gunbuses, which had seemed so familiar to me once, long ago, now looked like enormous prehistoric creatures. However, I knew that they were sturdy and would hold their own. They might not shoot down many Germans but they would be hard to kill.

The two Jastas arrived thirty minutes after the other two squadrons. I realised I would have an hour at the most and then I would have to return to base. We had parity of numbers but not quality. We would be lucky to last an hour. The Gunbuses and the BE 2s could fly north to south and use their gunners to fire at the Germans. The DH 2 and I would have to fly at them or be shot down. Six aeroplanes headed east; one Camel and five DH 2s. It was not a bad tactic for we might be able to break up their formation.

I began to climb. I wanted to use my superior speed and ceiling. Surprisingly none of the German fighters followed. I was one lone aeroplane, what damage could I do? I felt suddenly free. I could fly as fast as I liked and twist and turn to my heart's content. I could not crash into any of my fellows for I was far faster than the DH 2. I had nothing to lose save my life. I touched my pocket watch and the lock of hair. Beattie was with me. I was invincible!

I dived at the advancing line of fighters. I flew obliquely at their line. I was causing them a dilemma. Did they adjust their line for one lone Camel? I further confused them by banking to port and flying obliquely in that direction. I risked the fighters to starboard but they had begun to adjust to my attack. I had, perhaps, thirty seconds grace; I used it. I opened fire at two hundred yards. My angle of attack meant that I was flying across the front of the line of fighters. I must have fired a hundred rounds and I struck four of their fighters. I knew I could not hope to destroy any in one pass but I wanted to disrupt them and give the BE 2s a chance. Miraculously I saw smoke pouring from a Fokker D.II. I banked towards it as it dipped its nose. I banked to starboard and flew through the gap; away from the German guns. I continued my turn and found that the fighters were still concentrating on the easier target of the BE 2s. The fact that I was alone worked in my favour.

I fired at the rear of each fighter as I passed. I was less profligate with my ammunition and no fighter took more than ten rounds. I had no time to see if I had done damage. My only hope was to keep moving and firing for as long as I could. I was now flying along their line and heading towards the Gunbuses. I saw a DH 2 as it spiralled in a death dive and a Gunbus with a smoking engine limping west. The BE 2s appeared to be holding their own. I saw an Albatros with a large yellow Edelweiss painted on its fuselage and a green rudder. It flashed before my sights and I gave a longer burst. I immediately saw smoke coming from the engine. I barely had time to lift the nose and avoid a collision. As I did so I saw the Fokker on my tail and its bullets hit my tail and then thudded into the Albatros; killing the pilot. The Germans were doing my job for me.

I looped my Camel. I saw the empty sky above me. I reached the top; then I was descending rapidly. I saw that my opponent, too, had tried to loop but the smaller Camel had turned inside him. I fired a burst into his tail. As I continued to loop, faster than him, I kept firing. The fighter suddenly lurched to one side and began to fall from the sky. Bullets began to strike me from every direction. The fighters were like angry wasps when their nest has been disturbed and they were attacking me from all points of the compass. Although they were hitting me they were also in danger of colliding with each other as well as shooting their own men. I knew that I was running out of ammunition and fuel. I dropped my wing and begin to dive towards the ground. I was aware of bullets hitting me as I passed through the maelstrom of lead. I gritted my teeth and endured it. I just hoped that the Camel would hold together on its steep dive.

I saw the trenches below me; they were the Canadian lines. I began to pull back on the stick. I found sweat pouring from me as I struggled to bring up the nose. I still had plenty of air space but I could see, in my mirror the four fighters which had followed me. As the nose slowly came up I saw the BE 2s who had survived heading west. I kept the Camel at two hundred feet. It was the Canadians who saved me. They put up a barrage of machine-gun and rifle fire which created a wall of lead behind me. In my mirror, I saw two Fokkers fall from the sky to their deaths. The rest withdrew. I waved to the brown uniforms below me. They would enjoy the victory as much as I did.

The field had never looked so welcoming as I brought in the battered and bruised Camel. It would need a great deal of work to enable her to fly soon. One thing was certain, I would not be flying on the first day of the Offensive.

The whole of the squadron raced to gather around my bus. Gordy shook his head, "We saw most of that. You are as mad as a fish!" He pointed to my wings and the engine which were riddled with bullet holes. "You proved one thing. The Camel is a tough aeroplane in the right hands."

We made our way to the mess. A report would have to wait. All of us were celebrating my survival. The last three bottles of brandy I had bought were opened and everyone toasted the Sopwith Camel. That was the true hero of that battle. Randolph was summoned to answer the telephone and when he returned he clapped me on the back. "That was headquarters. The Canadians and the two squadrons who were up today were singing your praises. The Germans did not get through. We only lost five aeroplanes and they reckon that is down to you."

"Well, I hope that means that tomorrow we have no Germans to face for we haven't any aeroplanes to send up."

I was woken in the night by heavy rain as it thudded on the tent walls. The Passchendaele Offensive would go ahead but we would not fly that day. As it turned out my flight and my fight were the last ones in the Passchendaele sector. We were sent back to Arras and replaced by a brand new squadron of SE 5s. Not that it really mattered for the rains meant that no one flew for the first five days of the offensive and the poor soldiers had to wade through mud to reach their objectives. The one thousand yards they gained was paid for by five hundred Germans, British and Canadians for every yard.

As I flew a much-repaired Camel south I reflected that the sacrifices had all been in vain. Our squadron had done its duty and we had bled just as much as the men on the ground but as with so many battles it had been for nought.

Epilogue

We had been back at our old field for a week when the news finally came through that the first Passchendaele Offensive had stopped. We had our replacement pilots and Camels but there was an empty feeling in the squadron. We had lost too many good men in the battle at Ypres.

We were at dinner one night when Randolph came in and whispered in Archie's ear. Our Squadron Leader held his hands up for silence, "Gentlemen, I have just been informed that Major William Harsker has been awarded the Victoria Cross for his rescue of Lieutenant Holt!" There was a tumultuous noise as everyone cheered. The sergeants came in to hear what the noise was about and the words spread like wildfire. Gordy and Ted hammered my back screaming like banshees. Archie roared, "Silence." Everyone went quiet. "All of you fill your glasses. No-one deserves this more. Our leading ace deserves a second one for Passchendaele. He fought as bravely as an eagle. Gentlemen I give you Bill Harsker, the Eagle of the skies!"

Everyone toasted me but I felt empty. There were too many eagles who had fallen. I raised my glass but I was raising it to the eagles who had fallen, Lord Burscough, Charlie, Harry and even Lumpy. I, for one, would never forget them. I hoped the country would remember them too.

The End

Glossary

BEF- British Expeditionary Force
Beer Boys-inexperienced fliers (slang)
Blighty- Britain (slang)
Boche- German (slang)
Bowser- refuelling vehicle
Bus- aeroplane (slang)
Corned dog- corned beef (slang)
Craiglockhart- A Victorian building taken over by the military and used to treat shell shocked soldiers. Siegfried Sassoon and Wilfred Owen both spent time there.
Crossley- an early British motor car
Dewar Flask- an early Thermos invented in 1890
Donkey Walloper- Horseman (slang)
Fizzer- a charge (slang)
Foot Slogger- Infantry (slang)
Gaspers- Cigarettes (slang)
Google eyed booger with the tit- gas mask (slang)
Griffin (Griff)- confidential information (slang)
Hun- German (slang)
Jagdgeschwader – four German Jasta flying under one leader
Jasta- a German Squadron
Jippo- the shout that food was ready from the cooks (slang)
Kanone 14- 10cm German artillery piece
Killick- Leading seaman (slang-Royal Navy)
Lanchester- a prestigious British car with the same status as a Rolls Royce
Loot- a second lieutenant (slang)
Lufbery Circle- An aerial defensive formation
M.C. - Military Cross (for officers only)
M.M. - Military Medal (for other ranks introduced in 1915)
Nelson's Blood- rum (slang- Royal Navy)
Nicked- stolen (slang)
Number ones- Best uniform (slang)
Oblt. - Oberlieutenant (abbr.)
Oppo- workmate/friend (slang)
Outdoor- the place they sold beer in a pub to take away (slang)

Parkin or Perkin- a soft cake traditionally made of oatmeal and black treacle, which originated in northern England.
Pop your clogs- die (slang)
Posser- a three-legged stool attached to a long handle and used to agitate washing in the days before washing machines
Pickelhaube- German helmet with a spike on the top. Worn by German soldiers until 1916
Rugger- Rugby (slang)
Scousers- Liverpudlians (slang)
Shufti- a quick look (slang)
Scheiße- Shit (German)
Singer 10 - a British car developed by Lionel Martin who went on to make Aston Martins
Staffelführer- Jasta commander
The smoke- London (slang)
Toff- aristocrat (slang)
V.C. - Victoria Cross, the highest honour in the British Army

Historical note

This is my fourth foray into what might be called modern history. The advantage of the Dark Ages is that there are few written records and the writer's imagination can run riot- and usually does! If I have introduced a technology slightly early or moved an action it is in the interest of the story and the character. The FE 2 is introduced a month or so before the actual aeroplane. The Red Baron is shot down six weeks before he really was. The Sopwith Camel arrived at the end of May rather than the middle. I have tried to make this story more character-based. I have used the template of some real people and characters that lived at the time.

an improvised affair. Here is a photograph of one in action.

Selected Specifications for the aeroplanes mentioned in the novel
FE2b
2 crew
47 feet wingspan
12 feet 6 inches height
Rolls Royce Eagle engine 360hp
Maximum speed 81 mph (up to 88 at higher altitude)
Ceiling, 11000 feet
2 Lewis machine guns and up to 517lb of bombs
AEG G1
3 crew
52 feet wingspan
11 feet four inches height
2 Mercedes 8 cylinders inline engines 100 hp each
Maximum speed 78 mph
Ceiling 7874 feet
2 machine guns
Aviatik B1/B11
Crew 2
Wingspan 40 feet
Height 10 feet 10 inches
Mercedes D11 Engine 99hp
Maximum speed 60 mph
Ceiling 16404 feet
1 machine gun
Bristol F.2A
2 crew
39 feet 3 inches wingspan
9 feet 9 inches height
190 hp Rolls Royce Falcon v-12 engine

Maximum speed 123 mph
Ceiling 18,000 feet
1 .303 Lewis (rear-facing) machine gun (+an optional Lewis on a Foster mount)
1 Vickers .303 (synchronised) machine gun
Fokker E1
1 crew
29 feet wingspan
9 feet 5 inches height
.7 Cylinder air-cooled rotary engine 80 hp
Maximum speed 81 mph
Ceiling 9840 feet
1 machine gun (later variants had a machine gun firing through the propeller)
Arco DH2
1 crew
28 feet wingspan
9 feet 6 inches height
Gnome Monosoupape 10 hp Rotary engine
Maximum speed 93 mph
Ceiling 14,000 feet
I machine-gun either fixed or moveable
Nieuport 11
1 crew
29 feet wingspan
7 feet high
1 Le Rhone Rotary Engine 80hp
Maximum speed 97 mph
Ceiling 15,000 feet
1 machine gun
Fokker D.1
1 crew
29 feet wingspan
7 feet 5 inches high
Mercedes D 111 160 hp Engine
Maximum speed 93 mph
Ceiling 11000 feet
1 7.92 Spandau mg
Albatros D.1
1 crew
27 feet 10 inches wingspan
9 feet 8 inches high
Mercedes D 111 160 hp Engine
Maximum speed 109 mph

Ceiling 17000 feet
1 x 7.92 Spandau mg
Albatros D.11
1 crew
27 feet 10 inches wingspan
8 feet 8 inches high
Mercedes D 111 160 hp Engine
Maximum speed 109.4 mph
Ceiling 17000 feet
2 x 7.92 Spandau mg
Albatros D.111
1 crew
27 feet 6 inches wingspan
9 feet 6 inches high
Mercedes D 111 160 hp Engine
Maximum speed 102 mph
Ceiling 18000 feet
1 x 7.92 Spandau mg
Fokker D.11
1 crew
28 feet 8 inches wingspan
8 feet 4 inches high
Oberursel 100 hp Engine
Maximum speed 93 mph
Ceiling 14700 feet
1 x 7.92 Spandau mg
Halberstadt D111
1 Crew
28 feet 10 inches wingspan
8 feet 8 inches high
Argus As.11 inline 120hp engine
Maximum speed 99.4 mph
Ceiling 14764 feet
1 7.92 Spandau mg
Sopwith Pup
1 crew
28 feet wingspan
9 feet 6 inches height
La Rhone 9C 80 hp engine
Maximum speed 105 mph
Ceiling 17,500 feet
1 synchronised Vickers .303 machine gun
Sopwith Camel

1 crew
28 feet wingspan
8 feet 6 inches height
Clerget 9 cylinder air-cooled rotary piston (130 hp) engine
Maximum speed 117 mph
Ceiling 19,000 feet
2 synchronised Vickers .303 machine guns

- I used the following books to verify information:

- World War 1- Peter Simkins
- The Times Atlas of World History
- The British Army in World War 1 (1)- Mike Chappell
- The British Army in World War 1 (2)- Mike Chappell
- The British Army 1914-18- Fosten and Marrion
- British Air Forces 1914-1918- Cormack
- British and Empire Aces of World War 1- Shores
- A History of Aerial Warfare- John Taylor
- First World War- Martin Gilbert
- Aircraft of World War 1- Herris and Pearson

Thanks to the following website for the slang definitions
*www.ict.griffith.edu.au/~davidt/z_ww1_**slang**/index_bak.htm*

Lyrics of That Daring Young man on his Flying Trapeze courtesy of http://lyricsplayground.com.

Bill will return with the fifth in the series 1918.

Griff Hosker November 2014

Other books by Griff Hosker

If you enjoyed reading this book, then why not read another one by the author?

Ancient History

The Sword of Cartimandua Series
(Germania and Britannia 50 A.D. – 128 A.D.)
Ulpius Felix- Roman Warrior (prequel)
The Sword of Cartimandua
The Horse Warriors
Invasion Caledonia
Roman Retreat
Revolt of the Red Witch
Druid's Gold
Trajan's Hunters
The Last Frontier
Hero of Rome
Roman Hawk
Roman Treachery
Roman Wall
Roman Courage

The Wolf Warrior series
(Britain in the late 6th Century)
Saxon Dawn
Saxon Revenge
Saxon England
Saxon Blood
Saxon Slayer
Saxon Slaughter
Saxon Bane
Saxon Fall: Rise of the Warlord
Saxon Throne

1917 Eagles Fall

Saxon Sword

Medieval History

The Dragon Heart Series
Viking Slave *
Viking Warrior *
Viking Jarl *
Viking Kingdom *
Viking Wolf *
Viking War*
Viking Sword
Viking Wrath
Viking Raid
Viking Legend
Viking Vengeance
Viking Dragon
Viking Treasure
Viking Enemy
Viking Witch
Viking Blood
Viking Weregeld
Viking Storm
Viking Warband
Viking Shadow
Viking Legacy
Viking Clan
Viking Bravery
The Vengeance Trail

The Norman Genesis Series
Hrolf the Viking *
Horseman *
The Battle for a Home *
Revenge of the Franks *
The Land of the Northmen

Ragnvald Hrolfsson
Brothers in Blood
Lord of Rouen
Drekar in the Seine
Duke of Normandy
The Duke and the King

Danelaw
(England and Denmark in the 11th Century)
Dragon Sword *
Oathsword *
Bloodsword *
Danish Sword*
The Sword of Cnut

New World Series
Blood on the Blade *
Across the Seas *
The Savage Wilderness *
The Bear and the Wolf *
Erik The Navigator *
Erik's Clan *
The Last Viking*

The Vengeance Trail *

The Conquest Series
(Normandy and England 1050-1100)
Hastings
Conquest

The Aelfraed Series
(Britain and Byzantium 1050 A.D. - 1085 A.D.)
Housecarl *
Outlaw *
Varangian *

The Reconquista Chronicles
Castilian Knight *
El Campeador *
The Lord of Valencia *

The Anarchy Series England 1120-1180
English Knight *
Knight of the Empress *
Northern Knight *
Baron of the North *
Earl *
King Henry's Champion *
The King is Dead *
Warlord of the North*
Enemy at the Gate
The Fallen Crown
Warlord's War
Kingmaker
Henry II
Crusader
The Welsh Marches
Irish War
Poisonous Plots
The Princes' Revolt
Earl Marshal
The Perfect Knight

Border Knight 1182-1300
Sword for Hire *
Return of the Knight *
Baron's War *
Magna Carta *
Welsh Wars *

Henry III *
The Bloody Border *
Baron's Crusade*
Sentinel of the North*
War in the West
Debt of Honour
The Blood of the Warlord
The Fettered King
de Montfort's Crown
Ripples of Rebellion

Sir John Hawkwood Series
France and Italy 1339- 1387
Crécy: The Age of the Archer *
Man At Arms *
The White Company *
Leader of Men *
Tuscan Warlord *
Condottiere*
Legacy

Lord Edward's Archer
Lord Edward's Archer *
King in Waiting *
An Archer's Crusade *
Targets of Treachery *
The Great Cause *
Wallace's War *
The Hunt

Struggle for a Crown
1360- 1485
Blood on the Crown *
To Murder a King *
The Throne *
King Henry IV *

The Road to Agincourt *
St Crispin's Day *
The Battle for France *
The Last Knight *
Queen's Knight *
The Knight's Tale

Tales from the Sword I
(Short stories from the Medieval period)

Tudor Warrior series
England and Scotland in the late 15th and early 16th century
Tudor Warrior *
Tudor Spy *
Flodden*

Conquistador
England and America in the 16th Century
Conquistador *
The English Adventurer *

English Mercenary
The 30 Years War and the English Civil War
Horse and Pistol

Modern History

The Napoleonic Horseman Series
Chasseur à Cheval
Napoleon's Guard
British Light Dragoon
Soldier Spy
1808: The Road to Coruña
Talavera
The Lines of Torres Vedras
Bloody Badajoz

The Road to France
Waterloo

The Lucky Jack American Civil War series
Rebel Raiders
Confederate Rangers
The Road to Gettysburg

Soldier of the Queen series
Soldier of the Queen*
Redcoat's Rifle*
Omdurman
Desert War

The British Ace Series
1914
1915 Fokker Scourge
1916 Angels over the Somme
1917 Eagles Fall
1918 We will remember them
From Arctic Snow to Desert Sand
Wings over Persia

Combined Operations series
1940-1945
Commando *
Raider *
Behind Enemy Lines
Dieppe
Toehold in Europe
Sword Beach
Breakout
The Battle for Antwerp
King Tiger
Beyond the Rhine
Korea

Korean Winter

Tales from the Sword II
(Short stories from the Modern period)

Books marked thus *, are also available in the audio format. For more information on all of the books then please visit the author's website at www.griffhosker.com where there is a link to contact him or visit his Facebook page: GriffHosker at Sword Books or follow him on Twitter: @HoskerGriff or Sword (@swordbooksltd)
If you wish to be on the mailing list then contact the author through his website.

Milton Keynes UK
Ingram Content Group UK Ltd.
UKHW021158020624
443508UK00011B/491